SO THAT HAPPENED

A ROMANTIC COMEDY

KATIE BAILEY

Cover Vectors by
JOANNEWHYTE AND MSANCA

ELEVENTH AVENUE
PUBLISHING

1

ANNIE

Bras with no underwire are all fun and games until you're racing through a crowded airport, leaping over rogue suitcases like an Olympic hurdler as you wave your boarding pass in the air (uselessly) and yell "wait for me" (equally uselessly). Like the pilot's going to hear you all the way from the flight deck and take enough pity on you to halt the flight.

Lucky for me, the useless yelling and waving lend me enough of a "move out of the way for the crazy person" vibe that the crowds at the Logan Airport part like the Red Sea. Unlucky for me, by the time I arrive at my gate in a panicked, sweaty mess, I'm wearing my breathable, non-cancer-causing, metal-underwire-free eco-bra like a necklace.

"Hi," I pant-gasp at the attendant as I shove my hands up my sweater to return my over-the-shoulder-boulder-holder back to an appropriate holding position.

Attendant lady's eyebrows raise dubiously as her gaze follows my hands' path under my sweater, her frosted pink lips frozen in a grimace.

"Oh, don't worry. I'm not a pervert," I explain wheezily.

"I bought this bra off a TikTok ad. Needless to say, it doesn't really work."

Frosty Lips looks momentarily stunned. "Pardon me?"

"I'm a sucker for those change-your-life marketing scams."

It's true. I am the ultimate target market for those click-bait-y social media ads—the millennial version of infomercials. I could explain further that I have drawers full of blackhead removers that don't work, no less than four weighted exercise hula hoops for slimming the tummy region that I've used a grand total of twice, lip gloss that's meant to have a plumping effect but really just feels like you've inserted your lips in a hornet's nest, and—

"Ma'am, your ID and boarding pass, please." Frosty is still staring at me, and I notice her fingertips hovering near an intercom. She's obviously ready to call for backup.

I hastily yank my hands out from under my sweater and proffer my rather crumpled boarding pass at her. She looks at it in disdain, then pinches her thumb and forefinger at the very corner like it's a used Kleenex.

But snooty and disdainful as she might appear, my driver's license picture sure pulls a smile out of her. Probably because I look like a young Elton John.

"This is you?" She doesn't even try to hide the laughter in her voice.

I sigh, waving a hand as I bounce forward on my toes. "Bad breakup last year. Wore pajamas for a month. Gained ten pounds. Cut off all my hair to release the 'bondage of self' or whatever Jennifer Aniston called it."

I don't know why I feel the need to explain myself. But I *do* know that I will be at the Georgia DMV ASAP first thing Monday morning wearing full makeup to get myself a brand-new, peach-themed license with an updated photograph.

"I see," she says in a tone that suggests she very much does *not* see, and wants me out of her vicinity, like, five minutes ago. The lady hands back my documents. "You're lucky we're letting you on."

Hallelujah, and thank you, AmeriJet!

"Thank you so much! Seriously!" I sing as Frosty Lips hands me my boarding pass, her little button nose crinkled. I choose to ignore it—there's no way I'm letting her rain on my parade right now.

I half-run, half-stumble, half-skip through the gates and onto the jet bridge, but right before I hightail it through the door, I swear I hear her whistling *Rocketman*.

Sick burn, Frosty.

Little does she know that she basically saved my life. It's Friday night, and this is the last flight of the day from Boston to Atlanta... where I start a new job on Monday morning.

Yeah, like three days from now.

Needless to say, my mother was none too impressed with my forward-thinking, life-planning skills. Or lack thereof.

I am excited to see my dear old mom tonight, though. Unlike me, she's very much a planner—to the point that she's texted me no less than six times to confirm that she'll be at the airport to pick me up. Like mother, *not* like daughter.

I step onto the plane and greet the flight attendant at the door, flushing a little to see the full seats along the aisle. Excited as I am to have made the flight, the rest of the passengers clearly don't share in my happiness. As I trip down the center aisle, muttering vague, non-targeted apologies to everyone already safely buckled in and ready for take off, judgy looks are cast my way.

One particularly kind gentleman (not) even starts a slow, sarcastic clap.

I can't stand situations like this. You know, the type that make you feel itchy in your own skin.

I *want* to be one of those devil-take-the-hindmost, own-the-situation-with-confidence people. And deep down, I truly believe that there will come a day where I could stride to my seat with purpose and dignity, making it seem like I don't care that I made 200 people wait because I am very busy and important with a great reason for being late.

But I'm one-eighth Canadian. And I'm late because I, a grown woman of twenty-six-and-a-half years old, just spent ten minutes hiding in the airport bathroom.

So instead, I'll be saying "sorry" a million times while wishing the ground would swallow me up.

I don't believe in throwing salt over my shoulder, or that breaking mirrors brings bad luck. If a black cat crosses my path, my only instinct is to pet it. But if I were a woman of superstition, I would say that the universe *might* be trying to tell me that relocating back to Atlanta is another mistake.

It's not, though. I *know*, in my bones, it's not. It's my chance for a fresh start.

The slow-clapper is still—a tad unbelievably—slow-clapping, and I almost stop and deliver my inspirational internal pep-talk aloud. But then I remember that I'm a bathroom-hider who's about to move back in with her parents (a situation that will inevitably prompt my mother to invite every single male from her church between the ages of twenty and forty for dinner to present to me as a "prospect").

My mother seems to believe that if I simply married myself off, I'd be substantially happier.

I beg to differ.

As much as I love my mom, I don't think she can

possibly understand what happened. Dad was her first love —they've been together since high school and she never wanted anything or anyone else. I, on the other hand, may know nothing of childhood sweethearts, but I did recently learn a valuable lesson about why you should never, ever get involved with someone you work with.

"Come on now, put a spring in your step!" The impatient flight attendant shoos me along to my seat. Which is, of course, all the way at the back of the plane. In the middle of a row.

By the time I've finished my catwalk of shame—and, horrifyingly, had to ask the elderly lady with bad hips in the aisle seat to let me by—the last thing I need is for my other seatmate to hate me.

"Oof," I say to the man in the window seat, adopting what I hope is a charming, jovial tone. "Bad day for a squirrel to break into your car. That leather upholstery will never be the same again."

I don't know why I say this. Nobody asked.

It's like that meme. You know, the one that's like "Nobody:" and then a picture of someone saying something really dumb.

I am a living embodiment of that meme.

But it's a real story, even if it's not mine. It happened to my ex-coworker Larry once. He had to get a rabies shot and a course of antibiotics. Those welts didn't fade for weeks. Now, it's my go-to excuse for my habitual tardiness, which is something I cannot seem to shake no matter how many books I've read about being "highly effective."

This time, my being late wasn't my fault though. I had no other choice but to hide in the bathroom until the last possible moment. You would, too, if you thought you saw your ex and his new wifey.

5

Sounds stupid to say aloud, obviously. So I'm sticking with the squirrel story.

Which, upon some light reflection, may sound equally stupid.

However, the man next to me doesn't react. Doesn't even seem to register I'm here.

I can't see what he looks like as he's fully shielded behind the massive *Wall Street Journal* he's wielding. But if his body language is anything to go by, he's *pissed*. The knuckles on his big hands are white as he grasps the paper, and he's practically radiating tense energy.

I sit back in my seat, but can't resist peeking over to try and get a glimpse of his side profile. I'm guessing he looks like a cross between an angry Squidward and Mr. Burns from *The Simpsons*.

I catch a glimpse of his profile and my breath catches.

Boy, my instincts were off.

It's not much, but it's enough to know that the angle of that stubbled jawline screams movie-star-hotness.

He finally seems to register me—well, register my stare —and he moves his paper to fully hide his face. I swear his nose wrinkles as he does so.

Good lord, to top it all off, do I *smell* bad?

As surreptitiously as possible, I pretend to adjust my seatbelt while taking a little sniff of my underarm. A little sweaty, maybe, but I still detect deodorant. Nothing gross.

Maybe he's one of those super-smellers that can detect a scent the rest of us can't. Kinda like a bomb-sniffing dog. Or one of those people who smell cow farts for a living to see if they're eating a good diet (it's a real thing, look it up).

Either way, who is this dude to make me feel self-conscious without even a single glance in my direction? Just because his crisp, white dress shirt has zero sweat stains under the pits, and he smells like what I'd imagine a sexy pine forest would smell like, it doesn't mean he needs to make me feel like a greaseball.

"You okay, dearie?" the elderly lady on my left asks in a thick Boston accent. "Crick in your neck?"

"Fine, thank you." I lift my head out of armpit-sniffing territory and shoot her a smile. *Bless her heart.* "Sorry, again, for making you get up."

She pats my arm with a wrinkled hand. "Nonsense. It's good for me to move around before sitting three hours in flight. I consider myself lucky that you boarded late."

On my right, Broody Man snorts.

I ignore him. Maybe it wasn't a snort in my direction. Maybe he was clearing that super-smelling nasal airway of his.

"Cabin crew, boarding is complete," the pilot announces over the speaker system.

Broody Man very slowly and obviously checks his watch and sighs. Loud enough that he must be doing it on purpose.

And this time, I *know* it's directed at me.

Seriously? I was, like, five minutes late.

Seven, tops.

Fine. Ten.

But no more than eleven.

Besides, it's not like they held the plane for me. I've been onboard for a few minutes now, and we still haven't even pulled away from the gate.

So this delay is abso-positivi-lutely not my fault.

In a little moment of indignance, I glare at the back of the guy's newspaper. Which is a slightly more-passive, less-aggressive form of glaring at someone who can actually see you doing it.

Also much more informative about the NASDAQ, as it would happen.

7

When I'm all glared out, I kick off my old leopard-print booties and stow them under the seat in front of me. I'm about to pull my new Brené Brown book out of my bag when I notice the elderly lady looking at me expectantly.

I bite my tongue. Honestly, after the excitement of Bathroomgate and the consecutive luggage-hurdling to my actual gate, all I really want to do is tune out the world in bookland and tuck into my trusty snack bag. But I have enough Haribo gummies to share. Plus, old people are always full of interesting stories.

"Are you visiting Atlanta for a vacation?" I ask her.

She sighs and claps her hands dramatically. "For love!"

"Wow." I'm suddenly invested; this lady's got to be pushing eighty. "Tell me more."

"His name's Walter." Her saggy cheeks become petal-pink with a flush that takes years off her appearance. "He's a veteran. Ever so handsome."

I decide the polite thing to do is to refrain from asking which particular war he's a veteran of, so I opt for a smile. "I'll bet."

"You should see his pictures from thirty years ago. He was a fox."

"How did you two meet?"

"Christian Mingle. Have you heard of it?"

Outwardly, I'm calm and nodding, but in my mind, I've jumped straight to swindlers and catfishers and horrible predators who would take sweet, old, technology-impaired ladies for a ride and lead them to financial ruin. *Damn you, Netflix documentaries, for skewing my views on internet love!*

"Have you met Walter in person yet?" I ask hopefully.

She gives her head a little shake, beams. "My first time."

My smile tightens.

The elderly lady leans toward me eagerly. "Do you have an account, dearie?"

"Pardon?"

"A Christian Mingle account."

I loll my head back against the headrest. "Never tried online dating myself."

"Not even Timber? I thought all you young folks were swiping on Timber these days."

I bite back a laugh. "Do you mean Tinder?"

"Potato, pot-ah-to." She shakes her head dismissively, fingers tapping on her armrest. "All that swiping ain't good for you, anyway."

She runs a critical eye over me, taking in my rainbow-striped sweater, mom jeans, mismatched socks, and beaded hoop earrings. I imagine my style to be bohemian and care-free. Starving artist chic. Minus the starving part because, like Shakira, my hips don't lie.

In reality, however, I usually end up looking less "boho princess," more "color blind kindergarten teacher who got dressed in the dark."

"So, if you're not online dating," she asks. "I suppose you have a boyfriend?"

"Very much single." I say this brightly and with finality, hoping this will put a pin in this particular portion of the in-flight entertainment. I open a bag of Haribo and hold it out, but the lady is undeterred.

"And why is that, dearie? Pretty girl like you."

I made a string of mistakes that led me to lose everything I worked so hard for.

Luckily, before I can think of how to respond aloud, I'm saved (kind of) by another announcement over the intercom. "Ladies and gentlemen, due to unforeseen issues with the plane's operating system, we will be stalling here at the gate until further notice. We hope to have an engineer clear us for take off in a few minutes, and I'll give you an update from the flight deck when I have one. In the meantime, thank you for your patience."

A collective sigh rises from around the plane. I can practically feel the bristling, prickly energy from Grumpypants (formerly known as "Broody Man"—he's been upgraded. Or downgraded, perhaps. It's kind of a Puff Daddy, P. Diddy, Diddy situation).

I reflexively glance at him as he sets down his paper, and for the first time, I get a good look at him.

Wowzers.

He's... hot. Like, super hot.

His face would be handsome to the point of annoying— all sharp angles and perfect symmetry and dark eyes that smolder for days—if it wasn't for an endearing imperfection that softens him. Makes him more interesting. The small, pale scar on his cheekbone, right above his stubble, is the only blemish on an otherwise smooth, olive-toned landscape. It's beautiful.

And I must have a death wish. Because my hand suddenly twitches with a crazy urge to run my finger over the scar.

Unfortunately, the hand that twitches also happens to be the hand holding my family-size bumper pack of Starmix.

A rainbow of corn syrup and gelatin flies into the air, sprinkling like confetti over us.

"Oh no!" I squeak. "My snacks!"

Grumpy doesn't say anything, just raises a large hand to silence me.

It works. Mostly because I'm, once again, stunned by his rudeness.

I take a deep breath, try to be empathetic. Maybe he has a reason for being like this... like his dog died this morning. Or he lost his wallet. Or he has really bad diarrhea.

You can't judge someone for being rude during a bout of the stomach flu, can you?

The guy opens his mouth and it almost looks like he might say something... but then, his eyes meet mine and we hold eye contact for a long, loaded moment.

He seems to think better of whatever he was going to say and his mouth presses into a stern line. He picks up the suit jacket draped across his muscular thighs and shakes it out, scattering the rogue Haribo candies on the floor.

"I can't possibly think of why you're single," he says flatly.

My psychotic urge to touch him fizzles like a match dropped in water as I stare at him in shock.

"And I can't possibly think of why *you* think I'd want your opinion," I retort. Because never mind not judging. I have every right to be the judgiest judge ever.

This guy isn't touch-worthy. In fact, he's kind of a tool.

But behind me, somewhere in the far, far, distance, the old lady cups a hand to her mouth.

"Wooo!" she whisper-hisses. "I could feel that tension. I believe this is what Timber calls 'a match.'"

I turn to the lady in the aisle seat, horrified.

"No, it's not," I hiss, more embarrassed than ever, as I scoop up the scattering of candy in my lap and start shoving it both into my mouth and into the bag to eat later.

Don't judge me—although I'm one to talk right now. I will live and die by the five-second rule. Ten seconds if it's a food item I particularly like.

I shoot a glance at Grumpypants to see if he overheard

—100% likely unless he's deaf as a post—but he's busy tapping away on his phone, dark eyes intent on the screen. I can see that he's texting someone named...

Legs?

Good gracious, life really isn't fair. Because clearly, the most attractive man I've seen in years—perhaps ever—is a grumpy, rude so-and-so who *still* manages to have so much female company that he can't be bothered to remember actual names, just body parts.

Is he one of those businessmen you see in movies with a hookup in every city?

Gross.

Involuntarily, I glance at my own short, squat limbs. Nobody would ever give me "Legs" as a sexy little nickname.

I idly wonder what Grumpy's actual name is. My guess is that he's a Brad, or a Chad. Ooh, or a Thad—Brad and Chad's slightly douchier counterpart.

Yeah, this guy definitely looks like he could be a Thad.

His phone rings.

"Hello," the guy who might be Thad answers, his voice deep and gravelly and positively dripping with surprising Southern charm. He doesn't say anything for a few moments. "There's nothing I can do, my plane's still on the ground in Boston. I'll be there as soon as possible." His coal dark eyes flicker in my direction. "Yeah, me too."

I feel a tiny bit of remorse that he's missing his date with Legs... before I remind myself that the plane's issue is in no way my fault.

Plus, couldn't he call Arms as a backup? Or Boobs? Surely they're both saved in his contacts, too.

"*Someone* can't keep their eyes off someone."

The elderly lady's whisper makes me jerk in my seat. I didn't even realize I was staring at Grumpypants/Maybe

Thad. She also says this so loudly, it's likely that the pilot heard, all the way at the other end of the plane.

Before I can stop her, she chugs on like a freight train. "I tell you, if I was fifty years younger... ooo-ee. But no harm in looking, right? I definitely did a bit of staring at Liam myself when I first sat down. You know, before you arrived late."

Thanks for the reminder.

"Shh," I plead through a gummy mouthful of sweets. Because despite absolutely, positively not caring what the rude man next to me thinks, I *do* care if what he thinks is that I'm hitting on him. I shove the last of the candies back into the bag, distracted. "Who?"

"Liam." She beams and points to Apparently Not Thad, who's finished his hushed conversation with his girl-friend, Lower Extremities, and is now scowling at the ground.

Dammit. Liam is a surprisingly nice name, a strong name.

"And while we're doing introductions, I'm Rosemary," the lady says with a smile. "My sister, Mildred, is up in first class now that Liam swapped seats with her. What's your name, dearie?"

"Nice to meet you, Rosemary. I'm Annie," I say politely before registering her whole sentence. I wrinkle my brow. "Swapped seats?"

"Yes." Her eyes twinkle. "You're supposed to be sitting between Mildred and me. But young Liam noticed Mildred struggling and gave my dear sister his seat while taking hers back here by the bathroom."

I blink as my brain struggles to process. This guy did something nice for an old lady? Seems unlikely.

Though it does explain why someone in such a nice suit is stuck by the pee-scented rear of the plane...

Maybe that's why Liam is so grumpy—he's regretting

giving up his fancy seat in first class. I steal another look at his profile. At first glance, he seems totally unaware of our conversation, looking out the window with an impassive, removed expression. But then, I notice a hint of a flush above his crisp, white collar. Like this chatter about his good deed is embarrassing him.

He cares more than he lets on. Interesting.

"Her arthritis is so bad these days," Rosemary continues. "And I need her fresh as a daisy to be my wingwoman with Walter this weekend. Did I use that word correctly?"

Despite myself, I laugh. "You did."

"Well. You know that saying 'everything happens for a reason?'"

"Mmhmm?" I say with a dose of skepticism because, as I mentioned, I'm not really into this way of thinking.

"If Liam hadn't swapped seats with Mildred, he wouldn't be sitting next to you. And Liam," she addresses Grumpypants, undeterred by his glare. "Annie wouldn't have spilled her food all over you."

Then, Rosemary leans further across me so she can pinch Liam's cheek. Which makes his jaw tighten and makes me smirk.

"Don't give me that surprised look, sonny boy! I know you're listening. And let me say that this wasn't an accident. It means something; everything does. In fact, you should take Annie to dinner tonight!"

"What?!" My voice comes out strangled.

And as if this interaction can't get any more awkward, Rosemary responds by shooting me a weird, flickery wink with one droopy eyelid.

Liam sucks in a breath and pinches the bridge of his nose, clearly over whatever *this* is. For the first time, I'm on his side.

"Rosemary," I say gently, shooting a vaguely apologetic

look in Liam's direction. "You can't ask a man out on my behalf."

Life isn't like the movies—full of meet-cutes and random romances and serendipity. This seat switch and candy crush explosion is just a string of bad luck for both of us. No hidden meaning attached.

But Rosemary is clearly high on internet love, and is therefore a danger to society at the moment. I'm also beginning to wonder if she's a little blind or senile. Or both. The tension between Liam and me is palpable, but it's more hackles raised than desire in its crackle.

"You said you were single, dearie," Rosemary replies. "I believe you said 'very single.' I thought you could use my help."

Good grief. This is my life—getting set up by an overeager, love-drunk octogenarian who's taken pity on my barren wilderness of a dating life.

"Liam doesn't want to take me to dinner tonight," I say reasonably. Then, for some reason—blatant masochism, perhaps—I swivel my head to look at him. "Right?"

"Right," he says without missing a beat, accompanying the word with a curt nod.

Well. I can't say I wasn't expecting that answer, but he could have at least *pretended* to consider it.

"Why not? What's wrong with Annie?" Rosemary protests, and I suddenly wish we were close to a nice, open sewer that I could jump into.

Anything but this horror show.

Why couldn't Frosty Lips have done me a solid and denied me boarding privileges? I'd rather be stuck in an airport paying money I don't have for a new flight and downing copious amounts of caramel iced coffee and those adorable little hash browns from Dunkies while killing time with TikTok videos.

15

Maybe I was wrong. Maybe this is indeed a warning sign from the Fates themselves that moving back to Atlanta is the biggest mistake of my life.

Stop the world, I want to get off!

I look around me, plotting my escape, just as Liam lifts a thick brow.

He appears to assess me. Is this guy really about to tell me what's *wrong* with me?

"Nothing. Nothing is wrong with me!" I blurt before he can say a thing. "I might be single, but I'm not desperate. And for the record, I don't want to go out with him either. I don't date people with no manners. So I think we're done here."

My monologue is slightly injured by the weird grumble my stomach makes (due to not having time to order said little round hash browns from Dunkies before boarding). But all in all, I feel satisfied with my confident outburst.

Liam's eyes spark with something resembling surprise, and his mouth sets.

I shoot him a wide smile, which I hope conveys a metaphorical middle finger I would never actually give—me being the bigger person and all—before I twist my body away from him. I resolve to spend the entire flight steadfastly ignoring him.

If this freaking plane ever takes off.

Three hours.

I need to sit next to him for three hours, and then I never have to see him again.

2

LIAM

"AmeriJet would like to once again apologize for the delay..."

I tune out the latest intercom update and rub my eyes. It's been three hours since a strange, red-headed woman with a very bright smile to match her very bright sweatshirt showed up on my flight, spilled candy all over me, and then shouted at me.

For no apparent reason, I might add.

Maybe she's a bit cuckoo. Beautiful, but unhinged.

Or maybe I really don't understand women.

Either way, it was a very eventful start to a flight that turned out to be very uneventful. In that it never took off.

Because it's three hours later, and I'm seated in the departure lounge.

In Boston.

I'm growing increasingly irritated by the second, and I lean back in my uncomfortable orange plastic chair. I take a large bite of my sandwich—steak on ciabatta. Smells delicious, but tastes more like wet cement than anything that was once a cow.

That'll teach me to eat airport food.

Not like I had any other choice.

I chew methodically as I glare around the lounge, my eyes settling for just a second too long on Annoying Annie With the Candy. Annoying Annie who was absolutely horrified when the old lady insinuated we'd be a good Tinder match. And then, she called *me* the rude one!

She's across the room, sitting in the chairs by the windows and chatting animatedly to the elderly sisters. Beside them, a family plays cards, while two rows behind, a group of teenage boys are playing a game that involves a lot of swatting paper balls out of the air and yelling.

Is *nobody* as bothered as I am about this delay?

After the week I've had, I'm exhausted. Like, in danger of passing out on this plastic chair level of exhausted. So, to avoid any sort of public sleeping fiasco, I swallow the thick, grisly bite of sandwich, toss the rest in the trash can, and get to my feet.

Coffee will help.

I weave through the crowd and find myself, once again, casting a glance in the direction of Annie and the Golden Girls. I'm surprised to find her looking at me, too. I quickly look away.

Must locate the nearest Dunkin and order the largest coffee they've got. STAT.

Five days straight of back-to-back meetings, seminars, and group workshops are pretty much any introvert's worst nightmare. Add on the fact that I actually had to *care* about making a good impression, and you're talking battery fully drained. Dead.

Then, there's Legs.

I slide my phone out of my pocket.

She still hasn't responded to my last text... and I can't say I'm surprised.

I should've never risked it. Shouldn't have pushed my flight back to take that 3pm meeting. It was an accident waiting to happen.

If I'd gotten on my original flight, I'd be back in Atlanta on time tonight.

But I won't be. And I'm as angry with myself as she is with me.

I round a corner and sigh with relief when I spot the pink and orange neon sign. The surrounding gates are packed with weary travelers—looks like AmeriJet is having bigger problems beyond our flight.

As I wait in a lineup that would make an extreme bargain hunter on Black Friday shudder, I catch a glimpse of a vaguely familiar man ahead. Slight build. Blond hair with a touch too much gel. Hawkish eyes giving off a slight predatory vibe. Glued to his cell phone to the point where he's not even registering the line moving in front of him.

Ah, yes. I saw him at Algorhythm several times this week. It may be Boston's biggest tech conference with tens of thousands of attendees, but I remember this guy specifically because he was a bit, well...

Slimy.

The type of guy that thrives on surface-level social interactions, shaking so many hands and rubbing so many shoulders that you can imagine they must have grease flowing from them to slip around so seamlessly.

It's the polar opposite of how I operate, which might be why I picked him out from a mile away. But honestly, I was the wrong person to be at the conference this week anyway. It should've been Luke, he's so much better at this stuff—loud, and cheerful, and great at first impressions.

I'm not good with first, or second, or even third impressions. My sister, Lana Mae, likes to say I'm an acquired taste. Like an anchovy.

I hate anchovies.

But at least, it's over. I got through it. And I managed to talk at length to the reps from Tim Wiseman's office. Which is really why I was at Algorhythm in the first place.

Tim is one of the tech industry's most infamous billionaire playboys, and he's got a fat (Bitcoin) wallet full of crypto to spend on a good idea. He's everything you could ever want in an angel investor, and if I have any hope at launching a successful Version 2 of the app my company created, we need his investment. Thanks to my attempts at "schmoozing" (really, just a lot of forced smiles and passionate speeches), I know exactly what I have to do:

Step 1. Create a strong, data-driven, realistic vision for the future of our company.

Step 2. Get our human resources in order.

I'll be honest, I don't really understand the fuss around the HR stuff. We already have a manual for employees to follow, but apparently human resources these days also constitutes things like free coffee, morning donuts, and team bonding activities—as all the other tech start-ups seem to be doing.

Seems a bit pointless to me, but if that's what Wiseman wants to see, then that's what we'll do. It's within reach.

And if—*when*—we get the funding, having to spend a week making—ugh—*small talk* at a conference, missing Legs's big day, and getting stuck in an airport for a million hours will have all been worth it.

I'm feeling a little more positive by the time I get back to the departure lounge, and I settle into my orange plastic chair. I take a sip of coffee—black, bitter, and burning hot, just the way I like it.

It's only then that I realize everyone around me is getting to their feet, collecting their bags.

Finally.

Must've missed an announcement. It looks like we're on our way.

3

ANNIE

After what feels like an eternity spent in the departure lounge, I've finally successfully tuned out the world.

I'm calm, zen. My focus is on a paint chip on the wall across the room, and not on how much I would rather be anywhere else right now.

But then, Liam comes into my line of vision and my attention zeroes in on him like a sniper.

He strides over to the customer service desk, spreads his big hands across the counter like he means business. He's not red-faced, or yelling, or making a scene. He doesn't even appear to be saying anything. He's almost rigidly calm, his body tense, his expression carved from stone. Only his eyes betray any inkling of heat, and an inferno rages in their depths.

The Liam brand of "I get what I want and I want it now" is much more advanced than the average broody hot guy's.

Frosty Lips is behind the desk, doing something between a cower and an eyelash-flutter—an expression I've never seen in the wild before—while saying something I can't hear, but can imagine to be a promise of VIP treatment.

Everyone else in the departure lounge is doing good old run-of-the-mill whining and complaining. Theatrically making passive-aggressive phone calls to loved ones while shooting furtive dirty looks in the direction of the nearest AmeriJet staff member.

Normal stuff.

Why does this Liam guy think he can demand special treatment? And why am I so bothered by him? I'm not usually bothered by this kind of thing—what is this hidden side of me that's rearing its ugly head?

And no, I don't want to admit that he touched a nerve with that charming "can't believe you're single" comment.

Rosemary grasps my arm. "Come on, dearie. We don't want the best rooms to be taken."

I blink, snapping out of my thoughts. "Pardon?"

"Didn't you hear the announcement?" She doesn't wait for me to respond before she leans toward Mildred. "And I thought *I* was hard of hearing."

Mildred looks up from her knitting magazine like a startled meerkat. "Eh?" she wheezes. "You want me to crochet you an earring?"

Rosemary sighs like she's carrying the weight of the world on her bony little shoulders. She looks at me again. "We need to get to the Ground Transportation area and take the hotel bus link to the Econo Hotel for the night. Our new flight is at 7:00 tomorrow morning."

"W-what?" I stutter, looking around wildly for something to confirm Rosemary's story. You know, in case she is a bit senile after all.

Funny enough, she gives me the exact same look.

I'm suddenly aware that all of my fellow passengers are

making their way out of the departure lounge. Rosemary must be right.

Why? Why is this happening to me?

And why is it happening now?

Yes, I knew that I was cutting it fine flying to Atlanta on the Friday before my new job started. But my best friend, Prisha, was kind enough to throw me a going-away party, and it would have been exceptionally rude to miss it.

Plus, I had packing to do. You try condensing your life into two suitcases after living in a city for eight years... it ain't easy. Especially when you're the type of person who owns fourteen pairs of ballet flats so that she can have one for every color of the rainbow. Or, in this case, two rainbows.

With a sigh, I send my mother the fifth update text of the evening, this one confirming that I won't be arriving until tomorrow.

My phone rings immediately, and I turn the sound off before dropping it into my bag. The last thing I need right now is for her to demand to speak to the pilot or something.

"Alright, Rosemary, let's go." I offer the elderly lady my arm, then do the same for Mildred, who looks like she'd be quite content sitting here with her magazine for the night. I shoot a look in Liam's direction and resolve to not be a Complainy McComplainerson like him. "No use getting upset. We have to make the best of the situation."

"That's right, Annie. Ooh, I hope the hotel room has chocolates on the pillows!"

Something tells me the Boston Airport Econo Hotel is the exact opposite of that kind of establishment, but I'm not about to burst the lady's bubble. I respond with a noncommittal "mmm."

With one last glance in Liam's direction, we're off.

And by "off," I mean "moving through the terminal at a snail's pace."

Walking with Mildred and Rosemary is no easy feat. But what am I going to do, abandon the elderly?

By the time we've stopped twice to use the restroom, stopped again to buy a souvenir teddy bear with an "I <3 The Boston Red Sox" shirt (Mildred took a liking to him), located the bus link, and made our way onto said bus with no small amount of tsking from Mildred, exhaustion is setting in. All I want to do is shower, find a TV channel playing the *Real Housewives,* and crawl into bed with the contents of the hotel's inevitable vending machine.

You know what I *don't* want?

To walk into the lobby of the Econo Hotel and see my ex and his aforementioned wifey.

Aka, the woman he started dating the day after we broke up.

For the love of...

Today really does seem to be the day that keeps on giving. Because he's here. It's not a mirage, or a doppelganger, or any of the things I convinced myself I saw earlier.

Nope, it's unmistakably Justin. Standing in the same lobby as me, breathing the same air. With his arm around his new bride who is visibly...

Pregnant?

What the?!

I don't even bother to wonder what they're doing here—I can't process anything past that round, blossoming belly. Everyone in the vicinity probably thinks I'm doing a world-renowned impression of a largemouth bass, but I can't bring myself to care.

The baby bump is proudly displayed under one of those floaty white dresses that all pregnant women who could double as interior design bloggers tend to wear.

Veronica's face is relaxed and smiling, her honey-colored waves long and shiny. Almost as shiny as that rock on her finger.

I feel a bit faint all of a sudden.

I need air. This lobby is clearly short of oxygen.

Must fill out a comment card suggesting they purchase a few air-cleaning plants.

I start to back away from the front desk, hands up in a position of surrender.

Maybe I have enough hidden ninja skills to creep out of here unseen. I'll take a greyhound bus to Atlanta instead. Worse comes to worst, I'll ride a greyhound dog there, if I have to. Hell will freeze over before I spend the night in the same hotel as my ex and his pregnant bride.

No siree. I'm out.

They haven't noticed me, and Rosemary and Mildred are distracted—cooing over someone's squishy little pug dog. I can make it.

I take another step back. One foot behind the other, there we go.

Avoid that large metal trash can, and the child playing with her Barbie on the (less than clean) floor.

Just a few more steps and I'll be in the clear. Away from this living nightmare.

I'll find a McDonald's on the way to the bus station and drown my sorrows in an extra large milkshake and fries. Maybe some chick nugs with that spicy dipping sauce. You know, the mayo-style habanero one, and—

"Oww!"

I yelp as my foot smashes against something hard.

And... moving.

Despite my valiant windmill-arm-flailing, I lose my balance and teeter over like a jug of milk.

As I fall, I spot the culprit: a sleek, metal wheelie suitcase left unattended in the entryway.

I wince, bracing myself for impact.

But the impact never comes.

Instead, a large pair of arms circle my waist, catching me deftly. Like I'm a football or something.

"Oof," I grunt as the arms crush me toward a firm chest. A chest that smells like...

Sexy pine forest.

Freaking dammit! Not again!

I keep my eyes closed for a moment, staying still and wishing I could evaporate into thin air, while also breathing in that deliciously moreish scent.

"You okay?" a now-familiar deep voice grunts.

I slowly open my eyes. Look up at that gut-wrenchingly handsome face. Nod sheepishly. "Fine."

Liam examines my face a second longer before apparently deciding to believe me. He releases his (actually quite nice) grip—quick enough that I stumble as I hit the ground but, thankfully, don't fall again.

He takes a step back, putting distance between us, and affixes his grip to the handle of the rogue suitcase. He glowers in my direction. "Why were you walking backwards?"

"Why did you leave your suitcase unattended for someone to trip over?" I retort.

He raises a dark eyebrow. His expression is flat, but his eyes are deep, dark wells of intensity. What's with this guy? And why can't I look away? "You're completely right. I should've anticipated that someone would be moonwalking through the lobby and not see it. My mistake."

I think he's being sarcastic. I can never tell with sarcasm. They say it's the lowest form of wit, but I would argue that it's actually quite advanced.

"Well." I clear my throat, even as my skin tingles all over. "You can't just leave your bags scattered around all willy-nilly. Especially not at the airport. It's a rule. Ask the TSA."

For a moment, something like amusement flashes in his eyes. Only, it can't be amusement—his mouth is still set in a grim line and he seems about as cheery as you would after a root canal. "And what do the TSA have to say about bags being left unattended at a *hotel* near the airport?"

Oh, yeah. We're not actually at the airport anymore, are we?

Shoot.

"They report it to the... Boston Hotel Association!" I throw out haphazardly, my heart beginning to throb.

Did I make up a company to justify my argument? Yes, yes I did.

I just hate altercations like this. I get way too flustered and can't think straight and say the wrong thing and spend hours in the shower later dissecting the incident and thinking of all the wittier things I could've said.

Besides. There probably *is* a Boston Hotel Association. And they probably *do* have a rule about leaving bags unattended.

"Better report myself, then," Liam says as he reaches into his pocket and pulls out his phone. "Tell them I'm guilty of leaving my possessions unattended for moon-walking women to trip over. I'm sure they'll be along to arrest me any second now."

He opens his phone screen and starts typing. My heart leaps into my throat.

"Well, you know, you might not be able to find them!" I squawk. "They're an ancient company. Old as the city itself. Your best bet is to find a phone book and call them."

Liam's dark eyes meet mine again. "That explains why there are zero Google results for this legendary BHA."

My cheeks are aching hot again.

Dang it. He got me.

I scramble for any shred of dignity. "When they arrest you, I hope you have a lovely time in jail. I hear the food's great."

Ooh, that was a good one. Mental high-five!

My rush lasts all of point one of a millisecond because I'm suddenly aware of how loudly I shouted that. My voice is literally echoing through the lobby in waves, and Liam is no longer looking at me, but behind me. With horrifying clarity, I remember where I am. What I was trying to do via moonwalking in the first place.

And a ninja escape is no longer a possibility. The entire lobby is watching our suitcase-shuffle-scuffle.

Even the little pug Mildred was petting is now staring, tongue lolling dumbly out of the side of its mouth.

Oh no.

Oh no, oh no.

My only hope now is for a lightning strike or falling meteor to put me out of my misery.

Unfortunately, neither comes.

"Annie Bananie?" Justin calls from across the room, voice tinged with incredulity. I automatically wince at the nickname. "What are you doing here?"

I turn to face Justin and Veronica, mouth flapping open, then closed, then open again.

Back to the fish impressions then.

Awesome.

Veronica stands close to Justin, looping one arm through

his while the other cradles her belly. She's pretty darn pregnant. Like, no-fly-list pregnant.

"Wow! Annie, it is you," Veronica coos. "Are you okay? We saw you tip over."

There's a flattering descriptor. Don't cows tip over?

Never mind.

I take a shaky breath and do a quick "one, two, three" count in my head. Then, I open my mouth, unsure what's going to come out.

"Hahahahahahahaha." I laugh like a lunatic, hardly caring that my cheeks are probably going an unattractive shade of merlot-red. I lurch toward Liam and punch him in the arm. "Oh, you! What would I do without you?"

Liam stiffens, his posture rigid as a board. He blinks at me slowly, his stern expression replaced by a look of complete bewilderment. His thick, dark eyelashes sweep his cheeks before he levels that coal dark gaze back on me. "What?"

Justin and Veronica are walking toward us.

I'm already on a roll, there's no going back now.

I wrap both my arms around Liam's bicep—wow, that is *firm*—and gaze at him adoringly. Sigh like I'm a woman infatuated. Try not to notice the grimace of surprised disdain on his face.

Then, I turn my attention to Jussy and Ron Ron—as their wedding invitation so vomit-inducingly referred to them. "Hey, you two! I barely noticed you over there. Had one too many G&T's in the departure lounge," I explain with a weird, high-pitched giggle that sounds more like I've been huffing helium balloons than drinking myself into a stumbling mess. An actress, I am not. "Thank goodness Liam has quick reflexes. He's always saving me. Benefits of dating such a big, strong man."

Catty? Yes. Yes, it is.

But Liam looks to be about five inches taller and fifty pounds of muscle heavier than my ex. It's literally the ONLY one-up I've got in this situation.

I beg Liam with all the crazy-eyes I can muster to play along with my charade. I'm sure Legs won't mind if it's all pretend.

His fiery dark eyes meet mine for one thrilling moment before he shakes off my hands. They fall to my side limply and mortification shoots through my body.

What was I thinking? No way is this grumpy so-and-so —who's already mad at me for being late and falling over his suitcase—going to play along with my admittedly desperate performance.

He opens his mouth and I screw my eyes up, preparing for the shameful death blow.

Instead, a warm, strong arm circles my shoulders and the pine forest scent surrounds me. My eyes fly open to see Liam standing next to me, his lips slightly less turned down than usual. I assume this is his equivalent of a smile.

He stands *just* close enough to appear intimate, but far enough for it to feel awkward. I get the sense this guy isn't exactly touchy-feely.

Shocker.

"The way she talks, you'd think she was just using me for my body," he says in this flat, deadpan tone. So deadpan, in fact, that it takes me a few seconds to register his words.

My eyes are wide with shock. Is he... going along with this? "What?"

He raises his brows at me innocently as if to answer my question. He is. He's actually playing along.

"I know, I know," he continues. "You love me for my impeccable manners, too."

Oh. Nice one, Grumpy.

Why not throw a jab at me while you're at it.

31

I'm so stunned by this turn of events that I can only stand there, gaping, as Liam offers me another of those not-grimaces of his. "Come on, let's check in. You know how I *hate* lateness."

That second dig at me prods my motor skills back into use, and I nod like a bobblehead figurine. "Yes, good idea! Um, nice to see you, Justin and Veronica. And congratulations again."

Did I say "congratulations" a first time? Doubt it. But it's time to skedaddle out of here while Liam seems to be in an uncharacteristically generous mood.

Unfortunately, Justin doesn't get the memo.

"I can't believe we're here at the same time. What a co-inky-dink," he says chattily, smiling like I didn't just try to exit this conversation and he didn't just use the word "co-inky-dink" without a hint of irony. "Ron Ron and I were meant to be in Aruba, like, five days ago, but we had to rebook our flights."

Come on, universe!

This has to be a cosmic joke—the type I didn't believe in until right this second. It's the only explanation for why Justin and I are both right here, right now, after everything that's happened.

And a lot *has* happened.

Like... I quit my job—a data analytics job at a cool tech company that I loved and adored—what, four months ago now? Yeah, right before Christmas.

That was a fun holiday season. I spent it newly single and jobless, alone in my basement apartment, babysitting the neighbor's hamster, Karl, while drinking copious amounts of eggnog and reflecting on the series of bad decisions that got me to that particular low in life.

Mostly, the decision to date, then break up with, then be forced to work alongside a colleague.

The icing on the cake of the whole situation was when Justin started dating Veronica immediately after our breakup.

As I was the one who ended things, I thought Justin moving on so quickly was a good thing, a sign that I'd made the right decision and we'd both be better off for it. But then, he made things so difficult and awkward for me at the office that I eventually had to bow out and quit.

Unfortunately, this meant that this very same ex of mine got the promotion that I'd worked so hard for. A promotion that was meant for me. It's almost funny how my decision to break up with him worked out so conveniently... for him.

On my end, on the other hand, there were many weeks of wallowing, applying for jobs and questioning all my life choices. Not that I think it's right to stay with someone for the wrong reasons. But if I'd known just how badly things would go, I might've done more to avoid Justin's weirdly piercing eyes in the first place.

"We missed you at the wedding. You should've been there, Annie," Veronica goes on sweetly.

"Why *weren't* you there?" Justin smiles, and I have a sudden urge to kick him between the legs.

Which I don't, of course.

I am zen. I am calm. I am centered...

Ha. What I actually am is super flustered. "Oh, I couldn't have, um—" I fumble.

Thankfully, Justin isn't listening. Which is not unlike him, actually.

I guess some things never change.

"That's a shame, Bananie. You could've brought your new man." He looks at Liam, beams that smile of his that I know now is about as real and substantial as cotton candy, and sticks out his hand. "I'm Justin Manson."

Yup, Manson. Like the serial killer.

They're not related, though. I googled it once to make sure.

"Wait a minute." Justin peers at Liam. "You look familiar. Do we know each other?"

Liam eyes Justin's hand. "No."

He looks away without taking it. Instead, he surprises the absolute heck out of me by drawing me closer, his fingertips on my shoulder making absentminded, lazy circles. My stomach is unreasonably fluttery at the motion.

"Ready, babe?" he asks, his tone almost bored. "Rosemary's waving us over."

Babe? Hahaha, didn't peg him for a "babe" sort of guy.

Justin's mouth stays open and I almost chuckle aloud. His Big Mouth Billy Bass impression is way better than mine. He frowns at Liam's rudeness.

Which, I must say, I'm rather okay with at the moment.

"Yes, heaven forbid we're *late*. But you know how it is in the early days—you can't keep your hands off each other." I chuckle lightly, patting Liam's taut stomach, a move that perhaps goes against my better judgment. "But you two have a good honeymoon." I wiggle my fingers at the happy couple. "Sayonara, then."

Ugh. I have never once used this in parting. What is wrong with me?

Before I can embarrass myself further, Liam takes my elbow and directs me toward the front desk. Away from whatever... that was.

"Babe?" I grin up at him, the bubbling laughter rising in my throat. "Really?"

"I could ask the same thing, Miss *Sayonara*." He gives me a glare so powerful, it makes my knees wobbly. Then, he turns away and continues his frog-march across the lobby with frightening purpose.

34

Rosemary and Mildred are waiting for us at the reception, and Rosemary looks positively giddy. She's flushed like a school girl. "That happened even quicker than anticipated. I knew I could spot a match when I saw one."

Liam looks at her in horror and drops my elbow like it's covered in leprosy.

Me? I hold my breath until Justin ushers Veronica and his unborn offspring into an elevator. Once the doors close, I let out a trembling whoosh of air and turn to Liam. "Thank you. You saved me back there."

He grunts in response.

Of course he does.

But, lucky for me, he doesn't ask me for an explanation. Which means that I don't have to declare myself crazy just yet.

"We're off to our room," Rosemary announces, then gives me a strange, fluttering, blinky-wink that makes her look like she's having a stroke...

Oh my gosh, I hope she's not having a stroke!

I step forward, hands out. "Rosemary! Are you okay?"

"Never better. Good night, you two!"

And just like that, the spasm-y winks stop. She and her sister head to the elevators, all smiles.

Weird.

I watch them curiously as the doors shut on their smiling faces, then rub my temples in slow, steady circles as the weight of what just happened finally hits me.

Veronica is pregnant. Pregnant enough that my mind is a mess of numbers and dates that tell me something I really, really do not want to know. After I threw that awful pity-invite to their wedding in the trash—actually, crammed it down the garbage disposal just to see it get shredded to a pulp—I fervently wished to never see either of them again.

But I guess you can't have everything.

"Care to enlighten me as to what on earth just happened?" Liam's deep voice pulls me from my spiral.

So much for getting away without an explanation. I wonder if he'd accept "clinically insane" or "I blacked out for a minute."

I still can't bring myself to look at him. To face those dark, mysterious eyes, that brooding expression. I shrug a shoulder. "Ex and new wife. Did not, however, know that new wife was bearing his child."

Liam shifts next to me and I finally look at him. He's gazing toward the elevators, and for a moment, I swear I see a touch of softness move over his expression. But then, it clears and he nods curtly.

"Right, what's the hold up?" he grumbles, turning to the reception desk. "You'd think these people were checking in an entire baseball stadium with how long this is taking. Can only hope that the people who work here are more competent than the AmeriJet staff. If I had—"

"Annie Jacobs," the receptionist calls.

Hmm. Maybe Liam's incessant grumbling really works.

"That's me!" I stride toward the desk.

"Great. You're the last two to check in," he says, looking from me to Liam. "One key or two?"

"One's fine, thanks," I say.

"One's good for me, too," Liam adds.

The young man frowns, seeming almost confused, then passes us each a keycard in a little white sleeve. "Room number and wifi password are in there. Enjoy your stay."

Liam makes his way to the elevator without so much as a glance at me.

But I can't be too put out by this brusqueness... he *did* just let me throw myself at him, and he even played along. I still can't fathom why. This guy's an enigma in a dark-and-broody package.

"Thank you," I say again to the receptionist. "Oh, and where's my luggage?"

"Pardon?" He sighs like he wants me to go away so he can get back to the worn Terry Pratchett book and Starbucks cup he's got behind the desk. I don't blame him; I'd be doing the same.

"My suitcase?" I ask.

"Ms. Jacobs, I'm not sure what you mean."

"I checked a suitcase onto the plane," I explain patiently. Maybe he's new.

The guy stares at me blankly for a moment. Rather similar to Rosemary's stare, actually. "It's still on the plane," he explains slowly. "The passengers were advised numerous times at the airport that they'd only have their carry-on baggage for the night."

Oh, *frick*.

This is what I get for watching Liam try, and fail, to get comfortable on an dinky plastic chair in the departure lounge instead of listening to the AmeriJet announcements. And unlike Liam—who travels with a silver-bullet-style carry-on capable of inflicting major leg wounds—all of my things are rammed into my two checked suitcases.

Meanwhile, my carry-on baggage consists of three packets of Haribo, two books, a half-knitted scarf, and my overflowing wallet (overflowing with receipts I haven't bothered to sort through, not cash. Which is a real pity). No toothbrush or change of underwear in sight.

Frickety frick.

"Oh," I say weakly. "Thanks anyway."

He nods once, already pulling out his book.

Liam's still waiting for the elevator, so I stand beside him and flip open my keycard sheath. Room 216.

It's not ideal that I don't have any of my things for bed, but I can make do without my thermal PJs for one night.

Maybe I'll be super crazy and sleep naked, like sexy celebrities claim they do in interviews.

Hopefully I'm not on the same floor as Justin and Veronica. I don't think I could cope if I had to hear them do... *that*.

Not even sure you can do *that* when you're so heavily pregnant. Again, should this woman be jetting off to Aruba tomorrow?

Not my business.

The doors *ping*, and Liam and I step into the elevator. We reach for the same button—second floor.

Hmm. Wonder if Liam's room will be next to mine. That would be very weird. Especially if he calls one of his long list of body part females to keep him company tonight.

Sigh. I guess I'm wearing my noise-canceling headphones to bed, no matter what.

Or am I making too many assumptions about my new pal?

He *did* save my bacon earlier, after all. Even made a few jokes at my expense. Maybe he has a Guys Gone Wild side hidden beneath that perfectly tailored suit.

Interesting thought.

The elevator doors open and Liam makes an "after you" gesture. Which, I guess, is nice.

Until he sighs like I'm taking too long.

He *really* doesn't like to be kept waiting.

"Thank you," I say as sweetly as I can muster, then I bounce out of the elevator and turn left. One more minute and I'll be snug in my room for the night, away from this rude little man. Well, big man.

I wonder if the Econo Hotel has cable? If the *Housewives* aren't on, I'd settle for a good *Cake Wars* marathon.

Liam walks in my direction.

Maybe we really *will* be neighbors.

Outside my room, I rummage in my bag for the keycard.

Liam walks up beside me, shoots me a sideways glance that isn't exactly warm or friendly, then whips his card out of his suit pocket. He steps past me... and slides it into the slot on door 216.

For the umpteenth time tonight, a bad feeling fizzes in my stomach.

Oh no.

Oh no, oh no.

There's been a terrible mistake.

4

LIAM

"No." I cross my arms and look squarely at the receptionist —Cyrus, according to his nametag. "Absolutely not an option. No way. Out of the question."

"B—but, that older lady said..." Cyrus splutters.

"I don't care what the lady said," I interject. My voice is calm and even, but Cyrus is shrinking back anyway.

The arms. Must be the arms. I've been going hard at the gym lately. I *told* Luke that there was such a thing as too many bicep crunches, but he said I was delusional.

I drop my arms to my sides. "There's clearly been a terrible mistake."

Beside me, for some absolutely incomprehensible reason, a smile tugs at Annie's lips.

I really shouldn't be surprised though. In the brief—and I mean, *brief*—amount of time we've known each other, the woman's caught me off guard more times than I can count. One minute she's falling over my suitcase and threatening to have me arrested, the next she's leaping into my arms like a salmon, claiming I'm the love of her life.

"Is there a manager who can sort this out?" Annie asks as she bounces up and down on her toes. She's been doing that—toe bouncing—practically the entire hour we've been standing here. She's like a spaniel. A spaniel who somehow smells like a fresh ocean breeze. Warm and sweet.

I couldn't help but notice that light, clean scent of hers when she jumped on me earlier. And I'd be lying if I said I didn't enjoy the way her huge hazel eyes widened even further when I went along with her "he's my boyfriend" charade.

I don't know why I did, by the way. Maybe because I've never been good at reacting to things in the moment.

I need time to process things, mull them over before being able to communicate how I feel. Or maybe because, annoying as she seems, Annie looked petrified to see Slimy Guy.

Yeah, the guy happened to be the same smarmy man I did actually recognize from the conference. Pregnant bride at his side. Not that he was acting like it at Algorythm—I assumed he was single and looking with the way he was chatting up female attendees.

Something deep in my stomach twisted at the thought of a guy like *that* causing a woman discomfort. So I stepped up.

And now I'm paying the price in the form of Hotel Hell, which I'm sure must be a reality TV show.

"I-I'm the only person here. My manager went home when everything seemed to be under control." Cyrus straightens his spine, seeming a little less intimidated now. In fact, he looks like he's got about the same amount of patience left as I do.

Meanwhile, Annie—my self-proclaimed new girlfriend with terrible timekeeping skills and apparently equally terrible basic motor skills—looks downright sympathetic to the front desk clerk's woes.

According to Cyrus, the Econo Hotel is full. We've

spent the past hour calling every other airport hotel at Logan, but unbelievably, they're full, too. Including all the suites and multi-bedroom units—I would gladly pay any amount of money to make this issue go away.

"Well, get the manager back here then," I snap.

I know, I'm being a jerk. But right now, it's easier to channel my anger into this situation than focus on who I'm really angry with: myself. I should be with Legs tonight, not trying to sort out this impossible room situation.

"That won't be necessary, Cyrus," Annie says to the receptionist.

I look at Annie in indignation. "Yes, it will."

She pulls a face, like this is just a tiny hiccup instead of full-blown heartburn and indigestion. "This isn't Cyrus's fault, it's mine. And Rosemary's. Quite the busybody, isn't she?"

As we've recently learned, Rosemary—who is no ordinary dear old lady—overheard that the hotel was filling up while Annie and I were otherwise engaged. She then proceeded to tell my good friend Cyrus here that Annie and I were traveling together, madly in love, and only needed one room.

All she had to do was point out the whole "Annie hanging off my arm and laughing like a drunken fishwife" situation going on in the hotel's entryway, and that sealed the deal. Cyrus—who apparently just wanted to get back to that sneaky book he's hiding behind the desk—obediently checked us into one room without thinking to check first.

Now, the last and final room in the hotel is long gone to another traveler. That room was also apparently the last viable dwelling place in the entire vicinity of the airport.

"I'm not sure 'busybody' is the word I'd use," I grumble.

"Cheerful thing, aren't you?" Annie smirks. Clearly, my

rotten mood won't be bringing her down anytime soon. Even though this particular predicament *definitely* affects us both.

I'm tired, irritated and don't want to be here. And I'm sure she doesn't either. The least she can do is act like it. All this bouncy-bouncy, happy-clappy, eternal-sunshine crap is getting to me.

"I'm a realist," I say flatly. "And I really don't want to share a hotel room with you tonight."

It's not personal, it's just the truth. I don't share intimate things—like hotel rooms—with anyone. Never mind quirky, cute strangers who seem intent on crashing into my life at every opportunity.

Instead of being offended, Annie turns to me with another one of those mad grins. Despite the late hour, her lips are bright ruby red. The sky might as well be falling down, and yet, she prioritized putting on a fresh coat of lipstick.

It is a good color on her, though. You know, if I was the type of guy to notice that kind of thing.

"Just like you didn't want to go to dinner with me," she says with that knowing smile of hers. Like she has a secret I'm not privy to.

I actually forgot I said that. Told you I wasn't good when I'm put on the spot.

Although, in my defense, it didn't sound like she had any interest in Rosemary's suggestion, either.

"No," I respond grouchily. "That was different."

"Ooh, which one's worse?" she teases. "The thought of eating with me, or the thought of being my roomie for the night? I don't snore, you know. At least, I think I don't. Guess you'll find out soon."

She says this like she can't think of a single other reason

I wouldn't want to have a sleepover with her at a grotty airport hotel.

"As long as you don't continue talking in your sleep, I'll live," I reply.

Annie seems undeterred. "Well, seeing as I owe you one for pretending to be the love of my life, why don't I see if I can sleep in Rosemary's room tonight? Least she can do for causing this mess."

I nod once, relieved. Tomorrow, I'll be sending a very sternly-worded complaint to both the airline and the Econo Hotel for this mess. But for now, we're going to have to make do. "That would be ideal. Or as ideal as it's going to get."

I turn back to Cyrus, who has given up any pretense of caring about our situation and has his nose stuck in his book. "What's Rosemary's room number?" I ask, tapping the desk to get his attention.

He looks up with a sigh. "'Fraid I can't give out that information, sir."

"Are you freaking kid—"

"It's okay," she says, looking at Cyrus. "We'll make do."

"We absolutely will not—" I start.

But then, Annie lays a soft hand on my arm. Her touch makes me jolt.

And I look at her. Really look at her.

Take in her weird, haphazard clothing, her halo of messy auburn hair and red lipstick now slightly smudged at the corner of her full bottom lip. Her otherwise makeup-free face is very pretty, all things considered—creamy, pale skin and perfect symmetry.

And her eyes. Big eyes with long, sooty lashes and delicate, purple-veined lids. Hazel irises ringed with yellow and gold, and filled with so much complexity and depth that I forget where I am for a moment.

My mouth dries, the rest of my angry sentence frozen on my tongue. I don't regret helping her out with Slimy Guy, I realize.

Even if the result means bunking with her tonight.

She nods in response to my unfinished statement. "How bad can it be? I'll even take the bed closest to the door so I get murdered first." I stare at her blankly and she adds, "you know, like in *Schitt's Creek*."

"I do not."

"Ooh, it's a great show. You should check it out."

Cyrus nods in agreement, suddenly capable of being readily involved. "It really is."

Annie smiles. "Come on, I'll tell you about it on the way to our room."

"Please don't," I respond.

Annie smiles wider.

"Old Walter's got his work cut out for him with that spitfire, huh?" Annie asks conversationally as we step into the elevator.

I'm not sure at what point I gave her the indication that I wanted to chat about Rosemary's love life, but it seems all the more imperative that we sort out this mess before I get an earful about Annie's dating life. We don't know each other, and I intend for it to stay that way.

I look at her, hoping she takes my silence as a sign to stop talking. Instead, she answers her question for me in a deep, fake baritone. "Why yes he does, Annie."

It's so ridiculous, it almost makes me chuckle.

Almost.

When we get to our floor, I stall in the hallway. "You go ahead. I need to make a call."

"Oh, yes." She runs her teeth along her bottom lip. "I hope your girlfriend understands that this is all just a big mixup."

I'm left to wonder, yet again, whether this woman lives in a world all her own. "What girlfriend?"

"Ah," she says, her eyes lighting like she's just figured something out. It's quite unnerving, and I again get the sense she somehow knows something I don't. "I see how it is."

"How *what* is?" I ask, but she's already striding down the hall toward her—our—room.

I shake my head as I watch her retreating back. Only her back.

No way do I notice that she has a nice butt. Nope.

I dial Luke's number and sink into a hideous pleather armchair that someone placed outside the elevator. Must be an attempt at decoration.

He answers on the second ring. "Yo. You really stuck in Boston for the night?"

The background noise makes it apparent that he's frequenting an establishment of the "serves alcohol" nature. I could go for a drink myself right about now.

"You got my texts."

"Yeah. Bummer," my brother half-yells over the noise. Then, "hang on, I'm going to step outside."

A series of muffled bangs and crashes later, he's back. "You missed a good party earlier."

"I don't want to talk about that." I sigh heavily. "I just wanted to give you a quick update."

"Shoot."

"I ended up getting another meeting with Tim's people this afternoon—it's why I rescheduled my flight."

"Oh yeah?" Luke perks up. "And?"

"It's good news. Basically, they love companies like ours, and if we're able to get them a comprehensive plan for a V2 launch of the app in the next couple of weeks, we're pretty much in the running. There's a few start-ups they're considering, and they're only going to choose one for their investment, so we need to stand out. Basically, they want to see our company vision, and we gotta make sure our HR is in order. Like, show them our 'fun, positive team environment.' And they don't want any liabilities."

"Ah, shucks. No more making the staff work mandatory seventy-hour weeks then," Luke replies with a wicked laugh. "And forget about that steamy affair you were having with the receptionist."

"Har har," I say dryly. Barb, our receptionist, is in her mid-fifties, and is happily married to Roy, who collects stamps.

"All jokes aside, this is great news! We got both those things locked down, especially with the new hire starting next week. It's gonna be easy."

My chest feels lighter, like the weight that usually sits there is being lifted for me. Talking to Luke always makes me feel this way—he's the eternal optimist to my blunt realist. He flies by the seat of his pants and always makes light of every situation, while I have my endless, very heavily detailed spreadsheets and neat, orderly way of doing every task.

"Yes. It's looking... plausible."

There's no need to get ahead of myself and use a word like "probable."

"It's looking sweeeeeeet!" Luke's clearly at that stage of tipsy where he starts talking like a teenage YouTuber. Better leave him to it.

"Have a good night, Luke."

"You too, little bro. Don't get in too much trouble."

For some reason, an image of Annie flashes into my mind, all sparkly eyed and smiling. I shake the thought away immediately.

"I won't."

5

ANNIE

Actions have consequences.

It's a fact. Whether you believe in karma, or what goes around comes around, or a celestial being, the fact doesn't change. For every action, there is an equal and opposite reaction. I can't remember exactly who coined that, but they certainly knew what they were talking about.

When I said that I would share a hotel room with Liam —formerly known as "Broody Guy," "Grumpypants" and "Thad," and now known as my new boyfriend who apparently gets me drunk in airport bars and saves me from falling over—I did not consider the fact that I was agreeing to share a dinky little bedroom.

A bedroom with zero floor space and...

ONE TINY DOUBLE BED.

ONE.

For some reason, in my mind, I was picturing a large, spacious suite with enough floorspace to turn cartwheels (so much room for activities!) and two large, comfortable beds at opposing sides of the room.

Obviously, I was off in Harry Potter world, thinking of the Hogwarts dormitories.

I stand in the doorway to the microscopic room and stare at the bed, which takes up practically the entire surface area. Off to the side, there's an equally small bathroom with a shower, sink, and a toilet strategically placed so that, if you want to use it, you have to swing your legs up to close the door.

Oh no. This will not do.

Even I can't spin this one.

"What are you doing?" a deep voice behind me says, clearly suspicious.

I whirl around and pull the door closed, blocking Liam's view into the room. "N-nothing."

He narrows his eyes. "Just hanging out in the hallway for fun then?"

I wince. Better to rip off the band aid. "Okay, we may have a teeny tiny problem..."

"How tiny?"

"Um, this tiny." I swing open the door.

Liam draws in a breath. Swears.

I remember his "what girlfriend" classic playboy comment, and try not to be offended. He's clearly not too attached to commitment, so why is the idea of sharing a bed with me this repulsive?

"It's fine," I insist. For some reason, I'm hellbent on proving a point at this moment. Grumpy, suited fake boyfriends bring out the worst in me. "It's... I'll, um, sleep in the shower."

Liam lifts his eyes heavenward, like he is very, very done with both me and this entire situation. "How do you expect to accomplish that?"

"I'm sure I read somewhere that humans can sleep standing up," I say, still on my stubborn streak. "Or wait, was that dolphins? Never mind. Dolphins can't stand, they have tails..."

Oh, my gosh. *Stop talking, Annie!*

My nerves have clearly gotten the better of me, because my mouth is moving at an alarming speed, but I have zero control of the words coming out.

Finally, I manage to lock up my motor mouth and step into the room. Liam follows me with a decidedly concerned look in his dark eyes. Dark, totally captivating eyes that are probably evaluating me as clinically insane.

He sighs deeply as he closes the door behind us, and I wonder what he's thinking.

"Dolphins sleep with one eye open, you know."

I tilt my head, surprised both by this information, and by Liam volunteering it at will. "Really?"

"To ward off predators. They rest one hemisphere of their brain at a time."

For some reason, the fact that he knows this cheers me. "What other fantastically useless facts do you know about dolphins?" I ask curiously.

Liam shoots me a dark glare and his mouth closes like a trap.

Whoops. Obviously touched another nerve there. You just wouldn't expect a tall, broody, businessman-type with disarmingly gorgeous eyes to have a random assortment of dolphin facts. But I'm here for it.

Or... maybe I'm not. What if he has a weird dolphin fetish—like in that show where people marry their cars and/or the Eiffel Tower?

Nope. That's too weird a thought to have about someone when you're about to sleep next to them.

I survey the dinky room again, coming to terms with the terrible reality that our options are for the two of us to share the bed, or that I camp out in the hallway for the night. And those carpets were covered in dubious sticky brown stains.

I'd rather not risk my health sleeping out there, and I couldn't ask him to do it either.

Although, judging by his suit, he likely has much better health insurance than I do (which is none… at least for the next three months, when my probation at my new job ends).

"Guess we're doing this." Liam gives the brightly patterned bedspread a glance, reading my mind.

I know it's the wrong thing to say, but something about his Grumpypants expression triggers my motor mouth anyway. "Do you always sound so excited when you take a woman to bed?"

He shoots me a look. It's not friendly or smiley or jokey, but maybe, there's a brief hint of amusement. "No. Then again, I'd never attempt to seduce a woman in a place as disgusting as this."

I laugh. "That checks out. You seem more Ritz Carlton than Motel 6."

Legs must be living the high life.

He runs a slow, careful eye over me, taking his time as he sums me up. I don't know if it's the tiny room or the fact that it's so stuffy in here that we must be sharing oxygen, but my body feels hyper-aware of his focus. I desperately want to cross my arms in a self-conscious manner, but I resist.

Finally, he quirks an eyebrow. "You look more like someone who'd rent a yurt on Airbnb than book a hotel."

My mouth stretches into a smile. I'm impressed by how shrewd he is, and what he said sounded adventurous and unique—a compliment, I decide. "Yes! That's totally me."

"Somewhere in the middle of nowhere, with no plumbing," he adds.

Oh. Not so much a compliment, then. More a… comment on my personal hygiene?

Frick. Maybe my armpits really do smell sweaty.

While he fiddles with the broken blind on the window overlooking a street light, I give my left armpit another quick sniff. Still can't smell anything, but now I'm revisiting the possibility of him having a German Shepherd nose.

Yet another reason not to share a bed with this man. He'll probably be able to smell my morning breath a mile away. Especially if I can't brush my teeth tonight. *Eek!*

Instead of revealing any of my internal stressing, I give him a bright smile, then gesture to the bathroom. "Want to shower first?"

I'm extending an olive branch—a chance for him to use the bathroom before I stink it up with my apparent B.O.

Or a chance for him to feel at one with his dolphin buddies, who knows.

"I do." He's already in the bathroom and closing the door.

What a charming human. But I've almost come to expect this behavior by now.

And it's kind of fun to push his buttons, poke the bear.

What can I say? I live life on the edge.

I make my way across the room, close the frilly curtains, then flop onto the bed (surprisingly comfy, by the way). I take the opportunity to dig through my handbag to figure out what I'm working with for the night.

As expected, it's mostly sticky candy, pens, and books. Nothing remotely sleepover appropriate, unless I want to knit myself some underwear for tomorrow.

Ughhh.

The shower turns on in the bathroom and I'm hit with the very real realization that there's a naked man not five feet away from me. A tall, muscular man with gorgeous eyes and an angular jawline. This makes me feel... things. In my stomach.

Weird, squishy things that I have no business feeling.

Things my stomach never felt with Justin.

Justin and I were partners in a more... convenient sense. More nerdy talk than dirty talk, if you catch my drift. We walked to work together in the morning, cooked dinner together in the evening. Discussed projects we handled that day while we ate. Rinse and repeat. We were similar, had similar interests, and it just made sense for us to be more than co-workers.

Until it hit me that it really didn't.

But that's a whole other can of worms. Right now, I have a situation in the bathroom and I do not want to think of him *rinsing and repeating* anything.

I need a pep talk, badly. And pep talks mean Prisha.

We've been attached at the hip since we were paired as roommates during freshman year at Boston College. We knew it was meant to be when we both showed up to the dorms with a year's supply of tampons, a Channing Tatum poster, and a shower caddy that could double as a shopping cart.

I decide to text her. I certainly can't risk calling and having Liam overhear.

Annie: SOS. Stuck in an airport hotel for the night with a hot grumpy stranger.

Prisha: That sounds like the beginning of a *very* good book. Is it the type with spicy scenes in it?

Prisha: *hundreds of chili pepper emojis*

Prisha clearly thinks I'm joking. Or she's been reading too many steamy romance books lately.

Annie: This is not a drill, Prish! It's an emergency. I have no toothbrush or hairbrush or clean clothes and the bed is tiny and we have to share it and he hates me and he knows way too much about dolphins.

Punctuation and grammar are not my best friends when

I'm stressed. My phone dings almost immediately with a response.

Prisha: I love your life. How hot is this stranger you speak of? Are we talking Henry Cavill hot? Or, like, Leo DiCaprio ever since he got old and his head got a bit big?

Maybe Prisha was a bad choice of pep talker.

Annie: PRISH, FOCUS.

Prisha: Does he look like he wants to have his wicked way with you?

Annie: No he does not. He looks like he wants me to go away. Very far away. And I haven't even told you the worst bit yet...

Prisha: *gif of Ted Lasso smiling and saying "How 'bout that"*

My best friend is behaving way too flippantly about this whole thing.

Time to bring out the big guns. Prisha always loathed Justin, so this is sure to get her juices flowing.

Annie: I ran into Justin and Veronica. She's pregnant. Like, super pregnant.

Annie: And I told them this guy was my boyfriend.

Wow. Reading over my actions makes them seem even more insane.

I wait while the dots keep popping up and disappearing. Over and over.

I may have achieved the impossible and rendered Prisha Singh speechless for the first time in her twenty-six years.

Finally, a message back.

Prisha: Sorry, I needed to have a little sit down to recover.

Prisha: VERONICA IS WHAT? YOU DID WHAT? I'm calling you.

The shower turns off. Shoot.

Annie: Don't call me, he'll hear!

Annie: I have to go anyway, he's getting out of the shower. Will update you in the AM if he hasn't murdered me in my sleep.

Prisha: He's in the shower????!!!!! SEND PICS.

That's what Prisha took from my last message? Totally her fault if I die tonight.

Also, surely her husband—who she's super duper happily married to—has something to say about this request?

Annie: I'm obviously not in the shower with him. There is a door separating us.

Prisha: Open the door! Seize the day!

Annie: Good night, Prish. Say hi to Raj for me. Remember him? Your loving husband?

Prisha: Of course I do. He's right here beside me reading this whole conversation. He's very invested and wants me to let you know that he hopes you don't die because he actually quite likes you.

Annie: What a glowing review.

Prisha: Annie, we love you. Justin is a loser and you're better off without him. All we want is for you to start having fun, enjoy being single!

My heart warms. I know that my best friend only wants the best for me, only wants to see me happy. Hopes as much as I do that this fresh start is beneficial in every way.

Annie: Thanks, Prish <3

Prisha: Sleep tight *six winky faces*

"Shower's free." His voice is frighteningly close and I drop my phone. The guy moves like a freaking cat; I didn't even hear him leave the bathroom.

I slowly, almost reluctantly, move my eyes to Liam. His hair's damp, his skin dewy, and he's dressed in fitted charcoal running pants and a long-sleeve black t-shirt that clings to his muscular frame. Somehow, this look is even more intimidating than the suit.

He looks... powerful.

Not any ordinary housecat, but a panther.

He catches me looking and shakes his head. "This is pure insanity, isn't it?"

If he's trying to offer me a return olive branch and make this whole situation a bit more comfortable, it's not working. I'm totally tongue-tied as I stare at him. Why does he have to look like *that*?

"It is," I say finally. "But it is what it is and isn't what it isn't."

Wow, I should be a philosopher.

I'm clearly the only person in the room who thinks this. Liam grunts in response, abandoning all attempts at conversation (if that's what that even was), then proceeds to oh-so-carefully climb onto the bed... as far away from me as possible. Which, let's face it, isn't far.

I might've been in his arms earlier, but sitting in this room together, marooned on a tiny bed and surrounded by the heady scent of his woodsy body wash, this moment feels strangely more intimate.

"I guess I'll shower," I squeak, trying not to breathe in again. It would be just my luck that my nose does that weird whistling thing it does in dry weather.

He fixes me with a look that's all business. Nods. "I'll sleep on this side, above the covers. That way, you should be as, um..." His cheeks redden a touch. "Comfortable as possible, given the situation."

I grin at this almost sweet sentiment. "Don't worry about it, feel free to use the covers. I'm totally used to sharing rooms at gross hotels with perfect strangers."

It's meant to be a joke. A funny, lighthearted injection of humor into this crazy situation.

But as per usual, I failed to think before I spoke. And therefore, I failed to realize that my attempt at a joke actually made it sound like I'm a call girl. One with lots of customers.

And judging by the look on Liam's face, he's taken my sentence to mean exactly that.

"I'm not an escort!" I blurt quickly.

"Um, okay?" He pauses, his neck reddening again. Interesting that this hulk of a man embarrasses so easily. Then, he nods at my bag on the bed. "I saw you weren't prepared for an overnight trip so I left you a t-shirt in the bathroom." Another pause. "If you want it."

That's the second nice thing he's done for me today, while I, in turn, have created nothing but chaos for him. Maybe I shouldn't have been so quick to judge him. Or call out his manners.

"Thank you," I say sincerely.

Liam nods. "Good night, Annie."

He flips off the lamp, plunging the room into darkness, and I retreat into the bathroom. As I have no clothes, no toiletries, and, apparently, no dignity left, I take a quick body shower. Think about using Liam's fancy body wash. Decide that's a terrible idea. Settle for the Pepto-Bismol-pink bar of hotel soap, which smells like my grandmother's house mixed with Dettol.

Maybe I could hide in here all night. Curl up on the floor in a nest of towels, like a raccoon.

No. I need to take a page from all of my self-improvement books. I deserve to sleep on a bed tonight. Even if it's a tiny bed, beside a man who's way too gorgeous for his own good. Brené certainly wouldn't be considering the raccoon life.

Liam left toothpaste on the sink. I'm not sure if this is out of kindness or because my breath is disgusting, but either way, I'm grateful. I rub some toothpaste over my teeth and then consider putting my jeans and wooly sweater back on. Ugh, what a day to wear jeans with zero stretch.

I spot Liam's t-shirt atop the counter. It's white and pristinely folded. It looks so soft. So clean.

It's dark in the bedroom, anyhow. He won't get a glimpse of my pale, stubbly legs.

I make another quick decision, fold my clothes, then pull his t-shirt over my head. It's huge and comfortable and smells like heaven.

Good choice.

I slip back into the bedroom and slide into bed next to Liam. But there's no way on earth I'll be falling asleep tonight.

6

LIAM

What was I thinking? How could I have let that happen?

I throw my suitcase in the back of my vehicle with a little too much force, and slam the trunk shut. Breathe in deeply as I walk around the car to the driver's seat, attempting to clear my head and calm my whirling mind. I have more important things to address right now than my intense stupidity.

Leaning my head against the headrest, I slip my phone out of my pocket and send a text.

Liam: On my way. Be there asap.

I wish I could go home to a hot shower and my perfectly plush bed. I never sleep properly when I'm traveling, and last night, I fought it off for hours. Just listening to the steady breathing of the woman beside me as I lay in the dark, forcing myself to keep my eyes open.

It didn't work, of course. But what happened should *never* have happened.

I still can't fathom exactly *how* it happened. Am I really that starved of physical contact?

As a general rule, I keep people at arm's length. Physically, emotionally, every -ally you can imagine.

So why did I wake up with my arms wrapped tightly around Annie Jacobs this morning?

I give my head a firm shake. Shove away the memory of her face pressed against my chest, my hand on her warm lower back, curled in the material of my t-shirt on her body.

This was clearly just a blip, a one-time temporary break in the matrix or whatever you call it. Cuddling a stranger in my sleep may not be my proudest moment, but it's not like I'll ever see her again. In a week's time, I'm sure this will all be forgotten.

With that comforting thought, I start the car and One Direction blares at top volume from the speakers. I almost jump out of my skin at the high-pitched, poppy sound, and I catch a smirk from the leather-jacketed dude securing his bags to the Harley Davidson parked next to my car.

Freaking Legs and her boy bands.

Despite everything that's happened in the last twelve hours, the thought of her warms my chest. Of course I won't go home first, I can't wait to see her.

I turn off the radio and wind down all the windows so the car fills with the balmy early-spring Atlanta air, thick with the sweet scent of impending rain.

It's good to be home.

As I drive toward the pay station, I dig in my suit pocket for my parking stub. My hand unexpectedly closes around something... sticky.

I retrieve the piece of candy, which I think is meant to be in the shape of a fried egg. A goopy orange blob in the middle of a gummy white circle. Leftover from yesterday's candy shower, I assume.

I can't help but smirk humorlessly as I look at it.

This morning was... awkward, to put it mildly. I wasn't sure what to say or do. So, in typical Liam form, I reacted in what was probably the exact opposite way I should have: I packed up and slipped away while she was in the bathroom. She didn't want to see me anyway, I told myself.

But then, of course, we had to get on the plane.

Which meant three more hours stuck next to Annie. I was rigid in my seat, all too aware of her sweet ocean scent and her warmth. Both of which were way too close for comfort.

The second the plane touched down in ATL, Annie gave Rosemary a hug, wished her luck with Walter, and then practically climbed over her to make her escape.

Proving that she can be early for things if she tries.

It's been an extremely confusing twenty-four hours, and I'd quite like to move past it all.

I just hope that, by tomorrow, the night we spent together will be a blip in her memory too. And I'll chalk up the strange emotions she triggered in me as being due to overtiredness and a lack of fresh oxygen. And maybe the workings of a meddling senior.

Never to be thought about again. Like it never happened.

I look at the candy one last time. Then, I pop the sweet in my mouth and chew it until it's gone.

I let myself into Lana Mae's house and I'm greeted by... silence.

"Hello?" I call as I step inside. I slip off my shoes and place them next to the suitcase that stands alone in the middle of the entryway.

Harry Styles, the giant orange tabby cat, appears in the kitchen doorway. I had to bribe Legs with twenty bucks not to call the damn thing "Liam." Which, apparently, is another band member's name.

The cat rubs his side against my legs and purrs noisily. By the time he walks away, a fluffy ball of ginger remains attached to my pant leg.

"Hello, Harry." I sigh, brushing it off.

"Give Harry a hug!"

The voice comes from the top of the stairs, and I look up to see Legs, her face twisted in a scowl that Lana Mae claims makes her look like me.

The nerve.

"I brought donuts," I say, ignoring the fact that I clearly won't be getting a hug myself, and proferring the box of fresh Krispy Kremes that I brought to get back in Legs's good books.

Legs continues scowling. She doesn't back down easily —something I love about her. My initial offer for her to not name the cat Liam was five bucks, and she talked me up to twenty before snatching the bill and saying her second choice had been Niall all along. Liam was only her fourth favorite One Directioner, it turns out. In third place was Louis, and Zayn came in last for being "a deserter."

Lesson learned.

"Allegra, *please* get dressed. Mommy's gotta go soon." My sister appears next to Legs, tripping slightly as she attempts to simultaneously put on an earring and usher her daughter back to her bedroom.

"Uncle Liam has to hug Harry Styles first," Legs insists, crossing her arms over her narrow little chest. Which is currently drowning in an oversized, slightly disturbing pajama top with a picture of Justin Bieber—or "Justin Beaver," as Legs calls him—plastered on the front.

I need to have words with Lana Mae about appropriate nightwear for children.

Lana Mae catches my gaze and looks over her daughter's head at me pleadingly. "Birthday present, she wanted

63

it. Don't start with me, the child has Bieber Fever. And for goodness sakes, hug the cat, Liam. I don't have time for an argument this morning, I'm already late."

"Fine," I grumble. "But you owe me big time."

Then, I steel my favorite person in the world with a *look*. This child inherited her excellent negotiation skills from somewhere, and they sure didn't come from her sweet, giving mother or her deadbeat father.

"If I hug Harry," I say slowly. "Will you get dressed and also forgive me for missing your party?"

"Only get dressed," she counters.

"What if I told you I brought you a present?"

A flicker of interest lights in those big, brown eyes. All of us Donovans have the same dark eyes—it's a family trademark. Her mouth sets in a line. "It's not the donuts, is it? Because you bring donuts, like, every week."

"It's on top of the donuts. And you'll like it, I promise."

"Stop encouraging her," Lana Mae says, then turns to her daughter. "Allegra Liana Donovan, for the fifteenth time this morning, will you please go to your room and get dressed."

Lana Mae points with finality in the direction of Legs's bedroom, then makes her way down the stairs, shrugging on her jacket as she goes. Legs ignores her mother, keeping her eyes on me. She pulls on one dirty-blond pigtail, considering.

"Okay," she says finally. "I'll forgive you, Uncle Liam."

"Hallelujah," Lana Mae mutters under her breath.

As promised, I pick up the cat as Legs watches me carefully. I clutch Harry to my chest for a split second—trying not to get clawed in the face for my trouble—and, satisfied, Legs disappears to her room.

Lana shakes her head. "I swear, that child will be the death of me. Anyway, good morning." She lightly pats my arm as she walks by. "How were your fifteen hours at the airport?"

"Unremarkable," I lie, following her to the kitchen and setting the box of Krispy Kremes on the island. "How was yesterday?"

Lana Mae moves around the kitchen quickly, opening and closing cupboards, spritzing the plants on the windowsill, brushing crumbs into the sink. It's a tiny duplex with a postage stamp of a yard out back, but Lana's done wonders to make the place cozy and homey.

"The visit or the party?" she asks.

"Let's start with the visit."

My sister shrugs as she pours coffee into a travel mug. "Allegra hated it, as usual. We went to a ridiculously fancy restaurant and she wanted french fries for her birthday treat. But of course, there were no french fries on the menu. On the plus side, though, I only cried once, and it was in the bathroom, where no one could see me."

"I don't know why you keep putting yourself through that."

"They're her grandparents, Liam."

"That's technically only fifty percent correct," I grunt as I take my annoyance out on a donut, ripping it clean in half before putting a piece in my mouth. It's still warm, the sugar coating perfectly melted.

"The party was good, though," Lana adds.

"Wish I'd been there."

"Me too. I would've loved to see you get your face painted like a unicorn."

She laughs at my horrified expression, then reaches into a drawer and pulls out a pink binder. "Okay, my Uber will be here in five minutes. Everything you need should be in here." She flips through the pages. "Phone numbers, flight information, schedules. Instructions for the washer and dryer. Contact info for Allegra's doctor, the address of my hotel—"

"Why would I need your hotel's address?"

"What if you need to call me?"

"I'd use this handy gadget called a phone."

Lana purses her lips. "Well, what if the house burns down?"

"It would still be the twenty-first century. Phones would still exist."

"But what if—"

"Lana," I cut her off, keeping my voice gentle. I reach out and pat her hand. "We're gonna be fine. You go and enjoy your course. Learn something, for once."

A small smile crosses Lana's lips and she swats my arm. "How is it that a person of so few words always knows just what to say to make me feel better?"

My lips tilt. If only she knew all of the *wrong* things I said last night.

"I'm dressed!" Allegra materializes from nowhere. The girl moves soundlessly, her footsteps light as a fairy's.

I can't help but smile. She always insists on picking out her own clothes, and today, she's chosen a floaty white summer dress over a striped pink and purple long-sleeve top, yellow tights, and blue sparkly rainboots.

I'm immediately reminded of Annie and her crazy get-up yesterday. Which leads me to think about Annie in my t-shirt, and...

Seriously, Liam! What is wrong with you? It's like I've never interacted with an attractive human female before. It's ridiculous.

"Granddad bought me an iPhone for my birthday," Legs announces.

"An iPhone?" I cock an eyebrow at Lana Mae. "For an eight-year-old?"

66

My sister rolls her eyes and sets a mug of black coffee in front of me. "That's our father for you. Upstage everyone else with an entirely age-inappropriate, outrageously expensive present."

"What did you get me, Uncle Liam?" Legs wraps her arms around my middle, her little face all soft and hopeful. It's an interesting thing about kids—they're so blissfully *expectant* in their ignorance to the world's problems.

"Not an iPhone, that's for sure," I grumble as I reach into my jacket pocket. In my mind, the kiddie-safe phone she had before—where she could text all of four people and had no internet access—had been perfect and would stay perfect until she was at least eighteen.

I retrieve a thick, white envelope and throw it down on the island. "Happy birthday, kid."

Allegra glances at the envelope with a skeptical look. "That better not be twenty dollars, Uncle Liam."

"It's better than money."

"Better than money," she repeats thoughtfully, carefully ripping the back. I watch her the whole time, strangely nervous.

I take a sip of my coffee as she reads.

Then another. And a third.

"AGHHHHHHHHHH!"

There it is.

Even though I'm half-expecting it, the scream makes me choke on a mouthful of coffee and Lana Mae swear in a squeaky, high-pitched yelp.

"Ohmygoshohmygoshohmygoshohmygoshohmy-goshohmygosh!" Legs yells, leaping up and down before flinging her arms around me. "I always knew I loved you best, Uncle Liam!"

"What is—" Lana Mae comes up behind Legs and peers

at the gift. Her face creases in a frown. "Oh Liam, you didn't... How on earth did you even get those?"

I shrug.

She narrows her eyes.

I shrug again, with conviction this time. My sister doesn't need to know that I paid someone to wait in line for Justin Bieber concert tickets, does she?

And yes, I know I'm a hypocrite for criticizing Legs's pajamas and her phone, and then buying the child concert tickets. But I couldn't help myself. The look on her face makes it worth it.

"Mama, I'm going to see Justin Beaver!" Legs squeals.

"Yes you are, baby. Uncle Liam spoils you." Lana Mae plucks the tickets from her daughter's hand and looks at them. "Three? You planning on coming?"

I nearly spit out my coffee. "No. I figured she could bring a friend. Or you could invite Mindy."

"Not Mindy," Legs says.

Mindy is our brother Luke's fiancée, and she's still in the "testing" stage with Allegra.

Legs tends to treat new people with suspicion at the best of times, which I relate to endlessly. Growing up, my older brother and younger sister were effortlessly social, outgoing and popular, seeking out and finding attention wherever they went. I, on the other hand, preferred to be alone. My mother (also a social butterfly) used to joke that I was her "wary little black sheep."

I always chose—and still choose—the people I surround myself with carefully. Don't let many get too close.

So Legs and I have a natural understanding.

"That's 'Auntie Mindy' to you, sweetheart," Lana Mae corrects.

"Fine, not Auntie Mindy. I want Uncle Liam to come."

I shake my head no. I'll get the tickets, but I draw the

line at actually going to see one of these hormonal, baby-faced, boy-band singers.

"You should see the look on your face, Liam." Lana Mae laughs, then turns to Legs. "We'll talk about who we can bring later, okay?" She shoots me an innocent glance. "Maybe Uncle Liam and Uncle Luke can flip a coin for the honors."

"Or you can stay home, Mama, and Uncle Liam and Uncle Luke can both take me," Legs says with an eyelash flutter—which has a cuteness factor that could rival a baby bunny rabbit.

Damn kid's got us all wrapped around her little finger.

"Deal," Lana Mae says. "As long as they promise to wear 'Belieber' t-shirts to the show."

Allegra gives her mother a gravely serious look. "What else would they wear?" She then turns on her heel and makes for the stairs. "I'm going to call Uncle Luke and tell him. Bye, Mommy!"

"You don't want to give your mother a hug?" Lana Mae raises her eyebrows and clasps her hands to her chest in mock horror. "It's only the first time I've left for more than a day since you were born."

Legs sighs deeply. "Okay, okay."

But when her little arms wind around Lana's neck, Legs clutches her tight, hands fisting in her mom's sweater. Legs might act tough, but she's soft-serve ice cream beneath that hard candy shell.

"I'll miss you more than you can imagine, sweetie." Lana Mae pulls back from the embrace and nuzzles her daughter's hair. "You going to be good for Uncle Liam?"

"Yesssss," Legs says with a conspiratorial eye roll in my direction.

"Course she is," I say, but confident as I sound, something clenches in my stomach. I love Legs to death, and I've spent endless hours with her, but it's hard not to be nervous. I've never carried the responsibility of parenting a child before. What if I screw this up?

I remind myself sternly that I can do this. I *have* to do this. Lana Mae's counting on me, and Legs is, too. I'll do my best to be a great parent to her while Lana Mae is out of town.

After a long, lengthy, tearful goodbye (on Lana Mae's part. I definitely didn't tear up. Not at all), the door shuts and it's just me and Legs.

"So..." I say slowly, turning to Legs. Her expression is so down-trodden, I almost call Lana Mae to come back. "Ready for me to kick your butt at mini-golf?"

Legs perks up immediately. She shoots toward me and tackles me in a hug. "We're going to mini-golf?!"

"Why do you think your mom wanted you dressed? Let's go!"

"Thank you, Uncle Liam!" Legs yells, taking my hand and dragging me out the door. She gives me a look over her shoulder. "By the way, you smell funny."

Huh. Maybe I should've prioritized that shower before coming over. "Funny like how?"

"I dunno. Kinda like a *girl*." Legs giggles behind her hands at what she thinks is a very funny joke.

And maybe it really is a joke—a grown man who's so unaccustomed to romantic female company that he keeps finding himself thinking about a freaking *cuddle*.

Joke's on me, I guess.

7

ANNIE

I woke up early. Extra early.

First day at a new job, have to "seize the day," as Prisha put it (though not in the context she'd intended).

But then, instead of getting out of bed, I snuggled up and opened TikTok. There was a video of a golden retriever meeting her human baby sister for the first time, so of course, I had to watch that at least five times. The next video was a tutorial on making maple syrup, so I lingered for a few minutes more, because what if I get stuck in a Vermont forest someday and need to make maple syrup to survive?

Anyhow, after my TikTok spiral and syrup-making education (turns out that it's, like, a million step process involving a lot of equipment so, if I ever *did* get stuck in a Vermont forest, I would still be unable to make syrup), I was no longer extra early.

Not at all.

"Annie! Breakfast's ready. Hurry up or you'll be late for work!" Mom hollers from the bottom of the stairs.

From the vantage point of my cozy bed—which is still draped with my favorite late-noughties-era sequinned turquoise comforter—you could sub out "work" for "school" and I could almost believe that the last decade didn't happen. That I'm still sixteen, equipped with my new driver's license and a recently de-metalled mouth of straight teeth. That I have my entire love life and glittering career ahead of me.

A whole world of possibilities. No rap sheet of failures.

"Coming," I call as I swat away a hot-pink pillow in the shape of kissy lips and get out of bed.

I stand in the center of the room, clad in a Green Day t-shirt I acquired during my ill-advised and short-lived emo phase (which amounted to little more than a few safety pins on my bag, a pink clip-in hair streak, and a whole lot of badly-applied eyeliner). I take in the collage of "hot guy" posters—mostly Chad Michael Murray and Robert Pattinson—taped to the pink walls; the outsized Minion stuffy I won at the fair; the shelves of *Pretty Little Liars* novels. The corner vanity still holds a collection of striped knee socks and every flavor of Victoria's Secret lipgloss.

The entire room is a relic. Frozen in time.

I almost wish that I could hide here, in the past. But living at my parents' place doesn't change everything that went wrong since I last called this house my home.

But today is the first step to putting my new life in gear. So, I'm going to forget about Justin, forget about Veronica and my old job at Financify. Forget that I kicked off this weekend by waking up pretzeled around a strange man, cuddling him for dear life...

"Annie?"

Mom pops her head in without waiting for my reply. By the look on her face, she's unsurprised to see me dithering in a band t-shirt instead of being dressed and ready. "You're—"

"Yeah, yeah. Working on it."

"Some things never change." Mom smiles, her eyes crinkling at the sides. Though she's being sweet and reflective, her words fill me with unease. "Now, do you have something smart to wear today?"

"It's a tech company," I reply as I make my way to the mirror. "I could probably just wear this."

I do this when I'm nervous—act avoidant, like I don't care. It's a horrible habit, and one I could do without right now. Because I do care. I really, really do.

This job opportunity is *exactly* what I wished for through multiple months of unemployment and Kraft mac n' cheese packets. I'll be working closely with the owners of the company, AKA my new bosses—so far only known to me as "The Brothers," thanks to the HR lady's practical swooning over Zoom.

"That's one way to make a first impression." Mom makes a face at me. More specifically, she makes a face at my white cotton boyshorts, which feature an adorable print of ice cream cones. "You should invest in some nice undergarments, dear. Every woman needs something to make her feel sensual. Feminine. Sexy."

Oh no. It's too early for this.

"You know, men appreciate a nice pair of—"

"MOM! Now is *so* not the time." My face is burning because, somehow, somewhy, my mind is once again back in the memory of Grumpypants Liam and his big arms, all wrapped around me like he was my nocturnal bodyguard.

Why must my brain go there? It was humiliating enough to wake up and realize that I was drooling all over his chest. Moreso when I noticed that the t-shirt I borrowed was adorned with a streak of my lipstick.

And then, the grand finale of humiliation—after having a minor panic freakout in the bathroom, followed by a quick session of pulling-myself-together and reapplying my favorite lipstick, I was ready to face him. Talk to him. Smooth over this entirely awkward situation.

But when I came out of the bathroom, all traces of him were gone.

Yup. He was *that* horrified by my apparent sleep advances that he took off before I could even apologize for invading his personal space for the second time in twenty-four hours.

I left the hotel room feeling like I was doing the colloquial walk of shame—complete with no goodbyes and yesterday's clothes.

So, basically, I don't need my brain reminding me of him every chance it gets.

Put the past in the past, Annie.

I can do that. And, on the plus side, I guess I scored a new t-shirt.

I squint at my Edward Cullen poster on the wall, trying to imagine cuddling him instead. But honestly, teenage vampires don't seem to do it for me anymore. I mean, have you ever rewatched *Twilight* as a grown adult? Forget bloodsuckers, and hellooooo Charlie Swan eye-candy, I say.

"And when *would* be the time?" Mom tuts away, snapping me out of my Forks policeman mental swoon. "I'm just saying. I bet Justin would've liked—"

I hold up a hand. "Please. No. Justin is married to someone else. We are nada. Finito."

"Well, honey," she says, all too reasonably. "If you refuse to talk about what happened between you two, we can only assume."

"Okay, let me clear it up. Justin and I did *not* break up over my underwear choices."

Mom shakes her head, still tutting. "Anyway, you shouldn't wear nice underwear only for men, you know. It's a good way to boost your own confidence! Want me to pop by Kohl's today and pick you up some of those lovely, lacy briefs with the tummy support and the—"

"I'm good. Thanks, Mom," I interrupt before she can start telling me which ones my dad likes her to wear or something.

My parents have never understood the concept of these wonderful things called "boundaries."

Don't get me wrong, I love that they're in love. I just don't want to hear... details.

"Hop to it, dearie. I made your favorite—pancakes! If you hurry, you'll have time to eat one."

I roll my eyes, but I'm smiling. Pancakes were my favorite meal at five years old, and are, indeed, still my favorite. A sudden, sharp rush of warmth fills my body—gratitude for having loving parents who support me, no matter what. Though I'm desperate for change, I can also see that it's good to have some constants in my life. Family support. Today may be the first day of my future, but this is the first time anyone's cooked me breakfast in years.

And so, I'm going to dress to impress, eat my pancakes with lashings of maple syrup I still have no idea how to make, and then go impress the hell out of these folks at Stay Inside the Lines.

"Hey, Mom?"

"Yes, dear?" Mom looks up from where she's now shamelessly rummaging through my underwear drawer.

"It's good to be home."

8

LIAM

I don't hate Mondays. In fact, I tolerate them fine.

There's something about getting back into the office and putting my brain in gear after the weekend that makes me feel better. In control of what's going to happen. The week is mine to shape and mold into something that can be viewed as successful.

My Monday mornings usually go something like this: Wake up at 5am. Drink a green smoothie with exactly one point five cups of casein protein in it. Drive seven minutes to the gym. It's a boxing gym—not one of those nonsense trendy places with pop music, glittery boxing gloves and people clad head-to-toe in Lalalemons or whatever those ridiculous leggings my sister likes are called. I'm talking about a boxing gym that smells like sweat and testosterone, and has first aid kits on hand for inevitable bleeding.

I spend an hour with my trainer before driving home. This leaves me with twenty-three minutes to shower, shave, suit up and scramble four eggs. At 7am on the dot, I drive to the office and get a large black Americano at Sugarland (stupid name, great coffee) on the ground floor before making it to my desk for 7:30am. I usually have half an hour of peace and quiet before everyone else rolls in.

This Monday morning, however, goes a little more like this:

"Legs, where does your mom keep your lunch box?" I move from one cupboard to the next, opening and shutting as I go.

"Uncle Liam, Harry Styles pooped on the carpet!"

Oh dear Lord in heaven, give me strength.

"He also coughed up a hairball." A pause. "Eww, it's all *slimy.*"

That damn cat.

I open the next cupboard a bit too forcefully, and a pink, plastic tumbler falls out and bounces off my head.

"Ow!" I swear under my breath. "Legs, I'll clean it up. Come down and eat your"—*crap, the toast!*—"breakfast."

Buzz. Buzz.

My phone vibrates on the counter.

Patience. I just need patience.

I race to the toaster—which has black smoke billowing from it—and carefully remove the two incinerated pieces of bread. I reach for my phone with the other hand. "Hello?"

"You sound flustered, little bro." Luke chuckles, then takes a loud sip of what must be coffee. I'm in dire need of caffeine, but I haven't had a moment to brew anything. How does Lana Mae do this? "Parenthood keeping you on your toes?"

"Good morning to you too, Luke." I rub my hand over my face. "And for the record, I'm not flustered."

Feeling, in fact, very flustered, I cup the speaker and turn to the stairs. "Legs, get your butt down here! It's breakfast time!"

"I heard that," Luke singsongs, his voice muffled through my clenched hand.

I snap the phone back to my ear. "Are you calling for the sole purpose of annoying me? 'Cuz if so, it's working."

Luke laughs the laugh of a man who was not up half the night checking for monsters under his niece's bed. "You focus on getting our girl to school, I'll make sure the newbie's set up at work."

Right. I totally forgot that our new data analyst starts this morning.

I don't know anything about her other than the fact that she's female and highly-qualified. Hiring isn't something I get involved with. Mostly because it requires charming-people skills, and I just don't have time for that.

I'm eager to meet her, though. Our app's user data will be fundamental in shaping the company vision that we present to Wiseman. I'm hoping that this new hire will give us the info we need to improve on the app, make it even more user-friendly and appealing. Thereby securing us much-needed funding from Wiseman's company.

No pressure.

"What're you burning, Uncle Liam?" Legs appears in the kitchen with a squirming Harry Styles under one arm. She's wearing a bathing suit, one sock and what looks like satin evening gloves.

"Gotta go," I mutter to Luke, even as I hear him cackling in the background.

"Don't be late!"

"I won't. Mark my words."

Luke laughs again, so I hang up on him, then focus my attention on my niece. "Toast. I'm burning toast. What are you wearing, Allegra?"

"Clothes," she smirks. "I'm wearing clothes."

Brat got that sass straight from her mama.

"You can't wear a bathing suit to school."

"Don't say 'can't'," she chides. "Mommy says I can do anything."

"Great. Can you sit down and eat your toast then, please? And do you know where your lunch box is?"

She grasps a corner of the bread and gives it a disapproving look. "I don't like burnt toast."

Yeah, me neither.

I rub the spot on my head where the tumbler hit me, and take a long, slow inhale. Time to change tactics. "Legs, if you change out of your bathing suit and put on shorts, a t-shirt, and sneakers, I'll take you to Chick-fil-A for a breakfast sandwich on the way to school. Okay?"

Her little face lights up. "Two."

"Two what?"

"Two chicken sandwiches. One for breakfast, one for lunch."

I glance around me helplessly. I haven't had coffee, the lunch box is nowhere to be found, and...

Oh, lovely. Harry Styles is making a violent choking sound. He unceremoniously throws up another hairball.

I look back at Legs, who's giving me her best gap-toothed smile.

"You've got yourself a deal," I say solemnly. "Now, hurry. I don't want to be late."

Half an hour later, I am indeed late.

Between Legs refusing to settle her butt into her booster seat after our stop at Chick-Fil-A, having to make an emergency trip to Circle K for Skittles (yes, another bribe. But poor thing got a bit teary again about her mom not being here, and I may or may not have had another minor panic), and then having to walk her to her class and sit with her until her friend Jenny arrived, I was already late when I hit 75 North. Which, of course, was backed up due to construction.

Who in their right mind okays construction on a major artery during Monday rush-hour traffic?

By the time I finally arrive at the office, I'm officially late for the morning staff meeting and have half a mind to lodge a complaint with the city.

I open the door to the boardroom at 8:04am.

They haven't started yet. Everyone's standing around drinking coffee and engaging in inane small talk (the exact reason my usual habit is to enter the boardroom at 7:59am), but the way Vanessa from HR is looking at me, you'd think I blew off the entire meeting.

"Mr. Donovan, there you are," she says in this high-pitched, breathy voice. "I was beginning to worry."

"Traffic," I mutter quickly. The eternal cover-all excuse that requires no further explanation. I look away, tugging on my shirt collar.

"Flustered," Luke mouths at me from where he's sitting on the boardroom table, chatting to Jamal and Todd, our developers.

I give him a stony glare in return. He knows I'm giving him the middle finger in my head.

"Before we start," Vanessa rocks back on her red leather heels and looks at me in that coy, head-tilted-down, pouty way that I've often seen women do and never understood. It just makes them look constipated. "I need to introduce you to someone."

Ah, yes. The new data analyst.

Vanessa gestures toward a quiet presence hovering beside her. I was so flustered—dammit, Luke—I didn't even notice her there. I turn to her almost eagerly...

My heart stops.

The blood drains from my face.

Because the person looking back at me with saucer eyes, face pale as a ghost's, is the very same person I shared a very small bed with this weekend. The same person I left alone in a hotel room after cuddling her all night.

It's definitely, unmistakably her.

Annie's dressed less like a children's entertainer today, but she still has that same cute, quirky look. Her bright red and yellow, poppy-patterned sundress, fastened at the waist with a thick leather belt, wouldn't be classified as "typical office attire," and yet, it works. Her wild auburn hair has been straightened and tamed into a neat ponytail.

I preferred the wild hair.

The thought comes to me unbidden, coupled with a workplace-inappropriate flashback of wild-haired Annie wearing little more than my t-shirt. The way her breathing slowed as she fell asleep. The sighs she made every time she rolled over in bed next to me. The way I held her close...

I swallow hard.

This is a freaking HR nightmare if I ever saw one.

We stare at each other for one second. Two. Three.

Say something, Liam!

"H-hello," I finally choke out.

Annie blinks, like a spell's been broken, and her red-lipsticked mouth stretches into a sudden smile.

"Hi." She glances at her wristwatch, and then—I kid you not—she says, "glad you could finally join us."

9

ANNIE

Of all the things I could've said, did I really have to say THAT?

My foot-in-mouth syndrome always flares up when I'm nervous. It's a super helpful, special feature that I've been blessed with.

Not.

I barely hear Vanessa's surprised snort at the words that slipped out of my mouth like a bar of soap slips through wet hands.

All I can think is that this cannot be real life. Things like this don't happen in real life. And if they do, they happen in *Gilmore Girls*-esque towns with tight-knit communities who get breakfast at a single coffee shop owned by a handsome, flannel-clad grump.

Things like this don't happen in major cities of millions —where you can bump into a hundred people every day of your life and safely bet that you'll never, ever see them again.

I sneak a thumb and forefinger to the soft part of my underarm and pinch. Hard.

Ouch!

Pain radiates through me, sharp enough to make my eyes sting.

Not dreaming, I guess.

Could it be that this is all a set up and I'm being Punk'd? I glance around for hidden cameras. Unless Ashton is crouching behind that fake cactus in the corner, there's nothing to indicate that this is a TV show prank.

No, it's really freaking happening. The man I woke up clinging to like a spider monkey not two days ago is here. In front of me. Not only that, but he's my *coworker*. And judging by the fuss Vanessa's making, he's pretty darn important around here, too.

The mathematical chances must be, like, millions to one. Billions, perhaps.

I close my eyes for a quick moment, and smooth down my dress as I compose myself.

Freaking Rosemary and her crazy fate talk. She must have had something to do with this.

Vanessa's expression, meanwhile, goes from abject horror to curiosity as she peers at me, then Liam. "Hang on. Do you two—"

"Liam Donovan," Liam cuts her off, offering one big, meaty hand to me. The gesture is totally at odds with his brusque tone, and when I finally dare look at him, I'm stunned to see the look on his face: eyebrows knit together, mouth neutral, eyes expressionless. Void of any recognition.

Vanessa swallows the rest of her sentence and chuckles. "Never mind."

I stare blankly at Liam for just a smidge too long. He's really going to pretend we've never met? Or does he truly not remember me?

I mean... there's no way, right? We spooned. Spooned!

Although, maybe he's a serial spooner who has so many spoonees that he can't recall them all.

Brain, would you ever shut up?

He must remember me; he's not a goldfish. He's doing this on purpose. Must be.

And two can play at that game.

I put on an easy, breezy smile and place my hand in his outstretched paw. His grip is firm, his skin warm, rough and calloused. For a shadow of a second, when that hand touches mine, I swear I see his dark eyes flicker with something that tells me I'm not the only one thinking about the Econo Hotel. That sexy pine forest smell is still radiating from him, and I have a very sudden, very primal urge to inhale deeply.

Which, of course, I resist doing. Because I'm no longer in bed next to him, but at work with my new colleague, for crying out loud!

Before I can make a further fool out of myself, I remove my hand from his vice-like grip and step back. Smile in a way that implies my heart isn't currently beating a thousand times per minute. "Annie Jacobs. It's a pleasure to meet you, *Mr. Donovan*."

He doesn't say "likewise" or "call me Liam." He doesn't even welcome me to the company.

Nope. He simply sets his jaw, looks at me like it's quite the opposite of a pleasure to meet me, then turns to talk to another suit—a graying guy who introduced himself as Jamal earlier. "Nader, you deploy the new code yet?"

On the plus side, at least I'm not the only one not to get a "good morning." Jamal must be used to this, because he simply nods and moves to the boardroom table. Liam—*Mr. Donovan*—bends over the desk to take a look at the code-filled screen.

I stand stiffly, unable to tear my eyes from the man at the end of the behemoth table. He's even taller and broader than I remember, has that kind of powerful stature where his suit jacket strains at the top button.

"Don't worry," Vanessa hisses as we take our seats. "It's not you, it's him."

"I figured," I say quietly.

"He's so sexy, isn't he?" She puts her pointy purple nails to her chest and sighs. "I love a silent, powerful manly man."

Isn't Vanessa meant to be in HR?

I don't want to get on the wrong side of another person at this company within five minutes of starting, so I don't question her questionable comment.

"He's really... something," I reply benignly instead of saying what I really want to say. Which is: "if a woman behaved like that in the workplace, everyone would assume she had PMS. But when a man does it, it's considered *sexy* and *powerful*."

Double standards are the worst. Especially when applied to men who refer to women as "Legs."

Vanessa and I slide into a couple of empty chairs and the meeting is called to order. A man named Luke speaks first. He's handsome, in a clean-cut, pearly white smile, Abercrombie and Fitch kind of way. A far cry from a certain moody, smoldering man sitting in my right peripheral.

I risk a glance at Liam across the table. He's steely-eyed and clenching his jaw so tight, it tics. He's also gripping a mug of black coffee (what a fitting drink for this man) with white knuckles. I'm amazed it doesn't shatter.

I look down at my own cream-and-sugar-with-a-splash-of-coffee and take a careful sip as Luke speaks. I should be paying attention, I really should—he's talking about their potential angel investor or something—but I'm completely out of sorts. My stomach is churning like I'm bobbing around in a barrel being swept toward the edge of Niagara Falls.

Think, Annie, think.

What would Brené Brown do? (W.W.B.B.D—a motto to live by)

I take a breath and try some positive thinking.

Maybe I won't have to work with Liam directly; there are about ten of us in the room, and from what I can garner, we all represent different departments. The chances of our roles crossing over are small.

If the Wall Street Journal that Liam was reading on the plane is anything to go by, he's probably in finance. Which means that I'll never have to talk to him because not a single sane soul would trust me with anything finance-related.

Yeah, I deal with data. But actual money management? No way. My credit card statement is all the proof you could ever need to that effect. You'd think I was trying to seduce the UberEats guy with the amount I spend on pizza delivery.

I think back to the research I did on Stay Inside the Lines. I remember wearing a stained pair of sweatpants along with a freshly-pressed shirt while doing my Zoom interview. I remember emailing back and forth with Vanessa, and discussing lengthy, detailed contracts, and viewing an "About Us" page filled with pictures of the employees.

I don't remember anything about Liam "Sexy" Donovan. Which he's apparently known as around here.

My heart gives a hopeful leap. Maybe he's new, too. Has started so recently that they haven't even added him to the website. And if he's not on the website, he hardly has the power to make my career go up in flames, right?

Pleased with my conclusion and now wanting confirmation, I tap Vanessa on the leg. "Psst."

She turns her head, her long blond hair falling in a waterfall over one shoulder. "Yeah?"

"What does Liam do here?"

She looks at me like I'm a little simple. "Do?"

"Yeah, like what's his job?"

She frowns. "Mr. Donovan owns the company."

My jaw hits the floor.

Quite literally. I almost topple out of my chair.

"What?" I hiss when I finally recover. "He's one of *The Brothers*?"

"Um, yeah." Vanessa peers at me with a wrinkled nose and an expression that says *keep up*. Which I am obviously not doing, because this is insanity. "He's THE brother. The OG."

Shocked doesn't even begin to cover how I'm feeling.

Not only is my weekend bed buddy—the one to whom I just said "nice of you to finally join us" all sassily—my new coworker, he *owns* the company.

You can't make this stuff up.

Vanessa sighs loudly. I'm getting the feeling that subtlety isn't in her wheelhouse. "He got Luke—or Mr. D, as we call him—involved a couple years back to handle the operations and marketing."

My jaw drops further. "Wait. Luke is the other brother?"

Abercrombie model and Grumpypants are related? How?!

"Luke and Liam Donovan," Vanessa speaks extra slowly as she points at the two men. She's clearly misinterpreted my shock for a lack of understanding. "AKA our bosses. AKA total hotties. Luke's engaged, but Liam's single. He..."

I tune out Vanessa's chatter, my mind in a spiral.

Of course he's my boss. Why wouldn't he be my boss?

Something like this could only happen to me. Other

people do things like win ten dollars on scratch-offs, and snag the last parking spot at Hooters, or however that country song goes... Is Hooters still a thing?

That's beside the point. Which is this—I am not that type of person.

Instead, I do things like spend the night in an airport hotel with a man who thinks I'm a legitimate Bundy-esque sociopath, and it turns out that he holds the keys to my entire career.

I guess I can safely assume that, like Taylor Swift, I'm about to be locked out of my own kingdom. The silver lining (because there's always a silver lining, no matter how thin and flimsy) is that I'm not the Kanye West of this particular scenario.

Aaaaand this explains why Liam pretended not to recognize me. I've read the very detailed HR manual that was sent over with my contract, and even though bed-sharing was not specifically mentioned, workplace romances were. And they appear to be frowned upon at best around here.

I wish there was a way to tell him that I didn't mean to leap on him in my sleep. That it was a total accident and that I wasn't hitting on him. Pinky promise. He should know that, of all the employees that he could've possibly spent the night with, he doesn't have to worry about me trying to pursue anything romantic with him. Another workplace romance? No, siree. Not for this girl. Only insane people repeat things over and over expecting a different result.

Maybe I can just stay as far away from him as possible to get the message across. I mean, the guy can't think I'm, like, madly in love with him or stalking him or something if he literally *never* sees me. I'll be as professional as can be. No HR intervention necessary.

I'm still clinging to that wispy gossamer tidbit of positivity when Vanessa—rather forcefully—pokes me in the arm with a pointy fingernail.

"Annie," she hisses, and I look up to see nine faces staring at me expectantly.

Make that eight. Liam looks like he'd rather watch a live decapitation than look at me.

"I'm so sorry." I go a hundred burning shades of hellfire red. "Was lost in my thoughts for a moment and I missed what you said. Sorry," I add a second time.

Because, yanno, part-Canadian.

Liam's face is set like a cold marble statue. Luke, on the other hand, looks thoroughly amused. Once again, how are those two related?

"Do you tend to miss things a lot?" Liam asks—the first time he's spoken in this meeting. "Planes, trains, automobiles?"

My eyes jump to him. His expression's still stony, totally impenetrable, and his voice is neutral and flat. But his eyes glint in a way that tells me he *knows*.

"Ignore Liam." Luke elbows Liam in the ribs, then gives me a kind smile. "He's extra cranky this morning for some unknown reason."

I glance at Liam and know that his "extra crankiness" is for a reason very much known to me. Might be something to do with the fact I'm here, in his office.

Luke continues, oblivious. "I was just saying that we're stationing you in Liam's office, Annie. You know, because you'll be working so closely together to gather data before our V2 launch."

Oh no.

I'll be stationed. In Liam's office.

How on earth am I supposed to stay far away from him while sitting across from the man?!

I open my mouth but can't think of a single coherent reply. So, I blurt out the first thing that comes to mind. "Um, be right back. Gotta pee."

Gotta pee?!

Nooooo, Annie. Not a meeting-appropriate turn of phrase.

But it's too late to backtrack, so I shove back my chair and shoot to a stand. At this point, I'm desperate to get out of here.

As I make for the door, I hear Liam mutter, "some things really shouldn't be shared."

I get the distinct feeling that he's not talking about my untimely, bladder-related exit.

⚓

"Pick up. Please, pick up," I mutter over and over like a mantra as the phone rings. When the real dire straits happen, a girl needs her best friend.

Eventually, a breathless "hello?"

"Prish!" I whisper-squeak, quiet as I can given my current hysteria. The sound still bounces around the bathroom like it's a veritable echo chamber.

This is what my life has come to—locked in a toilet cubicle like I'm in one of those 90s' high school movies and it's lunchtime on my first day at a new school and I'm trying to avoid all the good-looking bullies.

"Annie, hi!" Prisha shrieks. "How's the new job? You killing it down there?"

"No, I'm in the bathroom—"

"Oof. Told you not to eat the plane food. I don't know what it is about that pasta they always serve, but it goes right through me."

"No, it's not that."

"Be quiet, I'm on the phone!"

"Prish—"

"Sorry, not you. Alia's screaming like a banshee. My ears are bleeding." She grunts, moving around. "So why are you in the bathroom? Cramps or something?"

"No, I'm hiding," I admit. Not my first bathroom hideout of late...

"Why are you—HEY, DON'T BITE YOUR BROTHER!"

I love Prisha with every last bone in my body; she's the closest thing I've ever had to a sister. But I should've known that she was the worst person to call right now. Prish has her hands full with Alia and Rishi, her adorable, completely chaotic two-year-old twins.

"Something happened," I continue, not knowing if she's able to listen, but I literally can't hold onto this information any longer. "Something crazy, you won't believe—"

"One second."

I stop talking and hear a series of bangs, crashes and wails at the other end of the phone. Then, silence.

"Annie, you still there?"

"Still here. What's going on?"

"I turned on *Peppa Pig*, then hid in my bathroom too." A pause. "Don't tell Raj."

"I swear I won't say a word to your husband about the illegal screen time." I laugh softly, my heart happier for having my friend on the other end of the line.

"So what's going on?" Prisha's voice is gentle. "Since you're hiding in the bathroom, I'm assuming that... ooh, you've spilled coffee all over yourself? Or ripped your skirt in half?"

I chuckle. "How on earth would I have ripped my skirt in half?"

"I don't know, a paper cutter?"

"Prish, what do you think happens in offices?"

Prisha has been a stay-at-home wife and mom since she married Raj, her childhood sweetheart, six years ago, and moved out of the shoebox apartment she shared with me in the city, and straight into suburban picket-fence life in Wellesley. She wouldn't have it any other way.

"Hmm... well, isn't it all just good-looking people standing around and drinking coffee between giving presentations and having scandalous affairs?"

"You've gotta stop watching *Mad Men.*"

"Never."

"We're getting sidetracked. I'm hiding in the bathroom because I may or may not have slept with my new boss—"

"GIRL. It's not even 9am on your first day!"

"Not like that! My new boss is the stranger from the airport hotel." I lower my voice, even though nobody else is in the bathroom. "You know, the one I shared a bed with."

"Shower Hottie is your new boss?" Prisha is making the gulpy sounds she always does when she's trying—and failing—not to laugh. "Sorry, Annie, but... this could literally only happen to you."

I frown at the cubicle door for answers, but unlike a high school bathroom, it's graffiti-free. And the room doesn't smell like cigarette smoke and strawberry-vanilla body spray.

"But that's not even the worst part..." I quickly get her up to speed on everything that's happened since we texted. Starting with Liam leaving his t-shirt for me in the bathroom, the morning cuddle fiasco, and ending with me walking into the boardroom this morning and practically insulting him (AKA, my BOSS) first thing.

The only part is I leave out is the drool. And that Liam left the hotel room before I could apologize for said cuddle fiasco.

Even Prisha can't make me feel better about that.

"So. Do you think I'm still going to have a job when I exit the bathroom?"

Prisha snorts. "Abso-freaking-lutely. You're smart and you work hard and you're great at what you do. And you're a good cuddler, too. So it's his fault if he didn't like that."

Despite myself, I laugh.

"If he's a good employer, he'll judge you by the quality of your work. Which will give you an A+ employee ranking in anyone's book."

I shift on the toilet seat and cross my legs. Did Prisha actually just give out sensible workplace advice?

"And if he doesn't see that," she continues, "he's clearly an idiot and you should get even by loosening the screws on his desk chair, or... putting rat poison on his lunch. He can't be mean if he's busy dying!"

There it is.

"Ooh, yes, the good old murder your boss plan. Classic." I roll my eyes. "I guess I do look good in orange."

"Brings out the orange in your hair," Prisha agrees with the cheery confidence of someone blessed with long, silky black hair that never fuzzes around her head in the rain and makes her look like a human Cheeto.

"Remind me again why we're friends?"

"Because we love each other. And because I believe in you. You can do this, Annie. You didn't move a thousand miles to give up on day one. He's probably as embarrassed as you are about the whole thing. And yes, maybe it was a tad inappropriate, workplace-wise, but it happened before you officially started working there, so no harm, no foul. Just forget about it and focus on your job."

"You're right." I smile. Square my shoulders. "I can do this. Thanks, Prish."

"You can repay me with photos that you've secretly snapped of McSwoony."

Aaaaaand we're back to the Prisha I know and love.

"Anyway," she continues. "I gotta go, Rishi's losing his mind. Pray for me."

"Always." I laugh as she hangs up.

I unlock the cubicle door, step outside.

I can and will go back out there. And I'll be the best new employee Stay Inside the Lines has ever seen. I moved all the way back to Atlanta, unpacked my two suitcases into my teenage closet, and bought a monthly transit ticket and six boxes of chocolate chip Eggos for my lunches. I can't back out now; I've come too far.

A sudden nervous clench of my bladder has me stepping back inside the cubicle and locking the door.

I'll be the best new employee Stay Inside the Lines has ever seen... right after I actually pee.

10

LIAM

"Vanessa, get in here." I slam the phone down before she can respond.

My blood is pumping at a ferocious speed as I pace the length of my office, back and forth. Soon enough, the HR specialist knocks and sticks her head around the office door. She gives me a big, brazen smile. "Yes, Mr. Donovan?"

"Where's the woman who just started?" There's a hint of a tremor in my voice that almost betrays me, and I mentally slap some sense into myself. I need to stay calm, stay in control.

This is a workplace. That I run. That this woman has essentially entered without my consent.

"Annie?" she asks, pouting her lips.

"Did we hire another new woman I'm not aware of?"

"No." Vanessa looks at me carefully, then tugs at the hem of her skirt. "She's in the bathroom, I think."

Still? What do women DO in there?

"Who hired her?"

She lifts a tan shoulder. "Um, I did."

"Did Luke vet her application, too?"

"Of course. Regular hiring process. I reviewed resumes,

95

did elementary screenings, compiled my notes for Luke, and then he picked the candidates I interviewed on Zoom." Vanessa chews her lip and looks at me with fluttery eyes. "Mr. Donovan, is something—"

"Get me everything you have on her," I cut her off briskly. "Resume, cover letter, any email transcripts prior to her being hired."

I know I'm being abrupt, but can you blame me? I'm in full crisis mode. Tim Wiseman specifically suggested we tighten up our HR. He didn't ask for a veritable circus of inappropriacy.

And to have *her* working in my office alongside me... in this tight space.

It just won't do. There must be some way to get around this.

Not fire Annie, of course. But maybe move her to another area of the office. Somewhere we won't be forced to see each other all day, every day. I just have to make sure I can do it without alerting Luke. He would have an absolute field day with this.

Vanessa blinks at me. Raises an eyebrow. "You don't usually take this kind of interest in new hires."

Busted.

Aware that I'm very low on options for an appropriate response—and now dreading the thought of Vanessa telling Luke anything—I find myself saying, "Do I pay you to make useless observations?"

Nice, Liam. What a guy—opting for the class-act, douchebag special.

I honestly didn't mean for the words to sound so dick-ish. Like I said, I'm terrible when put on the spot. Liam in crisis is not a pretty sight.

But strangely, Vanessa doesn't seem bothered. Or maybe she didn't hear what I said. A wry smile plays on her lips as she leans a hip against my desk. Like she thinks I'm flirting with her or something. Which I'm very obviously not.

I'm about to say something more, backtrack or apologize or something...

Instead, laughter fills the room.

Vanessa and I spin around to see Luke chuckling away, arms crossed and propped up against the doorframe.

He looks at Vanessa. "Liam got his panties in a bunch about something?"

"Oh, I, uh—" Vanessa looks between Luke and me like a deer in the headlights. It's probably the first time I've seen the brash, confident twenty-something look awkward. After a few seconds of silent floundering, she finally shrugs. "Um, I don't think Mr. Donovan wears panties, sir."

Luke splutter-laughs so loud, he claps a hand over his mouth. A red, splotchy blush climbs Vanessa's cheeks.

Not for the first time this morning, I close my eyes and pray for patience.

"Please ignore Luke. In fact, I implore you to ignore Luke," I tell Vanessa without looking at her.

"Yes, Mr. Donovan."

I sigh. "You can go now."

"Thanks, Nessa!" Luke chimes in, giving her a cheery grin. Like this was a perfectly normal meeting to have with your bosses. "Get a coffee downstairs and use the company card, my treat."

"Thanks, Mr. D," Vanessa says gleefully. That's how it is around here. I'm the buttoned-up, formal Mr. Donovan. Luke is coffee-buying, joke-making Mr. D.

Vanessa shoots me a final furtive, flirty look before shutting the door behind her.

I pinch the bridge of my nose—HR is clearly not Stay Inside the Lines' strong suit. No matter how many times

I've pulled my supergrump act with Vanessa, no matter how many times I've confirmed with her that the HR rulebook explicitly states that romantic relationships at the SITL workplace are *strongly discouraged*, she still flirts with me like *that's* her job.

I sink into my ergonomic chair and massage my temples for a few seconds. "Might wanna lay off the pantie talk in front of the HR specialist, Anchorman."

Luke sits on my desk. Picks up a stack of post-its. "Ness knows I'm bugging you, not her."

But I'm the one she keeps giving those scary bedroom eyes to.

Instead of saying that aloud, I pluck the post-its out of Luke's hands and put them back where they belong.

He picks up my stapler instead. Moves it from hand to hand as he studies me. "How's Legs?"

"Had a dozen outfit changes this morning, then went to school covered in head-to-toe glitter. With a bag of Chick-fil-A in her backpack."

"'Course she did." Luke grins. "I asked Mindy to take her to get her nails done after school. They should be done around the same time we wrap up here."

"She'll love that."

"Speaking of my fiancée, you got a date to my wedding yet?"

I shake my head and interlace my fingers, crack my knuckles one by one. "What on earth gave you the impression that I'm taking a date to your wedding?"

Luke smiles slyly. "The look on your face when you walked into the office this morning."

Ah. Typical Luke. Segue the conversation into unchartered waters, then pounce like a hungry great white.

I shrug as casually as I can manage. "I have no idea what you're talking about."

I'm usually good at hiding what I'm feeling—so good that I don't even know what I'm feeling myself sometimes. "Unflappable" is basically my middle name.

But when I saw Annie standing next to Vanessa, I was flapped. Very flapped. So flapped, in fact, that I panicked and pretended we'd never met.

Another reaction for the books, there.

I need to wrap my head around the fact that Annie works here now. Works *for me*, to be exact. This is a professional environment, and I have to behave professionally. So, just like they don't talk about Bruno in *Encanto* (yes, Legs forced me to watch that movie. Twice. And no, I didn't hate it), we won't talk about what happened. Ever.

Problem solved.

Luke looks positively gleeful. "You're hiding something."

I don't reply.

"And you've been acting all *American Psycho* since the meeting. More so than usual, I mean," Luke goes on. Annoyingly. "Why?"

"Just tired," I lie.

"Liam, I saw you looking at the new girl." Luke points my stapler at me accusingly. "I understand that she's objectively hot, but you never react that way to hot women. You've never so much as looked at Vanessa twice, and she's always checking you out."

So Luke's not blind to it either. Small comfort.

He also has no idea when to shut up.

"We can't be talking about this," I mutter, my voice almost a growl. "This is breaking all kinds of HR guidelines. Vanessa would have a fit."

Luke rolls his eyes. "She'd have a fit because you weren't talking about *her*."

99

"Whatever." I wave a hand. "It's unprofessional to be calling the new woman 'hot'."

Luke sighs deeply, like I've rained all over his carefully curated, cotton-candy-filled parade. "I know. I've seen Annie Jacobs' CV—impressive, what she's capable of. But you need to lighten up, lil bro. I'm just giving you a hard time."

I grimace instinctively, my gaze falling on the glass door to my office. Barb is speaking to Vanessa and shooting glances my way.

Whatever they're saying about me, it doesn't faze me. None of them understand how important it is that we secure this funding. I've put years of blood, sweat and tears into this app, but my employees have given me this part of their careers. *And* my one and only brother gave the money needed to move forward at a crucial point in the app's development.

Stay Inside the Lines might be my passion project, but it's also my responsibility. Without this funding, payroll is going to be difficult to swing for the foreseeable future.

"So, do you know her?" Luke is still staring at me, wiggling his eyebrows expectantly.

"We have more important things to do than talk about our new hire," I say quickly, turning my attention to my computer screen. I'm desperate to take control of this wayward conversation and turn it to what actually matters: business. "Especially since you're going to be busy with wedding planning, and I'm going to be busy with Legs's schedule. We need to get our V2 renderings together, and we need a reliable foot soldier to get us the data so we can make these app upgrade decisions, not a distraction that leads to pointless speculation."

"You *do* know her!" Luke gloats, rubbing his hands together.

Alarm bells go off in my head. How did...? "No, I—"

"He doth protest too much!"

I hate my brother.

"Tell me how you know her." Luke is practically dancing around the office, pointing at me and shaking his hips. I'm tempted to record this moment for Mindy so she can see what she's getting herself into. For better or for worse, indeed. "Tell me!"

I sigh. "You've clearly gotten hit in the head one too many times at the boxing gym."

I don't like lying to him, but I need to figure this out on my own. This HR issue needs to disappear if we are to have any chance of securing the funding from Wiseman's company. Besides, Luke has enough on his plate with his upcoming nuptials—I can't exactly burden him with this ridiculous situation.

"Um, hi."

Her voice makes me jolt backwards in my seat, almost overbalancing.

Luke freezes mid-butt-wiggle, a hand on his hip and the other pointing in the air like he's doing the *Night Fever* dance by The Beegees.

Both of us slowly, oh-so-slowly, look toward the door.

And there she is.

Annie Jacobs, standing in my office doorway, eyes bugging out of her face. Luke uses his "pointing" hand to smooth his hair and I clear my throat.

"Sorry to interrupt..."

"You weren't interrupting," I interject.

She nods. "This is where I'm going to be sitting, right?"

"Yeah. Sorry you're stuck sharing an office with Liam," Luke jokes.

"Same office, different desk," I say quickly. "We don't share desks here."

Luke shoots me another quizzical look before patting the desk next to mine—brought in here after the meeting, no matter how much I wanted to protest. He smiles at Annie. "This one's yours, please make yourself at home. And don't worry, Liam doesn't bite."

Her cheeks redden.

Well. This should be fun.

11

ANNIE

Liam may not bite... but he does make the cutest breathing sounds while he sleeps.

STOP IT, ANNIE!

I swallow. Clear my throat.

"Thank you, Mr. Donovan," I say to Luke, not daring to glance at Liam.

"Please, call us Luke and Liam," Luke replies breezily.

"Speak for yourself." Liam shoots him a look. "Now, let's get to work. Annie's on a steep learning curve, and time is of the essence."

I resist saying "aye, aye captain" and saluting him, but only just.

"Woah, wait up!" Luke holds up his hands. "Liam, where are your manners?"

Exactly what I was asking myself all weekend!

"We haven't asked Annie if she has any questions." Luke fixes me with his dark eyes. Not as dark as Liam's, I note. "Do you? Have questions, that is?"

I pause.

Honestly? I have about a million questions. But most of them are not questions I can ask my two new bosses.

Luke is looking at me expectantly, and Liam, meanwhile, tugs on his collar. I realize that Liam has not told his brother about the events of the weekend.

So how do I find out if everything is good here without actually coming out and asking?

"Um, well..." I start. "I do have one question."

Liam's eyes flicker, but Luke nods. "Go ahead."

I choose my words carefully. "When you say that you don't share desks at SITL, do you mean sharing a desk with a colleague—or boss—is against the rules?"

Luke says, "can't say I've had that question before" at the same time that Liam says, "absolutely, it would be completely inappropriate."

Luke blinks at Liam. "What are you talking about? We have no rule about desk sharing."

"Some rules don't need to be explicitly spelled out to be understood."

I get his message loud and clear.

"But, let's say you shared an, um... desk with someone, and hadn't realized it was against the rules. Or even realized that the person worked here. And when you did realize, you moved to your own desk. Would that be okay?"

There's a long silence. A dead silence. Save for the hum of the AC and the distant clacking of staff keyboards in the offices beyond.

I lean against my desk, waiting for someone to say something.

Anything at all would be nice.

Luke looks from me, to Liam, and back to me before throwing his hands up. "To quote my dear friend, Courtney... what in the name of Kim Kardashian's surgically enhanced ass is going on here?"

Uh oh, it's happening again. The verbal vomit is rising in me like a fountain, ready to explode.

104

Must say nothing, must play it cool, must pretend it never happened...

"We slept together!" I blurt.

Liam slaps a hand to his face. A literal facepalm.

Luke, on the other hand... Well, Luke Donovan doesn't look like the type of guy who is often shocked. In fact, in the short time I've known him, I've pegged him to be calm, laid-back, and chill. Nothing like his straight-laced, buttoned-up brother.

But right now, he's having a hard time picking his jaw up off the floor. Once again, his head swivels from me, to Liam, and back to me, then he repeats the entire action in double time. "You *slept* together?"

Oh, dang. He thinks... he actually believes...

I really, *really* shouldn't have said that.

"*Next* to each other," Liam corrects him tiredly. He shoots me a curious look, like he's trying to work out what on earth I'm doing. The answer to which, I have no idea. My original plan was to pretend it never happened. "We slept *next* to each other."

"In an airport hotel," I add in a useless attempt to be helpful. "It was a tiny room. The floor was disgusting. Brown splotches, you know how it is."

Luke's eyes glitter as he looks at his brother. "You slept with our new employee. In a hotel."

"For the thousandth time, not *with* her, *next* to her!" Liam's voice is loud and forceful. He doesn't necessarily sound angry, just adamant.

He's a good leader, I bet. With a voice like that, I can see falling into line. Couple that with his powerful, smoldering stature and those intense eyes, and maybe I can kind of see what Vanessa sees...

Noooo, don't go there, Annie!

"What do you think HR will have to say about this?"

Luke continues, waggling his eyebrows. "Kinda makes Pantygate look like small potatoes, doesn't it?"

"Pantygate?" I can't help myself. What on earth happens in this office?

Aren't tech companies meant to be full of overeager video-game-enthusiasts in Star Wars t-shirts? Or have I watched too many early 2000s' college movies?

"Oh, it's a thrilling dispute about what underwear Liam wears to the office," Luke says conversationally. Like we're talking about the weather instead of my boss's under-garments...

Nope. I'm not thinking about it.

Liam, predictably, has turned an unhealthy shade of puce, but Luke motors on. "Actually, you may be the one to enlighten us with the answer, Annie."

He shoots me a knowing wink, and I relax a little. He's making a joke, too. Maybe this will all be A-okay. A not-such-a-big-deal incident that we can forget with ease. I decide to join in, glad that we're moving past the awkward-ness. "No can do, I'm afraid. Mr. Donovan here went to bed fully clothed."

Luke slaps his hand on his knee, laughing. "Of course he did."

"This is no laughing matter," Liam snaps.

"Re-lax, little bro." Luke is clearly enjoying himself. He takes a swig of water and gestures for me to sit down. "We're all just getting to know each other. Although it seems you two already know each other preeeeetty well."

Liam ignores him, steeples his hands and looks at me seriously. "Miss Jacobs—"

"Annie," I interject with a sunny smile.

Liam looks pained. "*Annie,* I do apologize for the most unfortunate start you've had here at Stay Inside the Lines. I

106

also apologize for my brother, who doesn't seem to know the difference between a corporate office and a frat house."

He stops, like he's not sure he wants to say more. But after a long moment, he continues.

"Obviously, this was a very unfortunate series of events, completely outside of our control. If this is all too strange, if the circumstances are too unusual for you to have a fruitful working relationship with SITL, we understand and accept any request to terminate your contract."

A hard iciness gathers in the pit of my stomach, sharp and stinging. After that lengthy interview process, Liam is willing to get rid of me over a simple wrong-place-wrong-time travel mix-up?

"We do?" Luke gapes.

Liam holds up a large hand to silence his older brother. "We do. The last thing we need is an HR scandal over a simple... misunderstanding."

He fixes me with that coal dark stare, and despite my urge to flinch or squirm under his attention, I square my shoulders and stare back boldly. Clear my throat and channel all my confidence. "That won't be necessary. I'm here to work, not create drama. You hired me because you believed me to be the best person for the job, and you were correct. The circumstances surrounding how we met are beside the point."

I hold Liam's gaze, watch his reaction—of lack thereof—to me laying my cards on the table.

What I said is the truth. I came here to do a job, not get involved with my colleagues. And I'm not going to run out of here with my tail between my legs because of some ridiculous mishap.

To my surprise, Liam's brows lift a touch and his face softens. Just the slightest bit. "I'm glad to hear that."

Something in his voice, in those words, makes my heart flutter. As his eyes meet mine, I see we've come to an understanding—bury the past, focus on the task at hand.

"Thank you," I say quietly. "You won't regret this."

I'll make it my business that he doesn't.

12

LIAM

You won't regret this.

In my experience, those are usually famous last words. Destined to kick off some ill-fated scenario that you very much DO regret. But it's Thursday—three days have passed since Annie said those words, and so far, they've actually been correct.

It also means that at, as of 6:47 this evening, Annie Jacobs will have been in my life for almost an entire week.

And what a week it's been. First off, learning the ins and outs of parenthood—which has mostly consisted of being a free Uber driver, watching princess movies, and sneaking vegetables into other, less healthy foods.

Second, there's Luke. My absolute joy of a brother has been teasing me mercilessly since Annie's "we slept together" comment, and generally making things as awkward as possible. Last night, for example, I told Luke that I was popping out to grab us all takeout for dinner, and he replied, "I know it's hard for you, but try not to sleep with the cashier."

Which is rich, coming from a man who, pre-Mindy, was

totally unabashed in the amount of female company he kept.

But I can't complain too much. Luke seems to think that the whole hotel incident is one huge, hilarious joke—he's wrong—and not that big of a deal—he might actually be right. Annie and I have apparently both chalked it up to an unfortunate accident, and have *finally* moved on to work-related things.

This brings me to my third point: while the woman might spread chaos like fairy dust everywhere she goes, she's good at her job. Damn good.

To the point that, over the last few days, my shoulders relax when I see the work she's producing. How her findings will contribute to our proposed upgrades for the Stay Inside the Lines app.

Though maybe it's just her sweet, beachy scent, which now lingers in my office. Ocean smells are relaxing, right? It's probably just that. Nothing else.

Definitely not the fact that Annie Jacobs is sassy, free-spirited and beautiful. I haven't thought about any of that at all.

She's smart, that's all I'm focusing on.

And I'm not the only one who thinks so.

"Nice," Luke says when he finally looks up from the computer.

Luke and I are huddled in the boardroom, as we've been for so many hours this week, trying to get a semblance of a proposal together for Wiseman. "I like what I'm seeing with Annie's findings but I'm not sure about a couple of the suggestions—whether they're on brand."

My brow furrows as my eyes skate across the screen again. "I had the same concern."

"It's worth exploring, though. And I want to get this ironed out before we send the elementary V2 deck to Tim's office tomorrow. We'll deal with the HR stuff next week, it's less important." He pauses. "We're going to be tied up in that code meeting all afternoon, so tonight's gonna be a late one. Let's see if Annie can stay back to go over her thoughts behind points two and three, and how we could market those features with our current branding. I'm not comfortable moving forward without more information."

"Agreed." Then, I press my lips together. "But we can't stay late—we have Legs to think about."

"Already taken care of. Mindy's taking Legs along to her dress fitting this evening so she can try on her flower girl dress. That should keep Legs entertained for a few hours. Mindy's hoping to rack up some brownie points with our girl, anyway." Luke chuckles.

"She'll come around," I say. "And that sounds perfect. I'll check if Annie can hang back with us until 8pm or so."

"You."

"Pardon?"

"Hang back with *you*. Singular. I have to pick up the tuxes. I'll meet Mindy and Legs at Lana's place after and we'll stay until you get home. But don't feel like you need to rush back." Luke winks.

Annie and I, alone in the office together? We haven't been *alone* alone since...

Well, you know.

Great. Now I'm thinking about her wild auburn bedhead.

I scramble for something to say, some way to get out of this. "No, you're the groom. I'll pick up the tu—"

"No, you won't." Luke smiles like he won the Georgia Lottery Jackpot. "I'm going, you're staying at work. Just try not to sleep with her again okay?"

My brother looks way too pleased with himself.

This was all a setup. And I walked right into it.

"Remind me again why I gave you a job?" I glare at him and his grin widens.

"Because underneath all that steel and muscle, you're a big squidgy old softie."

I sigh tiredly, roll my eyes. But I can't ignore the fact that he makes a good point. And I promised myself that this situation wouldn't affect work. "Funny as you *think* you are, that joke is very stale. But you are right in that we need to follow up with Annie on some of this, so I'll ask if she can stay. I'll be home at 8:30pm sharp, and I expect you to have given Legs a nutritious dinner, checked her homework, made sure she's taken her vitamins and brushed her teeth, and read her an educational story."

"You must be a barrel of laughs as a babysitter."

"I'm the best."

Luke doesn't need to know that, last night, I let Legs paint my toenails pink while we ate raw cookie dough (the kind safe for consumption. Don't worry, I checked), and watched *Frozen II* for the third time this week.

"Oh, you'll also want to feed Harry," I add as I rifle through my papers. "He likes the fresh salmon from the can."

Safe and happy in the knowledge that Luke literally throws up at the smell of fish, I make my escape from the boardroom.

But my amusement is short-lived as there's nowhere to escape *to*. These days, the woman occupying my thoughts in the most bothersome way also occupies my office.

If I'm being honest, though, I don't actually mind letting her share my space.

Not that much, anyway.

Because yes, it's freaking annoying that my office now contains a fluffy pink chair pillow, a desk calendar full of quotes from *The Office*, and a gold pot of pencils topped with dinosaur-shaped erasers. Not to mention the little brightly colored woman who owns all the clutter.

But I've come to almost... look forward to her tripping in late every morning, cheerful and smiling and telling some ridiculous story about how she missed the bus because she saw a praying mantis and had to take a picture. Or because she walked the long way and got lost.

She always arrives with a book tucked under her arm and a pink paper bag from Sugarland. This week, she's tried the almond croissant, the cinnamon bun, the banana nut muffin and, today, the apple fritter.

I've worked in this building for years, and she's already tried more of Sugarland's menu than I have.

I can't help but smirk as I make my way back into my office. Annie's apple fritter currently sits atop its paper bag on the carpet next to her. She's forgone her desk chair in favor of sitting on the floor. This is how she prefers to work —on the ground, legs at a ninety-degree angle, stack of paperwork resting between her thighs.

It would be almost indecent if she wasn't wearing about twenty-five tons of fabric on her petite, curvaceous frame. Baggy, parachute-style pants, coupled with a strange, white, multi-layered top. Like she's a human wedding cake.

She chews on the lid of her pen as she flips through the pages, making notes here and there. She's piled that wild auburn hair into a topknot.

I find myself watching her, wondering if she might pull at her purple scrunchie and let those waves loose around her face.

Not because I like the look of her hair down or anything. But because the moment she does, she'll be shedding all over the carpet.

"What is it?" Annie asks as she picks up her pastry and takes a huge bite. Her lips are red, as usual. Chaotic as she may seem, when it comes to her lipstick, Annie is a creature of habit.

The thought of a shred of common ground between us pleases me.

I avert my eyes, striding over to my desk while giving her a wide berth. "Sorry?"

We don't usually do a lot of talking. Well, I don't do a lot of talking (and Annie does enough for both of us). One, because I hate small talk. Two, because it's awkward as all hell to dance around the elephant in the room.

Plus, there's the whole "Mr. Donovan" weirdness.

It's too late to insist that she call me Liam. I have no idea why I made it seem I wanted to be called anything other than my given name, and now I'm in the slightly precarious position of not wanting to call *her* by her given name, thus creating another kind of power imbalance between us.

I swear, if anyone's going to win the award for "worst communicator," it would be me. Thank goodness we have Trevor in communications for all of that.

"You were looking at me like you needed something?" Annie's voice brings me back to the present. She tilts her head and wipes her sticky fingers on her pants. I try not to wince.

I grasp at mental straws until I remember what Luke and I *just* spoke about. And it's work related. Which is what's actually important here.

Not her lipstick, or her wild hair, or the fact that she has a consistent (almost endearing) habit of speaking before her brain fully engages.

Now that my head is focused again, I clear my throat. All business and perfectly professional. "Are you free tonight?"

Her eyebrows raise, and surprise flashes in her eyes.

Crap. As per usual, I've said the wrong thing. "For work," I tack on quickly, my voice gruff.

Annie seems to relax a little. "Better check my calendar. Since moving back in with my parents, I have a glittering social life."

I nod once. "Luke and I want to get an elementary outline of some V2 upgrades over to Wiseman's office tomorrow, and I'd like to dig into your findings a bit more before we do." I run my teeth along my bottom lip, strangely nervous. "Is there any way you could stay late?"

"Fine by me. My current, action-packed Thursday night plans involve watching *Murder, She Wrote* with the olds and finishing the scarf I'm knitting."

I glance toward the window, where warm, golden sunshine is pouring in.

She follows my gaze. "I started working on it before I knew I was leaving Boston."

"Why'd you leave?" I instantly regret my question. I'm not one to pry, but I can't help being curious about the woman. I backtrack quickly. "You don't have to answer that."

"I don't mind." She purses her lips thoughtfully. "Needed a change. New location, new me. You know?"

Judging by how she looks away, a shadow crossing her expression, I have a feeling there's a lot more to the story. Maybe something to do with that slimeball ex of hers. But I remind myself of my boundaries—I don't need to know anything more than this.

Especially given the... unconventional way we started our working relationship.

I'll admit that I'd like to know how she feels about it all, but I can't very well bring it up. I plan to stick to my Bruno rule.

Best not to talk about it. Any of it.

"I get it," I say. Professionally.

Annie faces me and crosses her legs. "No, you don't."

"Pardon?"

"I bet you've had your whole life planned out from day one. Knew what you wanted to do, who you wanted to be. Never let anyone hold you back."

She's so right, and so wrong, all at once.

I raise a brow. "What's the problem with knowing what you want?"

"Nothing. But spontaneity can be good, too."

"You could *spontaneously* decide to be on time once in a while."

She peers at me with comically wide eyes. "Did Mr. Donovan just make a joke?"

"I was in no way joking. You are chronically late for everything."

"And you are chronically running your life on military time." She pulls a face at me and gives me a salute that can't be related to any military on planet Earth.

She wants spontaneity? Luke says I need to lighten up?

Fine. Let's try it their way.

Oh a whim, I grab a pen and jot down my number. Hand it to her.

"What's this?"

"I'm spontaneously giving you my number." I almost smirk as she stares at the post-it in my outstretched hand. "I have meetings lined up all afternoon, but let's meet back here at 5:15pm to begin our evening stint. You can text me if—*when*—you're going to be late."

She snatches the post-it, quick as a flash, then grabs one of her ridiculous dinosaur pencils—a stegosaurus. "You take my number instead," she says, scribbling away. "That way, you can text me when your newly-spontaneous self is the one running late for our evening rendezvous."

This woman, I tell you.

I take the post-it from her with an eyebrow raised. "You know I can't stand lateness."

"Then don't be late, Liam."

Her laughing eyes meets mine and the sound of my name on her lips prompts a warm twinge in my stomach.

"Don't be late either... Annie."

13

ANNIE

I slip off my headphones, pausing the most excellent Broadway show tunes soundtrack that accompanied my afternoon of data crunching. I lean back in my chair with a smile and stretch.

It's been a good day. Things are looking up.

Finally.

It's been three and a half days of sharing an office (*not* a desk) with Liam Donovan, and we might actually be... getting along. Hard as that may be to believe given the first twelve hours we spent together, and the man's overall grump factor for most of those hours.

But I think he's finally relaxing a touch around me. And yes, Liam's version of relaxed looks very different from most people's, but he seems to be coming to terms with the fact that I work here. And (hopefully) that I'm not insanely in love with him or something.

I mean, he even gave me his cell number earlier. Which I proceeded to give back before handing him my number instead. Because an actual stalker would never do that, would they?

One of my smarter moments, I like to think.

Plus, all initial awkwardness with my new boss aside, I am totally hooked on the job.

Hook, line, and sinkered, actually. With each day that I stride into the industrial, bare-floored warehouse type space that SITL occupies, my heart beats a little louder, my palms get a little sweatier.

It feels good to be a part of something again, part of a team that's set to make a difference. The funding the Donovans are gunning for involves a presentation to investors. Which means that we're doing a *serious* push to create a cohesive, data-driven vision for SITL. The elementary plans for the Version 2 launch of the app are going to make things even better. It's going to be a lot of work to get there, but it's a challenge I'm up for.

All the more because SITL have an awesome product that the market deserves, and I'm excited to help give it its best chance. The design is beautiful, thoughtful, clever. It has the mark of a deep, critical thinker all over it. And I think I know which Donovan brother that may be.

It's been interesting, watching the brothers work together, bent over mock-ups on the boardroom table. Through the glass walls of Liam's—and my—office, I've noticed that Luke always has his shirt neck loosened, sleeves rolled up, blazer off. His hair's usually mussed and he looks to be cracking jokes and checking his phone. Liam, on the other hand, is forever in the zone. Jacket on, tie straight, words clipped and to the point.

They're like yin and yang.

Luke is smiling, Liam is serious. Luke asks me every morning how I'm doing. Liam usually avoids asking me anything—until he asked me if I was free to work tonight.

I'm happy to stay late, don't get me wrong (and not just because I was glad for an excuse to escape yet another Jessica Fletcher marathon. Turns out, there really *is* such a thing as too much true crime television). But I also feel a little nervous for the evening ahead. It'll be our first time being alone together since I oh-so-elegantly drooled all over him in the hotel room.

I've seen enough soapy TV dramas to know how this scenario plays out in the world of fiction: work turns into cozy chat. Cozy chat turns into eating Chinese takeout from white cardboard cartons on the floor, while our legs get closer and closer, and then...

Oh, gosh. Am I fantasizing that a night working with Liam will be anything like the time Sandy Cohen nearly cheated on his beloved Kirsten in *The OC*?

Sacrilege.

That scene made me want to come after his blond temptress colleague with a pitchfork. How dare she! Sandy and Kirsten were TV's golden couple back in the noughties. In fact, the bedroom I'm currently residing in still has a couple posters of Cohen family members on the walls (Seth, not Sandy. Although twenty-six-year-old me would very much like to rethink that choice).

But this is real life and not a soap opera, and Liam is (as far as I'm aware) not hiding a secret wife anywhere. Plus, I am the absolute opposite of a temptress of any kind.

This will be fine. Purely professional.

And besides, Liam doesn't cross lines. He draws lines. Precision-straight lines.

Nothing to worry about.

Speaking of Liam... he's been gone awhile.

I spin around on my chair and glance at the clock.

Wait, it's 5:30pm?! I was so sucked into my show-tunes-and-data combo, I didn't notice that the official work day ended a half hour ago. No wonder it's so quiet in here.

I crane my head around, and sure enough, most people

have already vacated. Any stragglers are leaving the office in dribs and drabs. Where on earth is Liam?

I smile slowly as I realize with a thrill that *he's late*.

"Hey, Annie." Vanessa pops her head around the office door, startling me. She peers at Liam's empty desk before looking at me. "I'm off for the evening."

"Okay." I nod once. "I'll be here for the next few hours, I guess."

"Really?"

"Yeah, Lia—uh, Mr. Donovan asked me to work late."

"Oh." A long pause. "Want me to stay with you guys? I could help, um... sort?" Vanessa offers weakly. I get the feeling that, despite the fact that she hired me, she knows very little about what I do.

I also get the feeling that her obviously raging crush on Liam is unreciprocated. Unless I'm reading everything wrong again, which is always a possibility.

Lucky for me, I refuse to have a crush on Liam, so I will never end up in unrequited love territory at work. Seems stressful.

"That's okay." I shrug. "It's just boring data stuff."

Vanessa's eyes spark, but with a flare of what looks like jealousy. She nods. "Okay. See you tomorrow."

"Have a good night."

Once Vanessa leaves, I'm on my own. The office is silent. Almost creepily so. The industrial space with its exposed pipes, glass accents, and concrete floors is cool during the day, but now, it looks like the ideal setting for a grisly murder.

Where is he?

At that moment, my phone buzzes, making me jump.

Unknown Number: Got held up. Back at the office soon.

Unknown Number: It's Liam, by the way.

Unknown Number: Donovan.

I laugh out loud. What other Liam could I be mistaking him for? The man knows the current status of my social life. I chew my lip as I add his number to my contacts and type a reply.

Annie: I don't know if I can tolerate this kind of lateness.

Oh wow, I really said that.

I hold my breath for a moment, fingers poised to send a "sorry, ignore me" text.

My phone buzzes again.

Liam: Let's just say you owed me one, and now we're even.

I smile.

Annie: Hmm... I was eleven minutes late, you're going on twenty...

Liam: Coffee? To make it up to you?

Liam: Slash buy your silence to never mention my lateness again.

Annie: Yes! I'll call it even in return for caffeine.

Liam: Three creams, two sugars, right?

He knows how I take my coffee. This guy pays attention to details.

Probably one of the reasons he's good at running a business. He must do stuff like this—notices the little things—for all of his employees. The devil's in the details, and all that.

Annie: I'm impressed.

Liam: You shouldn't be. You drink about six cups a day.

Ah. So maybe it's less that he's paying attention and more that my caffeine and sugar addictions appall him.

That checks out.

I shoot Liam a quick "thank you for indulging my addiction" text, then put my phone down. My stomach swirls with nerves and I bite my lip.

I've spent most of this week digging deep into the database, and a plan is forming in my mind. A plan I hinted at when I gave Luke and Liam my initial findings. A plan I intend to present to Liam in its entirety whenever he's back.

I've focused on identifying patterns in user behavior, time spent in every component of the app. The point of Stay Inside the Lines is to schedule your life, organize yourself and your time as well as possible. But what if a little flexibility is the key to making users feel more satisfied and successful?

A margin for error, if you will. A tiny little rule bend.

I think I know how Liam Donovan feels about bending the rules.

But as I always say, data doesn't lie.

My stomach rumbles. So loudly, you could probably hear it a mile away.

Liam looks up from his computer. "Hungry?"

"Famished," I admit with a flush. It's 7:30pm, and outside, the sky is a swirl of pink and orange as the sun descends on the city.

The past two hours have gone by so fast. After Liam showed up with our coffees (and, quite incredibly, two packets of Haribos), I bit the bullet and walked him through some of my plan.

It's nerve-wracking to tell someone where you think they went wrong with the first version of an app they created. But Liam listened intently and took notes as I presented my ideas. He seemed thoughtful, like he had follow-up questions, but he didn't interrupt me once. He just let me talk.

Strange as this might sound, it was empowering. Which is lame when you consider that all he did was listen. But as a woman in the tech world, I've been subjected to countless interrupters, mansplainers, and people who are just downright dismissive. I honestly didn't realize how much it bothered me until tonight, when my boss—a man who had the power to be any of those things—was instead respectful and attentive. Let me speak.

And apparently, let my stomach speak for me.

"Want to get some food?" Liam offers as he leans back in his desk chair. He's undone the top button of his shirt and taken off his tie—something I have never seen him do in the office before. "We could grab a quick bite and I'll ask you my questions."

He turns his computer screen to show me the detailed list he's typed out. I laugh. "That might take all night."

"I have all night."

His eyes go wide after he speaks, and we look at each other for a long moment, the implication of his flippantly-meant words not lost on either of us.

A beat later, he averts his eyes and adds, "I mean... I have a couple of hours, max. Better get home at some point."

"Me too. People to see, scarves to knit," I blabber. I'm still thinking about those dark eyes of his. About the fact that he has so many questions about my plan, but waited for me to finish without interrupting.

Such a small gesture can make such a big difference.

Or maybe, after Justin, my bar is just really, really low.

Either way, it's made Liam go up even more in my mental estimation. Right now, the scorecard is having a hard time balancing because, on the one hand, he's scowly and surly and impatient. But on the other hand, I've seen him this week with his employees, and he may be curt and to the point, but when it comes down to it, he treats everyone with respect.

And here he is, considering my rumbling stomach. Which is actually the last thing I want him to be thinking about.

He must think I'm one big bodily-function of a person.

And, right on schedule...

GRRumble.

Liam lifts a brow. "So, food break?"

It really does sound good. One cannot live on caffeine and sugar alone, it turns out.

Maybe food will settle my stomach, which is churning with something suspiciously similar to butterflies. It's just hunger, though. I'm not fluttery due to all this time spent with Liam. Not at all.

"Sure," I manage, banishing any wayward thoughts to the dark, squelchy, seaweed-ridden cave of monsters from which they came.

"I know a good place, and it's close." Liam stands and buttons the middle button on his suit jacket. I try not to look at him—it's an innocent gesture that shouldn't make me feel anything.

I pull on my jacket. Today, I chose a fringey western number that looks cute with my Esmerelda-style skirt and hoop earrings. We probably look like chalk and cheese with our outfit choices, but as Liam and I step into the evening together, I find that I really don't care. And I guess he doesn't either.

It's that magical, dusky time of day when the city looks like it's got a filter over it: all shimmering golden lowlights and textured shadows. I breathe in a gulp of air as we walk in silence for a few minutes.

Yup, I can do silence. I can definitely do silence.

Nooo big deal....

"Did you know there are one quadrillion ants on planet Earth?"

Oh, awesome. What a normal thing to say.

"I did not." Liam looks at me with an expression that says "you little weirdo." But when his eyes meet mine, there's a glimmer of softness that wasn't there before. One that suggests he maybe, just maybe, might be reevaluating his assessment of me from "little weirdo" to "charming little weirdo."

One can hope, at least.

I press on with more fascinating ant chat. He might know all the dolphin facts, but apparently, I'm the ant lady. "Yup. If you put them all on a scale together, they would outweigh humans."

"That's a terrifying thought."

"It is," I say cheerfully. "Let's hope they never stage a coup."

Liam snorts with sudden laughter, which he turns into a cough. But, I'm sure I heard it—I made him laugh!

A smile beams on my face at the thought.

Soon, we arrive at a tiny, hole-in-the-wall Mexican restaurant with peeling green and red paint and flashing neon signs. It's the kind of place I adore... and a place I never would've pegged for Liam. He looks like a lobster thermidor and caviar kind of guy. The sort of person who's never been blessed to know the true Atlantan joy that is a Varsity chili cheese dog washed down with a frosted orange shake.

"What?" Liam asks, peering at me.

"Nothing."

"You don't like this place, we can go somewhere else."

"No, I love it. I just..." Ugh, I can't exactly say that I

thought he was a food snob, can I? "I was worried Mexican food would give me gas."

Oh, great. Back to the bodily functions. How very attractive and charming, Annie.

As I go predictably red, Liam looks like he's holding back another laugh.

"I just need to make a quick call," Liam tells me. "Feel free to check the menu to see if it'll be, er, agreeable to your disposition." He's still got that slightly-pained, trying-not-to-laugh expression.

"Oh, I'm sure it'll be very... compliant." Oh, for goodness sakes. What the heck am I on about?

Before I can say some other ridiculously stupid thing, I step into the restaurant. My stomach rejoices at the smells of chipotle peppers, fried corn chips, and heaven.

Right before the door shuts behind me, I hear Liam say, "Hey, my girl."

A jolt hits me. Is that Legs on the phone? Or maybe Ears, this time?

Either way, not my business. What Liam does with his personal life is no concern of mine.

I shove away all thoughts of Liam and the gal-pal he's talking to, and focus on my surroundings. The restaurant is small, with only a few brightly colored tables along the walls. I slide into a cozy corner seat, and pull out my phone so that I, too, look like I have some kind of a social life whenever Liam walks in.

My only text is from my mother.

Mother Dearest: Hi, darling. How was work today? Would U like 2 go 2 Farmer's Market this Saturday morning?

My mother likes to text like its 2002, she owns a Nokia 3310, and she's going to be charged for going over her character limit.

Also... Farmer's Market? I smell a rat.

Annie: Work was delightful, thanks. And why, exactly, would you like me to go to the Farmer's Market?

Mother Dearest: Blaine will be there.

Annie: And Blaine would be...?

Mother Dearest: 34 and divorced, but still has his hair.

Of course. Because those things obviously belong on opposing sides of a person's pros and cons list.

I reply that I'm allergic to Farmer's Markets and set my phone on the table just as Liam comes through the door. He makes his way toward me and shrugs off his jacket, putting it neatly on the back of the empty chair. "What can I get for you?"

My stomach gives another loud rumble, and I hope the music is loud enough to disguise the noise. I look at Liam in puzzlement, and he tilts his head toward the front. "It's counter service."

"Oh! Um, don't worry. I'll get mine." I spring upwards, bumping my head into a row of low-hanging chili pepper lights.

"Sit down." His voice is so commanding that I obey immediately. "It's on me."

"You don't have to buy me dinner."

He looks at me again with a vaguely confused expression, and rubs the back of his neck. "It's on the company, I mean. A write-off."

"Oh. Right." I glance in the direction of the menu boards for a moment, too flustered to think straight. Why does this man's presence consistently send me off-kilter? "I like everything. I'll just have what you're having."

Lame.

Liam frowns, then nods. Strides to the front of the

restaurant with purpose. I, in turn, avert my eyes so I don't have to look at his butt in those well-fitting suit pants.

Okay, so I take a peek. But just a quick one.

Quick-ish, anyway.

My phone buzzes again.

Mother Dearest: No need 2 be rude. Blaine's in the men's choir, U know. Voice of an angel. U coming home soon? Made chili.

Annie: Sorry, Mom, I'm just not interested in being set up right now. Going to be home late, grabbing dinner out. Thanks!

Mother Dearest: OK. CU L8r. Dad says hi. Lol.

She thinks "Lol" means "lots of love." I've never bothered to correct her, but I often hope she never tries to send anyone a condolences text.

The sobering realization hits me that I'm texting my mom on a weeknight to let her know that I won't be home for dinner. Yet again, I feel like I'm back in high school.

Until my very manly boss comes back carrying two overflowing trays of food.

I'm talking, enough to feed a soccer team.

He sees me eyeing the pile. "I didn't know what you liked."

"So you ordered everything on the menu?" I demand, mostly joking... until I see a guilty flicker in his eyes. My mouth drops open. "You actually ordered everything on the menu?"

He ducks his head as he sits. "Not everything."

"What did you leave out?"

"The side order of refried beans."

I burst into startled laughter, and the smallest whisper of a smile crosses his features.

It's not a proper smile; it's hardly even the ghost of a

smile. But it's enough to make my stomach drop dangerously.

"How are we going to eat all this?" I continue to giggle. On the outside, I'm laughing at the absurdity of this gesture. But inside, I'm feeling more than a little mushy at how sweet it was.

Liam shrugs those broad shoulders. "Just eat what you want. We'll put the leftovers in the staff fridge."

He doesn't have to tell me twice. I'm starving, and the food smells amazing.

I dip a nacho chip in guacamole and crunch on it while I stack a fish taco and a chimichanga on my plate (because deep-frying things always makes them better. It's a golden rule, here in the South).

I'm so busy stuffing my face that, at first, I don't notice Liam. While I'm slopping dip on the table and rotating bites of deep-fried goodness, Liam is meticulously eating from a rather boring plate of grilled chicken strips, sautéed veggies and rice.

I've never seen anyone eat so methodically, so efficiently. It goes: bite of chicken, bite of rice, two bites of veggies, and repeat. Over and over. Powering through a single—albeit mountainous—plate of protein, carbs and vitamins like it's his job.

I drop my taco. "Are you seriously only eating that?"

He looks up in surprise. There's a dab of hot sauce on his lip, which he quickly swipes away with his finger. Watching him touch his lips is... hot. Weirdly. Because what's hot about someone with food on their face?

Nothing, I tell you. But here we are.

"What do you mean?" he asks, his dark eyes meeting mine.

"You're eating one plate of food. Which means the

other approximately thirty-six items on these trays are... for me?"

"I told you," he says slowly, like he's having to channel the patience of a saint. "You didn't tell me what you wanted. And I don't like to guess."

Of course he doesn't.

Liam Donovan is the kind of man who says and does things because he's sure of them. Sure of his facts, sure of his prowess.

My gaze travels back to his lips. I bet he's one of those super-confident kissers who knows *exactly* what he's doing. And makes sure you know that he knows exactly what he's doing...

"What?" Liam asks and I startle out of my thoughts.

I drag my eyes from his lips, praying my flush doesn't betray me. *What is going on with me? Snap out of it, Annie. STAT!*

"Nothing!" I blabber. "Um, I mean, thank you. For this, erm, bountiful selection of food."

Who in their right mind uses the word "bountiful?" Nobody in this century, surely.

Liam's very distracting lips do that whisper-of-a-smile thing again, the corners tilting upwards.

"Shall we go over your questions?" I ask, somewhat desperately.

He wipes his mouth with his napkin, then throws it onto his empty plate. "Let's do it."

I cast a wistful glance at an extra-cheesy-looking quesadilla I was hoping to work on next. I hope it isn't rude to keep eating... and isn't it a myth that men only like dainty salad eaters, anyways?

Liam, like a magical mind-reader, pushes the quesadilla toward me. "You can keep eating, though."

This man.

I take a huge bite. He nods in approval.

And then, the barrage of questions begins.

Twenty minutes later, I'm dripping with both stress and hot-sauce-induced sweat as we go back and forth over one of my key points—that people need more flexibility as part of their routine than this app allows for. V2 of the app *needs* to cater to this.

"But, the point of this app is to improve organization in every area of your life," Liam says for the fifth time. "Doesn't leeway defeat the point?"

"According to everything I've pulled, no." I stand my ground. I know I'm right on this one, know it'll help the user experience.

"What if your data's wrong? Or more digging produces different results?" Liam crosses his arms, looking at me for an answer. "Do you have a backup plan?

I get the feeling this is an important question. A lot hinges on my next words.

I summon all the bravado I can muster. Grin. "I don't need a backup plan."

"Why's that?"

"Because I'm right. And this is not going to fail."

Those dark eyes are on me again, and for a moment, I lose my train of thought. Gosh, Liam's a beautiful man.

Warmth creeps up the back of my neck as he keeps staring at me. His face is impassive, but there's a glint of something that tells me I've given the right answer. Passed some kind of test. This realization makes a thrill zip through me, head to toe. He's impressed.

He takes me seriously. Takes my work seriously. And if this is what impressing Liam Donovan at work feels like, then I'm already looking forward to the next test.

"Liam!"

The excited shriek startles us both, and we look up

from our massacre of cheese and guac (okay, my massacre). A drop-dead gorgeous woman wearing only a sports bra and capri leggings is prancing toward us. She has the most perfect complexion I've ever seen. Seriously, her skin is so clear, I can practically see my reflection in it.

My hand automatically goes to the pimple forming on my chin. Too late, I realize that my hand is dripping with grease, and all I've done is guarantee that this pimple will be big, red and glaring.

Wonderful.

I wipe my hands on my napkin as Liam nods at the woman. "Cassandra. What a surprise."

Is it just me or is his voice totally flat?

"It is! I'm just getting a salad to go—had a late spin class down the road." Cassandra holds up a very non-greasy box of chicken and greens, and she beams at Liam without casting me a glance. Not that I blame her. I probably look like the kid sister he brought out for dinner. "I haven't seen you in, like, three weeks!"

Her voice is casual, but I get the impression that she knows the exact date and time she last laid eyes on Liam.

"Probably about that," Liam says blandly. He doesn't ask how she is. Doesn't make any attempt to introduce me. Instead, he shoots me a quick, apprehensive glance.

What?

For the first time since she approached our table, Cassandra looks a tad unsure of herself. Not that I blame her.

Liam's being, well, rude. Which isn't super unlike him, but this woman looks like a goddess—shouldn't he be drooling and not glaring at the table like it personally offended him?

She finally turns to me. Frowns. "I'm Cassandra."

"Annie," I reply, and she wrinkles her nose slightly, like she's puzzled by my existence.

"Annie works with me," Liam says swiftly. Too swiftly.

Cassandra's eyes light with fresh enthusiasm. She touches her hair and giggles, turning all her attention back to Liam. "Well, we'll have to get together soon. I'll call you?"

He barely nods. "Sounds great. Good to see you."

Which might *sound* like a nice thing to say. But the way Liam says it is more "goodbye, please leave now" than anything else.

As she walks away, he turns to me. Sighs heavily. "Sorry for that interruption. Where were we?"

I blink a couple times, lick my lips as I get my bearings. Weird as that interaction was, Liam's intent was clear—move Cassandra along as quickly as possible while making sure she knows I'm his colleague. Which explains his apprehensive glance in my direction—he probably didn't want her to think I was on a date with him.

Which makes sense. After all, that's what I am: his colleague.

Actually, not even. I'm his employee. This is not a dinner date, it's a business meeting. And while I may never be a soul-cycling, salad-eating goddess, I'm a damn good data analyst.

That's what he pays me for. And that's what I'm here to deliver. Period.

As if to prove my point, I shove another nacho in my mouth.

"We were talking about bending the rules," I say through a mouthful of chip.

14

LIAM

Ways to make a casual dinner with your colleague awkward:

1. Panic order her every last thing on the menu.
2. Find yourself totally unable to stop looking at her mouth as she eats, so try to "fix" the problem by asking her a bunch of work questions with military-like precision and force.
3. Get approached by a relentless dance-mom from your niece's class who's asked you out no less than four times in the past year.

So, all in all, another typical interaction with Annie. Spending time with her is like holding up a giant disaster magnet to my life—one that sucks in carefully arranged things at an alarming rate and flips them on their heads.

We've finished our food, but we're still lingering at Maria's Cantina, talking business. Our current topic of conversation is about flexibility when it comes to the rules. It's a topic I am not happy with. One, because we already know what that leads to: inadvertent illicit cuddling of your pretty new employee. And two, because I can't focus on what she's saying when I know I need to explain what just happened.

I don't like explaining myself.

"Why don't we present this to Wiseman as something we're still exploring. Seeing if it would resonate well with existing users as an optional feature," I toss out as a compromise.

I also don't usually like compromise.

But Annie has done her homework. She knows her stuff, is confident in what she's saying. And I know better than to let a personal preference affect my ability to run my company. Plus, she maybe, just maybe, might have a point. It's unlikely. But possible. I'm not going to be a stubborn jerk and ignore her work.

Even though I'm not convinced she's right.

She offers a small smile. "Sounds good. I think you'll see it my way eventually."

"We'll see," I reply. I'm not sure I'm capable of seeing any way other than mine, but Annie makes me want to try. And that's more than I can say for most people.

She wipes her fingers on her napkin. "Thanks again for dinner. I'm so full."

"Should we get out of here? Walk and talk?"

"Of course. I'm sure you have other places to be. People to see." Annie's eyes flicker to the restaurant door as she speaks. The same door that Cassandra exited a few minutes before.

It's now or never.

I suck in a breath. "Sorry about Cassandra."

"Don't apologize." Annie frowns. "You didn't do anything."

"I was rude," I correct. Pause for a moment before,

136

perhaps against my better judgment, adding, "she's been quite persistent in, um, pursuing me. Romantically."

Annie's eyebrows fly up. "Oh?"

"Her advances are"—I search for an appropriate sentence ending—"flattering, but unwanted. As I've made clear to her more than a few times."

Annie's eyes widen further. I'm not sure who's more surprised that I'm revealing this information: me, or her.

"You don't need to tell me this," she says quickly. "You weren't rude to me."

"I just didn't want you to think that I make a habit of being rude to people."

Annie smiles cheekily. It makes her face sparkle.

"Ruder than I have to be, I mean," I clarify with an accepting nod of her teasing smile. "I, uh, told her I don't date."

Anymore.

But I leave that bit out.

"Oh," Annie says again, but this time, the tiny word manages to pack a whole different meaning.

There's a slightly awkward (what's new) silence before Annie nods. "Well. Should we get going? Finish work before midnight?"

"Absolutely."

The evening air has cooled significantly in the time we've been in the restaurant. In fact, time's flown by. I'm officially late to take over watching Legs for the night, but if I'm honest, the thought of Luke itching with curiosity pleases me. Serves him right.

I'm glad I called Legs before we went in. I had a feeling this evening would take longer than expected and I'd miss her bedtime.

It's not like this super-long-dinner business is a common occurrence for me. Most of my meals over the past few years have been about efficiency—optimal levels of nutrients and calories in the quickest, simplest way possible. I usually eat alone standing at a counter, or with my immediate family at my sister's dining table.

This meal was... different.

Beside me, Annie shivers in the breeze. I reflexively shrug off my jacket and hold it out to her.

"Oh no, I'm fine." Her jaw tenses as she tries to keep her teeth from clattering.

"I insist," I press.

I'm not being pushy, I don't think. I mean, she's shivering!

Annie smiles and moves to let me drape the jacket around her. She shivers when my fingers graze her shoulders, and I try to ignore the way my heartbeat picks up.

My jacket is comically huge on her, hanging off her petite frame. I like the way it looks on her. I just hope that Cassandra's not lurking behind a trashcan, ready to spring out and yell "gotcha!" before dragging me on a date.

Dramatic? Yes. But I don't like the woman one bit.

Annie's quiet as she walks. I usually like quiet, thrive on it. Most people say altogether too many words in a day.

But Annie is not most people. And I realize I like all the crazy, strange things she has to say.

To the point that, right now, I'm overly aware of the quiet. Disrupted by it. It's not like her.

"What's on your mind?" I blurt.

Annie looks up in surprise. Smiles. "Honest answer?"

"Yes."

"I was thinking about how, the last time we ran into someone, I told them you were my boyfriend." She snorts at the memory. "Did I ever apologize for that? Like you apologized for what happened with Cassandra?"

I shake my head, unable to keep a small smile from

forming on my lips. "No apology necessary. The whole thing was kinda funny, actually."

"You didn't think I was a crazed psychopath?"

"Oh, I definitely thought that." I look at her, dead serious, and her mouth pops into a little O before she bursts into that contagious laughter again.

"I have to say that this has been one of my less conventional starts to a job," she says, shaking her head. "But in a weird way, it's worked out."

"It's certainly been interesting." I like that we're having this conversation. Glad to hear verbal affirmation that everything is okay between us.

"I guess I should explain myself, too." Annie lowers her lashes. "Like you did."

"That's okay," I say, even as I find myself leaning toward her. I normally never take this much interest in the lives of my employees.

"I want to." She grits her teeth, and I wait patiently. Then, that determined look of hers—a look I've grown to like—moves over her face. "Justin and I were coworkers at my last job. We met, fell in love, dated for three years, then broke up. It got a bit messy after that."

"Is that why you moved to Atlanta?"

Annie wraps my jacket tighter around herself. Looks off into the distance. "Not... entirely." Then, she seems to grit her teeth. Straighten. "I moved because it was the right thing to do. And I got presented with the right opportunity."

"Well, I'm glad you did."

Her head whips around, sending auburn strands across her face in diagonal lines. "Really?"

I nod, amused by her surprise. "Yes. I can already see how much you bring to the table. And I'm glad we didn't lose you over last weekend's..."

"Accident?"

I almost chuckle. "I was going to say 'incident.' But I think I like accident better. There can be happy accidents."

"Was the Econo Hotel one?"

At this point, we're outside our office building. I meet her eyes, hold them for a long moment. "I think it was. You?"

She breathes out slowly, and the sound is almost shaky. It's a sound I want to hear again. "Yes, I do."

I slip my key out of my pocket. Push the door open. "After you."

She slips by me and I smell her shampoo. It's that sweet, totally unique ocean smell again. So typically Annie. I bet my jacket smells like her now.

I follow her into the elevator, which suddenly feels about six sizes smaller than usual. Six times warmer too, despite the fact that I'm missing my jacket.

We stand close. So close, our arms are almost touching.

"Annie?" I say, not looking at her.

"Yeah?"

"For what it's worth." I keep my eyes trained on the stainless steel door. "Sounds to me like you were too good for that guy."

Annie shivers and the motion tickles my arm, pricking it with sensation.

"Or maybe he was just the wrong guy for me." Her voice is scratchy.

I swallow. "Maybe."

The elevator hums to life, and as we leave the ground, my stomach drops from more than just the motion of gravity leaving my body.

15

LIAM

It is a truth universally acknowledged that elevators are not sexy.

Or at least, it should be. For some reason, people seem to fixate on those scenes in movies and TV shows where two people in an elevator together end up in a quintessential passionate embrace, all to set up for a B.S. happily-ever-after. Like in that *New Girl* show my sister watches, where the annoying, loud guy and the quirky girl end up kissing in the elevator after minutes of screen time showing them running around and missing each other again and again.

In real life, after all of that cat and mouse, I'd be feeling sweaty and annoyed, not romantic. It's total sensationalism.

The point is, elevators are for efficiency. You enter one for the sole purpose of moving from point A to point B.

A cold, hard, metal box. That's all it is.

I certainly wasn't feeling anything toward Annie during the ride in that cold, hard, metal box last night—a ride which took all of thirty-five seconds, but felt like it lasted an eternity. Didn't think about how her skin flushed pink as her shaky voice put the emphasis on her ex being the "wrong guy."

Like there was a "right guy" out there for her.

Wasn't thinking about that at all.

Okay, fine. It was all I could think about. And still am even *now*, dammit. Eighteen freaking hours later.

It's like I inhaled too much of her ocean scent and it drugged me.

It's not helping that she's currently splayed out on the floor again, mere inches from me. Has been for most of the day.

She's in my office, and she's in my head. Big time. And now that I'm actually admitting that to myself, I'm not sure how I feel about it.

At that very moment, Annie looks up and catches me staring. A small, questioning smile plays on her lips.

"I have to leave early today," I say suddenly, mentally kicking myself for getting caught. Unfortunately, my sentence sounds almost like a question.

Great. Now I'm asking our brand new hire for permission to leave early.

"Sure thing, boss man," Annie says easily. "Getting your Friday plans started early?"

"Nah, just being spontaneous," I joke.

Annie snorts with laughter, and my lips tip up at the corners. She watches my expression, and her deep hazel eyes draw me in for half a second. My stomach stirs as I remember the tension that zapped through me as we stood next to each other. Butterflies, I believe people call them.

I wouldn't know—before Annie, my romantic life was more stale, old and moth-ridden.

But when it comes to Annie, it *has* to stay this way. She's off-limits. Thinking of her in any other way is a disaster waiting to happen.

"Hot date on the docket?"

"I don't date, remember?" I reply reflexively. This is veering dangerously close to small talk territory. Of a rather personal nature.

I know I shouldn't get personal with Annie, but we had such a great conversation last night, I somehow want to keep talking. Surely *that's* not off-limits.

Even if it is much-detested small talk.

She blinks, tilts her head. "What about Legs?"

What does Legs have to do with my dating life (or lack thereof)?

Maybe Luke told Annie that I'm babysitting our niece for a couple of weeks, and she assumed that I'd be with her this afternoon. Which is a correct assumption. Legs has her dance class, and I'll be helping her get ready and driving her to the studio.

"Yeah, I'll be with Legs," I say with a shrug. "Playing chauffeur."

Annie gives me a strange look. "Is that a euphemism?"

"For driving?"

"No, for..." She stops, reddens. "Uh, never mind. Ignore me."

I have no idea what's going on, but for some reason, I find myself asking, "How about you?"

She frowns at me in confusion.

"I mean, do you have any weekend plans?" I clarify, feeling awkward. Serves me right for indulging myself. There's a special place in hell for small talk. Right next to people who drive below the speed limit in the fast lane, and door-to-door salespeople.

Bothering people in their homes—the nerve.

And yet... I genuinely want to know the answer to my question.

"Probably going to catch up on a few things, then be

accidentally-on-purpose late for a forced trip to the Farmer's Market tomorrow morning." Annie's lips pucker, like she has a bad taste in her mouth. What's wrong with the Farmer's Market?

Yeah, I'm a secret Market Man. Legs loves to go, too. We always find the best avocados.

"What's happening at the Farmer's Market?" I ask, genuinely curious what could elicit such a negative reaction to great coffee, reusable canvas bags, and homemade peach jam.

"Long story." Annie shakes her head, then scoots backwards and scrambles up off of the floor. "Speaking of late, I am currently three minutes late for lunch with Vanessa."

"It's 3pm."

"Lunch doesn't have to be chicken, rice and spinach from the same restaurant at precisely 12:30pm every day, you know."

"I get steak sometimes," I say, defensive. Then, I remember the meal I had at Maria's last night.

Fine. She got me.

Annie gives a light chuckle and shakes her head. Her auburn hair brushes over her shoulders. "Wild one, aren't you?"

"When I want to be."

Annie's mouth pops open, and two spots of pink appear on her cheeks. I can understand why—I didn't mean for that to sound so flirty.

Or maybe I did. It's like someone poured water on my carefully painted lines, and the spill is blurring all the edges. Making things murky.

She recovers quickly. "You may be gone by the time I'm back, but have a good weekend. And while you're at it, why don't you test out SITL's upcoming new feature and be a little flexible with your weekend schedule."

Her confidence is amusing.

"And how do you propose I go about doing that?"

Her eyes flash, and my stomach drops. "Do something spontaneous. I dare you."

16

ANNIE

Liam: Spontaneously letting you know that I was two minutes late for my first taxi service.

I stare at my phone, reading the text again. I still have no idea what he means by "taxi service," but I've spent enough time with Liam Donovan this week to garner two things: one, he does not enjoy talking for the sake of talking. And two, he hates being late.

A smile stretches over my face as I walk along the sunny city sidewalk. If this text is anything to go by, Liam has actually taken me up on my challenge, and I'm hoping this means that we're finally on the right foot after a shaky start.

I mean, things were already going better last night—he listened so intently to all my thoughts on how to improve SITL's features. Plus, the guy *did* give up half his office space for me (fine, maybe more than half. What can I say? I'm a spreader). He seems to genuinely care what his employees have to say—surprising given his cool, standoffish demeanor—and it just makes me more curious about him. Eager to know what else lies behind those dark eyes.

What makes Liam... Liam.

Because I guess we're on a first name basis now. And, yanno, texting.

My fingers hover over the screen before I type out a reply.

Annie: Wow! Letting your hair down this weekend, aren't you?

Liam: Actually, it's pretty firmly held in place right now with a whole bottle of hairspray.

I frown at the screen, uncomprehending. Is this a joke...?

My phone dings again.

Liam: Long story.

What the freaky-deak is happening? Liam never has any stories at all, never mind long ones.

Annie: I have many questions.

Liam: I'll answer one.

I smirk as I type out my question.

Annie: Do you moonlight as a Dolly Parton impersonator?

I wait. Patiently. With bated breath (can you blame me?)

But there's no reply.

Probably took that a step too far. It's not every day that I ask my boss if he does a cross-gender country tribute for fun on a Friday night. But I guess that's small-fry compared to what we've already been through.

After a few moments, I stash my phone away, cursing my stupid foot-in-mouth syndrome. There were literally a thousand less ridiculous things I could've texted him.

I sigh as I wander into Trader Joe's and pick up a shopping basket. Lonely Friday nights call for hipster junk food. At least I can feel young and cool while inhaling copious amounts of calories.

I reach for a package of Everything But The Bagel kettle chips, and then head to the dip aisle. I check my phone again. Still no reply.

Oh, well. It was fun while it lasted. And maybe it's a good thing that he didn't text back.

Because I know there's more to Liam Donovan than what I'm seeing. But I also know that digging is dangerous. I'm already intrigued by him—the last thing I need is to dig so far that I catch feelings. For my freaking boss. With the rock hard biceps.

And yes, I know this for a fact because I felt them that fateful morning.

My skin heats at the memory.

I remind myself that, even if I did like him like that—which I don't—it could never be reciprocated. I'm a totem pole of all that he despises: flightiness, lateness, spontaneity.

And even if I wasn't, *he's still my boss*. Who appears to be very interested in (but not dating) a woman known for her shapely calves.

Goodness knows, after what happened with Justin, developing anything other than professional interest in someone I work with is out of the question. I'm going to need a bucket of ice cream and a reread of *Rising Strong* tonight to get myself in order.

I stand in front of the freezer for way too long, staring at the flavors before selecting a black tea and boba non-dairy dessert. I want to try something I've never had before. New experiences, that's what my second chance in Atlanta's all about.

Not repeating mistakes.

Which means that I will have no more thoughts of Liam. Just me, my calories, and my good friend Brené.

Pleased with my decision, I head for the checkout.

Ding!

I balance my phone precariously on my basket as I open the text. My heart leaps a little when I see the name at the top of the screen.

Liam: Grease-era John Travolta, actually.

Dammit.

17

LIAM

"Ready to go, Leggsy?" I ask as I buckle into the driver's seat.

Getting Legs ready for her dance class was an experience. For one thing, I learned the hard way that you can spray a bottle of hairspray the wrong way.

My eyes will hopefully make a full recovery someday.

"Yes!" Legs chirps happily.

I start the car, but before I can pull out of the driveway, my phone dings. I almost leave it, almost let it rest in the console, taunting me...

I can't take it.

I stop the car and open the text.

Annie: Screw knitting. I'll be front row at tonight's show.

A smile tugs at my lips, and I start typing: *"It's a date."*

No. Don't send that, you idiot.

Definitely not that.

I try again. *"What did you decide to do tonight in the end?"*

No! Not that either.

Texting is stressful.

I stare at my screen for another moment, unable to formulate a single coherent thought.

"Can you please turn on my song?" Legs asks, kicking my seat lightly as she does so.

"Don't kick, Legs," I say with as much authority as I can muster. It's crazy—at work, I have people tripping over themselves to do exactly what I say, when I say it. But at home, I'm at the constant beck and call and mercy of a precocious eight-year-old. "We have a volume agreement in the car, remember?"

"Sorry," she says with a sweet smile. "But I can't hear the song."

The child clearly does not care about honoring our carefully negotiated pact regarding how loud we play her music while I'm playing taxi driver.

She blinks her big, dark eyes in the rearview mirror. "Pleaseeeeeeeeee Uncle Liam?"

My kryptonite. Seriously, how can you say no to a child who looks so forlorn, so eager for something you're depriving her?

I don't know how parents do it. I feel like I'd be constantly spoiling my kids, doing anything to see them smile.

But as Lana Mae always points out, there's a difference between making your child happy and doing what's right. So I leave the volume as it is and click my phone screen off, deciding that the text will have to wait. We have a Junior ballet class to get to.

As I pull onto the highway, I glance at Legs in the rearview mirror. She's pouting, big-time, her little arms crossed over her glittery-leotard-clad body.

Gah. She knows how to get me.

And so, because I'm in a very good mood—and absolutely not because I'm being manipulated by a pint-sized person—I give in and crank up the volume. It's synced to my phone and playing Legs's special playlist from my Spotify, as per usual.

I know immediately that the song is by One Direction. I don't love the fact that I know this.

Legs begins to sing along. Loudly.

Who knew so much volume could come from such tiny lungs?

An involuntary smile creeps over my face, and I turn up the music a little more.

Legs cheers, and I tap my index fingers on the steering wheel to the music. It's actually a pretty catchy tune, something about making the most of living while you're still young.

Immediately, I think of Annie.

Annie, with her wide smile and fiery eyes and thirst for squeezing every last drop out of every day. Annie, who's late for everything and makes a fool out of herself by speaking before she thinks. Annie, who manages to laugh it all off and move on because life's short, and if you get tripped up, the only way to keep going is to get right back up.

"Uncle Liam?" Legs yells over the noise.

I turn the music down, reach for my coffee in the cupholder. "Yes, sweetie?"

"What does 'get some' mean?"

I choke on my coffee.

And I'm caught so off guard that I don't brake early enough for a red light.

I slam my foot down to stop the car. The action jerks Legs forward in her booster seat and sends a gush of coffee all over my white button-down shirt. "Shi—!"

The vehicle comes to an abrupt, jerky halt.

I twist around in my seat, heart pounding. "Legs! You okay?"

"Fine." Legs giggles, totally unperturbed. Then again, her mother drives like she's the only person on the road, and everyone else can get out of *her* way. It would be impressive if it wasn't so terrifying. "The song says that tonight, they're going to get some. Get some what?"

Blood pumps in my ears and I press my head back against the seat. I don't know if I'm more rocked by my ill attention to the road or by Legs's question.

I turn the radio off.

Good grief. I blame Lana Mae for this. Letting her child listen to inappropriate music about casual sex sung by delinquent youth. Aren't these boys, like, fifteen? Where are their mothers? I have a good mind to write to the record company and...

"Uncle Liammmm, what are they getting?" Legs asks again.

"Probably chlamydia," I mutter darkly under my breath.

"What did you say?"

No! I'm not prepared to field this type of question. I'm only the driver!

"Um... clams from... India." I cringe the second the words are out of my mouth.

Good one, Liam.

Will have to make a very awkward phone call to my sister later to explain that one.

"Clams? Eww, that's gross." To my intense relief, Legs seems placated by my absolute nonsense of an explanation. "Turn the song back up?"

"Absolutely not."

Thankfully, we're pulling into her dance studio, and Legs forgets the lack of music as her little face lights up.

"You ready?" I smile at her in the rearview mirror.

"Ready, Freddie!"

I turn off the ignition and grab her sparkly unicorn

backpack from the passenger seat. "Come on then, princess."

I hold Legs's backpack over my coffee-stained shirt like a shield as we make our way into the packed dance studio. Girls in tulle and glitter hug and twirl and squeal while their moms gather in groups, jangling their car keys and sipping their Starbucks lattes.

Lana Mae hates it here. Says she doesn't fit in, and asks me to take Allegra most Fridays. Which means that I'm a Razzle Dazzle Dance Studio regular.

I don't buy her excuse. I think, deep down, she's trying to set me up with one of the single moms here. Clearly, my little sister thinks I need to get a life.

Speaking of single moms, there's (thankfully) no sign of Cassandra, but I do spot Debs—a bottle-blond lady with an overeager voice and a penchant for putting her hand on my arm and trapping me in one-sided conversations.

She pushes her sunglasses up and smiles. "Liam, hi!"

I give her a nod, then turn away to sign Legs in. I sit on the vacant chair furthest away from Debs and her posse, then unzip my niece's backpack to get her water bottle and dance shoes.

Once she's ready, I give her a hug. "You're the brightest star in the room, my girl."

"I know!" she chirps with all the wonderful confidence only an unjaded eight-year-old can have. She untangles her arms from around my neck and spots her friend Ruby across the room. She gives her a big, enthusiastic wave, then turns to me seriously. "You can go now."

"You don't want me to stay and watch?" I chuckle. I'm not hurt or offended.

Well, maybe a tiny bit.

She shakes her head. "Nope." She pops the "p" and puts

her hands on her hips sassily. "You can go do something else."

Obviously there's nothing I wouldn't do for Legs—including participation in the studio's annual daddy-daughter dance (an archaic tradition that's non-inclusive of many modern family set-ups, in my humble opinion). But I've had a long day, and am vaguely relieved that I don't have to sit here for the next sixty minutes watching thirty children stand on their tiptoes and twirl off-beat.

Plus, I need to get out of this coffee-soaked shirt.

Plus plus, Debs looks like she's making her way over.

I give Legs another hug and watch her skip over to Ruby, crossing my arms in a vain attempt to disguise the fact that I'm wearing my coffee.

"Coo-eee!" I hear Debs behind me. I make for the door at breakneck speed, almost tripping over my feet.

Once back in the vehicle, I slump in my seat and assess the damage.

Shirt status—ruined. Also, cold and sticking to my skin in the worst way.

Agitated, I slip it off and throw it on the passenger seat in a crumpled heap.

What now? I can't very well sit outside a dance studio full of children while I'm half-naked. I am most certain there are laws against that. And if there aren't, there should be.

I have fifty-five minutes to kill and I don't feel like going all the way home, so I decide to stop by the office. I have a clean shirt there—a whole clean suit, in fact—and everyone should be long gone for the evening.

I turn the key in the ignition and pull onto the main road. It's one of those glorious evenings where the sun is golden and warm, and the air is ripe with the promise of summer. The traffic is even moving smoothly, for once.

I roll the windows down and enjoy the breeze circulating in the vehicle, cool against my bare skin. I may have my careful, precision-based routine that runs like clockwork, holds no surprises, and provides the people I love with everything they need. But there's something strangely liberating about this unplanned moment.

Maybe there is some kind of method to Annie's madness...

On a whim, I take a left. It's not the way to the office, but I have time to kill. Driving aimlessly is spontaneous, right?

I bet she often drives with no destination, the windows cranked down.

I smile at the thought of her riding alongside me in place of my stained shirt, laughing as her hair blows in the wind.

She'd have the radio on, I'm sure.

I flip the car stereo back on. One Direction blares at top volume, right where they left off earlier. I stifle a laugh at the memory of my faux pas while explaining the lyrics to Legs. That girl is going to keep me on my toes these next few years, that's for sure.

But now that she's not in the vehicle and I'm no longer worried about her hearing anything her sweet little ears shouldn't, I find that I don't want to turn the song off.

In fact, I turn it up.

Tap my fingers on the steering wheel.

Fingers turn into whole hands. Hands turn into head nods.

The track ends and flips to the next on the playlist, and it's another one I recognize. One I even know the words to. It's the song about the girl not knowing how beautiful she is. Not knowing how much the guy wants her.

One person comes to mind at these lyrics.

The same woman who's been running through my thoughts all day, messing with me so that I've started to *like* the chaos.

For crying out loud, I sent her a spontaneous text. I never do stuff like that. But when it comes to Annie, it's like I don't have as much control.

I'm not sure what I'm doing right now... but I actually feel lighter. Freer.

I crank up the volume and start belting out the words.

The lady in the car next to me—who, to be fair, looks like she's been sucking on sour lemons all day—shoots me a strange look.

Is that how *I* usually look?

I don't know. But I do know that, sitting here, basking in the evening sunlight and singing at the top of my lungs, my world's suddenly brighter.

18

ANNIE

I'm hot.

I'm hot, and I'm tired, and I'm sweating profusely while cursing my adorable linen overalls and high-neck ribbed shirt. Both of which are sticking to every inch of my person in a decidedly unflattering manner.

I'm standing at the bus stop, laden with paper grocery bags and wishing I wasn't wearing another one of my stupid TikTok bras that I have to keep yanking down. After a ten-hour day in the office followed by a veritable mad-house at Trader Joe's, I just want to eat my pint of non-dairy dessert in my pajamas while wishing it was real ice cream. At this point, I'll be having it as soup.

This not-having-a-car business is a royal pain in my behind.

But I can't complain. I mean, it's snowing in Boston. Prisha sent me photo evidence in the form of Raj shoveling the driveway in his penguin pajama pants.

Which, of course, I will be posting on Instagram later.

Is this bus ever coming?

I stick my neck out like a gawker, and peer down the

street in that awkward way people do. Like looking harder for something will magically summon it.

As expected, I do not spot a bus.

What I *do* spot is a black SUV pulling up to the lights with the windows down and One Direction's "You Don't Know You're Beautiful" blasting so loud, I can hear every word.

I smile, instantly cheered. Love me a bit of old-school 1D.

I'd be doing the same. Yanno, if I had a car.

Because I'm bored, curious, and evidently, a gawker, I squint a little to see the person in the driver's seat. My eyebrows raise to see that it isn't a teenage girl and her gaggle of friends. It's not even a late-twenty-something lady rocking out (guilty).

It's a man. A very broad, very hot man... who is also very shirtless.

His skin is inked with a collage of beautiful tattoos—intricate, artful drawings that I'm sure have an amazing story. He's got his head back and is singing horrendously off-key. I've never considered that a muscular, tattooed man rocking out to a boy band anthem could be so unbelievably sexy.

I grin as I watch him, entranced.

Then, for some reason, the man glances my way.

And I'm staring into coal dark eyes I'd recognize anywhere.

My jaw hits the ground. I have to squeeze my eyes shut a couple times. Am I dreaming?

But it's him. Undeniably him.

Liam stops singing. Turns the music off.

And I do the only thing I can possibly think to do in this moment.

I wave.

Only, for some reason, I put my whole body behind it, flapping my arm and jerking my torso like I'm one of those blow-up things you see outside used car dealerships.

Then, to make it worse, I shout "Hi, Mr. Liam!"

Apparently, my mouth couldn't decide on "Mr. Donovan" or "Liam."

Fan-freaking-tastic.

Liam seems to debate something. I see the wrinkle in his brow, the intensity in his eyes. It's almost like he wants to keep going, keep driving, pretend this never happened.

Instead, he signals. Pulls over.

At the bus stop. Right in front of me.

His face is calm and impassive, but his flush gives away his embarrassment. It creeps along his neck and shoulders and that chest...

Oh my gosh. Don't look at his chest, Annie!

I jerk my wayward gaze back to his face. Away from that (totally expected) muscular form and (totally unexpected) display of ink.

My heart is beating so fast, I think it might explode.

Liam is looking at me, his eyes hooded. Like this is normal. "Need a ride?" he asks.

I blink. "You're offering to be my chauffeur?"

"Yes."

I stand for a moment, dithering like a mad woman.

The light turns green. The person behind Liam honks. He keeps his eyes on me.

"Get in the car, Annie."

I get in.

Keep your eyes where he can see 'em.

I repeat this to myself like a mantra as I try to keep my

eyes squarely on the road. Meanwhile, Liam steers with his knee as he pulls on the work shirt he was wearing earlier, now crumpled and coffee-stained.

"You have tattoos," I blurt stupidly. Apparently, saying something remotely smart isn't on the cards this afternoon.

Liam nods. "I do."

I scratch my head, struggling to process this. He's wound the windows up and that sexy pine scent, coupled with all that bare skin, is making it hard to think.

He's grumpy and stuffy and straight-laced, I remind myself.

But that image of him is so at odds with what I just witnessed. Tattoos covering his arms and torso, stopping just above his wrists so they're hidden under his work shirts. Or long-sleeve shirts worn to bed.

My head is spinning.

Liam isn't just hot. He's downright sexy.

And this is *not* making me feel things.

"I didn't realize..." I mumble.

"You've never seen me with my shirt off," Liam responds reasonably.

He gives me a sideways glance and this sheepish expression creeps over his face, making him look almost boyish. I haven't seen anything like it, and it's making my head spin all the more. "I was trying out your spontaneity challenge to see if it had any merits. Think I embarrassed myself... that seems to happen a lot when I'm around you."

"Right back atcha," I respond automatically. "I don't think I've ever had so many... ah, unfortunate incidents-slash-accidents occur around one person."

Liam smiles. Actually smiles.

Not just a lip twitch or a smirk, but a full-blown, teeth-showing beam that lights up his entire face, transforming him. And goodness me, it's a sight to behold.

161

I look away.

"So, um... good first week? You enjoying the job?" Liam attempts conversation valiantly. Like he wasn't topless mere moments ago, and I haven't been blushing uncontrollably ever since.

I opt for bluntness. "You really don't like small talk, do you?"

"Loathe it."

"Thought so." I laugh.

"But," Liam adds almost shyly. "I am interested to hear how you like working at Stay Inside the Lines?"

I smile. "I love it."

He doesn't react, his face predictably unreadable. Instead, he asks for directions to my place, and we sit in a slightly awkward silence until his phone rings moments later.

He answers it hands-free. "Hello?"

"You picked up Legs yet?" Luke's voice booms over the car speaker.

Liam winces and turns down the volume. "No, I'm just dropping Annie off."

"You're dropping Annie off?!" Luke practically shrieks. "From where?"

"Long story. And you're on speaker."

"Oh, good. Hi, Annie!"

"Hi, Luke," I call cheerfully.

"Glad I caught you both, actually. You haven't cooked yet for tonight, have you, Liam?"

He cooks? A tattooed businessman who can cook?

Jeez, Louise.

"Was going to grab a pizza," Liam says.

"Don't bother. The caterers at the ranch are packing all the food from the sample menus we tried today. There's a

162

ton of stuff, more than enough for all of us. We'll bring it round to Lana's."

Who the heck is Lana?

"Sounds good," Liam says.

"Annie." There's a strange, innocent note in Luke's voice. "You should come."

I glance at Liam, but his face is totally impassive, a neutral mask. These guys are my bosses and I've only been at SITL for a week. Having dinner with them is probably a little much. "Oh, I couldn't possibly. I have, um—"

"I insist!"

Liam gives me another of his sideways looks. "Luke, the woman has a life. She could be busy."

That's nice. He knows I'm the opposite of busy, but he's giving me an out.

Or maybe he doesn't want me there. Maybe Lana's another girl he's seeing.

He sure knows a lot of ladies for someone who "doesn't date."

Did that sound jealous? Totally wasn't. Obviously, my boss can socialize with whomever he wants.

"Annie? Are you busy?" Luke presses.

I scramble for words. "Well, no. But I—"

"Perfect. It's decided, then. We'll see you in forty-five minutes."

He hangs up before I can respond.

"I can still take you home if you want," Liam offers, staring straight ahead.

His sentence stirs something in me. What *do* I want?

If I'm honest, I enjoyed eating Mexican food with Liam last night more than I'd like to admit. And tonight, I'm being given the opportunity to eat dinner with him again. I find that I don't want to pass up on it. Especially not in exchange for my mother's leftover chili and another night of unseasonable knitting.

"I'd like to come," I blurt before I can think too much about it.

"Suit yourself," Liam says brusquely, but if I didn't know better, I could swear his lips tip up just the tiniest bit.

Why did my heart flutter a little to see that?

Reel it in, Annie. We are a flutter-free zone.

Liam turns off the main road. "We've just got to make one stop on the way."

"Let me guess," I say, attempting a joke to get my mind safely back in professional territory. "There's some super pressing thing you've gotta grab from the office?"

"Nope. Have to pick up Legs."

My smile drops off my face. "Oh. Right."

I guess I'll finally get to meet the famous Legs. And Lana.

Surely that'll be awkward, no? Unless there's a bit of a *Sister Wives* situation going on here.

We continue to drive in silence, my mind churning with questions about what I'm getting myself into. If we're picking up Legs, should I get into the back seat? Or would that be weird?

How does one handle a situation like this? It's not every day that you hear about a woman being invited to her hot, tattooed boss's house for dinner along with two of his potential girlfriends.

Annie, why?

Finally, we pull into a strip mall and stop outside a butter-yellow storefront with a rainbow sign that reads "Razzle Dazzle Dance Studio."

Huh?

Liam unbuckles his seatbelt. "You coming?"

I raise a brow. "To the dance studio?"

"Yeah," he says seriously. "Thought you might like to practice ballroom dancing with me."

He must be joking. And I want to laugh, I really do. But then, I think about having those strong arms around me again and the laugh catches in my throat. I let out a bizarre "urrrckle" sound that has Liam looking genuinely concerned for my health.

I clear my throat. Banish all thoughts of dancing with him.

"I guess so," I say, sounding more confident than I feel.

I follow him out of the car, more perplexed than ever. Legs must be a dance teacher or something. She probably does yoga. I bet she's insanely flexible and can do that move where you put your legs behind your head.

The last time I did that was when I was in diapers, probably.

Liam buttons up the top of his dirty shirt and I try not to watch, try not to wonder about the colorful, intricate drawings beneath that single layer of fabric. When we walk into the studio, the place is full of little girls and boys in dance gear, running around, shrieking and having fun. Gaggles of those yummy-mummy types in designer yoga gear are scattered through the room.

Is Legs one of them?

At that moment, a blond lady—who's dressed just like Cassandra was last night—breaks away from her group and walks toward us. She's very pretty, with, uh, *ample* assets. She seems like she'd be Liam's type... Maybe.

I don't actually know what Liam's type might be given our "I don't date" conversation. But this must be her.

I smile, ready for introductions, but Liam nods. Stands a tiny bit in front of me, almost like he's hiding me or something.

No, not hiding, but... shielding?

"Debs," he says curtly. Then, to my surprise, he side-steps her, grabs my sleeve, and tugs me along behind him.

He lets go so he can crouch just in time for a little pigtailed ball of glitter to launch herself into his arms.

I watch the scene in total, abject confusion.

The girl breaks away from Liam and they have a sweet little exchange where Liam's face looks softer than I've ever seen it. I watch with my mouth wide open, bringing back my world-renowned big-mouth Billy Bass impression.

But seriously... what is happening?!

It isn't long before the girl clues into my cluelessness. She looks up at me curiously with huge, familiar coal dark eyes.

"Hi?" she says it like a question, puckering her lips.

Liam ruffles her hair and stands straight. Faces me. "Annie, I'd like you meet my niece, Allegra."

She gives me a gap-toothed smile. "Uncle Liam calls me 'Legs' for short. You can too, if you like."

19

ANNIE

For the third time in my life—and the second time in the past twenty minutes—I'm stunned into speechlessness. The English language evades me as I gaze down at the freckled, dirty-blond pigtailed ballerina with Liam's eyes.

I then realize that both Allegra—Legs—and her Uncle Liam are waiting for me to speak.

"Hi!" I choke out. "I'm, um, Annie."

Legs tilts her head, assesses me for a moment. "Are you Uncle Liam's girlfriend?"

"What?!" I splutter. "No, I—"

"We work together, honey. Remember?" Liam gives me an apologetic shrug over Legs's head. "The women I work with are not girlfriends, they're my employees."

A fact that we all need to be reminded of, apparently.

Because the whole "tattooed Liam cuddling a little girl" thing is making my brain—and my heart—do a whole lot of gymnastics. And neither are processing the very real fact that this still CANNOT make me feel things.

"Like Barb?" Legs asks with an adorable little tilt of her brow.

"Exactly."

"But not Mindy?"

"No, sweetie. Mindy is your new Auntie."

"Oh." Legs falls into thoughtful silence for a moment, then launches into a story about her ballet class while the three of us walk to the car. I'm fine to stay silent though, I'm still not over the shock.

Liam straps Legs into her booster seat in the back, laughing quietly at something she said. When he gets back in the driver's seat, I finally ask, "So, who's Lana?"

Liam shoots me a funny look, then starts the car. "Lana Mae. She's my sister. She's—"

"My Mommy," Legs adds. "She's in Phoenix, Arizona."

"For a business trip," Liam clarifies. "She's taking a course there for a couple weeks."

Suddenly, the whole chauffeur chat makes a whole lot more sense.

There I was, thinking it was some kind of sexy euphemism for what Liam gets up to on his weekends, when really, he just meant... Babysitting.

"There's a lot of cacti there," Legs continues. "Did you know that cacti is the plural of cactus, Annie?"

"I do." I twist around in my seat to face her. "I learned it in school. You did, too?"

"Yup." She tugs at her leotard. "I'm eight now."

Something clicks in my mind. A phone call made by an annoyed man on a plane who seemed very upset to be missing something. My eyes dart to Liam, and while he's staring ahead impassively, I know he's listening. "Was it your birthday recently?"

Her eyes light up. "Yes!"

"Happy belated birthday." I smile. "Eight is a good number."

"How old are you, Annie?"

Liam rubs a hand over his face. "Legs, you can't—"

"Twenty-six," I answer, staring at Liam's profile.

He doesn't say anything, doesn't supply his own age. Just looks at the road, poker-faced, as he turns off the highway and into a neighborhood lined with large trees and walking paths. Very family-friendly.

I wonder if Liam lives close to his sister. I pictured something more, I don't know...

Dungeon-y. Like a batcave or something.

"Annie, are you coming to meet Harry Styles?" Legs pipes up.

Like, the celebrity? I'm about to respond when I glance at Liam. He's smiling. A small, closed-lipped smile, but a smile nonetheless. Maybe he's a big fan. A Styler, if you will.

It would make sense, considering his performance earlier.

"Oh, yes. You're going to want to meet Harry Styles," he adds with an uncharacteristic twinkle. "Let's just hope he's feeling better today, huh, Leggsy?"

"I hope so," she says earnestly. "Mommy hates it when he's sick."

"You could almost believe he's going bald with the amount of shedding he does."

What celeb news channel are these people watching?!

"Are you excited to meet Harry, Annie?" Legs asks sweetly.

"Uh, sure," I say slowly. "I'm more of a Swiftie myself, but I wouldn't turn down an opportunity to meet Harry. Is he coming to Atlanta or something?"

Liam makes a noise that sounds remarkably like the beginning of a laugh. "Aren't you a little old to be meeting teenage boys?"

"Teenage boys? Harry Styles is, like, twenty-eight."

Liam's eyes shoot wide open. "That doesn't seem possible." He gives me a side glance, then seeing I'm serious, his expression becomes horrified. Which makes me smile. "*I'm twenty-eight.*"

"Well, then," I tease, strangely glad to learn how close in age we are. "Aren't *you* a little old to be singing along to music by men who you thought were teenage boys?"

"Yes," Liam replies gravely. Apparently, my excellent humor was lost on him there.

"Uncle Liam was a teenage boy once! He told me. He liked math class and played baseball and he had a girlfriend. But now, he doesn't have a girlfriend," Legs announces.

A slightly awkward silence falls over the vehicle.

Liam drums his fingers on the steering wheel. "Legs, honey, Annie doesn't want to talk about me. I'm old and boring. Why don't you tell us what you learned today in dance class?"

"My mommy was a teenager once, too," Legs motors on, ignoring Liam. "And my daddy. Then Mommy had me and Daddy went away and now I'm eight and she's not a teenager anymore. She's a grown-up, like Uncle Liam, and she says I'm going to make her hair go gray early."

I hold my breath as I ingest all this information, provided so innocently, so casually, from the mouth of a child. Personal information about Liam's family.

"That would be cool!" I tell Legs. "Gray hair is trendy now. All the fashion bloggers are doing it."

Legs smiles, then busies herself with her backpack, pulling out a little Tupperware full of apples. They're neatly cut, and lined up in straight, even rows. I know immediately that Liam was responsible for that snack prep.

The thought warms my heart. Or it would, if I was allowing myself to feel these things.

Which I'm *not.*

Liam catches my eye. "Lana Mae had her young. Her dad isn't... involved," he says quietly.

A pang of sympathy hits me. I've always considered myself lucky to have two loving parents.

My thoughts must be clear on my face, because Liam gives a little nod. "She's the most incredible kid."

His face visibly softens as he speaks about his niece. It's the most handsome he's ever looked.

I swallow thickly. "You seem really close."

"I'd do anything for her."

I sit back against the seat and let out an exhale. This short conversation felt so personal, so vulnerable. I feel like I understand Liam a little better now.

He would make an excellent dad.

The thought comes out of nowhere, but with a blinding, aching certainty. I hurriedly stash it away. That is absolutely, positively, no business of mine. I've known the guy precisely one week—who am I to be judging his parenting abilities?

At that moment, we pull into the driveway of a pristine duplex with brightly colored planter boxes and windchimes on the porch. The kind of place that screams "welcome home!"

"We're here," Liam says, looking at Legs in the rearview mirror.

Legs scrambles about, excited to get inside, and I take a moment to assess the house. Look at the door that I'm about to open into another part of Liam's life. I realize that I can't remember the last time I had this much anticipation for a Friday night.

Oh, wait. I do remember.

It was last Friday night. In the bathroom at the hotel, about to share a bed with a stranger.

A stranger who's no longer a stranger... and I'm glad for it.

🧩

"Took you long enough!" Luke's cheerful voice echoes as we walk into the living room.

I stop in my tracks. It looks like Pinterest exploded in here... in a good way. The room is small, but sparkling clean and gorgeously decorated in warm, earthy tones.

Lana Mae has good taste.

Luke is seated on the couch and Legs barrels toward him. He swings her onto his lap. "How was dance class, rockstar?"

While Legs regales him with the stories she told Liam and me in the car, my eyes glance around the room. Take in the framed art prints on the wall, the plants, the tall, overflowing bookcase. My eyes then land on the pretty woman sitting next to Luke on the couch. She has fair, sandy hair and is holding a glass of red wine. She's also wearing cut-off jean shorts that show off killer legs I'd, well, kill for.

Her gaze zeroes in on me. "Hiiiii, you must be Annie."

She practically bounces off the couch with excitement. I'm not sure exactly what I've done to spark so much joy, but I'm sure Marie Kondo would be proud.

"Hi!" I say as peppily as possible, trying to match her energy. "You must be Mindy."

"Sure am," she twinkles.

At that moment, a huge, orange cat comes out of nowhere and brushes my legs, purring loudly.

"Oh, hi there!" I lean down to pet him, and as he saunters away, orange patches of hair cover my pants. I brush them off.

"Don't bother," Liam grunts. "You'll be covered in orange by the time we're finished eating."

"Mommy calls them gifts," Legs chimes in. "Special gifts from Harry Styles that make her late for work."

My eyes swivel to Liam and he gives me that closed-lipped smile again, his eyes glinting.

Well, that clears up a few things.

"He doesn't usually take to people so quick," Liam says, watching Harry Styles the cat come back my way.

"He must know I'm a big fan." I kneel so I can pet him better, then throw Liam another look from beneath my lashes. "Even if he is too young for me."

Liam snorts with laughter and looks away. I grin, happy that I elicited that reaction.

Mindy watches the whole interaction with an open mouth, like she's observing an alien life form.

"Annie, take a seat." She pats the chair beside her and I oblige. Then, she starts plying me with a million questions, which I happily answer. She's exactly what I would've expected for Luke's fiancée: sweet, warm, chatty and funny.

Meanwhile, Liam leans against the doorframe, looking around the scene as if it's entirely unfamiliar to him. I get a sudden uncomfortable inkling—Luke kind of put Liam on the spot, and *he* had no opportunity to say "no" if this was awkward for him.

"You okay?" I ask him when Mindy gets up to grab something, giving me a momentary pause in the barrage of questions on the nitty-gritty details of my life in Boston.

Liam's eyes flicker, laced with caution. "'Course. Why wouldn't I be?" It's apparently a rhetorical question, because he then straightens and announces to the room, "I'm going to get changed."

I can't help but feel a little bit thrown off. Liam should be in his element here, but he's reverted to his stiff, formal self. Distanced Liam. It's a bit of a reality check. Liam is the man I should be complaining about to my colleagues by the water cooler. Not having dinner with and thinking about his inked bare chest.

My cheeks warm at even a hint of that memory.

Maybe I should just make my excuses and—

"Come on." Mindy grabs my elbow. "Let's get you some wine!"

Luke winks at us as his fiancée drags me to the kitchen, where she proceeds to pour me an entire vat of wine.

"How're you enjoying working with Lukey and Liam?" Mindy is still bouncing like a jack-in-the-box as she throws open the fridge and cupboards, firing plates and bowls and boxes of food onto the counter at an alarming rate.

Her energy is chaotic and carefree. I dig it.

"Luke's a fun boss." I offer Mindy a careful smile. She may be barefoot and have a wine stain on her shirt, but she's still the boss's wife. Or, soon-to-be wife.

"I bet," she says cheerfully, still banging around. "He used to work at a marketing firm downtown but left to join Stay Inside the Lines when it started growing so fast."

I lean against the counter and cross my arms. "So, Liam started the company alone?"

"Mmmhmm." Mindy dumps a box of ravioli onto a plate and pops it in the microwave. "Workaholic, that one. And not much of a people person..." She shoots me a cheeky look. "As I'm sure you've learned by now. Luke came onboard to manage the staff, handle the everyday running of things."

"That checks out." I swirl my glass of wine and look at the mini whirlpool I've created.

"Nature versus nurture is an odd thing," Mindy continues her kitchen tirade. "Luke, Liam and Lana all went through the same thing, but they all responded to what happened so differently."

"What happened?" I ask, then realize how nosy that sounded. "Sorry, I mean—I probably shouldn't... umm, you know—"

"They had a bit of a rough go of it." Mindy, bless her heart, has the kindness to interrupt my dithering ramble for the ages.

"I'm sorry to hear that," I respond sincerely.

Mindy suddenly stops all of her zooming around and points a fork at me. Rather accusingly. "You like him, too."

I swirl my glass a bit too hard, splashing cabernet on the floor tiles. "Oh! Let me get a cloth."

I busy myself at the sink, wetting a dishcloth and then scrubbing the spill. I keep my head down so Mindy can't see my reddening cheeks.

"What do you mean 'too'?" I ask, oh-so-casually, as I stand back up, rinse the cloth and wring it out. Easy-breezy, nothing to see here. I'm the poster child for casualness.

In reality, though, I don't know which part's tripping me up more: her calling me out on liking Liam—which I obviously don't—or her insinuation that he likes me 'too'—which he obviously doesn't.

The conclusion is, well, *obvious*: Mindy is blind.

"Can't you see it?" Mindy widens her eyes. Pauses. "Well, I guess not because you've just met Liam. But I've known him for a while, and he's never, ever invited anyone home for dinner."

"Luke invited me," I correct.

Mindy waves a dismissive hand, then tops up my wine. Right to the brim. "Luke may have invited you, but Liam let it happen."

"How do you mean?" My voice goes up half an octave. *Great job keeping casual, Annie. Not.*

"Liam might let Luke do most of the talking, but he always puts his foot down when he's set on something. Believe me, if he didn't want you here, you wouldn't be here."

I blink at Mindy, once again lost for words.

I sense a pattern forming—Liam surprises the hell out of me, and I respond by losing my handle on my native tongue entirely.

Seriously, there have been too many revelations today. My head may fall off, it's so heavy with new information.

I want to ask approximately nine hundred and forty five thousand more questions, but do not want to be accused for the second time in five minutes of liking my boss inappropriately.

Because that's what liking him would be. Inappropriate.

I need to find my tongue. Regain control of the situation.

"I wouldn't be here if I didn't want to be," I say calmly, before realizing—too late, of course—that this sentence kind of makes it sound like what I want is Liam. "I mean, um, I came because it was nice that Luke invited me. That's all!"

Legs twirls into the kitchen, flouncing her skirt as she goes. "Is dinner ready? I'm so hungry, I might die."

"That's awfully hungry," I respond with a smile, grateful that she's caused a distraction from whatever... that was. "We better feed you, quick!"

Mindy surveys the mountain of reheated food, then looks at me. "You okay eating on the couch in the living room? We turn into uncivilized animals when Lana Mae's away."

"My lap is my plate of choice, always."

She laughs. "We're gonna get along just fine, you and me."

"Just pinky promise not to tell Mommy. That's the rule." Allegra extends her little finger to me solemnly.

"Done," I promise, wrapping my pinky around hers.

We carry the takeout boxes, plates and cutlery to the living room and line them up on the coffee table.

"Let's dig in," Luke says as he piles garlic bread on his plate. I take a plate too, and serve myself a scoop of the caprese salad, which features some particularly ruby-red, plump tomatoes and the freshest-looking basil ever.

"Smells good." The deep, unmistakable voice comes from behind me.

I look back so fast, I almost give myself whiplash. As I register Liam on the stairs, I also try not to pay any attention to Luke's smirk at my actions.

Liam comes downstairs, his powerful stride as businesslike as ever. But his hair is shower damp, he's barefoot, and he's wearing casual sweatpants and a black tee that shows off his sleeves of tattoos.

Holy cannoli.

"I'm starving," he continues, pushing his damp hair back as he surveys the trays of meat, pasta, veggies and salads. The whole thing looks and smells heavenly, but the real feast is the sight of Liam like this.

It's everything I can do to drag my eyes away from him. I don't know why, but I somehow expected him to come downstairs in a suit.

But of course he wouldn't. It's Friday night; he's here with his family.

Once again, I have an uneasy feeling that I'm intruding. A voyeur getting a glimpse of something I shouldn't.

Despite Mindy's obvious shipping, I need to write off all the events of this evening as par for the course. Like it's a normal, everyday occurrence that I see my boss shirtless, find him very attractive, then have dinner with him and his family.

Because even though my fresh start in Atlanta hasn't exactly gone according to plan—in more ways than one—this family is my work lifeline. So no matter what, all of my interactions with them *must* be all business.

I look to where Liam's sitting, now painstakingly making a plate for Legs and looking like he's carefully calculating how much protein, carbs and veggies her fifty-pound body needs.

No, my stomach isn't doing a weird clenchy thing that it has no business doing...

I'm so screwed.

20

LIAM

"Beer league softball."

I frown at the papers spread across my desk, then look up at Luke and Vanessa. "Doesn't sound like a real thing."

HR meetings first thing on a Monday morning are not my favorite way to start the week, but here we are. If Wiseman wants to see a fun team environment, then we're going to give him a fun team environment.

And we're going to do that without any of this softball nonsense.

"Of course it's a real thing, you halfwit." Luke spins around in his office chair and waggles his pages at me. "Sports are very important. This softball league is an active, healthy, team building activity that encourages—"

"Drinking," I finish for him. Pinch the bridge of my nose. "We are running a business here, not a frat house. I don't know how many times I have to say this when it's something that literally should never have to be said."

Luke rolls his eyes. "Well, I'm pro-softball. People love softball."

"Softball is a sport for high school girls."

Luke points a finger at me like a little gun, and I'm half-surprised he doesn't make a "pew pew!" noise to accompany the motion, like we used to do when we were kids. "Brother of mine, that is both sexist and ageist."

I scowl, not wanting to be either of those things, but also not wanting to commit to playing alcohol-infused-fake-baseball with my employees. I know we're meant to be making a big push with our HR, and that includes showing that we have a great team environment and atmosphere here at SITL, but we still need to keep things appropriate.

Because goodness knows I'm already developing very inappropriate feelings for a certain new employee. Especially after what went down on Friday evening.

I didn't miss the way Annie's eyes moved over my half-clothed body when I picked her up. A blind man would have seen that. And let's not even get started on the heat that licked my insides as I felt her gaze on me. It's a no-go zone. A no-go zone I spent the rest of the weekend trying not to think about.

"Why don't we just... order pizza?" I suggest lamely.

Vanessa gives me a wink. "I like pizza."

"Good thinking." Luke's lips tip up in a grin.

I breathe a sigh of relief. "Good. Now that that's settled, what I really want to discuss is—"

"Why don't we do both?" Luke cuts me off.

"Excuse me?"

"Pizza *and* softball. What do you think, Vanessa?"

Vanessa sits across the boardroom table, looking from Luke to me and back again like she's umpiring a tennis match. Badly, I'll add. Luke's suggestions are definitely out of bounds, and she's being awfully quiet about laying down the long arm of the HR law. Which should surely state that this is an awful idea.

She fiddles with her notes. Crosses her legs, then

uncrosses them. "Hm. Beer league softball *is* very common for corporate team building," she says eventually. "The 'beer' part doesn't promote drinking or anything, it just means it's casual. Fun. Not too competitive."

"We could get t-shirts made," Luke adds brightly.

I raise my eyes heavenwards. "Well, if there are *t-shirts* involved."

I mean it to sound sarcastic—because seriously, we have about a thousand actually important things to attend to today, and Luke's priorities are about equivalent to a toddler's. But now, my mind is on t-shirts, dammit.

Specifically, an event of late involving my t-shirt and the same new employee who shall remain anonymous. Does she still have it? Has she washed it, or does it smell like her skin?

And more to the point, why in the hell am I thinking about what her skin smells like?

"Liam!" Luke unceremoniously snaps his fingers in my face. "Wakey wakey. Vanessa and I vote for beer league softball. There's a tournament this weekend, and we'll provide pizza afterwards—as you so smartly suggested—and beer—which you can choose to partake in or not. K?"

I feel elated. "Sure. Though I can't make it this week-end. Lana isn't back until the week after." I give Vanessa as warm a look as I can muster—because this is really her fault, suggesting team sports and alcohol like a hooligan. "You guys have fun."

Luke claps me on the back so hard I almost choke. "Nice try. I texted Mindy while you were zoned out. She'll take Legs to the game to watch."

"Oh."

"Come on, it'll be fun. Take you back to college, the good old days. Plus, it'll be a great way for everyone to let off some steam after working so hard."

A pit forms in my stomach. I haven't picked up a baseball bat in years, haven't wanted to. I regret nothing.

Would change nothing.

I push the thoughts away and focus on everything I have in my life because of my decision. Everything I've built. I have a business and employees I'm unbelievably grateful for, and if they want to play softball, who am I to stand in their way?

Maybe I really do need to lighten up.

I give Vanessa a nod. "Okay, I'll be there. Could you send a memo around to everyone?"

Vanessa nods, blinking her long eyelashes at me. "Absolutely."

Luke gives me a sneaky, knowing smile. "Thanks, Ness. That'll be all for now."

Vanessa gives me a sideways glance that's full of... something. And even though I stare hard back at her, she doesn't seem the least bit ruffled. Just skips out of the room like she hadn't spent the entire meeting making her half-lidded bedroom eyes at me.

Hm. Talk about HR issues. It's bad enough that Annie came over for dinner on Friday night...

Crap. Stop thinking about her, you creep. Because that's what an employer who thinks about his employees too much is. Right?

The second the door to the boardroom closes, I round on Luke. "Okay, as I was sayin—"

Luke belches loudly.

"Excuse you."

"Excuse yourself." Luke twirls a pen in his hand. "And just ask her out already."

Apparently, my words have fallen on deaf ears and Luke's started his own conversation.

"Who?" I sputter. "Vanessa?"

"No, Britney Spears."

Luke's sarcastic tone is not appreciated. "I don't want to ask Vanessa out. Or Britney Spears, for that matter."

"Well, obviously... because you are totally into someone else. You think I didn't see your whacked-out starry eyes just now?" Luke gloats. "Not to mention you were practically giggling on Friday night."

"Giggling?" I demand.

"You sounded like one of Legs's little school friends."

"And you sound like you've had a frontal lobotomy."

"Admit it!" Luke points his little gun finger at me again. "You got it bad for Annie, bro."

"Annie," I repeat dumbly.

"Yeah, you know. Annie." Luke grins and levels his hand in the air. "About yay high, red hair... ate dinner with us on Friday night thanks to my stroke of brilliance?"

"Hilarious. Never quit your day job."

"I'd be a phenomenal comedian. But seriously." Luke's expression turns almost business-like. "I'm happy that you're into someone. Pining looks good on you."

"You're wrong," I insist. "And even if you were right— which you aren't—it's not something we endorse here at SITL. I've read the employee handbook."

"You wrote the employee handbook, idiot."

And we're back to juvenile name calling.

I snap my laptop shut and give Luke a hard look. "Rules are rules for a reason."

"Not when you wrote them for the wrong reasons."

"The rules are perfectly in keeping with usual business practices in the United States."

"Not what I meant." Luke's eyes are that irritating amount of big-brother serious. Most of the time, I'm the one who leads the charge among our siblings, but when Luke gets like this, he's not afraid to pull out his haughty "I've been on this earth longer than you" card.

Factually correct, but intensely annoying.

"It's just one more wall you put up," he says, shaking his head. "One more barrier. You and Annie are both grown ass adults. If you like each other, why would you let the fact that you both work at the same company get in the way of exploring that?"

"Not 'exploring' someone you work with is both appropriate and correct," I say with finality. "Especially as we own said company. And we need to keep our HR in order."

"I hardly think Wiseman would care if you and Annie are upfront about the fact that you're dating."

"We *aren't* dating. And I'm sure he wouldn't," I say, but I don't mean it. I just want this conversation to end already. And it doesn't matter anyway, because this will never be something we propose to Wiseman. A moot point, if I ever heard one. "But I would never do anything to jeopardize the investment."

"Investment this, investment that." Luke twirls a finger, kicking his feet up on the desk.

"Yeah, investors," I say coolly. "Like, the people who are willing to fund this company and make it so that everyone can keep their job."

And so I can give him back everything I owe him.

Luke sits up a little, suddenly paying attention, and I'm not sure if this is because of what I said, or what I left unsaid. "Okay, okay," he mutters.

I breathe a sigh of relief... a little too soon.

"One more thing, though." Luke holds up a hand.

"What?"

'There's no harm in getting to know her better. I get that changing the company rules right now wouldn't look great for Wiseman, but you're not doing anything wrong by hanging out. You gave her a ride home after dinner on Friday and hell didn't freeze over, right?"

"I..." I trail off. The little twerp might be right. "I guess not."

"Glad you agree. Because I *might* have told her we're taking her out to dinner tomorrow night."

"You what?!"

"I said it was something we do for new employees. Dinner with the bosses."

"We don't do that."

"We do now." A wink. "Part of our excellent new HR initiative for impressing Tim and Co."

I'm dumbfounded. For some reason, Luke takes my appalled silence to be approval.

"I know, I'm a genius." Luke grins. "Now you get to take her out without *actually* having to ask her out, you rule-abiding chicken. I'll even send her an official e-vite so you don't have to. Look at me, solving all your problems."

"Trust me. You're my biggest problem."

When I walk back into mine and Annie's office, she's sitting backwards in her chair—why?—talking to Vanessa, who's perched on Annie's desk.

Seriously, why do none of these women use furniture correctly?

They look up as I enter and fall quiet, their expressions guilty. The exact same expression Legs had after I caught her in the pantry, balancing precariously on a counter stool as she attempted to reach her mom's secret chocolate stash on the top shelf.

They were talking about me.

185

Probably complaining about how I'm zero fun in all circumstances following that HR meeting. Which I can hardly blame them for.

I clear my throat. Hover in the doorway like a lurker.

Great. I'm being awkward in my own office. At my own company.

"Am I interrupting?" I ask.

Vanessa shakes her head. "We were just talking about getting beer league softball t-shirts made. We won't have them ready for Saturday's tournament, but we'll have them for our next tournament, I'm sure."

My gaze automatically pivots to Annie. "What kind of t-shirts are you thinking?"

She reddens.

Hmm. Maybe I'm not the only one who's been thinking of t-shirts lately...

I hope I'm not.

Whoa. Easy there, Liam.

She pauses, then blinks innocently. "I think they could be inspired by the people we work for."

I raise my brows. "How so?"

"You know... oversized, soft... total lifesavers when you have nothing else to wear."

Annie's still blushing, but her eyes have this curious gleam to them. Playful, mischievous. I pause, suddenly sure that we're not talking about team t-shirts anymore, but one, very particular t-shirt.

I have no choice but to bite, no choice but to pursue whatever this conversation is about. "Will Stay Inside the Lines be providing these t-shirts for the team?"

Annie smiles impishly. "Oh, I should think so."

Here it is, my chance to find out if she kept my t-shirt after the hotel. I'm not thinking straight at the moment, but for once, I can't bring myself to care.

"And will I be getting said t-shirts back at the end of the season?" I ask.

Annie's blush is now practically purple, but she squares her shoulders, continues to hold my gaze. "I don't think so."

She did keep it.

All I can picture is the woman wearing my damn t-shirt and very little more.

And she's looking at me like she knows it.

Did someone turn the temperature up in here?

Annie's hazel eyes are dancing with mischief and sparkle and so much goodness that I never want to look away.

"I'd say one could consider that stealing," I say quietly, trying to adopt a "stern boss" look.

"What if the team want to keep them as keepsakes?"

"Then the shirts should read 'I played for the Donovan Brothers' softball team and all I got was this lousy t-shirt.'"

Annie snorts with surprised laughter. "Mr. Donovan, was that a joke?"

I love the way she says "Mr. Donovan" like that. Like it's our secret that she knows what I look like eating left-overs in my sweatpants. Knows how my breathing sounds when I sleep.

Knows too much for comfort, really.

"About keeping the t-shirts being theft?" I shoot back. "Absolutely not."

Annie smiles. It's a big, wide smile that makes me want to smile back. Makes me want to move closer and—

"Ahem!" Vanessa's sharp exclamation snaps me out of my insanity. The room slowly, fuzzily, comes back into focus.

I forgot she was here.

I whirl around to the blond HR specialist, who looks, well... miffed. Super miffed.

"Shall we go and look at some designs tomorrow after work then, Annie?"

I look at Annie. Remember our not-a-date dinner.

"I can't, sorry," she addresses Vanessa but her eyes flicker to me. "I'm busy tomorrow night."

21

ANNIE

"Prishhhhhhhhhh!" I wail in the direction of my phone, which is propped up on my dressing table, on speakerphone.

"Annnnnnnnnnnnnnnn!" she wails back, but in a high-pitched, poor imitation of my whine.

"That wasn't even close," I tell her, peering into the mirror as I attempt to contour my cheekbones. Pout the lips, suck in the cheeks, dust the brush over the hollows...

Ugh. Why, oh why, does my bronzer make me look like I spilled cocoa powder all over myself?

"It was perfect. An Oscar-worthy impression. Maybe I should go on your date tonight for you, Liam wouldn't even know the difference."

"It's not a date," I hiss, looking over my shoulder to see if there are any skulking eavesdroppers in the hallway (also known as my mother and her book club pals). Though the air doesn't smell like Elnett hairspray, Chanel Number 5, or Chardonnay, so I think I'm safe. For now.

"What are you wearing?" Prisha asks. There's rustling on her end of the phone, followed by munching. Clearly, this is dinner and a show.

"What are you, some kind of payphone pervert?"

"I'm just a bestie with an excellent B.S. detector." I hear the smile in my friend's voice. Followed by more crunches. "Who happens to know that this is, indeed, a date. Goodness, these chocolates are delicious."

"It's not a date. It's dinner with my bosses. Plural."

"Dinner with your two *hot* bosses... Seriously, Ann. This is sounding more and more like a saucy book to me!"

"Prish, that's disgusting. They're brothers. This is a work event."

"Okayyy. If it's just a 'work event,' what are you wearing?"

"Clothes."

"Nice ones?"

"Ish."

What Prisha doesn't need to know is that I spent three hours after work yesterday shopping for a dress. And then proceeded to spend way too much money on said dress.

She doesn't need to know that at all.

I only did it because Luke said that they had a reservation at Petit Soleil. I googled it, and it's, like, super fancy. I didn't own anything even close to appropriate so I *had* to go shopping, didn't I?

"Fine, prove me wrong!" Prisha warns, and seconds later, my phone buzzes with a request to switch the call to Facetime.

Foiled!

I stare in the mirror, analyzing my dress from every possible angle. It looks okay, right?

I hit accept.

Prisha squeals. "You look like royalty, Annie!"

I blush with pleasure.

And then, I consider her word choice.

"Um, define royalty?" I ask.

190

Because "royalty" could mean anything from *I'm channeling my inner Meghan Markle* to *this look has a touch of the Henry VIII about it* (and by that, I mean that I look particularly ginger and double-chinned today. Not that I'm in the mood to behead someone. Except Prisha, of course).

I squint at my reflection again, then let out a long sigh. Whether or not my royal counterpart is a TV star sex kitten or a portly, syphilis-riddled, guillotine enthusiast, there's no denying that this dress is a little tight in the butt region.

"Annie, you look hot. Smoking hot. Good enough to eat. Etcetera, etcetera, you get the picture. Wipe that worried look off your pretty face and quit overthinking." She pauses. "And maybe while you're at it, wipe off some of that bronzer. You look... dirty."

"Dirty?" I squeak.

"You know, like you were doing some heavy gardening earlier and didn't quite get all the mud off your face."

I knew it!

"Oh my gosh!" I grab a Kleenex and frantically scrub until I look shiny and red and apple-cheeked. Henry-VIII-style apple-cheeked.

"I'm just going to cancel," I wail.

Oh, good. Back to my whiny tone.

Prish grins knowingly. "You're making a very big deal out of a 'work event' with Liam. *Now* are you ready to admit that it's more than that? That you loveeeee him, you want to kissssss him..."

And she's off, singing away in her best *Miss Congeniality* voice.

How dare she use my favorite classic romcom against me?

"I do not!" I exhale hard, then focus on rubbing extra foundation on the reddest bits of my freshly-scrubbed face.

Prish raises her brows. "You want to marryyyyyy him."

"Fine! Fine! I give." I grab a perfume bottle and spritz myself, needing something to do with my hands. "He's hotter than hell and I might have a teeny tiny bit of... interest... in getting to know him better. He's... interesting. But nothing more. I'm not.... interested in him like that."

Which is what I have to keep telling myself. No matter how my heartbeat picks up at the sight of him, or how sweet he was with Legs the other night, or how he was clearly flirting with me about his darned t-shirt yesterday... and I was shamelessly flirting right back.

But shouldn't have been. I need to keep it together, professional.

So what if the guy is an onion—made up of lots of delicate, translucent layers to peel back? You know what else onions do when you peel them?

Yeah, they make you cry.

"You want to say the word 'interest' some more, or is it my turn to talk?" Prisha asks, sounding all too triumphant.

"Neither." I pull a sulky face at my phone screen. "Look, I can't be, um, interested—shut up!—in Liam. He's my boss, and after Justin, I swore that I'd never get involved with anyone at work again. Being taken seriously in my career is my priority. Not finding a man."

"That is a dumb way to live your life, Annie. What if true love is right in front of you, and you're not allowing yourself the chance at happiness? All because of a promise you made to yourself that doesn't apply anymore."

"Or what if, for once, I'm being smart and thinking ahead?"

"It's a gamble either way, I guess. I mean, if you really don't want to go for it with your sexy, tattooed, grunting, romance-hero-level, manly-man of a boss, you could always just ignore him." Prisha says this like it's so simple, so straightforward.

But nothing has been straightforward since I stepped on that plane.

And it needs to be. I'm done with complicated and messy.

"We're opposites, Prish." I say into the camera. "Even if something *did* happen between us, it would never work out."

"Opposites attract, my friend."

"As if that's true for *your* love life! Raj is literally you with a beard and a... male appendage," I respond delicately.

"And I like it that way. But you, my friend, are different. You and Justin were so aligned in terms of your routines and interests. You were like a frappucino—all blended and icy and kinda overly sweet and icky after a while. You need heat. Someone who will be the peanut butter to your jelly. The Simon to your Garfunkel."

"Simon betrayed Garfunkel," I say grouchily.

Goodness, maybe all this time with Liam is rubbing off on me.

Prisha waves her hands dismissively. "Good thing that Liam is neither Paul Simon, nor Justin. So, do me a favor and don't treat him like he is, okay?"

I nod. Because Liam's not Justin, is he? Not even close.

"Okay."

"That's my girl." Prisha lifts her wine glass in a toast. "Now go get 'em, tiger!"

The doorbell rings downstairs.

He's here.

22

LIAM

"Are you serious right now?" I hiss into the phone, blood heating as my wrath is met with laughter.

"As a heart attack," Luke responds cheerfully.

"I am hereby resigning from my best man position at your wedding. I cannot, in good faith, be there when Mindy marries the likes of you."

Luke laughs harder. "Oh, she was in on it, don't worry."

"You are both dead to me."

"You'll be thanking us later!" Luke crows as I practically punch the screen of my cell phone to end the call—the modern-day equivalent of slamming the phone down.

Luke is not only dead to me, he is actually dead. Or he will be, once I get my hands on him.

I'm still simmering when the front door opens. I try to adopt a mild, pleasant expression as I open my mouth to say hi to...

Good gracious, the woman in the doorway looks exactly like I imagine Annie will thirty years from now. Same round eyes, pale skin, auburn hair that looks like it's been wrestled into submission. Though her mom's is graying around her temples and looks more successfully smoothed into place than Annie's ever does.

I mentally slap some sense into myself and pull myself together. "You must be Mrs. Jacobs."

"Call me Edel," she twinkles. Her lips—a darker, shinier red than the lipstick Annie always wears—stretch into a wide smile. "You must be Luke? Or Liam?"

"Liam Donovan, ma'am." I stretch out my hand and she shakes it enthusiastically.

"Charmed, I'm sure." She doesn't let go of my hand once the shake is done. Instead, she pulls me over the threshold. "Please, Liam, come in. The ladies from my Rakish Rogues book club and I were discussing the plot of *Plundering Pirates,* and we'd love a man's opinion of—"

"MOM!"

The familiar shout makes me smile despite myself.

"Liam will not be giving an opinion on pirate booty of any sort, thank you very much!" Annie appears at the door in a soft cloud of her signature sweet scent. She shoots me an apologetic look, then glares at her mom. "Sorry about my mother. Boundaries were never her strong suit."

Like mother, like daughter.

Only, not quite. Because said daughter is, well... *wow.*

I'm staring again. I should stop, but my brain is drinking in everything about Annie like she's an oasis in the driest desert. I want to mentally log the way her emerald-green dress hugs her curves, moving like water as she brushes past her mother in the doorway. The way her hair falls in waves to her shoulders, shiny and bright. The way her big eyes keep glancing at me too, taking me in just as hungrily.

Ho-ly. I think I need to sit down.

Instead of collapsing unceremoniously in the Jacobs' entryway, I rip my eyes away. Give Edel a close-lipped smile. "Apologies, I'd love to come in, but Annie and I can't be late for our reservation."

"Of course." She finally untangles her hand from mine, but not before giving it one last squeeze. "Another time, then?"

"Absolutely." I nod, entertained by Annie's grim expression.

She looks like hell might freeze over before she lets me attend her mother's book club.

"Ready?" I ask her. Then, because I'm a gentleman, I offer Annie my arm.

She peers at my elbow for a long moment before threading her fingers through the space. Her hand spreads across my bicep, and I feel the heat of her palm through my jacket.

Annie's mother runs an approving eye over us, then winks. "You kids have fun."

"We will." We step outside and Annie waits for the door to close before saying, "Sorry about her."

"She's funny."

"She makes me revert to behaving like a hormonal teenager." She laughs suddenly. "But it's nice, in a way. Being home."

I look down at her pretty face. "I'm glad."

"Where's Luke, by the way?" she asks as we make our way to my car.

I open the passenger door. "Something came up," I lie.

"So, it's just you and me?" Annie's voice falters a touch.

"Just you and me," I confirm, trying to keep my voice casual.

What I don't say is that Luke bailed on us. He's meddling where he's not welcome. And while one part of me thinks that what I really need from Annie right now is distance, another (ever growing) part of me is delighted to have her to myself for the evening, sitting two feet away, smelling warm and sweet and tempting.

This is ridiculous. Forget Annie acting like a regressed teen, *I'm* the one who's acting like he can't control his hormones.

She's just a woman, Liam. Just a woman you work with.

Just a woman you work with in a very, very nice dress.

I swallow. Plenty of women are attractive, so how has Annoying (But Cute) Annie From the Plane become Annie Who I'm Thinking About Way Too Much and Also Workplace-Inappropriately?

"Excited for softball on Saturday?" I toss out, coughing over the words as I pull onto the highway.

Small talk. I'm literally initiating small talk.

Annie gives me an easy smile. "I'm going to stink the place up. I suck at sports."

"I doubt that," I reply quickly, once again impressed by her ability to make fun of herself while wearing a huge grin. She seems ready and eager to joke about everything except work, which she takes remarkably seriously.

Yes, work is safe. Turn the conversation to pastures that aren't packed with alpha predators waiting to strike.

"You're very good at your job," I say.

Annie raises her brows. Smirks. "Well, at least there's that."

"I didn't mean it like—"

"I know," she cuts me off, still smiling.

"I'm sure you're good at a lot of things."

I did not just say that. Did not just lay out the most thickly innuendo-laden statement of all time to my freaking employee.

"Like, um, Sudoku," I clarify quickly. "You look like a Sudoku fan."

What am I talking about?

I glance sideways at her, just in time to see that darned grin slip back onto her face. "Oh yeah? What does a Sudoku fan look like?"

Hot.

But I can't say that. For obvious reasons. I need to change the subject, fast.

Say something, Liam. Anything at all.

"So your mom's into pirate porn, huh?"

Anything but *that,* dumbass.

Our business dinner that is definitely *not* a date is going just fine.

And by "fine," I mean that we make it all the way to dessert without me making any further comments about adult movies or number puzzles.

We talk about how she's finding her time at SITL so far, about the office and what might change if we secure the Wiseman investment and roll out V2 of the app with all the bells and whistles. It's small talk, of sorts, but I find I don't mind it one bit.

It's nice, being here with Annie, though this is a pretty intimate, romantic setting (Luke totally picked this place on purpose, the jackass). But it feels somewhat comfortable—still within the bounds of the rules, still above-board.

And as long as I don't let my eyes linger on her face—illuminated and glowing under soft candlelight—everything will be okay.

Or, I think it's going to be. Until she flips the script on me and lets her eyes linger on *my* face for a moment too long.

She nods at my cheek. "How did you get that scar?"

My hand automatically moves to touch the small white

ridge that intersects my cheekbone. I remember it like it was yesterday—I was six and cutting up magazines at my dad's house to make him a birthday card. I got a little too snip-happy though, and cut a tuft of the living room rug off.

Scared that my father was going to get mad, I sprinted down the hallway in search of my big brother. Luke always knew what to do in those types of situations.

Unfortunately, I slipped, faceplanting on the floor. The scissors, still in my hand, ended up embedded in my cheek.

Six stitches.

Mom was furious. I don't think I've ever seen her so angry with Dad. Most of the time, she just seemed exhausted around him.

I look at Annie, who's watching me curiously, waiting for my answer.

"Nobody taught me not to run with scissors," I finally say with a shrug.

She blinks, like I've surprised her. Then, she smiles and it's like the whole world lights up. Monochrome becomes technicolor. "Liam?"

"Yeah?"

"Don't ever run with scissors."

I can't help myself. I smile back. "Lesson learned."

Our eyes stay locked, and an electrical charge moves through my spine. The air between us thickens, becomes weighty, and my thoughts move to her red lips. Lips that look so soft, so utterly...

"New York Cheesecake?" A waitress materializes out of thin air, proffering a plate with the world's largest slice of cake on it, accompanied by a mountain of whipped cream and strawberries.

I nod in Annie's direction, glad of the interruption. I have to remember that this is *not* a date.

The waitress sets the cake in front of Annie. "Enjoy."

As the waitress walks away, I take a sip of water. Annie tilts her head as she digs her fork into her cheesecake. "So you're really not a dessert guy, huh?"

"Not really. The only dessert I ever loved was my mom's pecan pie. I used to go crazy for it at Thanksgiving. She'd make an extra one she called 'Liam's pie.'" My heart is heavy with the happy memory, now tinged with sadness.

And I can't quite believe I just voluntarily said all that out loud.

"Does she still make it?" Annie asks.

The heaviness remains in my chest as I consider how to answer her. Usually, I'd pass over her question, avert the conversation. But for some reason—maybe the wine, or the fact that Annie's going to town on the cake with this unashamed abandon that's kind of endearing, or the candle-light giving this whole thing a dream-like quality—I decide to be honest. "She passed away. Back when I was in college. A few days after Thanksgiving, actually."

A Thanksgiving I missed, and can never get back.

Annie's eyes glow caramel as she looks at me somberly for a few seconds.

"That sucks," she says finally, her voice more serious than I've ever heard it. The reaction is so perfectly Annie that some of the heaviness lifts. It's empathy instead of sympathy, and the perfect words for what was a very sucky situation all round.

"It does," I agree. "She was my favorite person. Practically raised the three of us on her own, which can't have been an easy feat. But I don't think I ever heard her utter a single complaint."

Annie waits a beat, letting my words hang between us. "I'm sure she'd be super proud of you if she could see you today," she says quietly.

I look at her. "Thanks."

"For what? It's the truth."

"I mean, thanks for not going the pity party route."

She frowns at her plate. "There's nothing worse than other people's pity. Always makes me feel like I need a shower."

I laugh, surprised. "This happen to you a lot?"

I'm not sure how, exactly, this conversation went from business, to flirting, to personal... but I'm one hundred percent invested now.

She shrugs, brushes a crumb off the table. "It's the other part of the reason I moved here. Outside of taking this job."

"What happened?"

"My ex happened." A strange, almost sorrowful little smile forms on her lips. Then disappears. "The one I mentioned the other night after work, same guy you met in Boston at the hotel. After I broke up with him, everything went south. Literally."

I don't say anything, just wait. She continues.

"I don't know... I woke up one day and realized I wasn't sure if he really loved me or if this was just convenient for both of us. I started to question if I was happy. Realized I hadn't been for a long time. It was like I was going through the motions of a life with someone, without actually being aware of how I was feeling. I was living a reality that was born of convenience, not passion, and I wanted more for myself." She sets her jaw, resolute as ever. "I deserved more. And so did he, I figured."

I nod slowly, captivated by her story.

"I eventually worked up the courage to end things. He was angry, said I was making a huge mistake. But he began dating Veronica pretty much the next day. Replaced me with her. He made things so tough in the office afterwards, acting like he'd devastated me by leaving *me* for Veronica. I don't know why, but I played along with his version of events. Thought it might make things easier for both of us."

She exhales a breath, seems to deflate a little. Shakes her head once.

"Then, he proposed to Veronica. And everyone at the office started treating me like I was some fragile, heart-broken invalid. I became *known* for that. Pitied for that. Instead of being evaluated for my work, it was all about 'poor little Annie.' Eventually, I couldn't stand it anymore, so I quit." She smiles wryly, running her finger around the edge of her plate. "And he got the promotion I was working toward."

My eyebrows are completely raised. I had no idea... how could someone treat a person—treat *Annie*—like that? Slimy Guy is an even worse person than I thought he was. "Annie, that... sucks."

She grins humorlessly. "It does. Thanks."

We hold eye contact for a moment. Part of me wants to reach out to her. Touch her. Hold her hand. Be there. It almost feels like torture that I can't.

She looks away, rubs her upper arms almost self-consciously. "In the end, it was good for me. I spent a couple months in a wallowing funk, wondering how I could've lost the life I built for myself in Boston in one fell swoop. But it was the right thing to do. The mistake wasn't breaking up with him, it was dating him in the first place. And mistakes come with a cost. I paid that cost by losing my career at Financify, but I gained so much in that I could be myself again, have my own identity. Achieve my own goals. At times, mine and Justin's lives were so intertwined that I didn't know where his ended and mine began."

"I understand that," I say, because surprisingly, I do. Sometimes I don't know where Performance Mode Robot Liam and Human Hotblooded Man Liam intersect. Or if they should intersect more, but I refuse to let them. Bury one deep beneath the other.

Her hand is on the table now, and I have to actively stop myself from reaching across to take it.

"That's admirable, Annie," I say instead, speaking from the heart. "Brave. That was a terrible decision to have to make. It takes guts to walk away from something you've worked so hard for."

She pauses, considering. "I never looked at it like that before."

I think about my life. About everything that could've been, and everything that is instead. All because of a choice I made. My eyes meet hers, and understanding passes between us.

Because looking at it this way was the only thing that kept me going when everything fell apart.

23

ANNIE

"Vulnerability is not about winning or losing, it's about having the courage to show up even when you can't control the outcome."

I take a huge bite of chocolate chip Eggo and chew monotonously, repeating every word of my favorite Brené Brown quote over and over in my head as I attempt to psych myself up for the dreaded softball tournament.

I may be terrible at sports, but I will go out there with confidence today. Show up and be brave.

And I will not think about Liam Donovan once while doing so. Not about how hot he's sure to look in sports attire (a Liam look I have yet to witness). Or about how startlingly hot he *did* look the other night in his dinner jacket and khakis when he took me to Petit Soleil on our definitely-not-a-date business outing...

"Penny for your thoughts, honeybunch?" Mom waltzes into the kitchen wearing a bizarre fluffy vest that makes her look like she butchered an alpaca.

I swallow my mouthful of waffle thickly, like I wasn't just absorbed in memories of the way my boss looked at me during our entire not-a-date.

Like he wanted me, I swear that's what his eyes said.

But his actions said differently. We flirted, we laughed, and then, he shared that he'd lost his mom, and I, in turn, unexpectedly spilled my guts to him about Justin. In so many ways I felt closer to him. Except physically. He was the perfect gentleman in every single way, but I mean, was a stray finger brush too much to ask for? A hand on the small of my back on our way to the table?

Apparently, it was. Liam kept his hands very much to himself in the most professional of manners. And yes, I was a little disappointed. I couldn't help but recall the way every nerve in my body flared when his fingertips brushed my shoulder the night we worked late and he lent me his jacket. Since then, my body has been craving another touch. And the longer it goes without, the more it wants its next hit.

I'm amazed I was even able to make coherent conversation given how distracted I was by the desire to be closer to him. Clearly, any and all mental restraint went out the window even as I vocalized my very real reasons for needing to stay away from him—namely, the last time I didn't stay away from someone I worked with, my career went up in flames.

But no, none of that mattered. I was too tuned into the occasional smirk that crept across his lips, the little scar on his cheek and the story behind it, the way his eyes burned as he kept his careful distance physically, even as we moved closer together emotionally. We lingered over coffee and cheesecake for hours, talking late into the evening.

The next day at the office though, it was like nothing had happened. He was all business-as-usual. I, on the other hand, spilled my orange juice all over the floor when he walked in.

Now, I'm wondering how on earth I'm going to be today, when I have to spend the whole day with him—and at a sporting event no less. How am I not going to say or do something mind-numbingly stupid to embarrass myself?

What if I imagined he was flirting the other night? It was a work dinner after all... even if Luke bailed and there was the sort of tension (on my end, at least) that you could cut with a knife.

But it's highly possible I read into it—history has shown that I have an overactive imagination. Seriously. One time, I convinced myself that a wasp was following me and plotting my death.

I can hardly tell my mom any of this, though.

Luckily, at that moment, she seems to register me, seated at the counter. She stops dead. "Or, more to the point, penny for why on earth you're dressed like *that*?"

I wipe my mouth with the back of my hand and opt to answer only her second question. "It's sports attire."

"What sport? Competitive getting-dressed-in-the-dark?" Mom raises her overplucked brows at me.

"Says the woman wearing a dead llama."

Mom laughs airily. She may be in her late 50s but she's still making the same risky fashion choices as ever, believing that she's the height of sophistication. And no matter what bizarre style she wears, she always looks like she's put effort into her appearance. I definitely got my confidence, grit and determination from her.

"One hundred percent synthetic, sugarplum. No wildlife were harmed in the making of this high fashion garment."

"Well, that's one less crime committed, I guess." I say. "It's a... bold choice. Brave."

"Fashion *forward*." Mom tuts. "Which is more than I can say for those pants. You look like you got lost in 2008. And I can see your panty line through them."

Why, oh why, is my mother so obsessed with my under-wear choices?

I groan and loll my head forward, touching it to the kitchen table. "Ughhh. Is it that bad?"

"Yes." She sits in the chair next to me and picks up my waffle, takes a bite. Then, she reaches for my coffee. I swat her hand away.

"There's some in the pot, I made extra for you." I smile at her hopefully. "Do you happen to own any sports clothes fabricated this decade?"

Mom wrinkles her nose. "Darling, ladies don't sweat... at least, not since the Jane Fonda craze in the 80s'."

Interesting (read: bizarre) perspective... but that should also tell you where I got my lack of athleticism. Mom and I do not do sports. Or anything involving hand-eye coordination beyond putting on mascara. Both of us also loathe the athleisure beloved by so many.

Which puts me in a predicament for today's baseball game.

Our uniform t-shirts—not quite sure what design Vanessa picked out in the end—haven't arrived yet, so for today's game, we were told to wear our own sports gear. And while I know that the Vanessas and Mindys of this world will come decked out in cute shorts and tank tops, I don't have anything even close to cute. My only "sports gear" consists of a mid-noughties pair of Victoria's Secret flared yoga pants in—you guessed it—neon pink. Complete with a foldover waistband and the word "PINK" written in rhinestones across the butt.

I found them in the back of my teenage treasure trove of a closet, alongside some extra chunky, silver-accented Skechers Shape Ups.

Yup. Seriously.

If this was 2008, I'd be at the height of fashion.

"Please, Mom, I'm desperate."

Mom runs a critical eye over me. "Why?"

Because Liam will see.

"Because it's a work function," I say reasonably. "And I look ridiculous."

"You always look ridiculous! Just last week, you wore three clashing colors in one outfit."

"Gee, thanks Mom."

"What I'm saying is—what makes this different?"

I tear off a piece of my waffle and start breaking it into crumbs. "Why the third degree?"

She winks at me. "Because I know a woman with a crush when I see one."

I let out a long breath. "Mom..."

"Annie, darling, you deserve every happiness after what happened with Justin. And that Liam boy was just delicious." She makes an obscene face that I'm going to go broke having to work through in therapy. "A word of advice, dear. Don't change who you are for him. Be yourself. You're more than loveable the way you are."

I'm not too sure about being myself though because, since the night I met him, what myself seems to want is to leap on Liam at any given moment. And I obviously can't do that.

But what I *can* do is stop worrying about sucking at sports and embarrassing myself. Just go out there and enjoy my day. And even if I can't leap on him, I can still use every opportunity for Liam to see me for who I am:

The woman who's good at her job, and makes him laugh, and who I kind of, sort of, maybe think he might like to get to know better.

And I think I have an idea of how to do it.

24

ANNIE

The baseball diamond is an All-American dream.

The sun is shining, the sky is blue, and it's a beautiful day for a softball tournament. If you're into that sort of thing.

I'm not sure what I'm expecting when I hop out of the car my dear dad lent me for the day (ten minutes early, I'll have you know. Mostly because I'm sure Liam expects me to be late). Nerves tingle in my stomach as I make my way from the parking lot to the bleachers where the crowds are gathered.

I can confirm that, whatever I was expecting, it certainly wasn't this chaos.

I'm talking country-music playing, hot dog-grilling, beer-swilling chaos. This looks more like a tailgate party than an athletic event. There's probably a hundred people here, and everyone looks ready for a good time.

Vanessa's memo was right about one thing though: this softball league is more for socializing than actual competition.

Thank goodness. Because if it's not about winning or losing, like Brené says, then nobody can be too mad when my spectacular lack of coordination sends Team Donovan Brothers on a one-way trip to Loserville.

I rummage in my purse for my sunglasses and pop them on. Hold a hand to my forehead as a sunshield as I scout for a familiar face.

Eventually, I spot Jamal and Todd, Stay Inside the Lines's developers. They're hovering awkwardly near the bleachers, looking as pained and unathletic as I feel.

These are my people today.

"Hey, guys!" I greet them with a cheery wave.

"Hi, Annie," Jamal says, then his gaze drops over my body and his eyes practically bug out of his head. "Wha..."

I set my tray of homemade brownies on the bottom bleacher, drop my purse to the ground, then do a little twirl to show off my mom's glittery, green, 80s' relic leggings. And my t-shirt. "Just a little inside joke between Mr. Donovan and myself."

"You mean Mr. D, right?" Todd's brow wrinkles. "Luke?"

"No, Liam."

"I didn't know Mr. Donovan had inside jokes." Jamal coughs. "Or any jokes at all."

"Are... are you sure about wearing that?" Todd adds, an expression close to terror etched across his narrow features.

I give the boys a wide smile. "Maybe the boss man's turning over a new leaf."

"Who's turning over a new leaf?" Luke's booming voice calls from behind me.

I spin around to see Luke, Mindy, Legs and Liam walking toward us, laden down with coolers, camp chairs and bags of snacks.

"Annie!" Legs drops the huge bag of popcorn she's carrying and runs toward me.

I crouch to her level and open my arms for a hug. "Hey there, cutie. You ready to watch your uncles play softball?"

"I brought Barbie and Ken in my backpack in case I get bored."

"That's a good idea! Are they gonna play softball, too?" I address my question to Legs, but I have to admit she only has fifty percent of my attention because, behind her, Liam is shrugging off his hoodie. When he pulls it over his head, his t-shirt rises with it, revealing a slice of tanned, toned, inked skin.

Beneath the hoodie, he's wearing one of those baseball shirts with a white body and navy sleeves, pushed up to show off his muscular, brawny forearms.

Boy, oh boy.

"No, they're gonna kiss."

"Kiss?" I squeak, startling back to my senses.

"Yes," Legs repeats slowly, like she thinks I'm a bit dim. "Kiss. Like Mindy and Uncle Luke, and maybe like you and Uncle Liam, too?"

"Oh, I um... uhh..."

I seem to be lost for words a lot lately.

Thankfully, nobody seems to have heard the musings of this eight-year-old's overactive imagination. And double thankfully, Mindy's around to save me.

"Annie!" She moves toward me with her arms outstretched, wrapping me in a hug. Goodness me, she's friendly. "How are you?"

Before I can answer, she sees my shirt.

"Wait..." A slow smile spreads across her face. "What is this?"

"What?" Luke appears at her side and slings an arm over her petite shoulder. They're cute together. Very healthy and attractive, like a pair of prized racehorses or something.

Mindy nods toward my shirt and Luke's eyes widen for a moment before he chuckles. "Does this have something to do with Vanessa not being able to get the uniforms in time?"

I barely hear his question, though, because I'm focused on Liam.

Liam Donovan, in all his mussed-hair, baseball-shirted, tattooed glory. Liam Donovan, who is staring directly at my t-shirt.

His eyes linger for a few long moments, and then he looks up to meet my gaze. Slowly, oh so slowly. Like his eyes are dragging up my body.

When they finally lock on mine, the anticipation is worth it. Because the smile that follows—the glorious smile that spreads over his handsome face as a result of my efforts—almost makes my knees give way.

He's smiling.

At me.

Thank you, Brené Brown, for giving me the courage to show up as myself today.

And thank you, Mom, for not letting me leave the house in those Skechers.

25

LIAM

I've learned another thing about Annie Jacobs today.

She is truly *terrible* at sports.

It's like her arms and legs and body don't communicate, and every time she tries to hit or catch the ball, she ends up in a tangle of limbs, galloping around like a newborn deer.

It's the most amusing thing I've ever seen... and adorable. Which is odd. I've always considered myself an athlete, but I never thought that athleticism—or lack thereof —would be something I'd be drawn to in a woman. But I guess there's a first for everything.

Annie seems to give me lots of firsts.

And today, for the first time in years, I'm not thinking of all the negative memories that come with standing on a baseball diamond. I'm thinking of her instead.

I can't help but feel attracted to how she does things her own way, not caring what anyone else thinks. Case in point: all the other women from the office—plus Mindy—have arrived to the field wearing some variation of leggings and a tank top. There's a scale, ranging from little more than a bra (Vanessa) to flowing, oversized floral patterns (Barb).

Annie, on the other hand, is wearing glittery green

tights and legwarmers that give off bizarre, retro-aerobics vibes. And she's paired these with a t-shirt I'd recognize anywhere. Because it's MY t-shirt.

Or what used to be my t-shirt...

She's given her keepsake from the hotel a new look. In bold, sharpie-printed letters, my formerly pristine, white, organic cotton shirt now reads: "I played softball for the Donovan brothers and all I got was this lousy t-shirt."

I should be pissed. First, she stole my shirt. Then, she vandalized it.

The cheek of the entire thing!

But honestly, I couldn't care less. For the first time in forever, a woman caught me so off guard, I couldn't help but smile.

Couldn't help but fall a little more.

Plus, she looked so hilarious during our first game, prancing around in the outfield and missing any ball that came her way by a mile. I could barely keep my head in the game because all I wanted to do was watch her instead.

I find I'm often watching her, like there's a magnetic pull directing my attention in her direction. I suppose when it comes to magnets, opposites always attract, and Annie and I? We couldn't be more different. I'm a carefully drawn, ruler-straight grid. She's a Jackson Pollock painting. A colorful ray of sunshine. And when that ray shines on you, there's no hiding in the dark.

I watch her now as the SITL crew sit in a circle of camp chairs between games. Luke has a portable barbecue going, and Annie's eating a hot dog while talking to Mindy and Legs, who's now graduated to sitting in Annie's lap.

She's taken to Annie like a duck to water. It's a good omen; Legs is a good judge of character.

I get another Coke from the cooler, then stand off to the

side, taking a few cool, sweet, fizzy sips as I look over the scene.

I'm grateful for my employees, but I'm not one for socializing outside work. I always believed that work and personal life should be kept separate. But as I survey so many important people in my life laughing and eating and joking together, my insides feel warm.

It's... nice.

"Hey."

Annie's voice is close—so close, a shock runs down my spine. She's rummaging in the cooler.

"Hello," I say, wishing it didn't sound so stiff and formal. Well, more stiff and formal than usual.

She finds a can of lemon Lipton iced tea and straightens. Chews on her lower lip as she stands next to me, surveying the field. "You're really good at softball."

"I used to play baseball." I keep my eyes on the field, trying to focus on anything but the fact that she's close enough to touch.

Instead, I think about how nice the sun feels on my face. How the smells of freshly-cut grass and hot dogs are like a precursor to summer. But whatever I do, I won't think about how Annie's grasshopper spandex tights are very... uh... let's just say *asset hugging*. To the point of distracting. Must not think about that.

Can't not think about that.

Okay, fine. No point in denying a fact: she has a nice butt.

Now, can my brain please go back to regular-scheduled programming?

"Oh yeah, Legs said that." Annie cracks open her iced tea but doesn't drink any. "Was it in high school?"

"College, too."

"When did you stop?"

"I dropped out junior year."

She doesn't ask any further questions, just tilts her head up, bathing her skin in a golden glow of sunlight. "My old company had a beer league softball team. It's pretty popular among tech start-ups, I guess."

My eyebrows fly up in surprise. Not at the fact that her company had a team—she's right, it is common—but at the fact that she's played this sport before and still remains so unbelievably bad at it.

I'm not exaggerating. I watched her wind up, swing for a pitch, and let go of the bat. It almost nailed the third base-woman in the face.

She chuckles when she sees my expression. "I was the water girl, I didn't play. My job was refreshments."

She's smiling, as usual. But her eyes are a little tighter than usual around the corners, like she's straining to keep that sunshine in her voice.

"Why?" I ask.

"Uh, I guess you could say I didn't help the team's points average. They were able to win more games without me playing."

"But it's *beer league softball.*"

Annie shrugs. "My ex was very competitive."

That douche.

I try to think of something positive to say. Something helpful and encouraging. Something that'll make her feel better.

"You know you're holding the bat wrong, right?"

Oh for saint's sake, Liam, you went with that? *Real smooth.*

"I'm pretty sure I'm doing everything wrong." Annie smiles self-deprecatingly. "Sports ain't my forte."

I check my watch. We have fifteen minutes before our next game. I survey the bleachers until my eyes land on

Legs. She's sitting with Luke, munching on dill pickle chips and studiously ignoring Vanessa, who's trying and failing to win her over.

I can, and I will do something.

"Come with me," I say brusquely.

"Where?"

"Just come with me, Annie."

"Okay." She pauses. "What are we doing?"

I reach for a spare bat. Give it a spin. Then I take a step toward her.

"I'm going to show you how this is done."

26

ANNIE

I'm going to show you how this is done.

Sounds like an innocent sentence, right? It could apply to anything from filing your taxes, to applying a perfect cat-eye liquid liner, to making French onion soup.

But when that sentence comes out of the mouth of a tall, tanned brick wall of a man, who's looking at you with intense smoldering eyes and wielding a baseball bat like he could do some serious damage, well... let's just say I'm practically a wobbling heap of Jell-O.

In fact, it is with severe effort that I trot next to Liam on my jelly legs as he leads me across the field to a row of batting cages.

"Umm... why are we here?" I finally ask.

Liam points at the first cage. "You're going to learn how to swing a bat."

Oh. Well, this isn't going to go well.

I follow him into the cage, watch wearily as he adjusts the machine that's going to start spitting balls.

"I'm not sure this is a good idea..." I trail off hesitantly.

"Don't worry, I programmed it to slow pitch. It can't hurt you."

"I beg to differ." My pale skin doesn't just give me the gift of instant sunburn when exposed to a single ray of light. Noooo, genetics also blessed me with the ability to bruise like a peach.

"I'll be right beside you," Liam says.

Somehow, this seems even more dangerous.

"Okay, step up to the plate," Liam instructs.

I do as he asks.

"Now, grip the bat here and here." He points, then hands me the bat.

I try to recreate his hand position.

"Closer together. Down a little with your right hand," he offers.

I slide my hand down the bat.

"More like this..." He steps close to me—like, sexy pine forest flooding my senses close—and this time, I don't resist inhaling his warm, clean skin. My heart speeds double time.

He places a hand on top of mine, and drags it down a little. I forget to inhale.

"Yeah, you got it," he murmurs, and all I can think is that I might as well have stepped into a romcom movie. Just call me J Lo, or Reese Witherspoon, or one of the actresses in a movie where the tall, hot hero teaches a girl to wield a bat. I've never been a fan of the whole "girl is hopeless at sports but a big strong man shows her how it's done" thing.

But now? I finally understand why the scene is so cliché. There's something so hot, so intimate, about having Liam's arms wrapped around me like this, his torso grazing my back.

Reminds me of another time we were in this exact position...

Breathe, Annie, breathe! I remind myself frantically. Sirens are going off in my head. We are well and truly in the danger zone.

I should step away. But dammit, he smells so good! Maybe just a few more seconds of lingering...

"Lift the bat and move it backwards. Yup, keeping that elbow up." Liam moves his hand from mine and drags it past my wrist, up my bare forearm, and to my elbow. He presses lightly where he wants me to angle my arm higher.

A line of fire follows in the wake of his fingers.

Holy moly double cannoli with extra chocolate chips.

He's touching my elbow. My freaking *elbow*.

Who knew elbows were a turn-on? Not me.

"Good, good." His voice drops a couple notches in a way that makes me wonder if he, too, could be affected by the feeling of his palm on my bare skin.

Surely not. We're in a public place; there are children here, for crying out loud.

And he's my BOSS.

The hefty reminder strikes me like a slap to the face, and I lurch forward, out of his grip. Just in time for the first ball to come shooting out of the machine.

It flies through the air and... hits me square in the stomach.

"Ooof!" I groan as I fall to my knees, coughing and spluttering.

"Annie!" Liam is right behind me, kneeling in the dirt. "Annie? Are you okay?"

"Yes," I wheeze. "Just a bit... winded."

I don't know how I force the words out. There's no oxygen in my body at the moment.

"Annie, I—"

There's another wheezing noise, but it's not coming from me. It's coming from Liam.

Is he... crying?

With serious effort, I turn my head toward him.

His eyes are screwed up, his cheeks are red, and he's trying, and failing, not to...

Laugh.

He holds up his hands in surrender. "Annie, I'm sorry. I don't mean to laugh but you went down like a sack of potatoes..." he trails off as his body begins to shake with laughter.

The sound is incredible. Deep and musical.

I'm so entranced, so spellbound by his laugh, by the joy on his face, that I forget I'm winded and I join in.

"Ouch," I groan again. It hurts to laugh, so I keel over in the dirt, lying on my back.

Liam rolls onto his back next to me, and the two of us lie there, looking up at the sunny sky and laughing until our ribs hurt and tears run down our faces.

I don't think about the fact that we're going to have to explain our ridiculous outburst. Or about the fact that I'm having feelings I can't possibly have. Feelings that I resolved to never, ever let myself catch for someone I worked with again.

I don't think about anything at all.

I just focus on the sound of Liam's laugh.

And laugh right along with him.

27

LIAM

I feel bare. Naked. Exposed.

And also... elated.

Today was a good day. The best I've had in a while.

It was all thanks to Annie. I can't remember the last time I laughed like that. Can't remember the last time I forgot about the world and lived in the moment, did what I wanted to do simply because it *felt* right.

Of course, lying in the dirt next to Annie and laughing my head off means that my dignity has gone to the dogs.

And right now, Luke and Mindy are like a pair of rottweilers with an extra juicy steak.

We're in Luke's car on the way home from the tournament and the happy couple are bugging me relentlessly (a tournament we won, by the way. I won't say that this was mostly because of me but...)

I roll my eyes, heaving a deep sigh. "It was funny, okay?"

Legs reaches forward from her booster-seated position and pats my shoulder. "It's okay, Uncle Liam."

At least someone's got my back. It was bad enough dealing with Vanessa's glare, Barb's wide-eyed, ill-concealed whispering, and Jamal and Todd looking at me like I announced I was uploading my consciousness to the cloud to live forever in AI form. But my brother and his fiancée are the worst of the bunch.

"It wasn't *that* funny," Luke says. "Nothing's *that* funny."

"I like her way better than Vanessa," Mindy adds.

"Who on earth said anything about Vanessa?"

"Well, that's who Luke was *trying* to set you up with before Annie came along and we saw what you looked like when you actually like someone."

"WHAT?"

Mindy winks at me. "Don't sweat it, Liam. I got your back."

I swear, my head is about to explode. "Why on earth do you two keep trying to set me up with my freaking employees?"

"Um, same reason Lana Mae keeps trying to set you up with those dance moms—we're trying to capitalize on your only contact with women."

"I contact women!"

"Liam, your dry cleaner doesn't count."

"You are an insane person."

"I'm a romantic. You should try it sometime."

Luke gives Mindy the goo-goo eyes. "You turned me into a romantic."

I roll my eyes. "Pull over, I'm about to be sick."

"But seriously, Liam," Mindy says. "Look at Luke and me. We happened because I was chasing one of his best friends at the time like an idiot." Mindy flushes at the memory. "I thought Luke was one of those guys who didn't want a relationship, didn't want to settle down, but when we finally got together, that changed. Things change when you meet the right person. You've changed, Liam.

And I think it's because you might've met the right person."

Mindy, who I love dearly as a sister-in-law-to-be, is not usually one for sage advice. But against my better judgment, that little speech is getting to me.

For so long, I was convinced that doing things my way—carefully organized, perfectly precise, comfortably predictable—was the only way that worked for me. But Annie's turned this on its head. Using data gathered from my company, for crying out loud!

She's thrown a lot of my firmly-held beliefs into question. My firmly-held protective shields.

Could Luke and Mindy be right? Could it be that, when you meet the right person, the rules of the game themselves can actually change?

I'm not totally convinced yet... but for the first time ever, I'm open to it.

Luke smirks at me in the rearview mirror as he pulls into Lana Mae's neighborhood. "We just want you to be happy, dude. We all do. You deserve something for yourself."

"I don't know."

"Trust me."

Legs grabs my hand. Squeezes surprisingly hard. "Trust him, Uncle Liam."

A strange calm settles over my body.

Maybe, just maybe, it might be okay to stop trying to control everything, for once. Maybe I can let myself trust the process.

Twenty-four hours later, my sense of calm has evaporated into thin air.

Poof! Gone.

"Legs, honey." I knock on the bathroom door for the fiftieth time. "Please let me in."

"No," her voice catches in a little sob and my heart fractures down the middle. "You can't come in."

She's been in the bathroom for about thirty minutes, and though my voice is calm and soothing, I'm panicking.

I picked her up from a dance friend's birthday party an hour ago. Cassandra's daughter's birthday party, to be exact. And the cheerful little girl I dropped off at lunchtime had become a wide-eyed, hiccuping, tear-stained ball of sadness.

The second I arrived at the door to collect Legs, she ran out of the house, flew past me, and scrambled into the car. Cassandra claimed total ignorance as to why Legs was in such a tizzy. In fact, she was downright dismissive about the whole thing. Any time I tried to ask a question about what could've happened, she suggested we "go inside and talk about it over drinks."

Never have I ever come so close to raising my voice to a woman.

But getting angry wasn't going to help Legs.

When I got to the car, Legs wouldn't talk to me. She just stared down at her hands, face pinched and sniffling. When we got home, she ran straight upstairs, locked the bathroom door, and wouldn't come out.

I've never seen her like this before. Lana Mae isn't answering her phone—I know she has an important seminar this afternoon. Luke and Mindy are staying at their wedding venue overnight to do final prep with the wedding planner, and the ranch is two hours out of the city.

So, I'm sitting on the floor outside the bathroom at a total loss.

Possibilities fly through my mind. I recently watched *Turning Red* with Legs, but surely it's a bit early for her first period? Google sure seems to think so, especially as Legs is small for her age. And it's highly implausible that she's turning into a giant red panda either, so that movie knowledge is officially useless to me.

Bullying at the party? I doubt it. As much as I don't like Cassandra, that doesn't equate to her daughter being a bully. Plus, Legs is good at standing up for herself and for what's right. She has a strong sense of justice, which makes me incredibly proud of her. If she was being bullied, I doubt she'd react like this.

I have no yardstick here; I've never been a little girl before. I stare at my phone, still open to my unhelpful Google search of "why would an eight-year-old lock herself in the bathroom?"

Then, I dial a number.

28

ANNIE

Liam greets me at the front door of Lana Mae's duplex and he looks like an entirely different Liam yet again. Not buttoned-up business Liam, sports-casual Liam, or tatted-up, shirtless Liam.

This afternoon, he's... regular Liam. Liam in dark wash jeans and Nike sneakers, just like that Taylor Swift song. The one where she thinks the guy looks so good, she can't help but imagine all of the fun things she could do with him.

I get it. This relaxed look suits him.

And it doesn't hurt that those jeans hug his butt just right.

His face, however, tells me that this is no time to be thinking about his butt. It's etched with worry (his face, not his butt) and he's got a nervous, fretful energy about him that I've never seen before.

"Thank you for coming," he says gravely.

"No problem," I say with a tentative smile, shoving my mom's car keys in my pocket and bending to pet Harry Styles, who is now purring aggressively while rubbing his side along my bare ankle (I wore capris for this precise reason).

I have no idea why Liam's summoned me, but I assume it's work-related, and I'm painfully aware of the fact that I was able to show up at the drop of a hat on a Sunday afternoon. True demonstration of my lack of any kind of a life (although the episode of *Antiques Roadshow* I was watching with Mom before he called was a good one. Crazy what people pay for creepy clown dolls).

I have to say, though, I'm a little flattered that he seemed to need me so urgently. That I'm on speed-dial for potential data emergencies.

"I didn't have anyone else to call," Liam adds.

Oh. Scratch that. I was a desperation dial.

"What's up?"

"It's, um, Legs."

My body tenses with worry. "Is she okay?"

"Well, the thing is... I don't know."

My brow puckers. "What do you mean?"

"She's locked in the bathroom and won't come out."

Well. I can't say I was expecting that.

Liam shifts from foot to foot. He looks so intensely worried and vulnerable, I almost want to give him a hug, tell him everything will be all right. "Can you talk to her?"

"Sure, I can try." I nod. "But she might not want to talk to me."

"She won't say a word to me either, so I figured this was worth a shot. You're my Hail Mary here, Annie."

The words slip out before I can think them. "Just what every girl dreams of."

Awesome, Annie. Make a joke in a serious situation—foot-in-mouth for another win. Not.

"Where's the bathroom?" I add immediately.

"Upstairs. First door on the right."

I slip off my flip-flops, and make for the stairs. Liam starts to ascend behind me, and I hold up a hand. "Nuh uh."

"What?"

"You should wait downstairs."

His dark eyes smolder with intensity. "Why?"

"You know. Give her space in case she needs some... girl talk."

Understanding dawns on Liam's face and he nods jerkily. "Right, right. I'll, um, be in the living room if you need me."

Moments later, I hear the distant roar of a Braves game coming from the TV. I smile at the thought of him sitting there, pretending to relax.

Again, I'm struck by two things—one, what a good dad he'll make one day; and two, how accommodating he is beneath that gruff exterior. Like, when he gave me space to talk the night we worked late, and now, he's giving Legs space *not* to talk to him. Not demanding anything from her simply because he's in charge.

"Legs?" I murmur as I tap the bathroom door. "It's Annie."

"Hi, Annie." Her little voice is reedy and sad.

"Can I come in?"

Silence.

As a lifelong bathroom-hider myself, I get this. In my experience, one only locks oneself in a bathroom when they're feeling desperate, and sometimes, desperation does not set the stage for conversation.

"I don't have to come in, if you don't want me to," I tell her. "But I'll sit on the other side of this door for a while. If that's okay with you?"

A sniffle. "Okay."

I sink to the floor, tuck my legs under me. "I once locked myself in the bathroom after I cut my own hair," I say conversationally. "I was a little older than you, and all the girls in my class had bangs. My mom said I shouldn't get bangs because my hair was too springy and they wouldn't sit flat on my forehead. But I felt left out. So, I took my mom's sewing scissors and chopped my own bangs. I cut them way too short. So short, they stuck straight up."

"Oh no," Legs says.

"I didn't want anyone at school to see, so I hid in the bathroom as long as I could before class started."

"I didn't want Uncle Liam to see me tonight."

I know that her offering this information is progress. And I also know not to push.

So instead of asking why, I simply say, "Sure, sometimes we need some time alone. Uncle Liam understands that. He's just worried about you, that's all. He wants to know you're okay because he loves you."

There's a silence, then the door opens a crack.

Success.

I step into the bathroom, where I'm greeted by the saddest little face I've ever seen. On instinct, I open my arms, and Legs crumples into me. The two of us stand in the middle of the bathroom, her arms circling my waist as she presses her face into my shirt and lets it all out.

Eventually, her sobs subside, and I run a hand over her matted gold hair. "Do you want to talk about it?"

She chews her lip, considering, and I sit on the edge of the bathtub. I smile encouragingly at her, not wanting to push. I remember having huge emotions at her age.

Okay, fine, I still have huge emotions. But as an adult, I'm now able to self-medicate with candy and ice cream.

Lucky me.

"Okay," Allegra finally says. I pat the spot next to me, and she sits.

She sniffles and wipes her nose on her sleeve. I wait.

"I told them I liked Finn a-and"—*hiccup*—"then Georgina"—*hiccup*—"called him to ask if he liked me too. And he said no because I was too... weird..." Legs gasps out the last word before dissolving into tears again.

Ah, unrequited love and weirdness. Good thing I'm an expert in both of these particular fields.

After a few careful questions, I learn that Georgina was the birthday girl at today's party, and Finn is the class stud. Apparently, he's good at soccer and all the girls in the class gave their Valentine's Candygrams to him.

"I knew a boy like Finn once," I say.

"You did?" Her dark eyes—so like Liam's—are full of curiosity.

"Yeah. Toby Barnett. He had, like, three Tamagotchis."

"What's a Tamagotchi?"

Ho-ly, I must be old.

"Um, kind of like a robot pet from the past, I guess? Anyhow," I continue hurriedly. "I liked Toby Barnett so much, it sometimes hurt. You know?"

She nods. "Did he become your boyfriend?"

"Not even close. I made him a really cool picture in art class and put it in his locker with a note asking if he wanted to go to the Sadie Hawkins dance with me. And you know what he did? He laughed and said there was no way he'd go to the dance with 'Weird Annie.' All his friends laughed too. Then, Toby took the prettiest, most popular girl in the class to the dance instead."

"No!" Legs gasps.

"Oh, yes. Her name was Hayley and she had the shiniest hair I've ever seen. Perfect, flat bangs, too. But you know what I realized soon after?"

"What?" She's invested, cupping her chin in her hands as she listens.

"Just because Toby was popular and cute, it didn't mean

231

he was nice. Or that we had anything in common. And I realized that... maybe I didn't actually like him, I just liked the *idea* of him. In reality, he didn't measure up. He hurt my feelings, and I don't like people who hurt others. No matter how cute they are."

Legs shifts around to look at me better, eyes wide as I continue to talk.

"There are more important things to be in this life than popular. It's about what's inside, if a person's heart is good... that's what really matters." I shake my head, even as thoughts of Liam dance through my mind. He was so cold and rude at first, but then I saw the soft, kind heart beating beneath. "And if Finn doesn't like you, it's his loss, but it's also your gain. Better someone likes you for who you are than wants you to be something you're not."

Almost immediately, I realize that I'm passing on the advice my mom gave me a day ago.

I am literally turning into my mother.

"Plus," I add with a smile and a nudge of my elbow. "Aren't guys like Finn kind of boring? Girls like us, we need guys who are more exciting, more complex. More than just a pretty face, you know?"

My mind flashes to Liam once again, and I feel myself start to blush. Legs, luckily, doesn't appear to notice. And also luckily, seems to have resonated with my speech because she's smiling. "Like Hassan?"

I grin. "Who's Hassan?"

"He has a pet flying squirrel, isn't that cool?"

Ah, to be eight years old and in fickle first love.

I sling an arm around Legs's shoulder. "A flying squirrel?! He sounds way cooler than boring, old Finn."

"Right?" Legs beams.

As she starts chattering about her apparent newfound crush on Hassan (seriously, I don't remember hitting the boy-crazy stage until I was, like, twelve. Kids these days are growing up so fast), I hear a rustle at the door.

I glance up in time to see Liam hovering in the doorway, and the look on his face makes my breath catch. He doesn't know I can see him, see his soft-eyed, dreamy-smiled expression. It makes my heart ache in the best way.

Honestly. Beneath all his complicated layers, this man is more cinnamon roll than extra-crunchy granola.

He slips away quickly, but he's too late.

I saw the look in his eyes.

And I don't think I can unsee it now.

29

LIAM

"Is she asleep?"

When I come out of Legs's room, Annie is standing at the foot of the stairs, wearing her jacket and staring up at me curiously.

"She is." I walk down the stairs as quietly as possible. Last thing I want to do is wake her. "Still a little tearful, but she's had a rough week with her mom being away."

"I get it." Annie shoves her hands deep in her pockets, making the bottom of her jacket fan out.

"Thank you for coming over. You were... great."

The understatement of the century. Annie was phenomenal this evening. A lifesaver.

I may have snuck up to the bathroom while she was talking to Legs, and eavesdropped at the door. Annie managed to simultaneously comfort her, validate her feelings, empathize, and cheer her up.

It was downright impressive.

"She's a great kid," Annie says.

"And I don't have to hunt down this Finn character and rough him up?"

"Rough him up?" Annie snorts, her eyes dancing. "Are

we in a Hardy Boys novel?"

"Depends who's asking."

She cocks an eyebrow at me brazenly. "Just how much did you snoop on our *private* conversation?"

"I may have overheard a thing or two."

"Eavesdropped, you mean?"

I give her a little smile. "That's a strong word."

She crosses her arm and juts her chin. "That's an accurate word."

She's got me and she knows it. I cross my arms and lean against the wall, getting comfortable. "Well, now that the cat's out of the bag... Toby Barnett, huh? Was he a stud?"

Annie throws back her head and laughs. "Oh, he was only the studliest little stud muffin Miss Jawinski's fifth grade class ever saw."

"Need me to hunt him down for a little roughing up, too?"

"Tempting." Annie smirks, and I could swear her eyes drop to my biceps for a moment. I can't help myself, I cross my arms a little tighter, suddenly grateful for those endless bicep curls. "But no need. Back in fifth grade, I killed his best Tamagotchi for revenge."

I let out a chuckle. "How exactly did you go about that?"

"Held down the reset button while Toby was in the bathroom."

"You cold-blooded little robot pet from the past murderer!"

"I'm not to be underestimated."

"I could never underestimate you." The words come out more loaded than a steakhouse baked potato. I immediately wish I could cram them back in my mouth.

Her eyes latch onto mine and a crackling silence stretches between us.

She shifts on her feet. "Well, I guess I should get going."

I don't want her to leave.

"Want a drink?" I find myself spontaneously asking. Logically, I know I shouldn't have asked. It's Sunday night, we have work in the morning. Of course she wouldn't want to stay for a drink wi—

"Like a glass of wine?" she asks.

"That is an example of a drink, yes." My lips twitch as I watch her face. Watch the way her brow softens, the small smile tugging at her mouth. "Or beer, coffee, a juice box, whatever you prefer."

I'm filled with this weird, nervous energy. Something that feels a lot like anticipation.

There's a battle raging in Annie's eyes and I wonder which way she's going to go. Maybe tell me to take my drink idea and shove it. But I have the feeling she won't.

"Wine," she finally says, her eyes locked on mine. "If you have any. Please."

My lips pull up at the corners. "Red or white?"

"I'll have what you're having."

My eyes travel over her auburn hair, flushed cheeks and arms. "Definitely red."

I'm gratified to see her skin deepen to a delicious shade of burgundy.

It's a beautiful night, so we end up sitting on Lana's back porch (with the door closed—Harry likes to make night-time escapes if given the chance). Annie slips off her shoes and curls her legs under her while I uncork a bottle of Shiraz. It would be perfect, except that Lana's doll-sized wicker loveseat feels like it might collapse under my weight.

The little couch is barely big enough for one person, let

alone two, but it's the only outdoor seating available. Which means that we're sitting so close, I can feel her every move. Sense when she wiggles her toes or shifts sideways. It's... cozy. Intimate.

The starry sky and the wine add to the effortlessly romantic mood.

Just what on earth do I think I'm doing?

Luke would howl with laughter if he could see me now.

I shove all pesky thoughts of my brother away as I pour two glasses of wine and pass one to Annie, my fingertips grazing her hand as I do. Roughness on cool, silky skin. The sensation is almost unbearable. An itch I need to scratch.

I slowly, reluctantly, pull my hand back, and Annie shivers a little as she cradles her glass. She takes a sip. "When does your sister get back?"

"In a couple days. I'm sure Legs will be glad to see the back of me and have her mom back."

Annie makes a face. "Don't be ridiculous, Liam. Legs adores you."

I grunt in response. Like a flipping caveman. Honestly.

"She does," Annie insists.

"I do my best."

"She's lucky to have you. Lucky to have Luke, too. But she seems especially attached to you."

My stomach twists, and I take a drink of my wine. "I'm lucky to have her. All I want is to be there for her. I was, uh, away for the first year of her life. I regret that now."

"Brené Brown says that regret is necessary to facilitate change and growth."

I ponder this for a moment, then nod. "Brené Brown sounds like a clever person."

"She is." Annie smiles this sweet, private little smile that makes my heart skip.

"It's, um, important to me. That I'm always here for

Legs." My eyes trace the rim of my glass, surprised I'm giving this information so easily, so willingly. And yet, it feels like the easiest thing in the world. Something about Annie encourages me to open up. To feel in a way I never let myself feel. "Her dad left Lana before she was born. He hasn't been in touch since."

"What a loser," she says.

"Agreed." I nod. "Allegra may not have her real father, but she'll grow up knowing she always has me. And it's my goal for her to never want for anything."

"*Real father*," Annie muses as she swirls her wine. "There's a big difference between fathering a child and becoming a father. And this man may have fathered a daughter biologically, but if he's never done anything to earn the privilege of a role in her life, then he's no father."

She sets her glass on the ground and twists to look me in the eyes. "A real father is the man who shows up. The caring adult who's there through everything, good and bad."

My brow furrows as I look at my own glass. I get what she's saying, and I appreciate her kind words.

"I just wish I'd been there from the beginning," I say quietly.

"But you're here now."

"Yeah. I guess I am."

I look at Annie, look into those hazel eyes, at once so playful and light, but filled with this energy I can't help but feel drawn toward. I'm suddenly very glad that I'm here right now. In this moment. With her.

I've had approximately two sips of wine, but I feel kinda drunk.

Bold.

"Speaking of regret," I say, my voice low. "Do you... regret the way we met?"

She cocks her head. "You mean what happened at the

hotel?"

Memories of her body pressed against mine, of her slow, heavy breathing fog up my brain. Her skin was so soft.

I wonder if it still feels so soft.

I banish those thoughts, clear my throat. "Yeah. I, um, I've been meaning to apologize for all of... that."

She runs her tongue over her teeth, her brows drawing together. "I think I should be the one apologizing."

"No apology necessary. I thought I made you uncomfortable."

Her eyes take on a heavy-lidded quality as she lolls her head slightly.

"Oh, I was very comfortable," she says quietly. "Too comfortable, perhaps."

A rush of warmth floods my body and I find myself moving closer. I can't resist. "I think I understand that."

"It was unprofessional though, wouldn't you say?" She widens her eyes at me, but she replicates my movement, shifting closer.

"Very," I reply.

Her gaze drops to my lips as she continues. "We deserved a verbal warning, at the very least."

My fingertips find her wrist, and the pad of my index finger skates along her forearm. Just as soft as I remember. "Oh, I'd say a written warning. Especially after what you did to my t-shirt."

Her eyes lock on mine and something strong and tangible passes between us. Her breath catches as her eyes drop to my lips and my heart picks up speed. She's so close now, her face mere inches from mine.

"Maybe I wanted more than just a lousy t-shirt," she whispers.

I can't stand it another second.

The rational part of my brain knows that this can't

happen. But I've sent it packing on an all-inclusive vacation to Cancun so that the primal part of my brain—the part that needs to know what her mouth feels like on mine—can take control for a few sweet moments.

My fingers tighten on her arm as my other hand slides over her thigh. I lean closer, close enough that I breathe her sweet smell and feel the warmth of her skin. I'm just inches from finding out what she tastes like, and my heart is hammering so loudly, I wouldn't be surprised if she can hear it. The wild, brazen, almost hungry look in her eyes tells me her heartbeat's matching mine.

"Annie," I say, her name trailing off on my lips.

Her eyes close, her chin tilts, and—

"Uncle Liam?"

The voice in the distance may as well have been a nuclear bomb exploding. I spring backwards so fast, I almost topple off the sad excuse for a loveseat. Annie hurriedly sits up and adjusts her shirt.

"Legs!" I gasp, turning to see my niece in the doorway, backlit by the kitchen light.

"I had a bad dream," she says feebly.

"Oh, honey. I'll come right up."

Her eyes move from me to Annie.

"Can Annie come too?"

Annie and I share a long, lingering look that's full of something so heavy, so weighted, that I feel moored to the spot.

"Annie's got to get home, sweetie," I say.

She nods. Stands. "I do. But I'll come back and see you soon, okay?"

"I'd like that," Legs says.

I cast one last glance at Annie, taking in her mussed hair, smudged lipstick, and wild, fiery eyes.

Yeah, that makes two of us.

30

ANNIE

Drip... drip... drip...

I stare at the brewing coffee as it trickles through the filter—rich, treacle-dark and scalding hot.

Kind of like Liam's eyes the other night. Eyes that captured me, drew me in. Liam Donovan's eyes are the human equivalent of a Venus flytrap.

Only, you know, masculine. Though I'd kill for those long, dark eyelashes.

Did we really almost kiss?

My heart says yes, my body practically screams the affirmative...

But my brain is torn. Unsure. Because that was Sunday —three days ago—and over the past seventy-two hours, I've barely seen Liam. He and Luke have been huddled in the boardroom, heads bent over their laptops and spreadsheets as things gear up for our push for the Wiseman investment. Apparently, it's down to just four companies now. SITL has a real chance.

Every time he comes into our shared office, Liam looks tired. Dark circles surround those incredible eyes.

I've been tempted to stalk over to his desk, shove everything off of it with one, big movie-esque hand sweep, then drag him onto it by the perfect silk tie so I can kiss the face off him...

"Annie?" Vanessa's voice startles me out of my fantasy and back into the present, where I am not wanton and wicked and throwing myself at my boss, but fetching coffee at Sugarland.

Heat pools in my cheeks and floods down to my chest. "Y-yes?" I squeak guiltily, sure she can somehow tell what I was daydreaming about.

Vanessa gestures an impatient hand at the girl behind the counter, who looks thoroughly bored by our presence. "Want to tell the lady what you'd like?"

"Um, just a coffee."

The girl snaps her gum. "What size do you want?"

"Large," I say automatically. Then I blush harder, like I've just said something obscene.

Isn't there a coffee spill somewhere that I can slip on? Maybe hit my head to put me into a nice, quiet coma?

Gum-snapper raises an eyebrow, like she can see right through me.

Vanessa peers at me. "You okay, Annie?"

"Ju—just need caffeine."

I wish I could know what he's thinking, whether he's second-guessing what almost happened the other night. Liam has been nothing but professional this week, maybe I should be the same. Forbidden, sexy workplace romances might look glamorous on the TV shows Prisha binges, but in reality, the stakes are higher. Bigger stakes means there's more to lose.

But that's not what's on my mind now, because all I can think about is sexy pine forests and black coffee eyes and soft lips framed by a hard jawline. Lips that look entirely kissable and...

FRICK, I'm doing it again!

Luckily, my coffee is ready. I swipe it off the counter and take a huge, throat-scorching gulp.

"Ow!" I whimper as blisters explode over my tongue.

The counter girl shakes her head at me. "You gotta wait, let it cool off. It's too hot to handle when it's freshly poured."

I'll say.

Hopefully my brain will cool it with the boss fantasies soon so I can actually focus on all the work I have to do this week. Free of all dirty thoughts.

Great advice, actually.

"Thanks," I tell the girl, rummaging in my jacket pocket and then tucking a ten into the tip jar.

Her eyebrows shoot up. "Thanks, lady."

"No, thank *you.*" I shoot her a cheery grin. Maybe a bit too cheery, because she's gone from surprised to slightly frightened.

Must stop scaring people.

"What was all that about?" Vanessa demands as we make our way out of Sugarland armed with our cups of java and a family-size box of donuts for the office.

Because sharing is caring. Not because I want to see Liam get powdered sugar on his totally NON kissable mouth.

Yes! That was better. Ish.

"What was what about?" I ask as we hurry around to the front door of the building. It was raining this morning, but now, the sun's out. I breathe in the warm, damp smell of sunshine after rain. I really do like Atlanta in the spring.

"Um, when you basically blacked out in the coffee shop just now, and then tipped the extremely rude and obnoxious counter staff?"

"She was insightful."

"I'd be surprised if she didn't spit in one of our coffees," Vanessa says with a roll of her eyes as we step back into the lobby. "It's like you weren't even in the same shop as me."

"I'm just distracted today."

Luckily, I'm saved from having to explain myself further by the lady in the elevator across the lobby. She's holding the door for us, so Vanessa and I hurry through, heels clicking on the glossy floor.

"Thanks," I pant as we dart inside, sloshing coffee as I go.

"Which floor?" The lady smiles, showing off perfectly straight teeth. She's wearing cute, oversized sunglasses, and has honey-colored hair. She looks like one of those people who could be wearing a garbage bag and everyone would assume it's a new trend they weren't cool enough to know about yet.

"Two. Thanks." Vanessa digs one of her heels into the ground, swiveling her attention back to me. "You've been distracted all week. Away with the fairies."

Is it that obvious?

Vanessa purses her lips and gives me the side-eye. "Did something happen last weekend?"

"Last weekend? No, nothing. Just the tournament, obviously. After which, I went home and slept." I nod convincingly. This sounds good, believable. Vanessa studies me, and a flustered feeling stirs in my belly. "Alone. Slept alone."

Nooooo. Why would I add that? Now it sounds like I'm lying.

"I see," Vanessa says with an eyebrow raise that tells me this is *not* over.

I look away sheepishly... right into the eyes of the stylish lady.

At least, I think she's looking at me. Hard to tell with those sunglasses.

The elevator pings and the doors open. Vanessa clacks out, and the lady gestures to me. "After you."

"Oh, thank you!" I rebalance my donuts and coffee, and step into the hallway. I didn't even notice that only one floor was selected on the elevator ride up. Is she here for Stay Inside the Lines? There's one other office on our floor, but this lady doesn't look like she needs hair plugs.

When we reach the doors to SITL, the woman follows Vanessa and me into the reception area. I'm about to ask her how we can help when she takes off down the hall with a confident familiarity.

Okay, she's clearly been here a million times.

I place the box of donuts on the table in the breakroom and select a raspberry donut for myself. Just as my mouth closes around a huge bite of doughy, sugary goodness, my eyes fall on sunglasses lady through the window-walls.

She throws open the glass door to mine and Liam's workspace and practically throws herself at Liam, hugging him tightly.

What in the?

"Who is *that*?" Vanessa squeaks, her hands clenching her coffee cup so tight, I'm surprised we don't have a volcanic coffee eruption on our hands.

"No idea. Maybe a contractor?"

Liam pats the woman's back, then smiles at her affectionately. His eyes crinkle at the corners, shining with warmth. He's magnificent when he smiles, and I'm momentarily dazed.

She chatters away, and he listens attentively. His body language is calm, relaxed.

The two of them are clearly well-acquainted. Comfortable.

Who is she?

"I can't believe this." Vanessa sniffs, pursing her lips.

I'm about to look away, bothered that I might be in any way bothered by this, when Luke appears. The lady springs up and Luke wraps her in a huge bear hug, lifting her off her feet.

Aware that I can't exactly stay here, gawking, in the breakroom forever, I sidle slowly toward the little reunion. When I get to the door, I hover for a moment. Liam looks up and waves me in, and I step inside, weirdly nervous.

"Hi, again," I say to the woman.

"Annie," Liam says. "I'd like you to meet Lana Mae."

Oh!

"Lana Mae!" I say, way too loudly. "Liam's sister, Lana Mae."

I'm ashamed of the amount of sweet relief in my veins right now.

"Hi!" I tack on for good measure.

Lana Mae whips off her sunglasses and turns to me. Fixes me with big, dark eyes. She's the spitting image of her daughter.

"I thought that might be you in the elevator! I'm so happy to finally meet you, Annie." Lana shoots a cheeky look at Liam. "I've heard *so* much about you."

"Really?" A glow rises in me. He's talked about me?

"Just a normal amount of things," Liam adds hurriedly, shooting his sister a warning glance.

Luke laughs heartily and slaps his brother on the back. Hard. "Whatever you tell yourself, bro."

Something about the way Liam looks at me, carefully taking in my reaction, makes my heart feel full.

31

LIAM

"Come onnnnn," Lana whines in a tone that sounds startlingly like Legs. We're standing downstairs in the lobby. I want to go back upstairs to work. But my sister apparently has other plans. "You totally have time for lunch."

Luke checks his phone, chuckling. "We won't even grill you too hard about Annie."

"Shh," I hiss, glancing around to see if anyone heard.

"You're coming. My treat." Lana loops her arm through mine. "I have to thank you guys for taking care of Legs."

I let out a sigh. "Fine. I have thirty minutes."

"You own the company. You have as much time as you want."

"Forty minutes, final offer."

"We can do an hour, no sweat." Luke then leans toward Lana conspiratorially. "We'll need *at least* an hour to cover everything. Just wait until you hear about the One Direction debacle."

Lana clasps her hands. "There was a debacle?"

"Liam had his shirt off."

"Oh, this is going to be good."

I press my lips together. "Changed my mind. I'm not going anywhere with you two."

"Sure you are." Lana Mae laughs as she drags me out the door.

A few minutes later, we've ordered a pizza and are sitting in the park nearby. I would never admit it to my siblings, but I'm glad to be outside today. My head feels clearer here. It's warm enough for me to take off my jacket, roll up my sleeves.

"Look at this guy, getting all unbuttoned during the work day," Lana Mae jokes. "Who are you and what have you done with Liam?"

"He's in lurvvvvvvve," Luke says giddily around a mouthful of pepperoni and cheese.

"You have tomato sauce on your shirt," I tell him.

Luke ignores me. Turns to Lana. "So, you ready to hear about the pickle Liam's gotten himself into?"

She rubs her hands together, all shiny and bright and eager. "Am I ever."

I concentrate on my pizza, methodically making my way through three slices: one veggie, two barbecue chicken. Not the most nutritionally-balanced meal, but the basics are there—protein, carbs, fat, veggies.

Lana Mae listens with wide eyes as Luke gleefully recounts the less-than-professional night Annie and I spent together, the dinner at our house, the baseball...

I say nothing. I know how my siblings operate: the more I protest, the more they're convinced I'm guilty. Or lying.

And right now, I'm both. Because I nearly kissed her the other night.

Kissed her, for goodness sake. What was I thinking, calling an employee to help with a personal situation, then offering her wine and inappropriately touching her?

Well, I'm not sure "inappropriately" is the right word.

Is touching someone's arm inappropriate? It sure felt like it when I touched Annie's.

Entirely inappropriate... but so right.

How can something so wrong feel so right? Did it feel right to her, too?

"Seriously, Liam." Lana crosses her legs and dabs grease off a pizza slice. She then stares at me with that slightly manic look she gets when she's using her annoyingly accurate motherly intuition on me. "Are you into this woman?"

"Um, I—" I falter.

"Because she's into you."

I can't help myself, I'm asking the question before I can even consider the repercussions—i.e. my human vultures for siblings. "She is?"

Luke smirks. "There's your answer, Lana. Same thing I've been saying about you and Carter for years."

"Shut up, Luke." Lana glares at him. He grins in response.

Nothing like sibling love.

"This is totally different. Carter and I are friends, that's all, and we barely see each other with all his traveling." She smoothes her sundress and looks at me seriously. "But Liam... I've been back for half an hour and I can already see that something's different. *You're* different."

"How?"

Lana pokes me in the side. "You're happy."

"I'm always happy." I scowl.

She rolls her eyes. "You're in the park, eating pizza, on a work day. This is not the brother I left two weeks ago."

"Fine." I hold my breath for all of two seconds. Then, "I like her."

The words are liberating on my tongue. Confessing them feels sweet. A relief.

"I KNEW IT!" Luke crows. He whips out his phone. "I have to call Mindy and—"

I swat the phone out of his hand.

"Hey, that's a brand new iPhone!"

"*Was* a brand new iPhone."

"Are you going to ask her out?" Lana Mae asks.

"It's complicated. She's my employee, and we've already accidentally shared a bed. She could report me for sexual harassment if I make a glimmer of a wrong move."

"Like kissing her in my backyard?"

"What?" Luke whips his head around to look at me so fast, he almost upsets the pizza box.

I frown at Lana. "How do you—"

"I stopped by Legs's school to see her before coming here." She smirks. "She might be young, but she ain't no dummy."

The heat is rising to my collar. I scratch my neck, not sure where to look.

Meanwhile, Luke is smiling like I just announced that I found the solution to world peace. "You kissed her?"

I shake my head. "No. But... almost. I think. Legs came outside just as we, um...'

Luke hoots. "Oh, this is good! This is too good!"

"Seriously, shut up, Luke." Lana Mae punches him lightly on the arm. He punches her back.

"You should ask her to my wedding," he says all too gleefully.

"I couldn't."

Luke wiggles his eyebrows. "Maybe I'll invite the entire office then."

"You are a serious douchebag sometimes, you know that?"

It's strange—usually, Luke drives me crazy with his

antics. But even as I insult him, I notice the smile in my voice.

I'm happy that he's happy for me, I realize.

And I'm happy that something other than my family is making me happy.

Or some*one*, I should say.

I take a breath, processing the sensation. I can't remember the last time I leaned into anything I was feeling.

Luke leans over and ruffles my hair. "I just want my wittle Liam to be happy."

"I'd be happy if you went to play in traffic for a bit." I jerk away from him, but I can't help it. The smile isn't just in my voice anymore, it's on my face.

"If you don't ask her to be your date for the wedding, maybe I'll ask her to be mine." Lana Mae grins cheekily.

"I hate you both." I smile. "But I'll think about it."

"That's a start," Lana Mae says happily.

"Well don't think for too long," Luke says. "We got laser tag tonight—it's the perfect romantic setting to ask a woman out."

I groan and scrub my face with my hand. "Ugh. I forgot about laser tag."

Yet another one of SITL's new HR initiatives to convince Wiseman we're "fun."

"Vanessa says it's mandatory. No excuses."

"I'll be there," I promise wearily. But my heart betrays me as a little thrill zips through me. Because not only do I secretly love laser tag... but the thought of running around a dark room with Annie?

It's not so bad. Not at all.

32

ANNIE

"Who came up with the idea for *laser tag*?" I ask Vanessa and Barb from the backseat of the car. Vanessa lives by the office and I'm still public transit dependent, so we're both bumming a ride with Barb to tonight's team bonding extravaganza. "My money's on Luke."

"Got it in one. I wanted to do an escape room, but Liam refused to be locked in a room with all of us for an hour." Vanessa sniffs. "Which is kinda rude, isn't it?"

A week or two ago, my vote would have been one-hundred percent yes. Now, I simply chuckle and roll my eyes. I'm actually excited for laser tag. I've never played before, but I'm not really focused so much on the game as I am on the fact that this will be the first time I've seen Liam outside of the office since we almost kissed the other night.

Vanessa peers at me in the rearview mirror. "What?"

"It's just so Liam, isn't it?"

"Liam!" Barb exclaims. "You two must be getting close, all cozied up in that office together. I've been working for Stay Inside the Lines for almost a year, and I still can't manage to think of Mr. Donovan as 'Liam'. He looks like he came out of the womb as Mr. Donovan."

This makes me cackle with laughter.

"I think he's got a soft side," I say innocently, like it's the first time I'm considering it. "Under all that bristliness, I bet he's sweet. Like a lychee. Ever had a lychee?"

I loved lychees growing up. Those odd-looking, exotic fruits that only occasionally appeared at the grocery store. The ones with the rough, spiky outsides and deliciously juicy, smooth insides.

"No," Vanessa says a tad coldly.

"I think Liam's a lychee," I say. "Or, like, a sheep in wolf's clothing. At first glance, he looks like a predator, but really, he's just... fluffy."

"Fluffy," Vanessa repeats.

"Like a lamb."

When you first meet Liam, he's all sharp teeth and snarling mouth. But if you look a bit closer... there's the fluffiest lamb you ever saw. And all I want to do is coax that lamb to come out and frolic with me. That's what lambs do, right? (And just to be clear, by "frolic" I mean "kiss.")

"I think you've been sniffing paint," Vanessa says with a smile and a flick of her hair. "He likes you, you know. Said in a meeting this week that you were the best thing to happen to this company in a long time."

"He said that?" I squeak. I was definitely not in that meeting.

"Maybe you actually have a chance with him," she says lightly, then flips down the sun visor and begins to apply lipgloss.

I can't work out Vanessa sometimes—whether she sees me as a peer or a rival. Whether she's aware that my heart speeds up at the sight of Liam.

"But I have to warn you," she continues. "I don't think he's a lychee or a sheep or whatever. I think Mr. Donovan's a brick. Hard on the outside, hard on the inside. And sometimes, when you're really mad, you want to throw him through a window."

"That's dark, Ness."

"Blood-chilling," Barb adds.

Vanessa sighs, looks at her hands. "I don't know if you know, but I kind of had a little... crush on Liam."

I feign surprise. "No!"

"But not anymore," she adds quickly. "I've decided that I'm not into guys who don't see me like I want to be seen."

My mind spins back to Justin. "Smart, Ness. I get that."

"So I've decided that I'm going to put all of my focus on the guy I'm dating."

"You're dating someone?" I practically choke. The woman has been visibly drooling over our boss since I started.

"Yes. And I wasn't sure about him, but I've decided to go for it. Put my all behind it and see what happens, see where it goes. There's no point in thinking about all the things I can't have. I need to focus on what I *do* have." Her voice is softer than usual.

I reach forward and put my hand on her arm. "That's a great plan."

"Thanks." She gives her head a shake. "Anyway. Think there'll be drinks at this thing? I'd kill for a Sex on the Beach right now."

As Barb and Nessa talk cocktails, I slump in the back-seat, lost in thought.

Vanessa may be taking a step back from crushing on the boss, but me? I can't stop thinking about what it would feel like to take a step closer.

In my twenty-six-and-a-half years on this planet, I've managed to avoid playing laser tag. And now that I'm here, it doesn't seem that I've missed much.

The building is dimly-lit, dingy, and smells vaguely of dirty socks. A bored teenager checks our group in, and as he does so, a herd of little boys come flying out of the "arena," as it's called, shoving each other and making farting noises with their underarms.

Vanessa stares at them in horror, then looks at her stiletto sandals. "I don't think I have the right footwear for this."

"Didn't you plan this?"

"Luke wanted to go—I just booked it," Vanessa splutters. "I didn't bother to look into how it actually works. I thought it would be kinda like a nightclub or something."

"A nightclub?" I repeat. At least I'm not the only laser tag virgin. And thankfully, I'm wearing my trusty tie-dye canvas sneakers.

Although the billowy white maxi skirt I've paired them with was probably not my smartest choice of attire.

"You know. Dark room, pulsing music, laser lights flashing. I thought it would be kind of..." She casts another horrified eye over the hoard of boys, zeroing in on where one boy is currently giving another a wedgie. "Sexy."

I sputter out a laugh. "Safe to say you were wrong?"

"One thousand percent wrong," she concedes. "But at least Mr. D looks happy."

I glance at Luke, who's strapping himself into one of the weird chest harness-y things we've all been given. He's grinning from ear to ear and heckling anyone within a five-foot radius. "Guy looks like he's a regular here."

Vanessa pulls a face. "Not what I would've expected."

I smile as I focus my attention on Liam. He's changed out of his work suit and into a black t-shirt and charcoal jeans. Which means those gorgeous, colorful arm tattoos are in full view. I soak in the sight as he sits on a bench and clips himself into his harness with ease.

"I think Liam's done this before, too," I say, surprised.

Vanessa's jaw slackens. "Holy moly. Those tattoos should be illegal. Not that I'm looking."

I don't reply. I'm too busy trying not to swallow my tongue.

I like to think I'm not a shallow person, that I value depth. That physical appearance isn't important, that...

Oh, who am I kidding? When it comes to looking at this man, I'm practically a puddle.

Ten minutes later—with no small amount of effort—we're all clipped into our harnesses, armed with large, bulky plastic guns, and being ushered into a "training room." There, another teenage boy gives us a rundown of how the game works, how to shoot our guns, and what to expect when we're in the arena. All between sneaking surreptitious glances at Vanessa's legs.

"So remember, you guys are playing our Mega Death game—which means that there's no limit on how many times you can shoot another player when they've been temporarily stunned."

Luke and Liam share a maniacal smile at this information.

The boy checks his clipboard. "The teams are as follows..."

Apparently, this has all been pre-arranged, because Luke and Liam step forward as team leaders right away. Luke even jostles Liam a little as they make their way to the front. I'm amazed to see Liam grin at his brother and mutter a few words I can't hear, but lip-read as something along the lines of "you're going down" with an unrepeatable expletive thrown in.

Wow. Mr. Donovan is full of surprises today.

Vanessa pouts a little as she's called onto Luke's team, but then seems to catch herself, like she's just remembered her vow to no longer pine for Liam. Luke practically pouts too when he takes in her shoes and short skirt. "Can you run in those?" he asks doubtfully.

Jamal, Barb and a few customer care people also get called to Luke's team, while Liam gets a couple of the accounting guys, Trevor, Todd, and me.

When I come to stand beside him, he nudges me in the side. "Ready for battle, Jacobs?"

Who is this guy and what has he done with Liam? I blink up at him, and his dark eyes dance all over my face. "Born ready, *Donovan*."

"Good." He smiles that heartachingly gorgeous smile of his again. "Because losing is not an option."

"Might've been a mistake to have the girl who's never played before on your team, then," I tease, keeping my voice light.

"Not a mistake," Liam says, his eyes darker than ever. "A happy accident."

My heart skips a beat.

"Sounds like you've had enough practice for both of us, anyways." I smirk, trying to make my heart rate return to normal. "You come here a lot?"

"Luke and I must've played laser tag a thousand times when we were kids. Mom used to take us." He smiles softly at the memory, then chuckles. "We were obsessed. So this is quite the blast from the past."

I see the nostalgic flicker in his eyes. He's so at ease—loose-limbed, smiling and full of fun competition. Almost like a trip down memory lane, back to a part of his childhood that was carefree and happy, is lifting whatever weight he usually carries with him.

My eyes linger on him as he sidles up to Luke and the two of them start smack-talking each other. Meanwhile, the boy stops checking out Vanessa long enough to count us down.

Our teams are led down separate passageways. Then, we're in the arena.

For a moment, I'm disoriented. It's dark, and it takes my eyes a few blinks to adjust. I hold up my gun tentatively, feeling like Katniss Everdeen after she rose on her platform into the Hunger Games arena for the first time.

And that's when I hear squealing. I catch a flash of laser light streaming across the air, followed by a red flash on a chest nearby.

Someone's been hit.

Time to get moving.

I use my free hand to hike up my maxi skirt and run as fast as I can. I spot a neon-painted piece of scaffolding and dive behind it. Just as I'm poking my head up, I see a light flicker and I take aim at my target.

The light flashes, and I hear the enemy team member groan.

Yes! A hit.

I could get into this.

A loud curse word, a flashing light, and nearby footsteps tell me I'm not safe here, so I dart forward, brandishing my weapon defensively as I head for what looks like a structure with a second floor platform. I'll have a good vantage point up there.

I jog toward a ramp, but the footsteps behind me are gaining. All of a sudden, I see a flash in my peripheral.

I look down to see my chest light blinking. I've been hit!

I pick up my pace, laughing as I go.

This is too much fun. What was I thinking, not playing laser tag all this time?

A laser light flashes to my left, warning me that I was almost hit a second time. Shoot!

Flash!

Ahh... another hit. Dammit. Maybe this plan wasn't so smart after all.

Gotta get to safety. Fast.

Flash!

Another hit.

I scramble forward, tripping over the hem of my skirt as I go. And then, out of nowhere, something closes around my arm.

A hand. A big hand.

"Agghhhh!" I scream as I'm pulled sideways in one swift motion, off the ramp and down a little side alley I hadn't seen.

The hand moves from my arm, clapping over my mouth as a body covers mine, pressing me into an alcove.

Suddenly, all I can smell is sexy pine forest, all I can feel is warm skin against mine. Darkness cloaks us in the alcove, totally hidden from sight, and my inability to visually orient myself serves to heighten my other senses, which are all in absolute overdrive right now.

Through the darkness, my eyes meet Liam's. Inky, sparkling, endless pools. I focus on his gaze—still dancing playfully—boring down on me.

I suck in a sharp breath, but this just has me breathing in more of his intoxicating scent.

He lowers his face so his lips are almost at my ear.

"Shhh," he murmurs, his breath tickling the sensitive skin on my neck as he gently removes his hand from its firm position on my mouth. "That was Luke behind you."

He pulls back and he's grinning, his face inches away. Painfully close. And his big, hot body, wide and hard as a brick wall, is still covering mine. His hands have moved to press against the wall, one on either side of my head, caging me into position. Protecting me.

Every square inch of my skin is tingling, whipped into a hyper-alert frenzy.

"Don't worry," he breathes, lowering his lips back to my ear. "He didn't see what happened. Nobody did."

I let out a nervous, high-pitched laugh. I feel woozy. "Thank you for saving me."

His smile turns wry. "Couldn't let you be the reason we lose the game, could I?"

I grin back, heart beating a million times a minute. "Should've worn my Team Donovan shirt."

Liam's eyes darken, his pupils dilating into depths of that deep, rich brown. "I can't stop thinking about you in that shirt."

My stomach clenches. "I can't stop thinking about you in general," I whisper back.

It's Liam's turn to suck in a breath.

His arms tense against the wall and the next thing I feel is his stubble scraping my cheek, sending shockwaves through me. His lips follow, the contrasting softness spurring a thousand butterflies in my stomach.

He gently kisses my cheekbone, then presses another achingly sharp and sweet stubbly kiss next to it. My hands reach up to fist in his t-shirt, pulling him closer. His lips move again, on a path to where I'm desperate for them, and I tilt my mouth hungrily to meet his, not caring where we are or what's going on around us, just desperate for more of *him*.

His lips skim mine, featherlight, and I begin to part mine....

Flash!

"HAHAHAHAHA, GOTCHA!" Luke screams like a psychopath.

Liam and I spring apart, and my eyes fly open to see burst after burst of green light. Liam's chest lights up as his brother fires mercilessly.

There's nothing we can do. We're trapped. Cornered. Sitting ducks.

Liam looks at me and smiles as he gets murdered over and over.

"You got killed because of me," I say.

"*You* kill me," he says softly, running the back of his calloused hand softly over my jawline. I'm not sure if it's his words or his touch that send a bigger jolt of electricity through me. He pushes a stray lock of hair behind my ear tenderly, and I look up into that gorgeous face. Trace my eyes over the stubble and scar and eyelashes and mussed up hair.

"And *I'm* gonna kill Luke for interrupting that."

He grins. "That's the spirit. On three?"

I peek around Liam and see that I'm currently concealed from Luke. The perfect sneak attack.

"One, two..." I count.

"Three!" Liam finishes as he darts sideways, moving his body away from mine and offering me the perfect kill shot.

"Gotcha!" I cackle as I shoot repeatedly at Luke, who whirls in horror to try and take me down.

Bursts of light explode all around me.

Fireworks.

33

LIAM

"Good game, Jacobs." I give Annie a nod as we exit the arena, then turn to acknowledge the rest of my team.

We're a motley crew after that insane death match. Luke is positively drowning in sweat—the man looks like he went for a swim fully-clothed. Todd is taking hit after hit of his inhaler, stopping between each one to let out a wheeze. Vanessa's broken a strap on her shoe, and I'm pretty sure Barb is half-drunk after smuggling in a hip flask.

But Annie?

She's glowing. And looking at her makes me glow, too, because I'm pretty damn sure I know what's making her smile that secret little smile she keeps sharing with the floor.

What happened in there was... hot. Like, crazy hot.

I'm a tangled mess of thoughts that involve full lips and shaky breath and soft skin.

I need to get her alone. Like, now.

"We lost by a million points." Annie raises her eyebrows at me, then bites that lip I can't stop thinking about. "But I will say that it was very... eventful."

"Not quite eventful enough, I'd say."

She flushes prettily, then attempts to unbuckle her

harness. A futile attempt. Her damp, messy hair tangles in one of the clasps, and it's so hilariously predictable that I laugh. She looks helpless, like a turtle on its back. "Need a hand?"

"Please."

I step toward her and gently take a lock of her hair between my fingers, trying to be as delicate as I can as I unfurl it from the clasp.

"How are you getting home tonight?" I ask quietly, trying to distract myself from how close we are. I remind myself sternly that everyone can see us.

Act normal, Liam. Or, as normal as possible.

Annie bites her lip and gives me a look that's so loaded, it's all I can do not to just grab her and kiss her. "Um," she says. "Well, I was *going* to ask Barb."

Going, past tense.

I glance in Barb's direction. She's swaying dangerously as she talks to Jamal. "Yeah, no. I'll call Barb an Uber."

Annie follows my gaze from under her hair knot and chuckles. "Good call. I guess I can get an Uber, too? Or the bus?"

I love how she makes these sentences questions... like she knows we can come up with a better plan.

"I'll drive you."

"Don't you have to get home to Legs?"

I smile. "Lana Mae's home, remember? I'm back at my place."

Annie's mouth pops open. "I just realized I have no idea where you live."

I try to hold back a smile. "Is that surprising? People don't often know where their bosses live."

"You know where *I* live."

Touché. I nod, eyes on hers. "True. I live in Midtown."

"But that's, like, the opposite direction."

"I like to take the scenic route."

Annie's lips twitch. "There is no scenic route."

I run my eyes over her pink cheeks and glittering eyes. "There most definitely is."

Behind her head, Luke points at Annie, then points at me, and makes an obscene gesture.

I flip him off before unhooking the last strand of Annie's hair from her harness. In the process, my fingers accidentally brush her cheek, and she sucks in a breath. The sound makes my insides flip.

"Annie and I can Uber together," Vanessa says brightly, popping up beside us with her heels in her hand.

"Nah, I'll take her." I try my best to sound casual.

"But I..."

"I'll take her," I repeat, this time in my boss voice. The one that says "that's final."

Vanessa stops arguing.

Luke mimes giving himself a high-five. I swear, who agreed to marry this idiot?

"Let's get out of here," Annie says as she shakes out her hair and tosses her harness in the returns bin.

It's cold out this evening, and when we get to my car, I crank the heat. We sit for a moment while the air circulates, blowing her sweet ocean scent around the vehicle.

Great. I'll just refrain from breathing for the foreseeable future. No big deal.

We pull onto the main road and sit in silence for a few minutes. Not a comfortable silence, but the tense, almost electrical silence you can physically feel.

"Annie, I—" I say at the exact same moment as she says "Liam."

We look at each other.

"You first," I offer.

She nods. Swallows. "About what happened..."

I give her a lopsided smile, one that I hope disguises just how hard my heart is beating. "You're going to have to be more specific. Lots of things seem to happen when you're around."

She snorts. "My best friend Prisha used to call them shen-Annie-gans."

My smile grows wider. "I've never heard such a perfect description for anything. So which shen-Annie-gan are you referring to, specifically?"

She gives me a side-eyed glance. Licks her lips. Then braces slightly, like she's not sure if she should say what's on her mind.

"I don't know where to start." There's a flirty, biting edge to her tone that's almost painfully sexy.

The stomach dropping sensation is back in full force.

I suck in a breath. "Shall we start with the fact that we spent a night holding each other, and even though I didn't know you, I've never in my life wanted to get closer to someone like I did you?"

"Really?"

I nod. Drum my fingers on the steering wheel. "Really. I don't get... close to people easily. Physically or emotionally. You, however, make me want to do both."

"I feel the same," she says softly. "Not a day has gone by that I haven't thought about that night. Thought about how I want to get that close to you again."

I know just what she means.

After what happened to my mom, everything I did became about control. If I couldn't control my surroundings, I could control what I was doing, control what I chose to focus on. If I couldn't control my shortcomings, I could control what I excelled at. Practice could make perfect.

And if I couldn't control what had already come to pass,

I could do everything in my power to control what happened next.

I was good at it, the whole control thing.

Until Annie came along.

"It's hard to control myself around you," I admit.

She lifts a shoulder, and when she speaks, her voice is breathy. "Then don't."

It feels like another dare. A challenge I won't hesitate to take.

"Fine. I won't."

I swerve suddenly, turning the car off the main road and down a side street. I pull into the first parking lot I see—a closed strip mall. I park the car and my hand tightens on her arm. She makes a strange little noise, and I, in turn, make the mistake of dropping my gaze to her lips. They're parted.

Lord have mercy on me.

"Good," she breathes. "I don't want you to."

This back and forth is ridiculous. But it's enough to make me forget every single last rule I've carefully lived by for so many years.

In this moment, the remainder of my control is slipping away. All I can see are those endless golden eyes, all I can feel is that silky smooth pale skin, all I can smell is her warm ocean scent, and all I can hear is her uneven breathing. Jagged enough to tell me that she, too, is feeling a little out of control by our proximity. A little reckless.

I move closer, my hands sliding over her forearms to her shoulders. My hands eclipse her narrow collarbones as I lean toward her, close enough that we're sharing air.

"Do you want me to kiss you, Annie?"

It's a rhetorical question.

I already know the answer.

34

ANNIE

Everything about this situation—those rough, calloused hands wrapped around my shoulders, his body so close to mine, the sandpaper edge to his low voice, the smell of his skin—it's almost too much to handle.

I'm lightheaded, drunk on him. And he hasn't even kissed me yet.

My eyes lock on Liam's, which are so dark, so intense, they look like black holes. A shiver dances down my spine. He's so close, I can almost—*almost*—feel him.

The anticipation is killing me. I'm putty in his hands.

We stare at each other for a few seconds, the only sound is of my increasingly quick, unsteady breaths.

All of my natural instincts tell me to run. This has gone too far; it's a slippery slope that's not going to end well for me. Again.

But right now, I'm done thinking about the past. Done thinking about anything, if I'm being honest.

Liam's eyes are twin coal fires, fueled by desire. "I want to hear you say it."

And so, I murmur, "I want you to kiss me."

His hands leave my shoulders, cradle my face. His

touch is tender, light, as his fingertips spread over my cheeks, sending flames across my skin.

He makes a sound in his throat—a groan, almost—and then, his mouth is on mine. Carefully, gently, the searing heat of his lips brushes against mine and shocks my senses. His lips are softer than I anticipated. Sweeter.

All too quickly—painfully quickly—he pulls back, palms still cupping my face as his eyes search mine.

Mere inches separate us and my mouth is on fire. But his eyes never stray from mine.

He's waiting for me, I realize. He's backing off so I can be in control of making the next decision. My heart warms with emotion. I've never made such an easy decision in my life.

"Get out of the car," I say in a strangled voice.

He obliges.

I climb out of the car and fly around to the driver's door, meeting him there.

"Hi."

He smiles, eyes wild. "Hi, yourself."

I surge forward, arms wrapping around his neck as I move toward his mouth, needing to kiss him again.

As if anticipating it, his hands trail from my face, over my neck, collarbones, and then skim down the sides of my body, leaving a trail of icy cold fire in their wake.

He picks me up in one seamless movement, as if I weigh no more than a feather. My legs wrap around his waist, and one of his hands moves to support my weight while the other trails lazily up my spine and into my hair, eliciting further shivers. My entire body is ablaze before my lips even skim his, but this time, when they do, he doesn't hold back.

Not one bit.

I've never been kissed so thoroughly. So hungrily. My arms tighten around his neck, pulling him against me, and our kiss goes from sweet to spicy in a matter of seconds as he gently tugs my hair and nips at my lower lip. I'm so wrapped up in everything Liam—the way he smells, feels, tastes—that I can barely tell where I end and he begins.

Every little thing that's gone unsaid between us is right here in his kiss. This man might be the Fort Knox of emotions, everything stowed away and locked safely out of sight, but for now, I hold the key. And I see him.

He's beautiful. Golden. A canvas displaying a priceless work of art.

And he wants *me*.

When we finally pull apart, I'm giddy and lightheaded.

Lighter still, when Liam aims the full force of that incredible smile at me. "I'd better get you home," he says, almost regretfully. "It's a work night."

I smile too. "Wouldn't want my boss to get mad if I'm late tomorrow."

"Who's your boss? He sounds like a total jerk."

"Ah, he's all right once you get to know him."

We're both laughing as we climb back into the car. The air between us is electric, buzzing with life and happiness. There's a lightness that feels like relief—the relief of finally leaning into this thing that's been building between us, almost painful in the anticipation it held.

As we pull out of the parking lot, Liam rolls down the windows and the sweet spring air swirls through the vehicle. His hand reaches for mine. "Hey, Annie?"

"Yes?"

"How would you feel about coming to Luke and Mindy's wedding?" He pauses. "With me, I mean?"

Butterflies fill my stomach to the brim. He wants me there?

"And here I was, hoping Legs was the one inviting me," I joke.

"Oh, believe me, I'm just getting in there before she asks you."

I tuck my mussed up hair behind my ears as I consider Liam's question. "I'd love to come, but is that... allowed? Us going to the wedding together?"

He runs his teeth over his bottom lip. "Technically, yes. The rules state that romantic connections in the workplace are not encouraged... but we wouldn't be at work, would we?"

"We would not." I grin at him. "Look at you, taking my data to heart and finding a little flexibility with the rules."

"I can readily admit now that you were right and I was wrong about that," he says gallantly.

"Wow. I'm going to need you to say that again."

"I was wrong." Liam smirks. "And I say we write the flexibility feature into the V2 launch as a definite."

"Told you—data doesn't lie." I smile so big, it hurts my cheeks. But then, I have a thought. Something we need to address. "Um, speaking about work and the investment and everything, I'd imagine it's best for both of us if we kept, um... well, if we kept a bit quiet about"—I tip my head toward him and swallow before continuing—"what just happened while we're at the office."

I say this because it's what I think Liam would want, sure. I know that getting SITL's HR in order is important, and the boss suddenly dating an employee might not look too wonderful.

But I also say it because it's a layer of protection for me. What if everyone found out about the two of us, and then Liam decides he doesn't want anything else to do with me?

Aside from the actual heartbreak of that potential scenario, I can't bear to be the subject of everyone's pity again.

I can't do it.

I like Liam. Like him so much, it almost hurts. But I'm also all too aware how much my past mistakes hurt.

"I agree," Liam's voice cuts through my thoughts, stilling them. "But that being said... I'd very much like for what just happened to happen again."

My heart leaps at these words. "That makes two of us."

35

ANNIE

The week that follows those earth-shattering kisses is a whirlwind of Liam in every form.

There's the Liam who strides into the office in the morning with frightening purpose. Spends hours in the boardroom with Luke, face pinched and eyes focused as the investment pitch comes to a head. There's the Liam who asks how my day is going, listens intently to my ideas, compliments my work.

And then, there's the Liam who gives me lingering sideways glances in the hallway, texts me sweet little messages when no one's looking (technically not a rule break). Who sneaks his hand onto my leg under the desk in meetings, moving his fingertips in dizzying patterns (also, technically, not a rule break). The Liam who drags me into the copy room when the coast is clear to kiss me senseless (okay, definitely a rule break. But well worth it).

This is also the Liam who insists on having lunch with my parents to officially meet them before whisking me away to his brother's destination wedding.

He's old-fashioned like that, apparently.

I'm not complaining. Every new side of Liam I discover is one I am totally here for.

Ding-dong!

And now, he's here. On my front doorstep.

Heart pounding with anticipation, I race down the hallway, sliding in my sock feet. I throw open the door.

"Hi," I say breathlessly.

Liam peers down at me, hand aloft and clenched to knock again. His expression turns from surprised to amused almost immediately as he takes in my disheveled appearance. "Hello."

"Okay, I'm gonna talk real fast cuz I have precisely two point five seconds before my mother appears and I just want to say I'm sorry about them in advance," I pant out in a rush.

He gives me an exaggerated frown and cups his ear. "Sorry, didn't catch that."

I roll my eyes and open my mouth to repeat myself, but right on cue—

"Helloooooo!" My mother materializes in a cloud of perfume and a frilly apron. "So lovely to see you again, Liam *darling*. Ooh, and you brought wine!" Mom manages to air-kiss Liam's cheeks, pluck the bottle of burgundy from his hand, and usher him into our entryway in one seamless motion. She makes a face at the French label on the bottle and gives Liam a too-bright smile as she pats his hand. "Mmm. It's not quite Kim Crawford Moscato, but I'm sure it's great."

Height of class and sophistication, my mother.

"Thank you for having me." He smiles as he steps inside, looks around the entryway. "You have a lovely home."

I love how much he smiles lately. I could watch him smile forever. Especially when it's aimed at me.

Mom giggles like a schoolgirl as Liam—quite admirably—admires her framed needlepoints.

"Oh, stop! Interior design is just a little hobby of mine. Learned it all from Good Housekeeping. Now, take off your coat. Stay awhile." Mom then proceeds to practically undress the man.

"Told you," I mouth at him with a grin as he obediently shrugs off his jacket. Underneath, he's wearing the softest looking charcoal-gray sweater I've ever seen.

I want to put my hands all over it. All over him.

He raises his eyebrows flirtily in response. "Worth it," he mouths back.

I feel giddy at the thought of going away with this man for a long weekend.

Luke and Mindy's wedding is at a ranch a couple of hours outside the city. Talk about a romantic setting... although, to be fair, anything would top laser tag, a strip mall parking lot, and a copy room with rattling pipes.

On paper, at least. My flutter-inducing memories of his mouth on mine might beg to differ.

Liam gives me a lingering look over his shoulder that's seared with heat as he's dragged past me by my mother, who's holding onto his arm like a kid clutches a balloon at the fair. His gaze makes my toes curl as I recall each of our kisses, and a soft smile settles on my face as I follow them into the living room to greet my dad. In typical Dad fashion, he's more interested in his newspaper than our lunch guest—who may or may not be his only daughter's new beau.

He's a man of few words, my father. The two of them will probably get along great.

As Mom buzzes around the living room like an over-excited bee while Dad does his best to nod along and look vaguely interested, I notice something—notice how odd a couple Mom and Dad are. But while they may be opposites, they *work*.

Balance each other out.

The thought gives me hope. Maybe Liam and I—different as we are—really could make this crazy, sexy, sweet little thing between us into something that's really real.

"Coming, Annie?" Mom calls, gesturing at me. "We don't want the casserole to get cold, do we?"

"Nope, we certainly do not."

After approximately sixty-five tons of chicken-broccoli casserole, four Tupperwares of "just in case you get hungry on the drive" leftovers, and a laundry list of questions that included Liam's blood type, family history, and SAT scores, we have finally escaped my parents house. Liam and I are pulling out of the driveway, with my bags (yes, plural. Packing is hard) stacked in the backseat.

Mom, of course, is waving away, making a big show out of it. "Bye now, God bless! Drive safe, young man!"

Liam raises a hand as we drive away. Meanwhile, I put my head in my hands.

"I'm sorry about her," I groan. "That was painful. I owe you one."

"How do you mean?"

"Um. Were you at the same lunch as me? It was like she was checking a dog for its pedigree."

"I like her." He shrugs. "She reminds me of you in a lot of ways."

"How?!" I demand.

Liam chuckles. "Asks inappropriate questions. Laughs a lot. Takes a genuine interest in people."

I glance back at my still waving, perma-smiling mother. "She took a stalker-level interest in you. Seriously, she's probably going to text me in twenty seconds asking how the drive is going."

"I think it's nice that she's waving us off."

I roll my eyes. "She's only doing that for our next-door neighbor Laura Lynn's benefit. Her daughter's dating a *surgeon*."

Liam's brow wrinkles. "I'm not sure I'm following," he says as he retrieves a pair of sunglasses from the center console and slides them on.

Damn. The man can wear the heck out of a pair of shades.

Tom Ford, too. Impeccable taste.

And great multitasking skills. I've always been impressed by people who can do other things while driving. I have a hard time keeping the car moving in a straight line on a road at the best of times. Easily distracted by squirrels, etc.

"It's like a neighborhood competition," I explain. "Whose offspring has mated the most successfully."

Liam's lips curl up. "Mated?"

My cheeks fill with heat.

Wow. Great word choice, Annie. Way to jump the gun.

"Dated! I said dated."

"No, you didn't." Liam takes my hand and his thumb brushes the sensitive skin along the edge of my palm, giving me goosebumps. "So I should take it as a compliment that she wanted to show me off to the neighbors?"

"Absolutely. By the time she's on her first Moscato of the evening, our entire cul-de-sac will know all about *Annie's new friend.*" I add air quotes around the last bit.

"Well, as long as they hear only good things. I don't want that to be the last time I come by."

My stomach twists in the best way. "Well that's nice, because I'm pretty sure my parents are way weirder than your family."

Liam smiles. "My mom was the sweetest, friendliest person on the planet. You would've loved her. My dad and stepmom, however, are..." He coughs slightly. His jaw tenses. "Different. You'll meet them this weekend. We're not close."

I bite my lip and mull over this information. Remember Mindy's words about the Donovan kids' childhood. How sad and pensive Liam looks every time he recalls his mom. I don't want to pry, but I'm curious about Liam's family. He's so close-lipped about, well, everything. The more he opens up, the more I want to know. "I'm guessing there's a reason for that?"

Liam's jaw is tight and he screws up his nose for a few moments, like he's carefully choosing his next words. "Several reasons. I've tried to have a relationship with them over the years, but my father... he doesn't approve of a lot of my life choices. Of the business Luke and I are running. Of Lana Mae being a single mother. It can make things... difficult."

Noted. Mr. Donovan Senior is a bit of a jackass.

"And your stepmom?" I ask tentatively.

Liam makes a face. "She's married to my dad."

The statement is somehow loaded and final all at once, and I get the sense that Liam's done talking about this. I don't want to push him, so I change the subject. "What's the agenda like for the wedding?"

The cloudiness lifts from Liam's expression and he relaxes as he runs me through the bachelor events, rehearsal dinner and girls' spa day that I'm invited to at Mindy's insistence.

The thought makes me feel warm as a tray of freshly-baked brownies. As an only child, I've never experienced the fun of having sisters. Justin had a sister, but we didn't see a lot of her. When we did, I got a straight-laced, pouty-faced sort of person who sneered at my outfits with open disdain, never asked me about myself, and generally expressed zero interest in getting to know me.

The Donovan siblings seem like a whole different ball game: fun, warm, bubbly, and welcoming.

"Wow, it's going to be a busy weekend," I say, excited.

Liam's eyes glint mysteriously. "Ah, I'm sure we can find some free time in there."

"Yeah?"

His expression turns wicked. "Well, I'd rather like some alone time with you."

That stupid smile is back on my face and butterflies fill my stomach. For some reason, my mind gallops off on a daydream of Liam and me on gorgeous white horses, riding off into the sunset. Leather chaps tbd.

"Can our alone time involve horses?" I ask, somewhat breathlessly.

"Horses?" Liam drums his fingers on the steering wheel. "Sure. It's a ranch, after all. You ever been to a ranch?"

"Negative. You?"

He thinks about it for a moment. "Me neither."

"Poof goes my Liam the Cowboy fantasy."

He shoots me an amused look. "That sounds like something your mom's book club would read."

I squeeze my eyes shut, horrified. "Oh my gosh, is nothing sacred? Stop giving me traumatic mental images of my mother ogling your oiled-up abs!"

He snorts. "Why are my abs oiled up?"

"I don't know, they just are. They're always oiled up in my head."

Liam laughs so hard, it makes me laugh too. I love seeing him this relaxed and carefree.

"Well, remind me to go buy some oil, I guess," he rasps when he finally stops laughing.

"Please," I agree with a grin.

He shoots me another look, this one so tender and sweet, it takes my breath away. "Annie, would you like to go on a horseback riding date with me while we're at the ranch?"

"Liam Donovan, are you asking me on a date within a date?"

"I most definitely am. Our first *official* date."

I'm smiling from ear to ear. "So, our not-a-date at Petit Soleil didn't count?"

"No way, Jacobs. You ain't seen nothing yet."

My heart picks up speed at the thought of what's in store for this weekend with Liam.

Although I've never actually been on a horse in my life. And now that I think about it, I envision my experience being less "riding off into the sunset" and more "getting bucked off immediately."

But, oh well.

If it's with Liam, I'm there.

36

LIAM

A couple years ago, if my brother had told me he wanted to get married, I would've laughed.

And if he insisted it were true, I would've had no choice but to assume that he'd lost a bet or that it was all part of some elaborate prank.

But then, I saw him with Mindy, and everything changed.

Changed to the point that my older brother—the former ultimate bro, ladies' man, and party boy—made the announcement that he was permanently forgoing the lothario lifestyle. And then, subsequently decided that he was going to take this step without indulging in a bachelor party.

My jaw dropped so hard that it almost fell off when he vetoed my (albeit very reluctant) suggestion of a bachelor weekend in Vegas (too loud, busy, and dirty for my tastes. But, I'm the best man, so if Luke wanted to go, I would've made the sacrifice).

Luke also didn't want to rent a limo and go down to Panama City Beach or Daytona, thank goodness. Or even have a boys' night out at home in Atlanta. He'd had enough of those over the years, he said.

The one thing he did want?

Ax throwing.

Yup. You heard me right. He wanted to go chuck sharp blades at targets on the wall like we were lumberjacks.

I was mildly surprised. I didn't think Luke had ever even been to a forest, never mind cut down a tree. He's a city boy, through and through.

But he was set on his decision. Apparently, Mindy has a thing for lumberjacks—which was something I obviously asked zero follow-up questions about.

This is why, four hours after pulling up to the most gorgeous, picturesque guest ranch you could ever imagine, I'm spending my Friday night in a field with a bunch of grown men. Throwing things.

Even more unbelievably, everyone seems to be enjoying this. It's a warm, balmy evening, and the dusky air is sweet and heavy. There's about twenty of us, standing on a huge lawn adorned with targets. In the distance, the sun dips below the rolling hills, pouring a golden hue on everything.

For an athletic guy, Luke is surprisingly awful at the activity—though that may be the four shots of tequila. I chuckle as he winds up and chucks the ax so haphazardly that one of his buddies yells "Duck!" and falls to the ground in a stop-drop-n-roll motion.

In contrast, the guy on my left wields his ax over his head and fires with ease. It spins through the air in a graceful arc before sticking dead in the wooden target. He lets out a "Whoop!" and punches the air.

A dark-haired man stands behind him, sipping his beer and looking on in amusement. "Easy there, Conor. Don't throw your back out, old man."

The ax-throwing guy smirks. "Your sister already threw my back out last night."

"Gross, dude!"

A lot of shoving follows that comment, and I smile as I look away.

I love how these guys can casually laugh and joke about their relationships in public—even if the joke is just that one of them is apparently sleeping with the other's sister (though he's wearing a wedding ring, so I assume it's serious).

Annie and I have been keeping things between us on the down low, at her request, until we see where things go. I was a little surprised when she asked... I was prepared to go straight to Luke to work out a solution for our company HR. But, I guess, for now, it makes sense. I'm just glad to be away from the office this weekend so we can be out in public together.

Soon—once the funding's in place and Annie feels more comfortable—we can take next steps at work. Or I hope we can take next steps...

And now my mind is squarely on a certain auburn-haired spitfire. What she would say if she could see me right now...

Probably a lot of inappropriate lumberjack jokes.

I turn back to my target and fire the ax. It moves quickly, like a bullet, before piercing the heart of the target.

Bullseye.

"Nice one, man!" The dark-haired guy gives me an appreciative nod. Behind him, the guy he called Conor is still steadfastly pounding ax after ax into the target.

"Thanks." I stick out my hand. "Liam."

"Aiden." He grins. "You must be Luke's brother."

"I am." I raise an eyebrow. "Not sure that's a great association at this minute."

Aiden chuckles and we both turn to take in my drunky-pants brother stumbling and wielding axes willy-nilly.

How does this ranch have the insurance to allow drunk people to throw weapons?

"He's so happy," Aiden says with a small, nostalgic smile. "I used to think that Luke and I would be single forever. That everyone else would get married, and we'd still be hitting up the bar every Friday night. It's funny how things change." He pauses. Sighs happily. "It's *good* how things change."

"Agreed," I say immediately, surprising myself. But I mean it. I used to be so averse to change, so rigid in my perfectly scheduled routine. Always making sure I was meeting all my responsibilities and being there for everyone else. I never stopped to consider if I was truly happy.

Then Annie came along and colored outside all my carefully drawn lines.

And I've loved every minute of it.

Loved how she makes me feel. How I see I make *her* feel.

Aiden seems to read my energy because he leans in. "You seeing anyone?"

I nod, and the motion is surprisingly comfortable given how long it's been since I said yes to this question. "Yeah, it's pretty new, but she's incredible."

Aiden smiles down at his ringed left hand. "I know the feeling, bro."

"LIAM!" Luke's shriek has us both jerking our heads upwards.

My brother is running toward me, waggling his phone in the air.

"LIAM, CHECK THIS OUT!"

I smile apologetically at Aiden. "Um, better go. The groom needs my assistance."

Aiden chuckles and claps me on the shoulder. "Good to meet you, dude."

"Likewise."

I dart through the cluster of people until I reach Luke. "What's up?"

He shoves his phone in my face. "It's down to us and one other company!"

"What?" I almost drop the phone I'm so surprised. "When did you...?"

"Email just came through. Check it out."

My heart picks up speed as Luke slings a delighted arm around my shoulders, shaking me and cheering as I read.

It's true. It's all come down to two companies. The funding from Wiseman's company is almost within our grip.

We just need to beat out... Financify.

Huh.

The app sounds familiar; where have I heard of it? After two beers, I'm not as quick on recall as usual.

The email has a link to a profile on both companies. I click on Financify's.

And come face to face with a picture of Justin Manson.

Annie's ex-boyfriend from the airport hotel. And also the Director of Analytics and Growth at Financify.

My body tenses so hard, I almost drop the phone again.

Of course... Financify was where Annie used to work. This job title must've been the promotion Annie was working for.

"Whoa, buddy. You drunk or something?" Luke, the one out of the two of us who is *actually* drunk, tipsily reaches for his phone. "Aren't you excited?"

I blink hard a couple times. "That's Annie's ex. Justin."

Luke's eyebrows raise in surprise. He looks at the photo on his screen again and smirks. "This guy?! You're *way* better looking than this guy."

Despite myself, I laugh. "You're just saying that because we look so alike."

"'Course I am. Consider yourself lucky that you took after me in the looks department. And Annie's ex or no Annie's ex, it doesn't matter. We could be up against Bill Gates or Elon Musk, for all I care. We've *earned* this. We deserve that funding, and we're getting that funding. Okay?"

I feel myself relax, feel the tension slide away.

Luke's right. It doesn't matter who we're up against. And it certainly doesn't matter who Annie dated in the past. It's irrelevant.

What matters is *now*. Things change.

And, like that Aiden guy said, it's *good* that things change.

Having Annie in my life is the best change that's occurred for me in years.

I glance at the now-dark sky and smile. "Hey Lukey, I'll be right back."

He narrows his eyes at me. "You're so obvious, you know that?"

"How do you mean?"

Luke holds up a hand. Though with the swaying, his palm smacks unceremoniously into my chest. "Leave. And don't come back."

"Excuse me?"

"I know you'd rather go see Annie." He winks. "*I'd* rather you go see Annie."

And then, because people change and things change, I give my brother an impromptu hug.

For a moment, he freezes. A hugger, I am not.

But after he recovers from the shock, he hugs me back with a fierceness that warms my heart.

37

ANNIE

"Wowee," I say aloud as I flop on the massive bed in my room on the third floor of the ranch house.

Truly, I've never seen anything like this. I have no idea if other ranches are posh, but this one sure is. The room Liam booked for me is positively palatial, with a plush, four-poster bed, a vintage chandelier and two overflowing vase-fuls of freshly-cut wildflowers on the dresser. I feel like a tiny human ant standing in the middle of the room.

But the best part is the large, cushioned bay window seat overlooking the stately home's gardens—complete with a weeping willow with a rope swing tied to one extended limb—and the paddocks where the horses graze. AKA, the nicest place in the world to curl up and read a good book. Which I plan to do first thing tomorrow morning.

Right now, I'm so tired, all I want to do is be in bed.

When Liam and I arrived at the venue earlier this after-noon, we went straight to the meet-and-greet welcome barbecue with the friends and family of the bride and groom (except Liam's folks—I have yet to meet them). It was so wonderful to meet so many people who know and love Liam—hear his aunt Tracey recount stories of his T-ball days, laugh with his childhood neighbor about the time Liam tried to adopt a duckling he found in the pond at the local park.

It was beyond lovely to see Liam smiling and relaxed and happy. He put his arm around me every time he introduced me to someone—always as his date, never as his employee. I can't even begin to describe the warm, glowing feeling when he did that. Like this was all just... right.

Eventually—too soon—Liam was off to throw an ax or something (it sounded sexy enough that I wanted to spy, but I was told it was strictly boys-only). So, I decided to put this amazing room to full use (seriously, the man spoiled me. He insisted that all guests have a room this nice, but I'm not sure I believe him. It would be so Liam to act like he didn't go the extra mile).

So here I am, one eucalyptus steam shower later, wearing the fluffiest bathrobe I've ever seen in my life. My plan is to veg on the bed all night watching reruns of the Kardashians with the Diet Coke and peanut M&M's from my travel snack bag.

I pull the huge comforter over my lap and shove a fistful of chocolate candies into my mouth, chewing as I flip through the channels.

I shuffle slightly, putting an extra pillow behind me, then pulling it away.

Roll onto my belly. Then back. Eat more M&M's, swap them out for Haribos.

Which makes me think about the night at the airport hotel with Liam.

I smile fondly at the memory of dodgy carpets and a single, doll-sized bed. Of a t-shirt that didn't belong to me but is now folded in my top dresser drawer at home.

Then, it hits me: I'd rather be there than here. I'd trade

this five-star luxury experience for a run-down budget airport hotel.

Because there, I was with Liam. And being in Liam's arms beats out every other luxury I can imagine.

I miss him, I realize. Selfishly wish I could have him to myself tonight.

I chew thoughtfully on another few gummies, looking at my phone. I could text him to let him know I'm thinking about him... but, I don't want to interrupt his boys' night. He's probably too busy having fun to think about me. And the thought of him out there having a good time makes me happy, too.

Knock, knock!

I startle at the thud on my door, sharp and insistent.

I'm not expecting anyone. Maybe they have the wrong room?

But it comes again, louder this time.

I slide off the bed and pad toward the door, tightening my robe as I go. I throw open the door and see...

Liam.

Specifically, a flushed, mussed-haired Liam, who looks beer-tipsy and sparkly-eyed and sinfully gorgeous in a lumberjack flannel shirt.

I blink, stunned. It's like my thoughts summoned him. *Magic!*

"Can't stay, gotta get back to Luke's party." He props himself in the doorframe, catching his breath. He's got a light glow to him, like he's radiating freaking gorgeousness.

I'm still trying to keep up, half-wondering if this is real or imagined. "Huh?"

"I ran all the way here," he explains with a grin. "I wanted to tell you that I was thinking about you. And I missed you. And to give you this."

He grabs my waist and tugs me toward him.

He kisses me. Hard.

I melt into him, winding my arms around his neck, pulling him closer as he kisses me breathless, claiming my mouth and my heart, all at once.

He pulls back all too quickly, and gives me a devastating smile. "That's better."

And before I can say a single word, he turns on his heel and takes off, running down the hallway and toward the stairs.

I'm speechless. Rooted to the spot as my fingers move to touch my sensitive, swollen lips.

I feel like Juliet after a stolen moment with her Romeo.

Stepping back into my room, I cross straight over to that beautiful bay window and curl up on the seat. Above, the stars are a sparkling canvas, lighting up the sky enough so that I spy Liam running across the gardens, making his way back to Luke's party.

At one point, he glances over his shoulder toward the ranch house, and he smiles.

38

ANNIE

I lean back and rest my toweled head against the wooden wall of the sauna, sighing happily. "Thanks again for inviting me."

"Of course," Mindy replies, like it's the most natural thing in the world for me—a woman she met just a couple weeks ago—to be here with her on the afternoon before her wedding day.

Lana Mae shoots me a glimmering, dark-eyed look that reminds me so much of her brother, I have to look away. "We didn't have a hidden agenda to pump you for Liam gossip. Not at all."

"Nope, not one bit." Mindy giggles and adjusts her skimpy bikini bottom. "But, now that you're here, you could tell us a few things. You know, if you want to."

I laugh. These girls remind me of Prisha with their easy banter and teasing. It's clear that the sisters-in-law-to-be are very close.

"Yeah. Like, how on earth did this all come to pass?" Lana Mae asks, her voice pitchy with excitement. "I was away for work for two weeks, and when I came back, I might as well have been gone for two years—hang on."

She interrupts her own tirade to unscrew the lid of her water and take a long drink.

"Much better." She smacks her lips. "I don't handle extended heat very well."

"Ten more minutes." Mindy pats her own toweled head. "Then the hair masks can be rinsed off."

They both swivel expectant eyes back to me.

"So?" Lana prompts. "You spent the night in a hotel?"

I've also been vaguely struggling with the heat, but now, I'm grateful for it. Surely my cheeks are already as flushed as they can get?

I drop my gaze to my hands. "We did... I thought he was a grumpy a-hole. And I'm sure he thought I was clinically insane."

Lana snorts. "Classic Liam."

I have to admit that I'm happy to be able to talk about Liam and me. It's so unlike our hush hush behavior at the office.

I describe the crazy debacle that was the night in the hotel, followed by the shocking realization that the man I shared a bed with (I left out the intimate cuddle-fest, of course) turned out to be my new boss. I explain that, bit by bit, I realized how different he is from the man I assumed he was. I tell them briefly about our first kiss, leaving out all the sizzling details because, eager as Lana looks right now, she's still Liam's little sister.

When I'm done, Mindy smirks. "So, it's serious."

"Oh... no. I don't know. I mean, I'm just here as his wedding date."

"Liam doesn't *do* wedding dates," Lana Mae says. "You're definitely not just that."

That now-familiar warm feeling fills my chest. I know Liam's focus is his company, his family. Know that he hasn't dated in a long time because of these priorities.

291

And yet, I'm here with him. That says it all really, doesn't it?

"When did you feel it?" Mindy asks, interrupting my thoughts.

"It?"

"You know, the 'it' factor. The moment when you realize you don't just want to jump his bones because your attraction is burning so bright, it's about to set your whole house on fire. It's the moment where, underneath all the flirting and sexual tension and butterflies, you realize with a sudden clarity that you feel so much more than that."

I don't even have to pause: the exact second she's talking about hits me square in the heart.

That kiss last night. The one that said more than a hundred words could.

"Annie?" Mindy prompts with a wicked grin. "Looks like you know the moment, huh? Or are you daydreaming about all the sexy making out you two have been doing?"

Mindy is brash and the exact opposite of subtle, and I like this about her. But I can't help but glance at Lana Mae to see if this conversation is officially TMI. Apparently not, because she's nodding along giddily.

I can't help but smile.

"I felt it," I confess. "The 'it' factor... I felt it last night."

Lana Mae claps her hands. "I *knew* this was serious. I've been wanting this for him for so long."

I take my opportunity. "Why doesn't he date?"

Mindy bites her bottom lip and glances at Lana, who sighs, her face suddenly serious.

"I'm not sure how much he's told you about our upbringing, but our family had... some issues," Lana Mae says quietly. "Our father wasn't the easiest person to be around. He was particularly hard on Liam—he had such high expectations of him."

"And this affected him dating?" I ask, trying to piece everything together.

"Liam's a complex person," she says slowly. "He takes things hard, carries the weight of the world on his shoulders, like he's personally responsible for other people's problems. He hasn't dated since his girlfriend in college, and over the years, he's put so much time and energy into SITL, I don't think he really had time or energy to date. Well, his company and also caring for and supporting Legs. He wants Legs to have a father figure in her life seeing as my ex left while I was pregnant."

Her shoulders slump slightly at the memory. I'm struck by how this beautiful woman has been through more crap than I can even imagine, and yet, she's so strong and resilient. I'm in awe of her.

"Luke helped out a lot too, especially in that first year," she continues. "Liam was away at college in California at the time."

"He said he played baseball for a bit?"

She smiles. "Is that how he phrased it? Always so modest, our Liam. He could've gone pro. He had a life out west—an athletic scholarship, working on his business degree, a gorgeous girlfriend..."

Lana Mae trails off, shifts in her seat a little.

"Then our mom passed away and he walked away from it all. Dropped out of college, quit baseball, came back home. Built a company. He was here for Legs and me in a way that's just... remarkable." She pauses, sounding a touch tearful. "He gave up everything and nobody could stop him. I just don't want him to have regrets."

Mindy puts a hand on Lana's arm. "Liam made the choice he wanted to make."

"I agree." My words come out barely above a whisper. This man I've fallen for, this man who has stolen my heart, is so different from any other man I've dated. In the best way possible.

Mindy glances at me and I see a glimmer of something that looks like approval in her sweet expression. "The path he chose led him to the right job. And now, the right person. No amount of baseball—pro career or not—could replace how precious that is."

Her words are balm to me. I love that they see what I see—how *right* this thing between Liam and me seems to be.

Lana Mae nods and looks at me. Smiles. "You make him really happy, Annie."

"He makes me happy, too," I say, meaning every single word.

"Plus, he's going to be even happier soon when they bag that investment—did you hear that they're down to two companies now?" Mindy sparkles.

I grin. "I did hear that."

"Luke made sure everyone within a ten-mile radius heard about it this morning," Lana Mae adds with a roll of her eyes.

"It's so exciting!" Mindy continues. "If SITL gets this, they'll be set. All of the risks will have paid off. They just have to beat out these Financify guys."

Despite the killer heat in the sauna, a chill runs through me. "Wait. Who?"

"Financify, I think they're called? Some finance app out of Boston." Mindy raises a brow. "You've heard of them?"

I give a stiff nod.

Oh, I've heard of them all right.

39

LIAM

If Annie Jacobs was a sandwich, she'd be a PB&J.

And don't take that the wrong way—it's most *definitely* a compliment.

Peanut butter and jelly sandwiches are the best. Universally loved by everyone, from little kids to octogenarians. They're satisfying and sweet, can be both a comfort food and a dietary staple. They can be fancy, with whole grain artisan loaf and fresh ground organic peanuts, or eaten as a Smuckers-and-Skippy-and-Wonderbread treat that reminds you of how the simplest pleasures in life can be the best ones.

They also happen to be my favorite.

As I stand in the foyer of the ranch, watching Annie attempt to walk down the stairs in her heels like a baby gazelle, I grin so hard, my face almost aches. Especially when she takes her phone out of her purse, checks it, and then almost trips over the edge of her dress. She narrowly avoids a tumble to the ground floor with an inelegant banister grasp.

She is most definitely my favorite. And it's so much more than just how gorgeous she is. Tonight, especially, in that long, breezy dress ("maxi dresses," I believe they're called) with her hair pinned up, leaving a few loose strands framing her face. Every little thing about her is attractive to me.

"Wow," Legs whispers from beside me, squeezing my hand. "She looks beautiful."

"She does." My dopey smile is still blazing center-stage on my face. "And so do you, sweetie."

Legs gives me a huge, gap-toothed smile and twirls. In true Legs fashion, she's wearing an odd, puffball-style dress that looks more like a Disney princess costume than formal rehearsal dinner attire. But the important thing is that she's happy.

I love that Lana Mae encourages her to be herself. It's one of the things I admire most about my sister, and about Annie, too.

Legs has great role models.

I glance around to see where Annie went, and spot her among a cluster of people at the foot of the stairs. She's laughing with one of Mindy's friends—a short, curly-haired brunette with a little kid on each hip. Annie seems so comfortable and at ease, even when she's surrounded by people she doesn't know.

She's like a chameleon. Seamlessly blends in anywhere.

Which is more than can be said for me.

As if on cue, a thin, reedy voice makes my smile instantly disappear. "Lana Mae! What on earth is Allegra wearing?"

Lana Mae turns away from our cousin Claire with a slight grimace—probably matching mine. She glances at her daughter, and then up at our stepmother. "Hello, Constance. You've arrived."

Our stepmother—who's been married to our father for about twenty years but still behaves like she barely knows us—steps forward and embraces Lana Mae awkwardly, gripping her arms in lieu of a real hug. "I sent Allegra a dress in the mail weeks ago. Why isn't she wearing it?"

Lana Mae gives a clenched teeth smile. "Because she wanted to wear this one."

Constance tuts, before turning to me and offering me an over-powdered cheek. "Liam."

"Hello." I kiss the air near her cheek and step away again. She looks the same as ever—perfectly pressed Chanel suit, pearls, stockings... and a look on her face like she's just stepped in cow dung.

"There you all are!" My father suddenly arrives into the conversation, his tone suggesting that we've been hiding from him on purpose or something. "Took me an age to park the car. Can you believe they don't have valet?"

"Yes," Lana Mae and I respond in unison. I shoot her an amused look and she crosses her eyes back at me.

"Stop that, both of you," Dad reprimands.

Great to see you too, Dad.

"Where is the man of the hour?" Constance barks. "A groom should be near the entryway at all times, ready to welcome his guests. Let's find him, Ed."

The two of them swan away, Constance's heels clicking on the marble floor.

I pull a face at Lana Mae. "I thought a groom should be focused on the bride, no?"

My sister rolls her eyes. "Not when Constance Donovan is in the room. I guess we can just be thankful they didn't arrive last night like everyone else."

Yup. My father and stepmother decided that they had more important things to do than be at Luke's wedding for the entire weekend.

I can't believe how hard I used to try and impress the guy. The thought almost makes me shudder now.

"My bet is that they leave right after the speeches tomorrow night."

"Please!" Lana Mae exclaims. "I give them 'til after the ceremony."

"You're on." I stick my hand out and we shake. And though we're both smiling, making light of it all, there's a sadness below the surface. For the person who's missing today, the person who'd be loving every minute of this. The sting of my mother's absence is particularly pronounced at big events like these.

"Should we get our seats before we have to encounter Dad again?" Lana Mae mumbles.

"Definitely." I nod, look down at Legs. "Wanna save seats for us? Annie too?"

"Yup!" Legs takes off for the dining room with Lana Mae in tow.

My gaze then zeroes in on the hazel eyes of my beautiful date.

She's finished her conversation with the curly-haired lady, and is making her way toward me with purpose. Her dress, coffee-colored, silky and gorgeous, moves fluidly over her curves as she walks.

"Wow," I breathe. "You look..."

"Like I might've broken my ankle on those stairs?" she finishes. "Yup."

I chuckle, already happier now that she's in my proximity. "I was going to say stunning."

She gives me a cheeky smirk. "That works, too."

"What was so terrifying on your phone that you almost faceplanted on the staircase?" I ask with a laugh.

Her face freezes for a split second. Then, she licks her lower lip before saying, "Maybe not the best time to talk about it."

My brow furrows. "Is everything okay?"

"Oh, yeah. All good."

I monitor her face, but she looks back at me placidly. Whatever it is, I know she'll tell me when she's ready. "Okay. Just as long as you're okay."

"I... it will be," she says with a bright smile.

I nod just as my eyes fall on an interaction across the room. My shoulders tense automatically. "In other news, I have something terrifying of my own to tell you: my dad and his wife have arrived."

She gives my arm a squeeze, then puffs out her chest and straightens her spine like she's preparing for battle. "Nothing I can't handle."

I stop in my tracks, spin her to face me. My hands slide over her shoulders and onto her back, slipping over the silky fabric of her dress. "Before we go in, I just want to thank you."

"For what?"

"For being here. You have no idea how much it means to me to have you here this weekend."

"Liam," her voice is soft and crackly, like bonfire kindling. "All I want is what's best for you. Always."

"I think *you* might be what's best for me," I reply, drawing her closer still.

That frozen look rushes back onto her face, but she blinks it away in a heartbeat.

"I hope so," she says seriously.

I know so.

I release her from my grasp and hold my hand out to her. She takes it, her fingers sliding through mine like we've held hands a thousand times.

"Let's do this thing."

40

ANNIE

Brené, my queen, what would you do if you were me? Telepathically deliver me your wisdom, oh wise one, I am begging you...

I offer up my silent plea as I shovel my dessert in my mouth to avoid talking. Boy, oh boy, am I in a picklier pickle than these weird pickled watermelon radishes on top of my otherwise perfectly good piece of chocolate cake.

I'll never understand fancy food. At the end of the day, I'm still my mother's daughter.

Despite the pickles on the dessert, this rehearsal dinner is beautiful—elegant, classy, intimate and just about perfect for Mindy and Luke. I'm so grateful to be here to celebrate the happy couple, and be with Liam in this moment.

But following the text message I got when I was making my way down here—the one that almost sent me tumbling down the staircase like a coffee-colored bowling ball—I also wanted to make my excuses, hop on the first plane to Boston, and personally deliver Justin a swift kick to the gonads. Or break into his apartment to put Nair in his shampoo.

That'd show him. The man was always so hung up about his hairline.

My blood continues to simmer as I glance at my phone on my lap. I'm not sure whether to be relieved or anxious about the fact that he hasn't texted again.

I take a gulp of my Prosecco to wash down my cake, full of nervous energy from having to sit through a three-course meal—a delicious one that I would've fully enjoyed had the nightmare ex not decided to make an appropriately nightmarish appearance.

Suddenly, I can't stand it anymore.

"Excuse me," I say to Liam, who's deep in conversation with one of Luke's friends. "Need to find the bathroom."

Tastefully chosen words as usual, Annie.

Liam looks at me with a smirk. "Don't hide in there too long."

Okay, so it might've been a lapse in judgment to admit to him recently that I hid in the bathroom on my first morning at SITL.

I pull a face at him, then practically sprint to the ladies, where I lock myself in a cubicle and check my phone.

Do Not Text Ever: Looks like your new boyfriend is my competition. May the best man win.

I read the message over and over, trying to work out Justin's angle. This text might seem innocuous enough, but I know how Justin operates. It was shocking enough to find out earlier that SITL was up against Financify for the Wiseman funding. But then, to find out that Justin himself was leading the charge in Financify's corner?

Horrifying.

There's something fishy about this. I don't trust it. Don't trust him.

But this is Luke and Mindy's weekend, and like I told Liam earlier, now is not the best time to talk about it. If we did, we'd only be speculating. I don't know what Justin is up to or what he wants, but he's clearly trying to cause trouble, and creating a scene by making a big deal out of what might just be a jealous, meaningless jab is not going to help anyone.

Besides, maybe I'm freaking out over nothing. Justin has a wife now, and a child on the way. Maybe he's just turned over a new leaf and this is his twisted way of showing it.

I don't know what his motivation is. But I do know that the only thing I can do right now is be the bigger person. And to do that, I need to stop hiding in bathrooms, get back out there, and be at the side of the man who brought me.

The only man I care to think about tonight.

The only man I care to think about in general.

I lock my phone and drop it back in my purse. *Bye, Justin.* You can't get to me.

I have more important things to think about.

Like Liam Freaking Donovan.

AKA, definitely the better man.

With that thought, I stride out of the bathroom with my head held high.

41

LIAM

It was all going so well.

We enjoyed our fantastic meal (yes, I indulged a little. Breaking all the rules here) at a long, barnwood table decorated with wildflowers and flickering candles. Annie and I were sitting with Lana Mae, Legs and a group of Luke and Mindy's friends, including Aiden—the guy I met last night—and his sister Jess—the curly-haired brunette Annie was talking to earlier.

Prosecco was poured liberally and toasts were made. Over salmon and baby potatoes and broccolini spears, Aiden's wife Courtney regaled us with tales from their honeymoon a year ago, which consisted of a roadtrip across the States and into Mexico with their three dogs ("fur babies," as Courtney called them). Plus a whole lot of making love in the most bizarre places they could find (Lana Mae had to cover Legs's ears a few times).

A giant flying saucer may have come up. I didn't dare ask questions.

But, as inappropriate as the conversation veered, Luke's friends were warm and hilarious and full of ridiculous stories.

At one point during the main course, Annie snuck her hand into mine, and though the gesture was small, the meaning felt enormous. How many events like this had I attended solo over the years? Or brought a woman I barely knew when I needed a date, a woman I didn't have any feelings for?

I never had a partner in crime, an equal, someone who was still there after the glitter of the evening was swept away.

I never realized it, but I was missing out.

And then, it all went wrong.

As dessert was winding down, people started mingling. Annie excused herself to go to the bathroom—right in time, it turns out. Because as soon as she left the table, Dad and Constance came over to say hello.

Or rather, tell us everything we're doing wrong with our lives.

"How's Allegra doing in school?" Dad asks Lana Mae now.

She sips her drink, sets down her glass, and tucks her hair behind her ear before she answers. "Why don't you ask her yourself?"

Beside her, Legs is happily playing Candy Crush and ignoring all the adult chat.

"Because I'm asking *you*, Lana Mae."

"Fine. She's doing just fine."

"And what is your definition of 'fine?' A's? C's? Skipping class to smoke pot in the bathroom?"

"Dad! She's eight, for goodness sakes."

"I hear kids start young these days. You've got to have a tight rein on your children. Bad grades are a slippery slope..."

Wow, this is rich. The Hypocrite of the Year award goes to Edward Donovan—the man who left us, barely saw us when we were growing up, and yet insists on managing our lives for us when he *does* show up.

And while I can't change who my father is, I can help Lana Mae out of this line of questioning. By volunteering as tribute.

"Dad," I cut in. "Did I tell you that I got a new tattoo?"

I did not get a new tattoo. But my father ranks tattoos next to getting C's and smoking pot in the bathroom on the list of behaviors he views as delinquent.

"Still doing that, are you?" Dad laughs humorlessly. "Thought you'd have grown out of that nonsense by now."

I could say the same to him. But I refrain.

"Nope," I say pleasantly.

"And who's that girl you're here with tonight?" Constance asks. "What happened to Tabitha?"

"Who?" I ask, taking an annoyed swig of my Prosecco. The bubbles go up my nose and I wish it was a whiskey on the rocks instead. I have a feeling I'm going to need something stronger than fizzy wine to get through this conversation.

"I sent you her contact information weeks ago. Her father is the CFO of a Fortune 500 company. Very wealthy family. Lots of connections."

"I have literally no idea who you're talking about."

Constance sighs deeply and purses her lips to take a sip of her lemon tea.

Dad—lucky him—*has* managed to acquire some whiskey, and he swirls the amber liquid in his crystal glass as he fixes me with a glare. "Maybe you should. Tabitha could've gotten you a good, stable job."

"I have a job," I say evenly.

Dad shakes his head and guffaws. "All this ridiculous gallivanting in 'start-ups' or whatever the word you young folk are using... It's not going to put food on the table, is

305

it? If you'd stuck with baseball, you'd have been set for life."

"I didn't want to stick with baseball." I wanted to be with my family. Like I said, no regrets. No matter what my father might think. "And anyways, it would have been a career in minor league at best. It's not like I was off to the MLB or anything."

Dad sighs. "You could have been, but you're too stubborn for your own good, Liam. And you need to think about your brother. He squandered an *excellent* career to join you in this little... endeavor. Gave up his job security and finances to pour money into your half-baked idea. But it's not too late; he could ask for his old job back. Make decent money to support his family."

The irony of my father's words is not lost on me. My mom raised three kids alone while working multiple jobs, and still, somehow, managed to make sure we wanted for nothing. Meanwhile, Dad was "so busy," he could only see us once a month. He missed multiple baseball games, swim galas, graduations, birthday dinners, you name it.

At some point, I simply stopped hoping that he'd come to my games. It was the right move, because he never did (until I got a full ride to college for baseball. Then, all of a sudden, he was very interested).

Sure, he provided us with grand gifts of laptops and designer sneakers when birthdays and Christmases rolled around, but what we actually wanted for was a father who was present. Who loved us and cared for us, instead of showing up once in a while to berate and criticize us. Got an A on an exam? *Why wasn't it an A+.* Won a silver medal at a sporting event? *Why wasn't it gold.*

Tonight is the first time I've seen my father in months, and it looks like nothing's changed. I've learned over the years to just shut it out, to meet his critical words with neutrality. Being upset or angry doesn't help anything—in fact, sometimes I think it prods him on. Like he secretly relishes the drama.

How he and my mother got along in the first place, I'll never know.

"Luke likes working with Liam," Lana Mae interjects, bless her heart.

I give my sister a grateful smile coupled with a small shake of my head. She shouldn't get involved. Her job as a group travel specialist is not *as* high on my Dad's complaint list—mostly because he gave up on her the second she became an unwed teenage mother. Now, he heaps all of his preposterous expectations on poor Allegra.

Dad fixes Lana Mae with a glare that is positively frigid. "Luke was on a path to success."

Was. Past tense.

What's left unsaid hangs in the air, heavy as storm clouds about to burst: after my failure to launch a baseball career, Luke was the only one he was vaguely proud of. Until I came up with the idea for SITL and screwed things up for him.

I scrub a hand over my face, mentally chewing over what sort of response I could possibly give to that. I refuse to let my father bait me like this.

But a sound cuts through my thoughts before I can open my mouth.

"Ahem!"

42

LIAM

I startle at the throat clearing, glance backwards.

Shoot, Annie!

What did she hear? I was so caught up in the conversation with my dad that I didn't even notice her.

By the look on her face, she's been standing there long enough that she's heard too much. I've got to find a way to get us out of this asap.

I step toward Annie. "Sorry you had to hear that, An—"

Annie's gaze is firmly on my father as she holds up a hand abruptly, cutting me off. Her expression is unlike anything I've seen in her before.

I shut right up.

"Mr. Donovan," Annie says, her voice clear and confident. She gives him a wide, slightly scary, smile. "You don't know me, but my name's Annie. You must be so proud of your beautiful family. To have a daughter who is smart and kind, and a wonderful mother to your granddaughter. To have a son who is so close with his brother that he gave up a job to work with him. And to have another son who has worked so hard to start such a wonderful company that he's able to employ a bunch of people—me, included—and garner the interest of a huge investor."

I swivel my head from Annie to my father, who is one hundred percent not used to being put in his place. Constance is pale, Lana Mae is hiding a shocked smile behind her hand, and my dad looks, well, vaguely stunned.

His eyebrows shoot up and he looks at me skeptically. "Investor, huh?"

"We haven't secured the investment yet," I cut in smoothly, not wanting to get ahead of anything.

Annie covers my hand with hers. Smiles. "But they will. They're a shoo-in," she says confidently, her eyes never leaving mine.

My gaze softens as I take in all her red-cheeked, indignant glory. Annie's got my back—got Luke's and Lana's backs too. And it feels, well... nice.

Unfortunately, the moment is short-lived. My dad's expression goes from surprised to smug as his eyes zero in on our clasped hands.

"Word of advice, *dear*," he says coldly. "If Liam is, indeed, your employer, I suggest you think twice about sleeping with the boss to get ahead."

Annie reels backwards like she's been slapped, and a surge of white-hot anger blinds me.

"Never, ever speak to her like that again," I say in a low, steely growl.

My father blinks. Dabs the corner of his mouth with a napkin. "Excuse me?"

I drop my voice to a hiss. My hand reaches for Annie's as I keep my eyes on my father. "You can go after me and criticize my life choices all you want, but don't you dare talk to Annie like that. In fact, do her a favor and don't talk to her at all. Stay the hell away from her altogether."

My dad's eyes are bugging out of his face, but he makes a strange huffing sound that I take to be an affirmation.

"Good." I glance at Annie, and my demeanor and voice both automatically soften. "Want to get out of here?"

She nods, her eyes huge.

I throw an apologetic look in Lana Mae's direction and I'm relieved to see that Legs is still happily locked into Candy Crush on her mom's phone, swinging her legs. She didn't hear any of that.

"Sorry," I say to my sister.

She smirks in return, clearly enjoying herself. "Not at *all*. Legs and I were just about to leave, too."

"Good night, everyone," I say, purposely not looking at my father and Constance, who are both still frozen in some kind of shock.

Annie gives a wobbly smile. "Nice to meet you."

She's a ray of sunshine even now. I don't deserve her.

And the least I can do is get her out of here. I kiss Legs on the top of the head, then drag Annie by the hand through the dining hall, into the foyer and out to the grounds of the ranch.

My hand tightens around hers as I stride forward, static buzzing in my ears. The night is cool and breezy, but I'm burning. Burning with shame and humiliation and... anger. The feeling is foreign. Heavy.

I can't remember the last time I let myself feel my anger. Feel the enormity of the screwed up situation that is my relationship with my dad. How much I miss my mom.

For so long after she died, I was emotionally drained. Shut down. But tonight, here with Annie, it's like she's torn down my walls.

Right now, she's silent at my side, skipping slightly as she overcompensates to match my pace. She casts a worried look in my direction but doesn't ask anything.

When we're at the creek, standing by the water in the moonlight, wind whistling through the trees and not a soul in sight, I stop. Drop her hand.

"Annie," I begin, unsure what to say. Where to start. How can I begin to explain?

She looks up with such a kind understanding in her eyes, it makes my heart ache. She presses her palm to my chest, spreading her fingers over my heart, which is pounding erratically.

"You don't owe me an explanation," she says simply.

There's a long, long pause that stretches through the night, carving a cavern between us. In the moonlit sparkle of her eyes, a million words pass unsaid between us. And because verbal expressions aren't my strength—because the words I want to say are stuck in my throat—my natural instinct is to shut down. Clam up.

But Annie deserves more than that. I can do better—be better—than that.

"I owe you so much," I say. "An explanation is just one of those things."

She nods, accepting this. "Okay."

"Shall we sit?" I nod to some Adirondack chairs nearby, and we take a seat. The evening breeze is cool and crisp, and I shrug off my jacket and hand it to her. She immediately accepts it, which makes me smile.

"So your dad really is difficult," Annie begins.

I take a deep breath, and then, finally, I let my guard down. Let my control go. And I speak.

"Growing up, I was always trying to impress him. My parents divorced when I was really young, and I didn't see my dad much. I think, in my head, I built him up to be this awesome guy who'd love me if I just got his attention by being better." I pull a face. "I was obviously wrong. My mom was constantly fielding his failures so we wouldn't be

311

disappointed. Drying tears over missed promises, visits, you name it. But for some reason, I still craved my dad's approval. And one day, it came. When I got my baseball scholarship—a full ride to UCLA. Suddenly, I was the apple of his eye. And, being the idiot I was, I was happy about this," I finish darkly.

Annie shakes her head, auburn waves blowing in the wind. "It's perfectly normal to want to feel loved by your parents."

"Maybe, but I put his approval ahead of other things that mattered. He was happy I was playing college baseball, happy I was majoring in finance. And I thought I was happy, too. I met a girl out there. Had a life. I put myself above my own family here."

I sigh, exhaling a long breath. "When Lana Mae got pregnant, I wasn't there for her. I stayed in California. Didn't even meet Legs until I came home for a week or two the following summer." My voice is getting heavy, laced with emotion. "That's when I found out that Mom was sick. Had been for a while. She, as usual, downplayed it. Made everything about me, not her. Encouraged me to go back to college when the summer ended, and I went."

Annie shifts slightly, moving closer to me, but she doesn't say a word.

"I was planning to come home for Thanksgiving." I swallow thickly. "But there was a big training camp, and I ended up choosing to go to the camp." There are tears in my eyes now, the foreign wetness rimming the edges. "And she died, Annie. She died and I wasn't there. I missed seeing the person I loved most on earth one last time because I was trying to impress a father who didn't love me. I've never been able to forgive myself."

I stop talking for a moment to catch my breath. I lost everything that Thanksgiving, and reliving it is physically painful. These feelings, these memories, have been buried deep for so long, and digging them up for the first time makes them fresh and raw again.

Annie's sitting stock still, eyes fixed on me.

"You must think I'm the worst..." I trail off. And then, her arms are around me. She's gotten out of her chair so she can crouch in front of me, and her cheek presses against mine as she pulls me close.

"You're a good person, Liam," she says fiercely, clutching me tight. "So good. And it's not your fault, what happened. It was never your fault. None of it."

"I should have been there." My voice cracks as I pull back to look at her, shame still coursing through me. "After that, I swore I'd never let my family down again. I quit college, broke up with my girlfriend, and moved home to Atlanta, where I belong."

"Your family loves you more than words can say," Annie's words are thick with emotion. "You've given Legs the father figure she didn't have—the father figure *you* didn't have. I've never come across a man like you in my life. You don't even realize how incredible you are."

I exhale slowly, feeling a strange, if a little embarrassed, relief to have finally spoken all of that aloud. All of the junk that I've been holding in for so long, trying to control every little thing in my life so that no more bad things happen.

Until Annie came along, and I realized that good things —truly good things—can't happen either if I don't occasionally let go and lean into the moment.

And this moment is one I want to lean into with all that I have.

I move closer to her, and her hands tangle in my hair as my arms wrap around her waist. My thumbs trace the curve of her ribcage as I pull her toward me. And then I'm kissing her. Kissing her like my life depends on it. I show her every little detail of the way I feel for her as my mouth moves over hers. She responds, arching her back and returning the kiss. It's soft, at first.

Then harder.

Her breath goes ragged and I breathe her in, pull her closer as I take my time with her. Our bodies press against each other and I kiss her with wholehearted purpose and intent as I lead the way in this star-soaked moment of pure bliss. Her fingernails scrape my shoulders, her lips are on my neck, my hands are in her hair as my teeth graze a sensitive spot by her ear that makes her shiver.

With every kiss, every caress, every touch and inhale and sigh and sensation, I pour all of my feelings into her, trying to communicate with every fiber of my being that I adore her. That I'd do anything for her.

And when we finally break apart, breathing heavily, skin hot and flushed against the cool night air, I see on her face that she feels the same.

43

ANNIE

I'm on fire.

I cannot for the life of me manage to get my body to cool off and relax: I take a tepid shower and change into my favorite purple space-themed pjs, brush my teeth and pop my retainer in. I wash my face and apply serum, moisturizer, and then a sticky layer of Vaseline to hold it all in (it's called "slugging," and according to TikTok, it stops you getting forehead wrinkles, okay?).

Then, I take my contacts out and peer blindly at myself in the mirror. You'd think a mouthful of plastic, a faceful of petroleum jelly, and frumpy pajamas with Jupiter on the front would put me in a less sexy mood. But apparently not.

Each and every one of those searing kisses left a brand on me. Burned me, marked me, to the point that, over an hour later, my skin is still hot, my lips are still swollen, and my head is still full of cartoon hearts swirling around in a dizzying circle.

After that disaster of a first meeting with his father, Liam whisked me away to the riverside, and poured his heart out to me.

Then, we kissed for what felt like forever before he broke away from me, checked his watch, and reluctantly commented on how late it was. Said that he should get me back to my room safe and sound.

I wanted to yank the watch right off his wrist and toss it in the river, scream at the top of my lungs "but I'm not done with you yet! You can't just get me all worked up and then suggest we stop kissing so we can sleep! Who needs sleep, anyway?!"

But obviously, that might've looked a tad insane. And it really was late—Liam was probably exhausted from putting those incredible lips to such good use.

So instead of having a tantrum, I let him walk me back to my room. I practically swooned in the hallway as he chastely kissed me goodnight, like he was a perfect gentleman who hadn't just spent the last hour devouring me. As he walked away, his eyes held a devilish secret glint that told me he was replaying every single second of it in his mind.

As I have been ever since he left.

Despite our obstacles—me being his employee, the unconventional way we met—this doesn't feel like a mistake at all.

I've never been one to believe in the universe and the stars aligning and all that nonsense. But I do believe I've found true love—and if the universe aligned for that to happen... well, I'll just have to be happy that I was wrong about all that fate stuff.

For so long, I focused on my mistakes. Was desperate not to make another one. But in this moment, I can see that my "mistakes" have led me here, to Liam.

It's where I want to be.

He's who I want to be with.

He's taught me so much about being selfless and putting other people's needs before your own. And right now, all I want to do is put him first. Let him know he comes first.

Before I know it, I'm on my feet and running down the hallway, barefoot and scrunchie-haired and greasy-faced as can be.

When I get to his room, I knock loudly.

Knock again.

Eventually, a bleary-eyed, tousle-haired Liam answers. Wearing only a pair of flannel pajama pants.

Holy freaking mother of all cannolis.

When Liam sees me, the corners of his mouth lift.

"Hey, you." He rubs his palm over his eye. "Nice space get-up."

Then, he sees my expression. Raises a brow. "Is everything okay?"

"Can I... come in?"

He doesn't hesitate. He simply steps aside, holds the door open for me.

His room smells like him.

I stand there, hovering awkwardly in the middle of the space and trying not to focus too much on the grand king bed at the center.

"So." He gives me a lopsided little smile as he comes to stand in front of me. "You're here because..."

"I love you!" I practically shout. "I love you, Liam, and I don't want to keep this quiet or keep things between us. I want to be with you, for real."

Liam's dark eyes soften, melt like chocolate. "I love you, too, Annie Jacobs. More than my words could ever say."

He opens his arms to me and I step in. I trace the white scar on his cheek, delighting in the way he shivers at my touch. Then, I nuzzle my head onto his shoulder, press my hand to his chest, and spread my palm across his heart. His inked skin is warm, soft above hard muscle. I feel that sweet heart pulse beneath my touch.

"Did you really get a new tattoo?" I ask.

His chest vibrates as he chuckles. "No, but I'm going to have to soon."

"What do you mean?"

"Well... I started getting tattoos after my mom died. It was hard to talk, to communicate, so I used them to tell a story. My story."

I move my head back so I can study the beautiful ink on his body. "And you need a new one soon because...?"

Liam smiles that devastating smile. "A whole new chapter of my story has just begun."

Tears prick the back of my eyes, and I pull him toward me. Everything he shared with me tonight broke my heart. I'm so sad that he had to go through what he did, but so grateful for the person he is.

"I might have to get a tattoo too, then," I say in a small voice.

He hugs me tighter. I've never felt as safe as I do right here, right now, in his arms.

"Do you want to stay here tonight, Annie?" he murmurs, holding onto me like he never wants to let go.

I nod.

Without another word, I climb into his bed. Without another word, he gently pulls the covers up over me, leans across to tuck me in. Then, he pushes a stray lock of hair off my forehead before sliding into bed behind me, drawing my body close and enveloping it with his.

His bare chest is hot against my back, and one of his big hands splays across my stomach as he holds me to him.

Before long, his breathing slows, gets heavy with sleep.

I, on the other hand, stay awake as long as I can, trying to savor every moment of this beautiful night.

44

LIAM

A sliver of sunlight streams through a crack in the curtains and dances over my eyes, pulling me from sleep.

I'm so warm, so comfortable... and Annie is in my arms.

I smile into her shoulder, dropping a kiss on the nape of her neck as I breathe her in. Her sweet ocean smell is a scent I would recognize anywhere, would be able to pick out of a crowd of thousands if I had to.

This is the second time I've held her all night, but waking up couldn't feel more different.

She loves me. And I love her.

Before, I was filled with panic, fear and uncertainty—about her, about myself, about the entire situation. But this morning, I have the most achingly perfect sense of calm imaginable.

Crazy that her run-in with an ex-boyfriend would put in motion the most incredible series of events. Events that I wouldn't change for the world.

I lie still a little longer, soaking in the moment.

Up until now, this thing growing between us has been a rocky road, filled with external obstacles, but that's all about to change. We both deserve better. Both deserve a proper chance at real happiness, real love... because that's what I'm feeling right now. Nothing but love.

I've heard that love can make a man do crazy things. But what I want to do, it's not so crazy, is it? What's crazy about stopping at nothing to be with the woman you adore?

I'm sure we can explain our relationship to Wiseman in a reasonable way. And if I have to choose between Annie and work, I choose her. I'll always choose her. Every single time.

Forget my rules, my HR policies, my carefully written manual. Luke was right all along: I wrote it for all the wrong reasons. Placed unfair constraints on both myself and my employees in an effort to keep everything neat and orderly.

But love isn't neat or orderly, is it?

So, the first thing I need to do when I get back to the city tomorrow is rewrite the rules.

Color outside the lines.

Stop living in fear of what might happen if I just let go.

Reluctantly, I check the time and realize I'd better get ready. My brother's getting married today and I've got a best man job to do.

I shift out of my big spoon position and prop myself on my elbows. Push a stray lock of hair out of Annie's angelic, peacefully sleeping face and lean down to kiss her goodbye.

"Screw HR policies," I say softly. "I want to tell the world you're mine, Annie Jacobs."

45

ANNIE

I wake up in Liam's bed alone.

"Mmm," I sigh aloud, as I roll over in the warm sheets and glance at the window, where bright daylight is glowing from behind the curtains.

Goodness me, what time is it? I slept like the dead last night. Down for the count. I can't remember the last time I slept so well. Liam's arms are now my official favorite place to sleep. Tried and tested not once, but twice.

I grin to myself as I throw off the covers, climb out of bed, and open the curtains. The sunshine is dazzling... and remarkably high in the sky.

Shoot! I bet it's so late, I'll have to rush to get ready for the wedding. Liam likely left ages ago to commence his best man duties for the day.

I can't wait to see him, standing there by Luke's side. Looking all sexy in a tux.

Cheerily, I practically skip back to my room, where my dress for today is hanging up outside the wardrobe, ready to go.

I grab my glasses from my nightstand and shove them on my nose. Then, I grab my phone.

Four unread text messages? Since when am I this popular?

I flop on the bed and open the first.

Liam: Good morning, beautiful. Hope you slept okay. Getting ready with Luke and the guys now. I love you.

Liam: FRICK it feels good to say that.

I laugh out loud at this.

Annie: Love you too, sexy tux man.

The next message is from Prisha.

Prisha: I am going to need picture evidence of your weekend getaway to the ranch with McSwoony. Seriously. Pics or it didn't happen. And there better be horses involved.

I laugh again. Great minds think alike. I snap a picture of the view outside my window and text it to her.

Annie: I've seen horses, but so far, no actual riding off into the sunset. Although Liam did promise to make that happen, so we shall see...

A reply comes in immediately.

Prisha: You are living the sexy cowgirl dream.

I snort. Close out of the message thread. With a breath sucked in through gritted teeth, I realize the last one is from Justin. What now?

Do Not Text Ever: No text back, huh? You're obviously not too concerned about a potential HR nightmare.

My heart picks up speed as I read, then re-read his words.

I stare at the message until the screen goes fuzzy.

I was able to pass off his text last night as an attempt to stir the pot. I was able to forget about it and move on. But maybe that wasn't the right way to deal with it... Because this looks more sinister. Way more sinister.

I mean, SITL and Financify are against each other for funding. Could he be trying to play dirty?

But I can solve this. Pretty easily, in fact. All I have to do is tell him the truth. I don't care what he thinks of me anymore, don't care how pathetic I'm going to look... all I care about is getting Liam and SITL out of the crosshairs of whatever *this* is.

Annie: Whatever you think is happening... you've got the wrong idea.

There. Send.

Buzz!

I drop my phone like it gave me an electric shock. Gingerly, I pick the phone back up and swipe open the screen.

Do Not Text Ever: Nice try, Annie Bananie. You checked into the same room.

I freeze, my palms so cold and clammy that I barely register the buzz as the next message comes in.

Do Not Text Ever: Sleeping with your new boss before you even start the job? Tsk tsk *winky face emoji* Honestly, I didn't think you had it in you.

Annie: You're wrong. That's not what happened. I was shocked to see you and Veronica at the hotel and I reacted by pretending Liam Donovan was my boyfriend. He went along with it to be nice. I didn't even work for him at the time.

There, the truth will set you free, or whatever they say.

Do Not Text Ever: Really though, does it matter if I'm right or wrong? Think about it. Whatever the context, checking into a hotel with a brand new employee-to-be doesn't paint your new boyfriend in a good light. Especially with Wiseman's interest in HR protocols.

My blood chills, dampening and cooling any residual heat from Liam's warm bed.

The sudden coldness is icy. Sharp.

Annie: What do you want?

Do Not Text Ever: Make your boyfriend pull his bid for funding.

My heart is in my stomach and my throat is raw and scratchy when I swallow, like I've been eating shrapnel.

Annie: You can't ask me to do that.

Do Not Text Ever: Well, let's put it this way: I don't think Wiseman plays with HR grenades ready to blow.

That weasel.

Annie: So you're blackmailing me.

Do Not Text Ever: Oh, Bananie. It's not blackmail. Blackmail's personal. This is just business.

My chest is pulsing and I feel sick to my stomach. I'm disgusted with Justin. Disgusted with myself that I could've dated a man like that.

Because it's not even a personal vendetta or a revenge plan. It's all business. Cold, calculated business. People like Justin stop at nothing to get ahead in their careers. People's feelings, reputations... they're all fair game as long as he gets what he wants.

Do Not Text Ever: Do it this way and everyone wins. Well, I win. You just avoid a senseless HR scandal. I know you're smart, Bananie. Be smart about this.

I feel like firing my phone at the wall. Watching it smash into the plaster and shatter into a million little insidious, vitriol-coated pieces.

But, as a pacifist with the throwing arm of an uncoordinated five-year-old, I settle for beating my fists on the duvet.

The flabby punches make me feel stupid, so I roll onto my back instead, staring blankly at the ceiling. The crown molding around the light is really pretty. Fancy. Pristine and perfect. The opposite of how I feel right now.

How could everything go wrong so quickly? Everything that felt so perfect between Liam and me last night now feels muddied by my past coming back to haunt me.

What have I done?

And, more pressingly, what am I going to do now?

It really is a beautiful day for a beautiful wedding.

Luke and Mindy are married in the mid-afternoon sunshine in an intimate outdoor ceremony under the willow tree in the ranch's gardens. She's radiant in white lace, and he's glowing with pride and happiness.

The smell of honeysuckle carries through the warm breeze, and the creek gurgles approvingly in the distance as the officiant pronounces the happy couple man and wife. Luke sweeps Mindy off her feet in a showstopping kiss. And from his position at the front, heartbreakingly handsome as he looks out onto the crowd, Liam's eyes find mine.

My heart constricts. This might be a celebration, but for me, it's the unthinkable: I've gotten myself into a situation that feels horribly familiar.

Only this time, I've fallen in love with a man who's an innocent bystander.

I bite my lip so hard I taste metal as Luke and Mindy descend the aisle hand in hand to a roaring standing ovation. Clap as hard as I can, palms stinging as I smack them together, trying to drown out the noise in my head.

The thoughts of the conversation I'll have to have with

Liam tonight, when the wedding's over, flip over in my head. I don't want to break this news to him today, on such a happy day, but I know I can't keep him in the dark.

When you strike a match and keep it isolated, it burns out in mere seconds. Extinguished in a couple of heartbeats. But if you hold that same match to something flammable —*boom!*—you can create an inferno. So really, when holding a lit match, you're actually holding the potential to set the world on fire, or to let it fizzle away to nothing.

It's how you apply it that matters.

Right now, that match is in my hands. And when this thing goes up in flames, Liam's going to be the one who gets burned.

That thought physically hurts.

Dinner and speeches follow the ceremony. Mindy's maid of honor—her sister Holly—is hilarious as she regales the crowd with tales of the girls' recent trip to Vegas. Then, Liam takes the mic.

His best man speech is impressive. Funny and heartfelt and clearly full of love. He honors their late mother, and his close bond with his older brother, and there's not a dry eye in the house when he's done. Even Mr. Donovan Sr., AKA my new least favorite person (well, it's a toss-up between Justin and him. They both deserve the Nair in the shampoo treatment equally), looks vaguely moved.

By the time the last toasts are given, the cake is cut, and the band makes their way onto the stage of a fairy-light-illuminated marquee, it's already getting late. Poor little Legs, who's stuffed to the brim with overexcitement and vanilla sponge cake, is trying to keep her drooping eyes open. She's wilting like a wildflower in her crumpled, soda-stained, floofy dress, while Lana Mae speaks sweet words to her.

I watch Mindy and Luke hold each other as they have

their first dance. They move in sync, gazes locked, bodies pressed together.

I can't tear my eyes away from them. I'm so happy for their happiness.

A warm hand slides across my lower back, making me jump. But I recognize the confident, strong touch almost immediately. Lean into it automatically.

"Hey, you," Liam says as he comes to stand behind me, wrapping his arms around me and resting his chin on my head. "Between photos and speeches and being Luke's errand boy all day, I feel like I've barely seen you."

I twist around so I can face him. Across the room, couples are making their way onto the dance floor to join the newlyweds.

"Do you want to dance?" I'm stalling. Like a coward.

"Sure."

Hand in hand, we make our way to the center of the swaying couples. He puts his hands on my hips, resting them on the small of my back. I wind my arms around his neck and draw him close, never wanting to let go.

"Annie, is everything okay?" Shrewd and intuitive as ever, Liam is peering down at me, concern flickering in those dark, dark eyes of his.

On this dance floor, in Liam's arms, it should be a perfect moment. But it's not. "Do you ever wish things could be different?"

"How so?"

"Less... complicated."

He pauses thoughtfully, running his fingers along my spine as our bodies slowly sway together. "Yes and no. I'm glad our complications have brought us to this moment. And on that, about what you said last night, I agree. I want to come clean to Wiseman. Tell him the truth, lay it out on the table. If it causes an issue with him funding SITL, we'll just have to handle that from there. But, honestly, if we're upfront about it, I can't see it being too big of a deal—it's not like we've committed a crime or anything."

Liam's smiling now, but my palms are sweaty, and I'm beginning to feel a little seasick.

If he goes to Wiseman when we're back in the office tomorrow, it'll be too late. Justin will have alerted him to our supposed indiscretion at the airport hotel, and it'll look like he's only coming clean because he got caught.

Nobody will ever believe that we got together naturally over the course of weeks. That nothing happened between us physically before I started at SITL. That night at the hotel will look the opposite of the innocent rooming accident it was. Liam will be painted as a boss abusing his power with a new female employee, and I will look like a woman who uses my sexuality to get ahead in the workplace.

No one in their right mind would touch that kind of HR nightmare with their investment money.

Liam brushes my chin with the backs of his fingers, gently tilting it upwards so he can look at me. "Hey, don't worry so much. Worrying is my job, remember? You're meant to be the spontaneous, carefree one. Every relationship needs one of each, right?"

He's so sweet, so sincere, and I'm holding back tears now. "Liam, what if us being together screws things up for your company?" I press. I need to know just how badly this is going to bruise him. "What if it all goes wrong and, because of me, you let down Luke?" I swallow. "Lose everything you've worked for."

He pauses, and I see a hint of worry in his eye. It's only there for a brief second, but I see it clearly.

"I'll figure out another way," he says resolutely. "We have a great userbase, there's money coming in. It just won't

330

be the scale-up we were hoping for. We might have to scale back a little, but I will make it work. I know I will."

And there it is: Not *we*, but *I*.

Liam still sees all of this as his battle to fight. He's carrying so much responsibility on his shoulders, has employees to think about. Luke to think about. And I know he's thinking about Legs and her future, too. Because he's Liam, so of course he is.

What he's been working toward for years is on the line. He wants to take care of his family. Feel like a success. His dreams are currently right on his doorstep, but I'm standing in the way.

It's actually almost laughable: the entire time, I've been worried whether it's a mistake for me to fall for him. I never, ever stopped to consider if it was a mistake for him to fall for me.

And that's when I know, in my heart of hearts, that I can't just tell him the truth and let this mess happen. I need to snuff out the match before anything catches fire. My stupid fake boyfriend stunt at the hotel caused this problem, so now, I need to fix it. Not Liam. Me.

Because if there's one thing I can't bear to be, it's Liam Donovan's biggest mistake.

And while I can't control the outcome... at least I can try.

"I promise that this will all work out just fine, Annie. For SITL, and for us." He's calm. Quietly full of hope.

I take a deep breath. "Liam... I need to go."

"Oh yeah? Why's that?" He thinks I'm joking. Looks down at me and smiles that devastating smile. The one that usually rips me into a thousand pieces then puts them all back together.

This time, the pieces stay scattered on the floor like confetti.

The night air is warm, cloying, beneath the twinkling stars. The breeze smells like sweetgrass and the promise of summer.

But in this moment, I feel nothing but cold, wintry disbelief as I stand in the driveway, staring at the dust still swirling above the gravel road that stretches toward the edge of the property as I attempt to make sense of what just happened.

Annie's gone.

She called an Uber to take her to the train station. And then, she just got in the car and drove away. It took everything in me not to run after her, waving my arms and shouting "Wait!"

I refrained. Obviously.

She wouldn't tell me what she was doing, where she was going—just that it was an urgent problem that she had to solve.

That I'd see her in a couple of days.

There was a weighted look in her eyes that told me something was wrong. That there was much more to this.

With all the questions she was asking as we danced, I thought maybe she changed her mind from what she said last night. I asked her if I was moving too fast, talking about telling everyone at work about our relationship. That we could put the brakes on if that's what she needed. But she insisted that wasn't the case, that she was fine. That I stay. "You don't always have to solve everyone's problems, Liam."

Her startling insistence shook me. I'm entirely perplexed by what on earth changed when everything between us last night had felt so right.

But she wanted to go, so I let her. I didn't like it one bit.

When my mom died—when I realized I belonged in Atlanta with Luke and Lana Mae and Legs instead of in California with my baseball career—that was an easy decision to make. It made sense. Sure, breaking up with my girlfriend sucked. Dropping out of college sucked. But I knew it was right. The choice was simple.

But tonight, watching Annie drive away without an explanation, I realized that, for the first time in many years, my priorities have shifted. Everything in my life is not in neat, orderly, carefully controlled boxes anymore.

I've allowed myself to feel. To experience love. And it's like realizing that I've been living in the dark all these years.

I am where I'm at today because of Luke quitting his job and getting behind SITL, both with his time and with his money. I'm finally in a position that, if we secure this funding, I can pay him back. Give our staff job security for the future. Start investing in Legs' future with a college fund for her—Lana Mae's a single mom on a small salary, and I want Legs to have the brightest future imaginable. It's a responsibility any good father figure would take for their daughter. And I love Legs more than life itself.

But I also love Annie.

Somebody finally flipped a light on, and everything is illuminated. Because of her.

"Hey!" Lana Mae's voice carries through the night. "There you are!"

I look up to see my sister making her way toward me, wobbling on her heels as she navigates the gravel driveway.

She stops when she sees my face. "Liam, you okay? Where's Annie?"

"She had to leave."

She stares at me in puzzlement. "What do you mean, leave?"

I feel weirdly closed-off, like I don't want to talk. Like all of the emotions I finally tapped into left me right along with Annie.

But they didn't. They're within me. And I know that, to move forward and grow, I have to not only be open and honest with Annie, like she's taught me to do, but also with the other people in my life that I love.

"She went to the train station. She had an emergency or something."

"An emergency? You let her take the train alone? What's wrong with you?" Lana's voice has gone up about two octaves with sheer indignancy.

"She didn't want me to come, Lana. And I don't know why she left in the first place." I rub the base of my hand over my eye, suddenly exhausted. "I told her I wanted to tell Tim about us, and she got all weird and bolted."

"Well what on earth are you still doing here, then?"

"It's Luke's wedding."

Lana clicks her tongue in indignance. "No, I mean, why haven't you gone after her?"

"I have to be here tonight. I need to be here for Luke, and for you and Legs. What if Dad goes at you again? I'll need to fend him off."

"Excuse me?!" Lana practically shrieks. She jabs me in the chest. "First off, I can fend for myself, thank you very much. Secondly, what kind of a man lets the woman he loves leave so he can be there for his SISTER?"

Well. When she puts it like *that*.

"That's not how it was. Annie wanted to do whatever this is alone."

"And I'm sure she's fully capable of doing whatever she's doing alone. I don't mean you need to be her knight in shining armor, this isn't medieval times. But for the record, you don't need to be mine, either. Or Allegra's."

"I'll always be there for Legs," I say staunchly. "I won't let her go through what we did with Dad."

"But she's not your daughter, Liam. She's my daughter. And while I so deeply appreciate everything you've done to give her a father figure, I'm telling you that spending your entire life trying to make up for something that she doesn't even remember is not going to help either of you." Lana Mae is the fiercest I've ever seen her. "You are nothing like Dad. Never have been, never will be. And I'm so thankful that she has you to look up to as an example of what to look for in a man."

She jabs me in the chest again. "But that means putting *yourself* first every once in awhile. The best thing for Allegra is for her to see you happily married with a wife you adore, and hope that one day she can find a good man to marry, too."

My head is spinning. I've never thought of it this way. Never taken a moment to consider that prioritizing my own happiness could contribute to fulfilling the needs of others, too.

"And if Annie is that woman for you, you need to be there for *her* first. Whatever this is she's dealing with right now. Not to save her, but to support her."

"What's with all the commotion?" I look up to see Luke striding toward us, bow tie hanging loose around his half-unbuttoned dress shirt.

"Annie left and Liam didn't go after her."

"WHAT? WHY?"

"That's what I said!" Lana Mae crows.

"It's your wedding, Luke, I couldn't leave."

Luke rolls his eyes dramatically. "No offence, little bro, but if this was your wedding and Mindy left, I'd go after her. I love you and all, but I love Mindy more."

His words are an icy water bucket of realization.

How on earth could I have let her leave?

"Liam," Luke goes on. "You do know that you owe us nothing, right? Literally and figuratively. I invested in SITL because I believed in it. Believed in you. Not because I wanted to have something to hold over you. I don't ever want you to feel like you're indebted to me. Whatever happens with the funding, I don't give a damn. I love you and all I want is to see you happy."

This touches my heart. Love isn't about paying back dues, or keeping score, or penance for things you wish you'd done differently. It's about not only forgiving others for being imperfect sometimes but letting them forgive you for the same. I may not have always been there for my family, but I'm here now. And I'm forgiven. And my happiness is important, too.

Annie is my happy. The love of my life.

Real love, love that makes you lose sleep, love that makes you say and do crazy things, love that makes you crave a person like a drug every time they're not near, that type of love only comes around once in a lifetime.

I'll be damned if I'm going to let that slip through my fingers.

"Um, hey guys?"

"Yes?" my siblings chorus.

"Two things." I clear my throat. "First of all, thank you. Secondly, if you'll excuse me, I gotta go. Like, now."

Luke raises his eyebrows smugly. "It's about time, idiot."

48

ANNIE

"Excuse me. Sorry. Coming through. Pardon me." I repeat the words flatly as I move down the center aisle of the train, trying my best not to whack all the unfortunate aisle-seaters with my duffel bag.

I'm right on time for this particular form of public transit. Nice to see I've finally broken the habit of a lifetime.

Unfortunately for me, though, when I get to my designated seat, I discover that there is no handsome, grumpy stranger next to me. Instead, there's a teenage boy with his finger up his nose.

Charming.

I sink into my chair and rest my head in my hands, breathing in the cold, stale AC that's blasting on me as I gather my thoughts. Or try to.

Since I left Liam at the ranch, since I ran away from the person I loved with no explanation, my head has been a jumbled mess. Forget coloring outside the lines, my mind is one big scribble.

Should I have told him? Let him help?

I so badly didn't want to heap yet another responsibility

on his shoulders, give him yet another problem to solve. But not being honest with him feels wrong.

Across the aisle, a pair of elderly ladies are drinking tea and reading Danielle Steel books. They remind me of Rosemary and Mildred, from the very plane ride that brought Liam and I together. The thought of them makes me smile despite myself.

Until that day, I never believed in wonders of the universe or fate or stars aligning. Thought it was all nonsense.

But now, I believe that everything happened that day for a reason.

I was meant to meet Liam. It's so clear to me that we're meant to be together. And I'm going to do everything in my power to fix this mess. Beating myself up about what I did in the past isn't going to help me right now, nor Liam. I need to take action, move past it. I quoted Brené Brown about this very thing recently when I was talking to Liam—"regret is necessary to facilitate change and growth."

When I really think about it, my regrets have shaped change in me that was good. Healthy.

And that change in me is what's empowered me to take action instead of wallow.

The thought is empowering: in this life, we're not summaries of our mistakes. We're merely shaped by them.

And what my past has shaped me into is someone who fights for who and what they love.

The train lurches into motion and a static-y crackle over the intercom announces that we're on our way.

I gaze out the window as the dark, shadowy scenery beyond the train begins to move.

There's a rustle of movement in the aisle as someone makes their way to their seat. Must've made the train just in the nick of time. Been there.

"Sorry I'm late." The voice comes from somewhere above me. "I'd say it was because a squirrel broke into my car, but it's actually because I was busy being the biggest idiot on the planet."

It's a deep, achingly familiar voice that makes me turn in my seat.

"Liam?" I can hardly believe it. But there he is, still in his freaking tuxedo, lurching and wobbling in the center aisle as he tries to stay balanced with the train's jerky movement. As usual, he is a sight to behold. "What are you doing here?"

"Taking a train to..." He pauses and squints at the little screen at the end of the train car. "Wait, Hartsfield-Jackson? We're going to the airport?"

Before I can reply, he slides into the empty seat across from me. Eyes the teenage nose-picker. "Hey, dude. Wanna make fifty bucks in five seconds?"

The young guy's face lights up. "Bruh! Do I!"

Liam hands him a folded up bill. "I'll pay you fifty dollars to go sit somewhere else."

"Dude, why would you do that?" The boy snatches the money in awe. "There are like a hundred empty seats."

Liam doesn't take his eyes off me. "It's part of my grand gesture... I need to show my girlfriend I love her. That I'm always here for her. And, you see, it all started with a seat swap."

There's a bubble in my chest, getting bigger by the second.

The kid doesn't need to be told twice. He beams at Liam, grabs his bags, and is gone in a flash.

With a satisfied nod, Liam moves to sit next to me.

"Hi," he says.

"Hi yourself," I reply, the memory of our first kiss tingling on my skin.

"Annie, I don't know where you're going or what you're doing right now, but I know that I want to be by your side for the journey. Whatever that looks like." He stops. Smiles. "It was a mistake not leaving with you tonight, because being by each other's side, through good and bad, is what comes first. It's what you do when you love someone."

Everything in my body is warm. Soft. Swirling with emotions.

But I have to tell him the truth.

"Liam. I love you. But there's something you need to know. I left because Justin's blackmailing me. He threatened to tell Wiseman that we hooked up before I started working at SITL and get us kicked out of the running for the funding."

Liam looks at me blankly. "And sorry, forgive my ignorance, but how was going to the airport going to solve that?"

"I was going to fly to Boston so I could kick Justin in the nuts."

Liam nods in approval. "That's my girl."

I sigh. "Um, I guess I didn't really have a plan. I knew I couldn't let Justin blackmail me, but I was at a loss. I thought that if I could just talk to Wiseman first, let him see in person that I'm sincere and I love you and that this isn't some sleazy, seedy boss-employee affair, that he'd see our side of the story and not Justin's."

Liam is smiling now. "So, let me get this straight... It's Sunday night, you are wearing a cocktail dress, and you left a wedding so you could catch a train to the airport. To fly to Boston to look for a random dude called Tim Wiseman so you could tell him you love me."

I consider this. "Correct."

He shakes his head in total wonderment. "Do you even know where to find Wiseman? Have an address? Phone number?"

Definitely hadn't thought this through.

"Nope," I say resolutely. "But I would've found a way. I knew that I couldn't fail, couldn't have our happy accident of the way we met lead to something so negative. I love you way too much to let myself become your biggest mistake."

"It could never be a mistake to love you, Annie. Loving you is a privilege. An honor I don't take lightly. And I want to keep on loving you every single day, for the rest of my days."

I look at him through teary eyes. "Same, Liam. I just wish I could have solved this mess for you."

"You already did."

"Huh?" I blink at him.

"I placed a call to Wiseman on the way here. Told him everything." Liam grins. "Guess I beat Justin to the punch, because he told me that my forthright honesty was admirable. Refreshing. In a way, I almost think it gives us an edge."

"Really?" I sniffle, looking at him in wonder. He actually took that risk for me. Without even knowing what was at stake.

"Really. And whether we end up getting the funding or not, I'm going to change the rulebook right when I get back to the office," Liam continues. "Because nobody should have to choose between love and their career. And I want you to have the best of all worlds, Annie. You deserve the best of everything."

My heart is full.

49

ANNIE

Six Months Later...

"We're baaaaaacccckkkkkkkk!" Luke sings as he swings open the front door of Lana Mae's duplex with theatrical gusto.

I look up from my spot on the couch—where I'm curled up with a glass of red wine in my hand and Harry Styles in my lap—and burst into surprised laughter.

Mindy, who's on the chair across from me, groans, then covers her eyes and peeks through a gap between her fingers. "Oh, my eyes!" she yelps.

Lana surveys the scene and smirks. "Well well well, what do we have here?"

Luke, Liam and Legs are all standing in the doorway dressed head to toe in Justin Bieber concert merch—glittery hats, graphic t-shirts, flashing glowstick necklaces and all. There's even a cardboard cutout of Bieber himself tucked under Luke's arm.

Goodness gracious.

Legs squeals and runs to her mom. "Oh my gosh, Mommy, it was so fun! You should've been there..."

I smile at the sweet thought of the little girl finally

getting to attend the long-awaited concert with her two favorite uncles. Then, I turn my attention to the man I love, who's still hovering in the doorway unreasonably attractive for a man wearing a pair of flashing space boppers on his head and a t-shirt with a shirtless Biebs on the front.

"We may have gone a bit overboard at the merch table," he announces, a tad sheepishly.

"Speak for yourself." Luke points a ginormous foam finger at his brother before flinging his cardboard Bieber aside and sitting down right in Mindy's lap.

"Hey!" she squawks, trying to push him off her.

"Did you have fun, at least?" I ask, keeping my attention on Liam. He seems to be buzzing with some kind of nervous energy. He shrugs. Waits a moment. Then, he nods. "It wasn't so bad."

Legs's ears perk up. "Really? So you'll take me to see Harry Styles—the real one—when he comes to play in Atlanta?"

"Don't push it, kid." He smiles at his niece, then turns to me. "I'm beat. You ready to head out?"

"Sure thing." I delicately scoot Harry Styles—the cat—off my lap and get to my feet. Lean down to give Lana Mae and Legs an awkward group hug. "Thanks for having me."

Lana Mae looks at me over Legs's bedazzled Bieber baseball cap and smiles. "Thanks for coming over this evening."

"Dude, I'm always up for a Channing Tatum movie marathon," I say in return. I've been spending a lot of time with Lana Mae and Mindy over the past few months, and having good girlfriends here in Atlanta has filled at least part of the huge gap in my life now that I live so far from Prisha—who's still my bestie, and still sends me ridiculous texts daily, don't worry.

Mindy climbs to her feet and stretches her arms above

her head before picking up her empty La Croix can. "We gonna head out too, Lukey?" She gives a little shimmy in his direction. "Ain't too late for some you know what, dontcha think?"

"I think I'd rather not hear you say anything of the sort again," Liam responds at the same time as Luke says, "It's never too late for *that*, babe" with some terrifying wiggly eyebrows to accompany the sentiment.

"People, there is a child present," Lana Mae pipes up with a glare. But she's smiling. She's always smiling, and though I know she's blessed with the most wonderful brothers and daughter in the world, I can't help but hope that she finds her own romantic happy ending someday soon.

"Hopefully we can add to the child count after tonight," Luke replies, totally unabashed, with a slightly jarring hip thrust to accompany his almost equally jarring sentence.

"Wait, you're trying?" Lana Mae shrieks, as I clap my hands together in delight.

Mindy nods. "Yup. Early days still, but yes. We're officially trying."

"Congrats, guys. Crossing my fingers for you." I beam happily as Liam gives his brother one of those bro handshakes—a deliberately masculine gesture that does nothing to disguise my boyfriend's misty eyes.

He's a sensitive one underneath it all, my big old cinnamon roll.

Legs looks up eagerly. Right at Liam. "What does 'trying' mean, Uncle Liam? Trying what?"

Liam snorts out a laugh. "I'm very happy to be able to say 'ask your mother' to that one. And on that note, I'm tapping out. Goodnight, family."

It takes a full five more minutes of hugs and congratulations and goodnights before we actually end up by the front door.

Warmth fills me as we leave Lana Mae's place, and we do so hand in hand.

Once we're in the car, Liam immediately yanks his space boppers off his head, and I jab him in the ribs playfully. "Okay, fess up—on a scale of one to ten, how much did you hate it?"

He groans and shifts out of my stabbing range, before he lolls his head back against his seat. His fingers tense on the steering wheel. "Was it that obvious?"

"Yes." I grin.

"Fine. I'd give it an eleven."

I snort. "That bad, huh?"

"I loathed every moment of it. It was 70,000 tweenage girls screaming for three hours. All the songs sounded the same. And the decibel level in there was surely breaking all kinds of regulations."

I can't help the huge smile that spreads across my face. "There's the grumpy man I know and love."

"I don't know what you're talking about." He smirks. "I'm a delight."

"Yeah, you are." I reach across and put my hand on his bare, muscular, tattooed forearm. It's the sexiest forearm I've ever seen. And it's all mine. The new tattoo on my own wrist—the one that reads "No mistakes, just happy accidents"—is just visible from this angle.

Liam has the same one right above his heart. We got them together. It hurt like all hell and I cried like a baby while Liam tried (and failed) to conceal his amusement, but I don't regret it. I never could.

Because no matter what, I'm human. Imperfect. And imperfect things will happen, guaranteed.

But loving Liam Donovan has been the most perfectly imperfect journey of my life so far. The best happy accident ever. And I want to remember it always. Even if it means having a Bob Ross quote inked on me permanently.

When we eventually pull up to my place, I'm yawning.

And yes, I mean my place.

After Liam and I signed the new SITL paperwork saying that we were in a relationship, things went from good to better. SITL got the funding from Wiseman and, with a secure job future, I was able to put a deposit on a great studio apartment rental in Virginia-Highland—a stone's throw from Liam's place in Midtown.

I joked that it was a compromise, seeing as we no longer shared an office at work. After the funding came through, SITL rented out a whole other floor of the building and got to work scaling up the app for V2. The main new feature being the "Color Outside the Lines" addition, which allows users to be flexible enough with their schedules to balance having the best of all worlds in their lives.

The launch was a roaring success, resulting in tens of thousands of new users. Now, I work on a completely different floor from Liam, managing the SITL analytics team. Technically, I still report to him, but I have all the job autonomy I've ever desired. And even though I work my tail off every day to do the best job possible, I no longer feel the need to prove myself through my work. Because, just like my mistakes, my career doesn't define me.

The person I am does. And the person I am puts people before success.

Luke tells me this is one of the qualities that make me a great team lead. And I have one person to thank for teaching me that.

"Wanna come in?" I ask as Liam parks.

Another smile. He bounces his knee as he says, "Thought you'd never ask."

We get out of the car and walk into my building. Call for the elevator.

Liam's still got this nervous energy radiating off him. When the doors ding open, he practically drags me in there. Pulls me toward him with no small amount of force and kisses me like we haven't got a moment to spare. Kisses me with all the certainty and confidence I've come to expect from a kiss from Liam Donovan.

AKA, pure magic.

"What's gotten into you?" I laugh between kisses as my lips move along his jaw. "Biebs concert got you all horny or what?"

Liam nips the skin at the base of my neck in response. "No, it just got me thinking... Got me thinking about how much I love you. How, even though I hated every second of that damn concert, I'd do it again in a heartbeat. With you, if you wanted to go. But also with our future kids."

He draws back so he can look into my eyes. My heart is beating a million times a minute.

"I love you, Annie Jacobs," he says quietly. "I'm trying to be better about expressing my feelings, so I'm going to tell you how I feel. And that's that one day, when you're ready, I'm going to ask you to marry me. Consider this your warning."

Every bone in my body seems to melt into the floor. "I love you too, Liam. And I want to love you always." I smile giddily. "I consider myself warned."

"Good. Now that the emotional stuff is out of the way, can we talk about how I've been wanting to kiss you like this all freaking night? You were all I could think about." He moves his head so his stubble drags along my cheek deliciously. He murmurs into my ear, "I don't even want to wait 'til we get into your apartment, I just want to keep kissing you right here."

My body heats immediately, but I try to keep my voice cool. "Hey now, I thought you believed elevators weren't sexy."

"I used to." Liam turns and presses the emergency stop button with a spontaneous *thwack* that thrills me. He then rounds on me, caging me into the corner and up against the steel railing. My pulse picks up at his proximity, at the heat coming off his body and the fierce, resolute look in his eyes that tells me he loves me no matter what.

He skims his fingertips down the side of my jaw, scorching my skin with desire as he moves closer. Dizzyingly closer.

"But, like a lot of other things, I was very wrong about that, wasn't I?"

I don't reply. I just kiss him.

Thank you so much for reading!

If you enjoyed this book, please leave me a review. As a new author, reviews mean everything to me. I appreciate each and every one of them.

A NOTE FROM KATIE

OH MY GOSH YOU GUYS!

First of all, I love you so much! Thank you thank you thank you for reading *So That Happened*. I am so grateful you picked up Liam and Annie's book and I really hope you enjoyed reading their love story.

While I adore Liam and Annie, a whole set of circumstances meant that this book was a massive mountain to climb for me, and I would have never summited the peak (understatement of the century—I would actually still just be lying at the base of the mountain ugly-crying) if it wasn't for a few people that I absolutely have to thank for making this possible. They say it takes a village to raise a child, and I think the same can be said of writing a book:

To my ARC readers—THANK YOU! Your time is so valuable, thank you for choosing to spend it with my characters. Your feedback, suggestions, love and support always fill me to the brim with gratitude. You're all wonderful.

To the entire Bookstagram community, who were so quick to rally around me with my debut almost a year ago, and have been so instrumental in my success as an author since. Every post, comment, share, story and reel means the world to me. I love seeing how my books have reached your lives. And a special shout out here to @bookwithcollins and @chelseas.book.channel—you have both been particularly kind in supporting me and my books. Thank you!

To my family. Especially you, Kurt. Even though you'll never read this coz you don't read my books. You have always believed in me, and I love you so much for that.

Finally, to all of my fellow indie author friends who provide me with such incredible community, support and friendship. I'm so thankful to have found this space of the world and to be in it with you all—the mutual support, love and encouragement I've seen here is so inspirational. And while I love and appreciate so many people who are part of this community, I do definitely have to thank a few people personally:

First and foremost, Sara Jane Woodley. You are not only the best editor, copyeditor and talk-me-off-a-ledge-r that I have ever met, you are also the best friend a girl could ask for. The Prisha to my Annie. Or something. I love you so much! Thank you so much for your tireless efforts to help me write this book and bring it over the finish line. You are seriously incredible.

Leah Brunner, for so much accountability and so many hilarious message threads of despair—you kept me on the straight and narrow for this one, and I'm truly grateful for that, and for our friendship.

And to Kiki, aka Emma St. Clair, for being such a wonderful mentor and friend, and tirelessly blessing us all with your wealth of bookish knowledge... everything you do definitely does not go unnoticed, and I am so grateful for the time you've spent answering my million and one questions about everything!

I'm sure I've missed so many people, but basically, I am

just an eternal big ball of gratefulness. So if I didn't mention you by name, know that I still appreciate you so much.

Thanks for letting me be here and share this space with so many incredible humans. That's the biggest gift of all.

Big, big love,

Katie B x

ALSO BY KATIE BAILEY

The Quit List

Donovan Family

So That Happened

I Think He Knows

Only in Atlanta

The Roommate Situation

The Neighbor War

Holiday Hockey Rom Com

Season's Schemings

Printed in Great Britain
by Amazon

43688777R00202